# GHOST

## FORGE BOOKS BY JAMES SWALLOW

*24: Deadline*

*Nomad*

*Exile*

*Ghost*

# GHOST

## JAMES SWALLOW

A TOM DOHERTY ASSOCIATES BOOK

NEW YORK

GHOST

Copyright © 2018 by James Swallow

A Forge Book
Published by Tom Doherty Associates
120 Broadway
New York, NY 10271

www.tor-forge.com

Forge® is a registered trademark of Macmillan Publishing Group, LLC.

Library of Congress Cataloging-in-Publication Data

Names: Swallow, James, author.
Title: Ghost / James Swallow.
Identifiers: LCCN 2020032128 | ISBN 978-1-250-31877-0 (hardcover) | ISBN
    978-1-250-31875-6 (ebook)
Subjects: GSAFD: Science fiction.
Classification: LCC PR6119.W355 G478 2020 | DDC 823'.92—dc23
LC record available at https://lccn.loc.gov/2020032128

Our books may be purchased in bulk for promotional, educational, or business use.
Please contact your local bookseller or the Macmillan Corporate and Premium
Sales Department at 1-800-221-7945, extension 5442, or by email at
MacmillanSpecialMarkets@macmillan.com.

First published in Great Britain by Zaffre Publishing

First U.S. Edition: November 2020

Printed in the United States of America

10  9  8  7  6  5  4  3  2  1

*For all those who fight to hold the line
for freedom and reason.*

*This book is dedicated to the memory of
my father, Terrance Swallow.*

# GHOST

# — ONE —

The panic filled him. It was fluid and heavy, choking his lungs and pooling in the pit of his stomach, weighing him down. As Lex walked, the hazy, midday air turned into a tidal drag and his knees weakened. He had to stop to catch his breath, so he lurched toward a pharmacy closed for the siesta, ducking out of the high sun and into cooler shadows.

He hid there for a few moments, trying to moderate the fear and failing. He ran a hand through the hair framing his corn-fed features. His haunted, terrified eyes blinked behind his glasses as he fiddled with them, smearing the lenses.

Lex looked down at himself, and for the first time he saw the tiny dots of rust red that speckled the white T-shirt beneath his baggy black hoodie. The vise clamped around his heart tightened a little more. He touched his cheek and it came away smeared with flecks of crimson. Quickly, Lex rubbed his face clean with the hoodie's sleeve and fumbled at the zipper, pulling it all the way up to hide the rest of the spatter.

It was the Greek guy's blood. Lex didn't even realize that it had got on him. His mind was so focused on running away.

*It all happened so fast.* They had set the meet for a wide piazza on the outskirts of the old township of Rabat, toward the southern end of Malta. Lex had been on the Mediterranean island for days and it seemed to be getting smaller with each passing hour. He wanted to be gone. When the message came, he was falling over himself to get to the rendezvous.

The information arrived in a chain of digital text, filtered through the encrypted Tor server Lex had set up on the day he started running.

Decoded, it was a promise from the Greek smuggler to get him out of Europe and on a plane to Canada. *Kyrkos, that was the man's name.* The deal had been agreed. It was going to happen.

It was supposed to play out with them connecting in Rabat and then driving down to Valetta, where Kyrkos had a boat moored. Lex had planned to end this day on the waves, watching the sun set over the ocean. He was going to have a little ritual, where he would have burned the identity documents he was carrying and toss the ashes into the water. Start anew.

Lex Wetherby would be buried at sea and gone forever. That was how it should have happened, because no one knew where he was. *He was safe.*

But after he had sat down across a café table from the Greek, the burly bodyguard positioned nearby did a weird double take. He moved like he'd seen something wrong, something dangerous. In the next second, the big man jerked backward as if he'd been kicked by a horse.

Lex had seen people get shot before, but there had always been noise, the thunderous crack of a gun. This time he'd heard nothing, and it made everything strange and unreal.

Kyrkos had bolted from his chair, knocking over a glass of wine. He had enough time to swear at Lex before a second silent round hit him in the face. The Greek tumbled over in a heap and some tourist on a nearby table saw the blood. A child screamed.

Lex fled, an innate sense of self-preservation making him flip the table aside as he dashed away. A third shot had splintered a corner of the wooden tabletop. Unable to help himself, he'd thrown a look over his shoulder as he sprinted toward the mouth of the nearest alleyway, toward the faint promise of safety.

Tourists and locals stood frozen with horror, hands to mouths, faces lined with shock. The only ones who'd looked his way were a man and a woman of average height, their identities hidden beneath identical light-colored baseball caps and big black sunglasses that covered half of their faces. He'd glimpsed the dark, angular shapes of compact pistols hidden in their hands and all reason in him dissolved. Up came the oily panic, like a boiling flood head.

He'd raced through a narrow, airless passage full of stale odors which spat him out on to Kbira Street a few blocks north of the piazza. He'd followed the old road, moving without thinking, skirting around the dusty flanks of the church of St. Augustine. Rabat stood atop a hill, and there was a steady breeze through the medieval streets that plucked at his hair and pushed bits of litter along the gutters. On all sides, terraces of sun-bleached buildings crowded in on one another, most of them closed up for the afternoon.

Running on autopilot, Lex almost doubled back before he realized he was on the verge of making a fatal mistake. He staggered to a halt in the pharmacy doorway, trying to catch up with himself, concentrating on what he could remember about the town. He knew there was a coach terminus not far from here, where Rabat met the walls of Mdina, Malta's ancient fortress capital. All he had to do was slip aboard a local bus and get away, lose himself among the other passengers. The rest he could figure out en route. For now, he was trying to concentrate on *not dying*.

The red ruin of the Greek's face flashed up in his mind's eye, and Lex gagged as he tried to blot out the image. Nestor Kyrkos was connected and the man had enemies, he knew that. He wondered if maybe the man and the woman in the baseball caps had come to end the Greek's life for some infraction that he wasn't even aware of. Maybe they weren't interested in him at all.

But then, reflected in the pharmacy's window, Lex saw an olive-toned face half-concealed by dead black lenses on the other side of the street, and he knew that he was the real target. Kyrkos and the bodyguard were just collateral. Their deaths had been the shooters clearing the field of anyone who could be a threat, before turning on their true quarry.

Lex slipped out of the shaded alcove and pushed through a group of aging English tourists coming the other way. Over their muttered complaints about his rudeness, he heard the low drone of a subsonic bullet a split second before a sand-colored block in the wall near his head grew an impact crater. The tourists reacted with mild surprise at the sound of splintering rock as Lex left them behind, hugging the yellow stone of the surrounding buildings, putting them between himself and the killers until he turned the corner.

*No sound.* Whatever weapons the two assassins were using, they were practically silent. No one else seemed to be aware of what was going on.

Lex moved as fast as he could without actually breaking into a run, afraid that giving in to the panic would result in his death. In his haste to escape, he had left his messenger bag behind at the café, but there was little in there that he couldn't replace. The most important thing, *the invaluable thing,* he had on him. The prize for which he had betrayed his comrades had not been out of his reach since he'd left Berlin.

His hand twitched and tightened as this thought ran through his mind, and nervously Lex ran his other fingers over the scars on his palm, picking at the old, healed wound. His right leg was starting to hurt, like it always did when he was stressed, but he pushed the phantom ache aside by patting himself down, taking inventory of what he still had on him in the pockets of his cargo trousers and hoodie.

*Not much.* Adrenaline soured in his mouth, leaving a metallic taste. This wasn't like the kind of fear he was used to, the rush of speed that washed over his body when he base jumped or rode a curl on a surfboard. *That* he could manage, because in those situations Lex was always in control. *This* was raw and hard and overpowering, and he was struggling to keep his head straight.

*These people want to murder me.* The reality of it finally hit him full-on, punching the air out of his chest.

The fateful choice Lex had made weeks ago, while in Germany, had come back to bite him. The people he lived with, partied with, the people he thought he had known . . . Now he wondered if he had never really understood them. He'd been willfully ignorant of what was actually going on, of the plans being made. He had deliberately looked the other way and ignored the hard questions that threatened to spoil the fun of it all. Until the day had come when he couldn't gloss over it anymore.

Lex hated himself for that. When it got too much, when he couldn't sleep at night for all the fear in him, he ran. He ran to here, into *this*. And now the killers his former friends had sent to deal with him would do their jobs, and Lex's too-late attack of conscience would be rendered worthless. He cursed under his breath and tried to shake off the sick dread that threatened to choke him.

He started to jog, deliberately going around the ornamental gardens at the north end of Rabat and through the parkland. He slipped behind the trunk of a large carob tree to catch his breath, and dared to take another look back in the direction he had come.

The man in the cap and glasses was close, a few hundred meters away in the shade of a road sign. He was looking in the opposite direction, scanning the street for any sign of his target. Lex saw his mouth moving, but couldn't hear any of the words. The man had two fingers pressed to his neck, as if checking his own pulse. When his fingers dropped away, Lex saw what looked like a nicotine patch on the assassin's throat.

The man glanced in the direction of the bus terminal and nodded, listening to a voice that only he could hear.

Lex followed the line of his gaze. His gut twisted as he saw the second shooter, the woman, emerging from between two white-roofed single-decker buses. She had her hands clasped together, holding her gun out of sight under the folds of a light-colored jacket.

Her head turned, dazzling sunlight flashing off those big glasses, and she looked right at Lex. Her body language changed in an instant, as if a switch had tripped inside her. She started walking his way, slow and unhurried. She had the same kind of patch on her neck as the other guy, and her mouth shaped more words that Lex could not make out.

The matter of his survival collapsed down to one single option. Lex couldn't head for the bus terminal, he couldn't go back the way he had come or down the road that descended the hill. Those routes would take him right across the paths of the assassins.

But there were clumps of people going in and out of the old walled city, more groups of tourists crossing the stone bridge that led to the historic gate into Mdina, enough of them for Lex to use as cover. He moved as quickly as he could, the old pain in his leg biting anew, and screened himself behind a clutch of laughing sightseers busily taking selfies.

He felt a strange moment of dislocation as he threaded his way toward the baroque portal rising up in front of him. He knew little about Mdina's real past, but he remembered that this place had doubled for mythic castles in television fantasy sagas, shows that Lex had binge-watched on long and lonely nights as he waited for his code to compile. He half-expected the people on the bridge to draw swords and come at him; it felt like the whole world wanted him dead.

He tensed with every step he took, waiting for another silent shot to strike him between the shoulder blades, but it didn't come. As he passed into the shadowed streets of the medieval fortress, he shivered involuntarily.

On the far side of the gate, the road split into three, and the milling tourist crowd went straight ahead, following Villegaignon Street past the entrance to St. Agatha's Chapel, the first of half a dozen churches crammed inside Mdina's millennia-old ramparts. Lex broke off from the group, slipping away into the side street that followed the line of the fortress's southern wall. There was another entrance into the old city that he had seen from the taxi which brought him here, to the west. If he could reach it and double back, he still had a chance to get away unseen.

He started sprinting, but the pace didn't come easily. With each slap of his trainers on the cobbled street his bad leg jolted him. Soon the walls began to close in, near enough that he could have reached out his arms and touched both sides at once. The narrowing passage captured some of the daylight, reflecting off the sandstone walls and casting precious few shadows where he might have halted to get his bearings. Off the main thoroughfare, Mdina seemed deserted, reinforcing the strange movie-set aura of the place, but Lex couldn't afford to stop, not when the assassins were so close on his heels.

He skidded around a shallow corner and spotted the arch concealing the western gate. The locals called Mdina the "Silent City" because of a preservation edict that forbade the use of cars inside the walls for all but a few residents, but there was more to it than that. The old battlements seemed to channel sound into odd, ghostly echoes or soak it up entirely. Lex couldn't be sure if the rapid steps he heard behind him were his own footfalls reverberating back at him or those of a killer, and he didn't dare to slow his pace to find out.

He made it to the gate and dashed though, emerging once more into the full brightness of the day at the top of a ramp leading down to the highway.

The woman in the cap and glasses had anticipated him. She was coming up the ramp to the western gate in quick runner's strides, her face flushed with effort. She held her gun close to her waist. They both stopped short in surprise as they saw one another.

She recovered first. Her weapon came up, the blocky black shape of the revolver seeming too large for her long and delicate fingers. Lex was briefly dazzled by something—then saw that the pistol had an integral laser sight beneath the barrel, sending a crimson dot dancing down his face, across his throat and chest.

He threw himself back toward the gateway as she fired twice. The pistol let out a low metallic clatter, more like the sound of jangling keys than the thunder of a gunshot. Divots of yellow stone splintered out of the arch, hot fragments nicking Lex's cheek as a bullet almost struck him.

He veered back the way he had come and ran deeper into the city, jackknifing into the first side street he found to get out of the woman's line of sight. A third bullet cracked into the flagstones at his feet as he lurched around the turn. The narrow thoroughfares of Mdina had been designed to be no longer than the length of an arrow's shot, so that invaders couldn't get the drop on local soldiers, but against modern firearms that conceit counted for little. Lex's headlong flight took him up a shallow rise, beneath lines of colored glass lanterns hanging out over the street, past windows barred by iron grates and locked doors. He saw the red splash of the laser off the wall ahead of him and dodged aside again before the assassin could draw a bead.

Lex skidded into a piazza, the wide-open space dominated on the far side by the bright frontage and bell towers of the Cathedral of St. Paul. More clumps of tourists were dithering here, groups of elderly folk up from the cruise liners moored in Valetta or parents with their animated children in tow, snapping pictures or listening to fast-talking guides leading them about on walking tours. Lex looked past the travelers, trying to find another escape route.

The few cars that were permitted inside the city walls were parked here, and he scanned them, desperately looking for one he could steal.

His gaze caught on the other assassin. The man halted across the way from him, pretending to be interested in the complex ironwork of an ornate second-floor balcony. One hand curled across his belly, hidden under his jacket. The man rocked off his heels and turned in Lex's direction, the motion calculated to look casual and non-threatening.

A fresh surge of panic came over Lex and he searched the faces of the oblivious holidaymakers. He wanted to shout at the top of his lungs, scream for help. But if he did that, what would happen? In his mind's eye he could see the two killers firing wildly into the crowd, slaughtering people in a mad rush to end him.

Lex started walking, quickly and purposefully, pulling his hoodie tighter around him. He did have one last card to play, one final risky gambit that might get him out of this. But he needed height and distance to make it work.

He passed a boutique selling expensive ornamental glassware, on the ground floor of what had once been a medieval hostel. He looked up, briefly wondering if he could access the building's roof from within. Outside the boutique stood a life-size mock-up of a Maltese Hospitaller Knight. Without warning it was thrown back, slamming against the wall, falling into pieces at Lex's feet. He saw the bright silver edges of a bullet hole through the knight's chest plate and staggered back, catching sight of the woman standing at the mouth of the side street. She had her gun concealed in the same way as her partner, and the shot she fired had passed through the gaps in the crowd and nearly struck its intended target. All the tourists were looking in Lex's direction now, surprised by the commotion but still utterly unaware of the assassins in their midst.

At last, Lex's reserve snapped and he gave up all pretense of trying to blend in. He started running again, weaving through the people ambling along the main street, ignoring the curses and shouts left in his wake. He gambled that his hunters would follow him at a more careful pace, knowing that the narrow road he followed only ended in one place. Lex was deliberately boxing himself in, cutting off other avenues of escape.

The street emptied into the Piazza Tas-Sur, an open space more commonly known as Bastion Square. Around the edges, restored palazzos with red-fronted doors had been turned into museums or terraced restaurants, making the most of the superlative view out across the northern ramparts of the city. Visitors stood on the broad steps that led to the top of the battlements, taking in the sheer drop down the side of the hill to Mdina, the outlook over the village of Ta' Qali and the vineyards beyond. On a clear day like today, it was possible to see out to St. Paul's Bay and the resort town of Buggiba on the northern coast.

The pain in Lex's bad leg collected around the knee joint and he winced as he slowed to a walk. He started checking the zips and fasteners on his clothing, making sure they were secure. Under different circumstances, what he planned to do now would have excited him. He would have a GoPro clipped to his shoulder, and the action camera set to record everything. But here and now he was more afraid than he had ever been in his life, driven by abject terror instead of a thrill-seeking impulse.

Lex closed up the hoodie and tugged a canister from the thigh pocket of his cargo trousers. The size of a large beer can, it attached to a web of expanding bungie cords that he spooled out and looped over his shoulders, snapping them together with a spring-loaded D-ring. He pulled it tight and the canister sat high on his back, between his shoulder blades.

Lex took a deep breath and climbed the stairs up to the battlements two at a time. As he reached the top, he felt the distant twitch of his stomach swooping before the sight of the drop.

*If I do this wrong it will end me*, he told himself. But if he didn't do it, the shooters would put him down right here in front of everyone. He turned his head and closed his eyes, feeling the breath of the wind on his face, sensing the direction of the gusts.

Then Lex reached up his back for a red plastic toggle on the bottom of the canister, and stepped over the cautionary signs warning not to approach the unguarded edge.

Behind him, Lex's pursuers held their guns sideways on and low. They kept them down by their hips, hidden in the folds of their jackets. Both of them fired, but even with their specialized training, their shots were off-target by too great a margin. One round blasted a discarded water bottle sitting on a step, the other blew up a puff of rock dust a few inches from the target's feet. Again, the faces of bystanders started to turn in his direction.

"*He is going to kill himself,*" said the male assassin through the wireless communication node adhered to his throat. This was unexpected.

"*No,*" said the woman, her reply tickling him through his skin. "*I don't think so . . .*"

The target's arm came down in a sharp motion, and the object he had strapped to his back snapped open into a blossom of bright orange fabric and fine white cords. The thin material immediately caught the steady breeze and inflated into a narrow rectangle with a kite-like cross-section.

"*A parachute?*" The man disregarded protocol and launched forward, hoping to get to the target before he could step off the ledge.

The compact canopy filled with wind, drawing shouts of surprise from the assembled tourists in the square, and the target pushed off the side of Mdina's battlements and into the air.

The woman grabbed her partner by the shoulder and pulled him back. "*Wait.*" She was already putting her weapon away.

He resisted, irritated at the idea of missing the kill. The chute was little better than a gimmick, a toy that would barely slow the target's descent. If he got to the edge, if the woman covered him, he might still be able to hit the mark. It was galling to think that this *civilian* would escape them.

"*Both of you stand away,*" said a third voice. "*I have this.*"

*     *     *

Lex had half-expected the micro-chute to flop out and tangle, leaving him with nowhere to go, but the device performed better than he dared to expect. A nasty shock went through his chest and shoulders as the canopy took his weight and the cords cut into his flesh, but that was a small price to pay for getting away from the silent shooters. An unexpected thermal from the base of the tall hill threw him up and to the side, slipping him away from the edge of the fortress city, carrying him toward the farms ranged out below. Elation shocked through his body.

It would be a hard landing, he could tell from the rapid rate of descent and the fluttering of the canopy, but it would be one he could stagger away from and that was all that mattered. Lex was already thinking about what to do next—find a vehicle, get down to the coast and get off this rock—when the wind boosted him up once again in a brief rise. He caught sight of the church spires and tiled rooftops across Mdina and Rabat.

In the tallest of the towers, the light of the sun glittered in reflection. A flare off the glassy eye of a telescopic sight.

A moment later, a single steel-cored 7.62mm bullet penetrated Lex's body a few degrees off his sternum and tumbled violently as it passed through him. In the brief instant it took to enter through his chest and burst out through his back, the round spun and ripped through the tissues of his lungs, and tore open the bottom of his heart. Blood gushed into the ragged void created by the passage of the sniper shot and his body twitched as it went into brutal, fatal shutdown.

Lex died as he sank toward the ground, his life ended in an instant. When his corpse finally crashed into a row of vines down in the valley, his clothes and the orange chute were soaked with a wet mess of dark, arterial red.

A tourist pointed over the edge of the battlements and shrieked. Others were holding up cell phones to record what was going on, and neither Cat nor Dog wanted to remain in the square a moment longer, for fear their faces might get captured on some idiot's video footage.

"*Back to the rendezvous point,*" Dog said, stepping back from the ramparts. He gave Cat the slightest of sideways looks as he walked away, acting as if they had no connection to one another. "*Leave through the main entrance. I will go through the west gate.*"

"*Understood,*" said Cat, speaking without speaking, the device on her neck sensing the half-constructed words as they formed in her throat and turning them into a droning signal. The sub-voc unit made her skin crawl and she resisted the urge to scratch her face, directing the motion into adjusting the sunglasses perched on her small nose.

"*I am making my way to the car,*" Fox said. Cat unconsciously looked up, although from where she was there was no way to see the high roost the sniper had used. "*Local law enforcement officers are at the site of the first engagement. Recommend we shift to secondary exit protocol.*"

Dog was team leader, so the decision was his, but both he and Cat respected the elder Fox's field experience and the answer was as she expected it to be. "*Agreed.*"

She passed by the cathedral and quickened her pace. Her fellow assassin had already vanished into a side street. "*What about the target?*"

"*I saw where he went down,*" Dog replied. "*We must act quickly if we are to get there before anyone else.*"

"*I had to leave the rifle behind,*" Fox admitted.

"*You sanitized it?*" said Dog.

"*Of course.*"

"*Then it won't be an issue,*" Dog added. "*Proceed.*"

Cat slowed her pace as she passed through the Mdina gate and stopped at a vendor to buy a bottle of chilled water, aping the tourists congregating nearby. As she paid for the drink, the green Fiat the team had been provided with came around the corner and slowed to a halt. Cat walked over and climbed into the back.

From the driving seat, Fox gave her a nod and then drove on, halting a second time at the next intersection to pick up Dog. As they rolled away from the traffic lights, a silver police car lined with a blue checkerboard livery raced past in the other direction. As soon as it was out of sight over the crest of the hill, Fox accelerated away, aiming the car toward Ta' Qali.

"Why was he not killed with the first shot?" Fox's voice sounded gruff when he spoke aloud. He didn't direct the accusation at either of them, but Dog stared out of the window and at first gave no indication he was listening.

"The Greek and his bodyguard were more dangerous," said Cat, after a moment, as she peeled the comm unit's self-adhesive pad from her neck. "They were armed. They needed to be neutralized first." She always felt odd talking immediately after removing the sub-voc—she had to consciously remember not to whisper each word she said.

Fox was going to add more, but Dog turned to him. "Just drive," he said. "If we don't get what we came here for, then we will have to consider our alternate options. That will extend the duration of the mission." He gave Cat a look. "None of us want to be here any longer than we must be, no?"

Cat shook her head, and began reloading her weapon, swinging out the revolver's angled chambers to insert fresh rounds. There might be witnesses at the landing site, she reasoned, and if that were the case it would be necessary to silence them as well.

# — TWO —

There had been a good fall overnight, so the morning's arrivals at Pont de la Flégère had come up the mountain eager to race the runs and make the most of the fresh powder. Across the valley from the majestic peak of Mont Blanc, the skiers and snowboarders were already carving paths back and forth before the sun was high in the clear blue sky. There were no clouds, and the thin air was crisp and dry. It was going to be another perfect day on the slopes at Chamonix.

Among the early risers were a couple who kept to themselves, free-styling on a pair of fast CAPiTA boards, looking for kickers to jump and natural drop-offs at the periphery of the blue runs. The guy was white, in his late thirties, tall and whipcord-thin with a scruffy mop of dirty-blond hair, and he had a ragged excuse for a beard that aged him more than he wanted to admit. Now and then he let out a whoop when he caught some air, and he spent most of the time grinning out from behind a pair of mirrored goggles. He took risky turns that planted him in the snow every few runs, as he rediscovered old skills faded with disuse and worked at finding the limits of his abilities. The woman with him took it more cautiously. She was East Asian, maybe ten years his junior, and slightly built. Her small frame, the blue highlights in her black hair poking out from under a cherry-red helmet and her round face made her look more like a teenager. Her matching crimson jacket was a size too large for her, accentuating the impression. She made languid, geometric lines in the powder and rarely got herself into a spill.

Their path brought them toward a cable car station rising further up the peaks, close to a lounge bar with a wide terrace looking out over the valley.

"Race ya," she said, with a challenging nod.

"You think you can keep up with—?" He didn't get to finish the question. Out of nowhere, his partner made a rapid push off a low slope and flashed by him, digging in a little to spray snow as she passed. "Funny. Ha," he called after her, pivoting on to the same line.

"Loser buys!" She sang the words over her shoulder, deliberately mimicking his boarding style, cutting back and forth in tight traversals.

He pushed into the headwind rising up from the valley and closed the distance. Up ahead of them, pennants raised over the lounge bar's frontage flicked and snapped in the breeze, marking their makeshift finish line.

Another group was at the bar's entrance in the process of removing their skis; an elegant couple in expensive, fur-lined snow gear, along with an assistant and three gray-jacketed men of heavy and intimidating build. One of the heavies detached himself from the group and walked into the path of the snowboarders.

They didn't appear to notice him, both of them too busy trying to outpace the other on the last few hundred meters of their improvised race.

The guy on the snowboard used his weight to his advantage and cut the line past the woman, tossing off a sarcastic wave as he left her in his wake.

"You're a dick!" she said, without heat.

The man looked back in her direction as the slope levelled out. "And you are—"

He was going to say *a sore loser*, but the tip of his board hit a mogul that he hadn't noticed and before he could correct, his balance shifted the wrong way and he wiped out. Face-planting in the white, he rolled to a stop and came up laughing at himself. "Idiot!"

The big man's shadow fell across him and for a second he thought there might be the offer of a hand to help him up; but the heavyset man just watched, waiting for him to rise.

"It's okay. I can manage," the boarder said dryly.

The man in the gray jacket moved to block the path to the lounge. "Bar is closed," he said, in a thick Eastern European drawl.

"Oh?" The guy made a show of looking over the other man's shoulder, watching the elegant couple as they took the best table on the terrace. The lounge's staff were in the process of ushering out the handful of other customers already there. "Doesn't look that way to me." Behind him, he heard his companion slide to a halt a short distance away.

"Bar," repeated the man in the gray jacket, "is *closed*." He said the words slowly, as one might speak to someone who was hard of thinking. Then to underline the point, he used his thumb to drag down the zipper on his jacket so it fell open. The knurled grip of a handgun was visible protruding from a belt holster beneath the coat.

"Whoa, whatever, pal." The guy raised his hands. "Be cool."

"Go away," suggested the other man calmly. "Now."

He shrugged and picked up his board, deciding not to argue the point. The woman fell in step with him as they carried on down the slope.


"That's her." Marc Dane dropped the Canadian twang he was affecting and switched back to his natural London accent as he hefted the snowboard on to his shoulder.

"Oh yeah." Kara Wei nodded, adjusting her goggles. "I got a good capture." The optic rig the Chinese-American woman wore concealed a digital image processor, and she tapped at a control pad on the brow of the frame. "Looks like she's brought her latest lover up for some of that clean mountain air."

Marc turned his head so he could steal a glance back toward the bar. The big man watched them walk off, and by now the lounge had been completely emptied of everyone but their target and her entourage. "How much d'you think it costs to buy out a place like that for lunch?"

"Pocket change for the rich and self-centered," Kara said flatly. "Meanwhile, we have to work for a living."

"Yeah," sighed Marc. "For a second back there, I actually remembered what it was like to take a holiday."

Kara made a face at him. *"Boo hoo.* Come on, we have crime to do." She dropped her board back on to the snow and stepped into the bindings, rocking on the heel side as she snapped them tight.

Behind her goggles, Marc thought he saw a flicker of anticipation. He looked down at the battered Cabot dive watch on his wrist, putting himself into a mission-ready mindset. "If she follows her usual pattern, that gives us roughly three hours before the limo meets her party at the cable car station . . ." He clipped on to his own board, gazing along the line of elevated cables down through the snow-dusted trees to the terminus in the valley below. "You ready to try a black run?"

"Race ya," Kara repeated, and launched herself with a burst of speed, hunching low and forward.

Despite himself, Marc grinned again and turned after her, guiding the rocker board into Kara's wake.

The descent passed in a blur of white and brilliant sunshine, the mountain depositing them back at Les Praz de Chamonix, toward the northern end of the valley. For Marc, the Evettes Flégère run concluded a hazy race through snow, rock and woodland that seemed to take only moments. Time became elastic on the track, contracting into one single extended instant of concentration as he guided himself down and down, crossing dozens of switchbacks and descents. Then it was over, and his heart was still pounding in his chest. The denser air felt oddly heavy in his lungs and he panted as his body adjusted back to it.

Kara shared a bottle of water as they walked quickly through the side streets toward the heart of Chamonix. They avoided the main drag, which at this time of the day would be choked with tourists and those late to the party on the mountains. Marc checked the countdown as they found their way to the back of a nondescript two-story office behind a hotel complex.

The building had been rented from a letting agency weeks earlier, and deliberately left to sit idle. Marc and Kara had arrived in the dead of night a few days ago, and they followed a careful routine to make sure the place appeared unoccupied to the outside world.

"I'll spin us up," said Kara, as she went upstairs.

Marc stripped out of his snowboarding gear and cleaned off. He changed into a dark-blue boiler suit, rolling it on over a fresh T-shirt, working his arms into the sleeves before pulling the brass zip to his neck. A match for the ones worn by the mechanics working in the garage down the street, Marc had weathered it by dragging the thing around the tarmac behind the office, making sure it had enough oil stains and scuffs to look lived-in.

He moved to the windows and peeled back the corner of a layer of sun-bleached newspaper taped over the glass, peering out at the garage a hundred meters away. Set back off the road, the collection of low hangar-like structures had the same arched roofs as the rest of the town. But where the residential chalets, hotels and shops sported wooden cladding, ornamental balconies and sprays of flowers, the garage workshop was bare corrugated metal and blank gray walls. Petrol pumps and a spare parts store took up the eastern end of the place, while the rest of the area had been given over to grimy work-shops and maintenance bays. It was a long way from the clean lines, expensive stores and classy restaurants a few blocks south.

He scanned the open mouths of the workshops, picking out the shape of a green Land Rover and a black Mercedes C-Class inside, but saw no sign of the target vehicle. His leg muscles were stiffening from the run down the mountain, and he walked in a circle to fend the aches off. He wanted to look at his watch again, but Marc knew that counting every second wouldn't make time move any faster.

He wandered up to the bare, unfurnished room on the second floor, where Kara sat in front of a camping table, staring fixedly into the screen of a military-specification laptop computer. Black cables snaked away from the machine, some coiling into a portable power pack, others connected to a collapsible satellite antenna that sat on the floor like a discarded, open umbrella. As with the floor below, the windows were papered over with yellowing pages from *Le Monde*.

Kara's expression was distant. Her eyes had taken on a hacker's robotic intensity, an aspect that Marc himself knew well from his own experiences of being stationed behind a keyboard. There was a strange kind of non-awareness that came on when you were glued to a screen for too long, a narrowing of the world that made everything fall away until the motions of your hands and the blink of the cursor seemed to happen of their own accord.

Getting deep into the code, losing yourself in the wires . . . There had been a time when Marc had found that *restful*. A part of him was envious that Kara was running support for this mission. Once, that would have been his assignment.

But a lot had changed for him since that time. Formerly a field technician for one of British Intelligence's Tactical Operations Teams, Marc had left that life behind after fate conspired to first make him a fugitive, and then cut him off from his country and the service that had trained him. In the wake of that, he might have been set adrift and lost all purpose, if it hadn't been for the intervention of others.

A man named Ekko Solomon gave him a chance to recover some of what he had lost, to get back into the world and make a difference in it. The enigmatic African billionaire owned a large corporation called the Rubicon Group, and a small part of it operated as a private military, security and intelligence contractor. Marc was officially listed as a "consultant" on the company's books, but that vague title covered a multitude of possibilities.

Rubicon's PMC arm specialized in close-protection details, kidnap and recovery and information security—or at least, that was the face shown to the world. The reality was that the company's so-called "Special Conditions Division" had a much larger mandate than fielding bodyguards for affluent clients.

Solomon made certain that Rubicon adhered to a staunch moral code. He was a man on a mission, using his wealth to do right, to reach out across the globe and take on threats that nation states were either unwilling or unable to oppose.

*Small actions with large consequences.* Rubicon's founder described their work in those terms.

It was a just cause, and Marc had willingly signed on to be a part of it. He promised himself that he would remain until the day came when he had cause to doubt Solomon's sincerity, if he ever did. In the shadow world of intelligence agencies, terror cells and non-state actors, where lines of loyalty and truth were often blurred, the suggestion of doing a thing because it was ethically *right* seemed like a quaint, almost naive notion. But there was a correctness about it, a truth that Marc Dane couldn't ignore.

"Five minutes out," said Kara, her voice pulling him back from his reverie. She studied video feeds from a series of co-opted traffic cameras. "You ready for this?"

"Yeah." He straightened, moving to another table where his mission kit was laid out, waiting for the go.

"All this build-up and then *poof*, it'll be over . . ." Kara said to the air. "A girl could be disappointed."

"You should be happy this is a low-hazard assignment," Marc noted. "Easier that way."

"Hope so," she said. "Of course, maybe Solomon doesn't think the two of us can handle the dangerous ops."

He eyed her, uncertain if she was joking or not. Kara's demeanor could switch from cat-eyed and grinning to flat sarcasm in a blink, and that made her hard to read. "You don't want to get shot at," Marc told her.

"You'd never say that to Lucy." She looked up, then back to the screen in front of her.

"Lucy Keyes was a tier-one Special Forces operator before she signed on with Rubicon," Marc countered. The ex–Delta Force sniper was another vital member of Solomon's covert agency, and while they usually worked alongside one another, right now the American was a world away on an assignment of her own. "I reckon Lucy's tolerance for mayhem is different from yours and mine, yeah?"

"Yeah," echoed Kara. "A gig like this would be way too boring for your girlfriend."

Marc stopped dead and glared at her, coloring slightly. "That is not, in any way, *correct*." He sounded out the retort so there was no equivocation. Marc had respect for Lucy and he trusted her, but he didn't like the intimation that there was something else going on between them. "We have a strictly professional relationship," he added, and didn't dwell on exactly why Kara's comment bothered him so much.

"I'm not judging." She worked at the keyboard, pulling up different video feeds. "I figured . . . you and she had . . ." Kara gave a lazy shrug, starting to lose interest in the thread of conversation. "I mean, after you cut loose from MI6 and abandoned them—"

"I didn't *abandon* anything." His tone hardened. "I didn't have much of a choice."

She heard the edge in his voice and became contrite. "Sorry. I didn't mean anything by it." Kara shot him a blank look, then turned away again. "My mistake."

"Not the time," he shot back, tamping down his irritation, forcing his attention back to the situation at hand. "Don't be fooled into thinking this'll be a cakewalk."

Marc returned to kitting up, completing his disguise with a grubby black watch cap and a plastic nametag that Kara had made up in a portable 3D printer at the back of the room. A folding Wingman multi-tool went into one of the boiler suit's sleeve pouches, an ASP air-weight collapsible baton into another. Marc checked his custom-made Rubicon digital notepad and then zipped it into a thigh pocket, along with a spool of data cable. The last thing to go on were a pair of black 5.11 tactical gloves.

"Comms," said Kara, and she threw a tiny object to him in an underarm toss. He snatched a flesh-colored radio bead out of the air. The device resembled a discreet hearing aid, and he put it in place in his left ear.

"Okay." Marc took a deep breath and tried to shake off some of the adrenaline rising in him. It didn't help.

"Nervous?" she asked him, without looking up from the screen.

"No."

"Liar." Kara tapped out a command and peered at the display. "One minute out. He's turning on to the street now."

Marc wandered back to the window and found a tear in the paper to look through. Approaching from the end of the road, the midnight-blue limousine was impossible to miss. That kind of car was a rare sight in all but the largest European cities, with most of the older continental avenues too narrow to accommodate the vehicle. Having such transport in one's personal fleet made a statement. The owner didn't care for the shortcomings of the world impacting upon their need for conspicuous luxury.

Here and now, the limo was empty, made clear by the way the driver bumped it over the curb as it pulled into the forecourt of the garage. Marc watched a roller door rise so the car could nose into one of the workshops. "We're sure that's the right vehicle?"

A digital camera encased in a non-reflective sheath was clipped to the window ledge and Marc heard its lens motor whine as it zoomed in. Kara captured hi-resolution images of the limo to compare with the surveillance shots they already had on record.

"Same plates. Getting a ninety-eight percent match on vehicle mass analysis," she told him, all business now. "That's Toussaint's ride."

"Okay." Marc pulled the watch cap down over his hair and scratched his chin through his beard. "Green for go. In and out in forty minutes, that's the optimal."

"Good luck," Kara said absently, already lost once again in the glow of her screen.


Marc exited the empty office by the rear fire escape and turned up the boiler suit's collar, hunching forward as he walked toward the garage.

"*Radio check.*" Kara's voice buzzed in his ear and he adjusted the fit of the radio bead.

"Five by five," he replied.

"*En Francais,*" she admonished. "*You're pretending to be a local boy, remember?*"

Marc gave a thumbs-up that would be seen by the camera in the window. "*D'accord.*"

The timing was good. Half of the garage's staff were still out at lunch, and at a distance Marc's disguise made him resemble any one of them. He could easily have been a guy wandering back early ahead of the other mechanics to get a start on the afternoon's jobs. *Nothing amiss here*, he told himself, willing it to be so.

The cover allowed him to cross the edge of the forecourt without drawing any attention and slip around the side of the workshops, where he knew a fire exit was situated. Two nights earlier, Marc had slipped carefully over a wall topped with broken bottles and done some in-person recon. The oil drum he had moved was still where he had put it, close to the wall where he could use it as the stepping stone to an escape route if the operation went badly wrong.

Of course, if that happened, then the whole mission would have to be scrubbed. The operation hinged on leaving as near to zero footprint as possible, and getting made by the targets would trigger a whole load of secondary protocols.

Marc had worked out the details before they had arrived in Chamonix. They would have to make it look like a failed attempt to steal a car, hiding one illegal action beneath another, but he hoped it wouldn't come to that.

He kept moving, carefully following a path that kept him out of the eye line of the yard's security cameras. Marc had their positions memorized, but he couldn't afford to take any chances. A stocky, bearded man over by the petrol pumps caught sight of Marc and threw him a languid wave, not really looking at him. Marc returned it and before the greeting could turn into something more, he was out of sight and at the fire door. It opened easily, and Marc slipped into the workshop.

Within, it was as unremarkable as it was outside. The garage's owner didn't draw attention to his place with big neon signs or gaudy advertisements. The business had a reputation for discretion and competence, which was why its customers paid handsomely.

The workshop was gloomy and heavy with the reek of engine oil. The black Mercedes and the Land Rover were up on jacks above the maintenance pits, undersides lit by electric lamps but with no sign of the mechanics working on them.

Parked between the two jacks, the target vehicle's bonnet was open to reveal the engine beneath. Even at a distance, Marc could see the anti-fragmentation baffles around the power-plant. The car had been hardened, fitted with heavy duty shocks, run-flat tires, sheets of high-impact armor and bulletproof glass. This kind of protection was usually afforded to vehicles that rode around in war zones rather than the French Alps. Nothing short of a rocket-propelled grenade would be able to pierce the passenger compartment, but right now the rear right door hung open as someone moved around inside.

Marc drew back into cover and waited. He tapped the ear bead twice, a pre-arranged code to let Kara know he had eyes on the limo.

*"Copy that,"* she replied. *"Be advised, I saw the driver go into the main office with one of the other employees."*

After a while, a ropey young white guy in his twenties with a shaven head and a glum expression clambered out of the back of the car, cradling a portable vacuum and other cleaning kit in his hands. The servicing of the interior done, he moved to the front and set to work on the engine, snapping on another work lamp to flood the compartment with light. That had the effect of dazzling the mechanic, allowing Marc to slip around the Mercedes and go low, out of his line of sight. He moved toward the limo's passenger door and eased it open again.

Marc waited for the right moment, and when the mechanic's attention was elsewhere, he climbed into the rear compartment and pulled the door shut.

"I'm in," he whispered. Moving low and slow to keep his weight evenly spread, Marc slid toward the panel that separated the driver's cab from the rest of the interior. The internal privacy blind was still up, and with the dark tinted glass in the side windows no one outside would be able to see him in here.

Next to a glass-fronted mini-fridge stocked with bottles of expensive Veen mineral water and tins of Beluga caviar, Marc found an access port that flapped open when he pushed at it. Behind the flap, he saw the limousine's electronics bay, a nexus for the circuits that ran the car's entertainment system, air conditioning, internal lighting and more.

It was the *more* that interested Marc. Plugging the data cable into the bay's mini-USB port, he connected the compact tablet from his pocket to the other end and booted it up.

The device quickly mapped the architecture of the limo's systems and auto-launched a piece of intrusion software. Within a few seconds, the program had found the vehicle's on-board satellite navigation system and set to work sifting through its limited memory. As Marc expected, the records of the previous journeys stored in the satnav were gone. He imagined the driver was dutiful about that, erasing each route map after it had served its purpose. But simply hitting the *Delete* key was not enough to destroy computer data. That would only erase the file's header, and the majority of the data would remain in the device's memory until actually overwritten by new information. If you knew where to look, that "deleted" map could easily be recovered.

A progress bar popped up on the tablet's screen and slowly began to fill as the intrusion program copied the satnav's memory. *Two minutes*, Marc guessed. *Then we'll have Toussaint's complete itinerary for the last month.*

Madame Celeste Sophie Toussaint was proving a difficult quarry for Rubicon's Special Conditions Division. She kept walled estates outside Annecy and down on the south coast, and the corporate headquarters of the media company to which she was sole heir occupied an elegant eighteenth-century building in the historic quarter of Lyon. All three were highly secure locations, protected by advanced security systems and guarded by well-paid forces of armed guards. Toussaint employed a Russian-based military contractor called ALEPH as her sentinels, and Marc knew them well. He had crossed paths with some of their mercenaries on an icy day in the Polish countryside and he had no desire to be in their sights again—hence this operation had been conceived to get the intelligence they needed on the woman by more indirect methods.

Over the course of the last year, Rubicon's digital intelligence sources had tracked payments going into Toussaint's accounts through several shell companies that were suspected fronts for militant groups operating in Central and Western Europe. They didn't have proof yet, but the intel strongly suggested that Toussaint was using her global network for the clandestine brokerage of classified information. While she overtly supported nationalists, manipulated politics and stoked the fires of dissent through divisive news programming and slanted media, nothing outside the bounds of legality could be traced back to the woman. Toussaint was suspected of deep ties to the leaders of far-right organizations and fanatic extremists on all sides of the ideological divide, but to date Rubicon had been unable to put her in the same place as any of those people. When she left her estate, she traveled below the radar, and her vehicles, like her homes and her office, were swept twice a day for listening devices. Tracking her was not a viable option, and the dense firewalls around the computers in Toussaint's offices and estate were formidable.

In the end, Rubicon applied an old but irrefutable truth to the operation: security is only ever as strong as its weakest link. Marc had found that weak link in the garage used to service Toussaint's cars while she visited Chamonix. It was impossible to remotely attack her limousine's on-board electronics, but a physical connection would get the intelligence Rubicon needed. If they could build up a picture of Toussaint's movements and map that on to information already in hand about her clients, things would come into sharper focus. Toussaint had a reputation for wanting to make deals face to face, and if that meant she had been meeting terrorists and criminals somewhere in the French countryside, her itinerary would be proof enough of her dealings. And then . . . steps would be taken.

Marc turned that thought over in his mind, watching the progress bar creep forward, listening to the mechanic working at the engine a few meters away.

The French media heiress was more than an amoral opportunist. She was part of a covert group called the Combine, a gathering of power brokers, industrialists and old money types who worked with the common interest of enriching themselves still further. The group had originally come together in the horrors of the First World War, profiteering off the sale of weapons to both sides in the great conflict. In the present, they sought to manipulate the unending War on Terror, stoking the fires of a fearful world and reaping the rewards.

For a moment, Marc lost focus, remembering. The actions of the Combine had set him on the path he now followed. They were responsible for killing the members of his MI6 team, when the unit had come too close to the edges of a Combine-supported terrorist plot. A woman he had cared deeply for, his friends and his career in the British secret service had all been lost in fire because of that.

These people, with their money and their power and their view of the world as if it were a chessboard for their games, were the ones who had struck the flame. A year later, he had been forced to work alongside Combine operatives during the frantic search for a missing weapon of mass destruction, and being directly exposed to their callous outlook had only hardened Marc's resolve to bring them down.

If Toussaint was just a criminal, then exposing her would restore a small measure of balance to the world. But if they could prove she was Combine, then the deed became a personal one for Marc Dane. He nursed an icy fury for the group and ruining their schemes was a victory he sorely wanted.

But Rubicon had to be *certain*. Ekko Solomon would not act against someone without being absolutely assured of their guilt.

"*Hey.*" Kara's voice sounded in his ear, drawing him back to the moment once more. As she spoke, the layers of digital encryption in the signal gave her words a flat, machine-like timbre. "*I'm seeing the guy who spoke with the driver. He's walking out to the front of the main gates for a smoke. He's alone.*"

"Eyes on the limo driver?" Marc whispered the words, letting the bone-induction microphone in the earpiece pick them up.

"*No joy,*" Kara told him, and a jolt of cold ran down Marc's back. As she said the words, he heard a mutter of conversation strike up outside the car, behind the open bonnet. He caught a few words in clipped, fast French. The mechanic complaining about a half-finished job. Then another voice, gruff and pissed-off, insisting that it was time to leave, *right now*.

Marc looked at the tablet. The progress bar was three-quarters full, and without the complete download the mission would be a failure. If he tried to get out of the car now, he would be seen. Possibilities spun through his mind, all of them untenable.

The downward spiral his day was taking continued unabated. The limo's bonnet came down with a slam and the car jostled on its shocks with the force of it. Marc glimpsed movement in the side windows and he heard the driver's door clunk open and closed.

"*What's going on in there?*" said Kara. "*I don't have a visual.*"

"Think I'm going for a ride," Marc whispered.

The vehicle's engine grumbled into life and a chorus of dull metallic thuds sounded around him as the doors automatically locked. The limousine lurched into reverse and crawled out of the workshop, back into the wintry sunshine.

"*Oh shit.*" Kara's reaction mirrored Marc's own, but he stayed silent for fear of doing anything that might alert the driver to his presence.

It would only require the man to drop the privacy shield and throw a glance into the passenger compartment for him to see Marc down on the floor, clutching at the data tablet. Toussaint's drivers were provided by ALEPH, and they carried personal firearms in defiance of French gun laws. Marc's folding baton would be no defense against a pistol.

He felt the vehicle bump the curb as it eased out on to the road, then lurch again as it moved into forward gear and away.

"*Dane, he's leaving early. Tell me you're not still in there.*" He tap-tapped the earpiece in answer and Kara's reply took a while to come. "*Shit. Okay. I've got your comms. I can track you.*" There was another long pause. "*This is not optimal.*"

Marc didn't respond, moderating his breathing to slow his racing pulse as he lay on the floor of the limo, staring up at the frost-spotted sunroof above him. The tablet in his hand vibrated gently, letting him know that the download had finally completed, but in the current situation that gave small consolation. He decided to risk sending a data signal, using the tablet's wireless functionality to compress the stolen information, then direct it in an encoded burst back to Kara's computer and a remote cloud server operated by Rubicon for exactly these kinds of situations. It only took a few seconds to run the subroutine, and when it was done, he took a deep breath. At least now, if he ended up on the wrong end of a gun, the intelligence they had come to Chamonix to capture was safe.

It only remained for Marc to get the hell out of the limousine without being discovered. He tapped silently at the tablet as the driver switched on the radio, the vehicle accelerating as it veered on to a main road.

The radio spat out a rapid-fire stream of French from a news-caster filling in the high points of the day's global events, concentrating on a terse report about a metro train crash in Taipei that had claimed the lives of a French fencing team visiting Taiwan for the Youth Games. Presently, the news bulletin concluded and a female presenter returned to hosting a chart show rundown. The music gave Marc the cover he needed to move around in the limo's rear compartment.

He shifted so that his legs wouldn't cramp up in the tight confines and ruin his chances of running if an opportunity presented itself. Trees flashed past the windows, but from his low angle Marc could see no landmarks. Instead, he used the tablet to mirror the satnav screen on the limo's dashboard and squinted at the display. They were moving south, back toward the far side of the valley. That meant that the vehicle was most likely on its way to the cable car station to pick up Toussaint early.

He ran through that scenario in his head, based on the surveillance data Rubicon had gathered on the woman's routine. The limousine would park, covered, at the side of the station and Toussaint would get in with her executive secretary and bodyguards before they set off to her next destination, either the airport or her estate. Given the annoyance in the driver's voice back at the garage, Marc guessed that this summons had not been planned in advance. He wondered if he could use that to his advantage.

Marc considered and rejected a couple of possible action plans; get Kara to drive out and intercept the limo before it reached the station; try to co-opt the vehicle's cell phone and fool the driver into redirecting them to a secluded spot where Marc could make a run for it. He shook his head. Both of those options were messy and they would leave Toussaint aware that her security had been violated. It was imperative she did not know her itinerary had been hacked, otherwise the woman would go dark and the intelligence Rubicon had painstakingly gathered would be rendered useless.

Waiting until the car reached the station was the worst choice of them all. Even with the element of surprise on his side, Marc estimated his chances as slim to nil. ALEPH's mercenaries tended to solve problems with the liberal application of bullets, as he had learned back in Poland.

"*I checked the maintenance logs from Haute-Savoie,*" said Kara, referring to the nearest airport, an hour away in Annecy. "*Toussaint's Gulfstream is being gassed up as we speak. Something has her rattled.*"

Again, he didn't reply. Speculating on the target's reasons for her rapid departure was, for now, of secondary importance. Instead, he opened up another window on the tablet and streamed the live feed of traffic bulletins pushed to the satnav, skimming them for anything he could use. There was information about a stalled coach out in Argentiére causing tailbacks, a notation about ongoing roadworks in Le Houches . . . And then he found what he needed. An advisory to motorists warning them to avoid police patrols with radar guns camped out along the N205 motorway. The cops were tracking reckless or inattentive drivers speeding out of the long Tunnel du Mont-Blanc.

Working quickly, Marc inserted a command window between the incoming traffic data and the limo driver's display. His grasp of the French language was good enough to craft a quick message to the effect that an overturned truck had blocked the road they were already on. He hit *Send* and a moment later, Marc heard the satnav ping as the message appeared. The driver gave a grunt of irritation and Marc knew the man was buying it. With a few more commands, Marc made the hacked satnav display show a new route that directed the limo on to the N205 and a roundabout route to its destination. He deleted all mention of the speed patrols and held his breath.

The limo rolled slightly as the driver pulled into a slip road and took the on-ramp. *Step one*, Marc told himself. *Now for my next trick*.

Retreating out of the satnav's programs, Marc went back to the basic maintenance menu and found the main virtual circuit for the vehicle's other electrical systems. Like most cars built in the last few years, the limousine used a device called a "controller area network" to run the power flow from the battery to the various devices. CAN access could be shielded from external wireless attacks, but from within the car with a hard line plugged in, it was wide open. Marc's eyes narrowed as he swung into the pace of the plan. He cued up a macro to activate the solenoid switches in the door locks and open them on his command, then tabbed to the controls for the limo's front and rear lights, and waited.

On the satnav screen, the crimson dart representing the car passed into the area where the police patrol lurked and Marc set the next stage in motion. With a couple of keystrokes, he started the exterior lights blinking on-off, on-off, hoping that the driver wouldn't immediately notice it. With more time, he might have been able to loop into the traction controls for the vehicle's brakes or even affect the steering, but doing so would have run the risk of causing a traffic accident. With the frost-slick road beneath the limo's wheels, it could have easily thrown them into a serious collision.

*If this doesn't work, that's exactly what I'm going to have to do.* Marc tensed, wondering how best to survive that, if it came to it.

But in the next second, the flash of blue strobes behind the car told him he had been successful. A white BMW police motorcycle roared up on the inside lane and Marc glimpsed the helmeted cop in the saddle jabbing a finger in the direction of the motorway's hard shoulder as he paralleled the limo.

The driver swore under his breath and Marc felt the vehicle slow as it slipped across the highway. In a moment, they had halted and the man up front began drumming his hands irritably on the steering wheel.

Marc cued up a last macro on the tablet, set the command running and then disconnected it. As he carefully replaced the flap over the access panel, the driver rolled down the window to talk to the police officer. Marc began counting down from ten.

"*Y at-il quelque chose qui cloche avec votre véhicule?*" Marc could make out the cop looking into the cab of the limo as he slid back over the floor of the rear compartment, toward the door nearest to the hard shoulder. The driver said something Marc didn't catch as his count reached zero. The limo's horn let out a long, loud blare of sound and the doors unlocked in the same instant.

In the time it took the motorcycle cop and the limo driver to react to the unexpected noise, Marc had opened the rear door just enough to slip through and roll out, face down on to the asphalt. Staying low, keeping the body of the car between himself and the police officer, Marc squirmed over a squat concrete barrier and into a weed-choked ditch. He lay flat, willing himself to remain unseen.

He didn't dare raise his head to look over the wall, for fear that he might be spotted. Instead he waited, gripping the handle of the collapsible baton and straining to listen. Minutes seemed to stretch into hours, and at any second he expected the shadow of the cop or the driver to fall over him and a voice to angrily demand, *Que faites-vous ici?*

At length, he heard the grumble of the limousine's engine as it pulled away, and after waiting another minute, Marc finally peeked back over the lip of the barrier. The vehicle and the motorcycle patrolman were gone. The tension of the situation drained out of him and a half-gasp, half-chuckle escaped from his mouth.

"Close one," he said aloud, looking around to re-orient himself. Trudging back down the hard shoulder, he set off in the direction of the staging area. Marc reached up and tapped his radio earpiece. "You reading me? Extraction is complete, over. It was chaotic as hell, but I reckon we did okay." Only silence answered him, and after a moment he plucked out the device, checking to make sure it was still working. "Kara? Are you on?"

The only sound that returned was the faint buzz of an open channel.

He wanted to get back to the rented office as quickly as he could, but Marc resisted the urge and followed the protocol that existed for any irregularity in the mission. He took a circuitous route, making sure he wasn't being followed, until he approached the site from the opposite direction he had left it hours earlier. He was cold and tired by the time he arrived, chilled by the icy mountain air even though the sun shone brightly.

Across the street, nothing seemed amiss at the garage where it had all started, the mechanics at work and no sign of any suspicious vehicles parked nearby.

Keeping out of sight, Marc came up the stairs to the office space with the ASP baton hidden in his hand, ready for anything. He found Kara alone in the bare, unwelcoming room. She was in the middle of stripping the place down, packing their kit into bags.

"You're back," she said, "good, help me with this." Kara thrust the portable satellite antenna into his hand and nodded at an open case on the floor.

Marc pocketed the baton and set to work folding up the antenna for transport. "You went silent on comms—" he began, but she spoke over him.

"Had to," Kara insisted. Her earlier mood, the mix of sly boredom and undirected energy, was gone. In its place she seemed distracted and sullen. "There was . . ." She stopped talking and then started again. "There's been a development."

As she said the words, Kara moved to her laptop and snapped it closed. Marc saw a flash of a screen filled with text. "Toussaint?" he asked. "I mean, are we blown?" His hand clenched. Had all his on-the-fly improvisation to get the data from the limo been for nothing?

Kara shook her head. "Not that." She flashed him a quick smile. "Smart play, very good." Then it was gone, flicked off like a light. "This is different. We're shutting down, Delancort's going to have a clean-up team come in and sanitize this place."

Henri Delancort was Ekko Solomon's executive aide and de facto chief of operations, a man who seemed to have the numerical value for everything stored in his head, and in Marc's eyes, someone who only saw the world in terms of losses or gains. It was usually his job to parcel out the tasks of the Special Conditions Division. "Delancort contacted you?"

Kara gave a nod, stuffing the mil-spec laptop into a backpack before snatching up a red leather jacket hanging on the back of a chair. "As of now, the Celeste Toussaint investigation has been pushed to secondary status. We've been re-tasked to a more time-sensitive assignment." She jerked her head toward the door that led to another room, where their personal gear and sleeping racks had been set up. "You ought to change. I got us flights."

Marc closed up the antenna case. "We're not going to debrief?"

"No time for that. Give me the tablet, I'll refresh the memory and load the data—you're gonna need on it. I have you on a plane from Geneva. I'll take the train across the border to Turin and get my flight from there, to maintain operational security."

"Where are we going?"

"Malta. Rubicon received an alert . . . Someone—a *person of interest*—was killed there today." She eyed him. "There's a Combine connection."

Marc felt a rush of cold run through him. "Probable, like Toussaint, or—?"

"High confidence," she cut him off again. "Look, there will be a briefing packet waiting for you on arrival, okay?" Her tone softened. "You know how it goes with these creeps. If they pop up on the radar, we have to take advantage of it. Solomon wants us to get this done. Low-profile. Minimum communications."

"There's no one else Rubicon can send?"

"SCD's other assets are tied up," she explained. "It has to be you. And me."

Marc nodded to himself. If there was a confirmed Combine lead in Malta, it would go cold quickly. The group were good at covering their tracks.

And after what happened today, he felt the gnawing rise of a familiar ache in his chest. The need to make the Combine pay for all they had taken from him, for all they had taken from so many innocents, never really went away. If there was a chance to strike back, for certain this time, he wanted to be a part of it. "The guy who was killed, he was with them?"

"He was their victim," she corrected. "We have to find out why."

"Okay," Marc said, at length. "I suppose this is what we get for complaining about low-hazard assignments . . ." Kara looked at him blankly. "Are you okay?" Studying her, he noticed her cheeks were flushed.

"Fine." She noticed his close attention and turned. "I was blindsided today. Getting complacent. Seeing you nearly get tagged out there brought me up sharp." Kara gave a low sigh. "It reminded me this isn't a game."

"Can't argue with that. All right, I'll get my kit and we'll head out."

"Marc." Kara called his name as he walked away. "You trust me, don't you?" It seemed an odd question and his confusion must have shown on his face. "Never mind." She brushed her words aside like they were a nagging insect, before he could answer.

# — THREE —

A bell over the door jangled as Lucy Keyes entered the diner, drawing a wan smile from the dark-haired waitress standing near the cash register. The woman gestured with the pen in her hand at the tables and booths, most of them empty this early in the morning. "Sit where you want, honey. Be with you in a second."

"Thanks." Lucy smiled back as she removed her expensive designer sunglasses, dropping them into the pocket of the bolero jacket hanging off her athlete's shoulders. She ran an ochre hand over the tight fuzz of her close-cropped hair, and wandered deeper into the restaurant. Instinct made her pick the booth closest to the fire exit and she slid into place where she could see the doors and observe the street outside. She pretended to look over the menu as she scanned the other people in the restaurant. A couple of early bird commuters getting in their carbs before heading downtown, a few solid blue-collar types tanking up on coffee and one or two bleary-eyed night shift workers stopping in on their way home. None of them set off her hunter's radar and she allowed herself to relax slightly.

Outside, the watery post-dawn light of the new day had the promise of sunshine behind it, but Lucy was distrustful of the weather in San Francisco. The winds off the bay could bring rain clouds in from the Pacific when you least expected it, or present clear blue skies at a whim.

The city was still waking up. A few blocks away, the residential streets around Alamo Square were shaking off a long weekend as the inexorable rush of a new Monday came upon them. She watched sparse traffic flicker past and found her partner on the far side of the street, pretending to smoke. Malte Riis was a good head taller than

Lucy's spare, athletic frame, with sandy hair and the kind of angular features that only Nordic genes could generate. He didn't talk much, and she liked that about him. When he *did* speak, she listened. Malte had been a Helsinki cop and then later a member of the Finnish SUPO intelligence service, and his instincts were always razor sharp. For her part, Lucy brought her sniper's eye to every situation, but she had a tendency to think only in terms of *targets* or *potential targets*, and sometimes the nuances could get lost behind her more military frame of mind.

The rosy waitress, whose badge announced her name as *Babs*, came to the booth and Lucy ordered coffee and waffles. By the time the order arrived, Lucy had spotted the car where the contact was waiting. A dark-blue Ford sedan, probably a rental, parked down the block in front of a vintage clothing store that had yet to open. On the dot of the clock striking the hour, the driver-side door opened and a Hispanic guy in a suit walked quickly across the street. As he entered the diner, he found Lucy and strode toward her. Over his shoulder, she saw Malte peel off from his position and vector in after him.

Lucy stiffened as she got a good look at the man, masking her dismay with a sip from her coffee. Her free hand slipped toward the butt of the Pulse pistol hidden in a paddle holster in the small of her back. The compact, non-lethal stun gun would be enough to take down a man of twice the new arrival's size.

The guy took the seat across the booth from her without waiting to be asked. "You're Keyes?"

"Could be," she said, with a sleepy half-smile, and put down the coffee mug. "I don't know you."

"Name's Gonzalez," he explained. "I'm with Rowan."

"Are you?" From the corner of her eye, she saw Malte enter the diner and come her way. "He never said anything about a new face." Lucy rocked back in the seat, as if she was preparing to leave.

"Don't," said Gonzalez, and the mask of studied calm he wore briefly slipped. "Give me a moment."

Malte was at the booth now, and slipped in next to Gonzalez so the other man had nowhere to go.

"I'm going to take something out of my pocket," said Gonzalez.

He produced a wallet and set it in the middle of the table, opening it to reveal a gold Department of Justice badge and a Federal Bureau of Investigation ID.

"Special Agent Lee Gonzalez." Lucy read his name aloud off the laminated card. "Like I said, I don't know you."

Gonzalez shot Malte a look and then put his attention on her. "Well, I know you, miss. Lucille Keyes, ex-US Army, dishonorably discharged, currently at large under an open arrest warrant—"

"Oh, stop it. I'm blushing." She ate some more of the waffles, and talked around a mouthful. "You look like a smart guy, so you clearly didn't come here on your own to take me in. Tell me why I am looking at you instead of Rowan."

Gonzalez blew out a breath. "People are concerned that Rowan has been operating outside his remit."

"People like you?"

The FBI agent shook his head. "He's just being careful."

Lucy saw Malte stiffen and reach for his own sidearm as a door behind her opened. A gruff voice, marbled with fatigue, cut through the air. "Good of you to come."

"Rowan." Lucy recognized the older man's tones immediately. She looked at Malte and shook her head. The Finn gave her a wary nod and put his hands back on the table.

"Keyes." In his mid fifties, with thinning hair and a face of weathered granite, Rowan looked like he should have been a senator or a general. Instead, his usual job was to keep those kind of men safe.

"How's the Secret Service treating you?" she asked.

"Poorly," he replied, sitting down next to her. "I don't need to draw you a picture. D.C. is a shit-show right now . . ." He trailed off. "That's why I reached out to you." Rowan signaled the waitress, and Babs came over with the coffee pot. She topped Lucy off and poured out mugs for the three men and, before she left, the woman gave Rowan's shoulder a squeeze.

"We okay here?" said Babs.

"Always." Rowan gave her a brief smile that sent her on her way. He saw the question in Lucy's eyes and answered it. "Barbara's husband was in my unit, back in the day. After he passed, the rest of the squad chipped in when this place had some landlord trouble. In return, I eat for free."

"And we get to use it for off-book conversations," added Gonzalez.

"Lee here is a good man," continued Rowan, "and he understands the situation. If you trust me, you trust him."

"All right." Lucy shot the FBI agent another glance, giving him a penetrating once-over. He didn't flinch from it, and she got the vague sense that she was staring into the eyes of someone who, like her, had been in harm's way more than once. "You served?"

"Marine Corps. Two tours in Iraq," Gonzalez replied without hesitation.

"Jarhead, huh? I guess I can make allowances."

"Don't give him a hard time," said Rowan. "He's sticking his neck out like I am."

"About that," said Malte, speaking for the first time.

"What do you want from us?" added Lucy. "After what happened with Al Sayf, I figured we wouldn't talk again."

Nearly two years ago, she had been in Washington, D.C., with Marc Dane, racing the clock to stop an atrocity engineered by the fanatical Al Sayf terror group and their collaborators in the Combine. It had almost been a total disaster, and if not for Special Agent Rowan—a former Delta Force operative like her—Lucy would not have been able to do her part in preventing the deaths of hundreds of innocent people. In the end, the shared conviction between two ex-soldiers had allowed her to avert disaster. That same trust had brought Lucy here to San Francisco, despite—as Gonzalez had rightly pointed out—her status as a fugitive under American law.

Rowan had contacted Rubicon via back channels and asked specifically for Lucy Keyes. She owed him enough of a debt to agree to the meet, but this cloak-and-dagger crap was getting on her nerves.

"Why am I here?" she continued. "Spit it out."

"We need your help," said Rowan, and the admission was hard for him. He leaned in. "Over the last six months, a joint operation involving the Secret Service and the FBI has been unravelling. We're tracking a radical militia group, but piece by piece, the op has been cut out from underneath us by the new administration. Now we're inches from being shut down completely."

"I'm the point man on it for the whole west coast," Gonzalez said grimly. "Everybody else in the Bureau has been ordered to prioritize external terrorist threats over domestic ones . . . But these creeps? We know they're planning an attack, possibly within the next forty-eight hours, right here." He tapped the laminated table with one finger. "But no one's listening."

"I can't get any weight behind this from my end," added Rowan. "Gonzalez has a couple of guys . . ." He paused for a moment, and when he spoke again, Rowan sounded like he had aged ten years. "We're mired in red tape. And I'm sick in my gut with the certainty that people are going to get hurt if we don't intervene."

Gonzalez anticipated the next question. "We've exhausted all our options. That's why Rowan threw in your name. Because you're outside the system."

Rowan's voice lowered. "I've heard the stories about Rubicon. I saw what you did in D.C. So I'm calling in a favor. A last resort. I need you to do some of that vigilante stuff for us."

"Who are the targets?" said Malte.

"They call themselves the Soldier-Saints," Gonzalez replied. "Your basic nightmare cocktail of radical Christian extremists, doomsday fanatics and white power neo-fascists. We got on to them because they were funding their exploits through a counterfeiting ring, but in the last couple of months they've gone through a step change. Upping the tempo of their operations in California, consolidating. They're getting ready for a big event, but with no manpower and no resources to help us prove it, all I have to show my ASAC is a bunch of circumstantial evidence. There's a location here in the city we scraped out of cell phone traffic, but without ironclad probable cause I can't get a warrant to go turn it over."

"Soldier-Saints . . ." Lucy gave a nod and beckoned Babs over for another refill. After the waitress had served them, she went on. "I know the name. If you ain't white, straight or male, they're looking to fit you with a collar or a noose. This city is gonna be like honey to them—hard to think of a place they'd hate more. But last I heard, they were pretty low-rent. What makes you think they're moving up to the big leagues?"

"Simple," said Rowan. "No one is there to stop them, and they've gotten bolder. And we're being forced to look the other way while they arm up."

Malte frowned. "Is someone helping their cause?"

"It's likely," said Rowan.

"Rubicon is a private military contractor, we know that," Gonzalez broke in. "But Rowan says you guys have a kind of *pro bono* attitude to this sort of thing. Is he right?"

"He's not wrong," offered Malte, pausing to take a gulp of coffee. He glanced at Lucy, raising a questioning eyebrow.

She found herself nodding. "There will have to be certain guarantees," she began.

"Whatever you need," said Rowan. "If it's in my power. Get us something actionable, something that the DOJ can't ignore."

Lucy sipped at her coffee and fixed the older man with a hard look. "We're not the police. People who get in my sights don't tend to end up in jail, you read me? What you're asking for here—what you're *sanctioning*—are you really sure you want to pull that trigger?"

The long silence that followed was finally broken by a sigh from Rowan. "I don't like it one damn bit," he said. "But right now, we don't have any other choice."


The shower in the Hotel Nova kept alternating between pulses of hot or tepid water, but the flow was powerful and Marc tried to wash away the sluggish after-effects of the flight.

It was late morning by the time he touched down in Malta, and the journey had made him itchy and uncomfortable. He wanted to clean off the adrenaline and refresh himself after the incident with the limousine, but it seemed now that the only chance to gather himself had been on the plane. It hadn't done the job.

Instead of snatching some much-needed sleep, he found himself going around and around down blind alleys of thought, picking at recent events like they were scabs.

The operation in France was the first Rubicon mission he had taken on where he acted as the lead in the field, and as much as he knew from previous experience that things never followed the plan you set out for them, the final execution had been disappointing. They had what they needed, but Marc felt like it was still undone. The abrupt *drop everything and go to Malta* orders from Solomon only served to make that worse.

Marc wanted to prove that he had made the right choice in accepting Solomon's offer of a job with the Special Conditions Division. Last year's situation in Mogadishu and Naples, where he and Lucy tracked and neutralized a rogue nuclear weapon, had left him feeling wrung out, questioning his place in the world. In the end, it was Solomon's simple perception of a truth that allowed Marc to find his way—*he wanted to be part of this, of something greater than himself, to work with a force for good.*

But there was more than that to it. Buried deeper beneath a drive to do right lay a colder, more pragmatic motivation. Marc understood the compulsion for justice—no, for *revenge*—that came from losing what mattered most to you.

There were still days when he closed his eyes and saw Samantha Green's smile in the darkness, fading from him like smoke. He would remember her touch on his skin and the bitterness would rise. Sometimes he would bolt awake in the middle of the night, convinced he could hear the jangle of a telephone ringing, knowing she would be on the other end of the line. But that phone was in a Camden Town safe house, half a world away.

Marc leaned into the water streaming from the showerhead and turned the dial toward the blue, embracing the cold. Icy needles burned out the thoughts plaguing him and he felt his skin tighten around the puckered marks of the healed bullet wounds on his arm and his belly. The exercise regimen drilled into him by the doctors at Rubicon's private clinic in Oslo had made a difference to his rail-thin form, giving back some of the muscle mass that his more sedentary time behind a keyboard at MI6 had stolen from him. He was nearly as fit as he had been back in his Royal Navy days. *Marc Dane 2.0*, he thought. *At least, that's the idea.*

He turned off the water and toweled dry as he walked out of the bathroom, although in the hot Maltese afternoon he hardly needed to. The basic, shabby hotel room had a good view of the bay. Settled in the Gzira district, close to the tourist hub of Sliema, it was ordinary enough to blend into the hundreds of other mid-range multi-story apartment blocks that lined the sea front. Security was a joke—Marc had already repurposed a spare towel to secure the door handle and blocked the balcony with a chair—but it was low profile, and after absorbing the new mission brief, that was exactly what they needed.

The file was unusually terse, but straight to the point. He assumed that was because this operation had been put together quickly. *Was that why he had been chosen to deal with it?*

Marc's skills were at their sharpest when improvising in a fluid situation, but that impulse always pulled against his conflicting desire to try and plan for every outcome, to weigh the numbers on each potential scenario.

The brief explained that an American civilian named Lex Wetherby was dead, apparently killed by a gunshot to the chest inflicted as he attempted to base jump from the battlements of Mdina. A known quantity in the world of data intrusion, Wetherby had previously been employed as an analyst for a major digital security company. At the start of his career, he ran "red team" sorties against the firewalls of major corporate clients in order to test their defenses, but eventually he came into conflict with his bosses and switched sides, dropping into the shadows of the so-called dark web. As a black-hat hacker-for-hire, he'd taken happily to the criminal life, but then his story became hazy.

In a world where bragging rights for those who pulled off the toughest hacks was precious currency, Wetherby became a phantom. Whatever he had been doing happened under the radar, unremarked and uncelebrated. Usually that was a sign of someone co-opted to work for a nation state's cyberwarfare force, but Wetherby didn't fit that profile. He was too much the console cowboy, too much the thrill-seeker.

And now he was dead, and the file said Rubicon believed that the Combine were involved in the killing. The mission orders were to sniff around and find out more about the circumstances of the hacker's murder. Marc grimaced as he thought about that. The briefing packet's text on exactly how that reasoning had come about was vague to say the least, and he made a mental note to press Kara for more information.

He sat on the bed, next to the large padded envelope that had been waiting for him at the lobby when he checked in. There was a machine-printed label on the front from a wholesale company, one small element of the Rubicon corporation's global structure. *Toy Box Supplies.*

The name made Marc smirk as he ripped open the packet and slid out the contents. The cardboard sleeve for a kit of construction blocks hid a small case made from gray armored plastic. He could have tossed it out of his fifth-floor window and it would have remained intact after hitting the road below, contents still undamaged. Flipping up a panel in the side of the case revealed a pinhole microphone where the lock should have been, and he spoke three words into it.

"Marc Dane. Nomad."

His choice of recognition word might have seemed mawkish, backward-looking even, but the name of his former MI6 unit still resonated with Marc in a way that nothing else could. It was also a constant reminder of where he had come from, and what would always be at stake.

The case accepted the voice print and concealed locks snapped open. Inside, dense foam padding protected the black glass slab of a satellite-enabled smartphone and a matching Bluetooth earpiece. Nestled next to the communication kit lay a Glock 29 subcompact semi-automatic pistol and a couple of additional magazines of 10mm ammunition. He considered the gun. Given the situation, Marc hadn't expected to be issued a "lethal pack" and again he wondered about what Rubicon was not telling him.

After checking and loading the weapon, he dressed quickly in some light cargo trousers and a loose khaki jacket over a T-shirt.

Marc fastened his dive watch around his wrist and glanced at the time. He was due to make contact.

The smartphone was a custom-made model bereft of identifying marks. It chimed as he activated it, and the micro-camera in the casing snapped a shot of his face, ensuring it recognized its user before it unlocked. A suite of apps blinked into life and he tapped an icon to activate the built-in end-to-end encryption software. A moment later, a bubble-shaped graphic flickered into life and the device vibrated.

He hit the *answer call* key and Kara Wei's voice issued out into the warm air. *"How d'you like the new spyPhone?"*

"Does it do more than the last model?"

*"Read the manual."* She took a breath. *"So, we're running this op under isolated protocol. I'm down the hall from you in room fifty-six. I'll act as base, you're the legs."*

"Got it." He considered what that meant. Under this mission profile, Marc and Kara would not interact directly except in the direst of circumstances. Each would operate physically separate from the other in order to maintain effective security. He looked at the gun as he paired the Bluetooth earpiece and put it on. "Are we expecting trouble here?"

*"A man is dead,"* Kara said briskly, her voice switching to his ear. *"Whoever shot him is still out there."*

"Right." Reluctantly, Marc tossed the weapon and the spare loads into a waterproof drawstring bag and slung it over his shoulder, heading out. As he passed Kara's room, he heard someone moving around inside. "So I reckon we start with Wetherby himself, yeah?"

*"His body is at the mortuary at Mater Dei Hospital, a few miles out of town."* Her voice was level now, back to "operational" mode. *"But there are guards on it. Leave that for a moment. I'm working on penetrating the local police headquarters in Floriana. I'll get what they have on the case, you check . . ."* She paused, and for a moment Marc thought he had lost her signal as he descended via elevator to the ground floor. *"Check out Nestor Kyrkos, the man Wetherby met with."*

"Okay." Marc slipped on the USAF-issue sunglasses he habitually wore as he walked out on to the street. The briefing had been equally thin on the Greek national and his employee, who had both been gunned down shortly before the hacker was murdered. He said as much to Kara, but she offered nothing more. "So where am I going?"

*"Kyrkos has a mooring at the Laguna Marina on the Valetta Water-front, near the cruise ship terminal. I'll send you a map."* He paused, and a moment later the phone chimed again, as new data arrived on the screen. *"We need to be sure what his part in all this is. Was he collateral damage, or involved in the hit somehow?"*

Marc accepted this with a nod and shot a look up at the Nova's fifth-floor balconies. Scanning across, he counted to the sixth room and saw a thickset surfer-type leaning on the balcony, sipping at a bottle of beer. Behind the guy, the inside of the room was hidden behind net curtains. "Who's the side of beef?"

*"What?"*

"The bloke on your balcony. Or did I miscount?"

*"No . . ."* Kara paused. *"I met him on the plane. I figured he'd be good cover. And I needed a little distraction. You have a problem with that?"*

That gave Marc pause, and he turned away, finding the red Maruti jeep he'd rented at the airport. "Just make sure it doesn't become a complication."

*"Sure,* Mom. *Whatever."* She cut the call with a snort.


Dog's nose wrinkled at the astringent scent of the cleaning fluid, as Fox moved around the living room of the cramped little villa, running a cloth soaked with the chemical over every surface that Cat or the men might have touched during their brief stay on the island. It was important to the operation to make sure that they left no traces of themselves behind for their enemies to find, should they be clever enough to trace the team back to this place.

Dog would have liked to burn the villa to the ground, to be thorough, but Fox argued that would draw too much attention. Even though the building was relatively isolated, away from Malta's busy coastal areas, there were enough witnesses around that such action might backfire on them. He reluctantly accepted the older agent's counsel, and while Fox worked, Dog busied himself packing up their equipment. Fox's sniper rifle, the Chinese-made AMR-2 that had taken the life of the American in Mdina, had been left behind in the departure and was now in the hands of the local police force, but nothing about it could be linked to this house. Cat and Dog's silenced weapons went into metal cases fitted with self-destruct charges that would obliterate everything within if opened by the unwary. The interiors of the cases were surrounded by special baffles that would mask the presence of the pistols inside from any cursory electronic scanning. The guns themselves were OTs-38s; five-shot revolvers originally developed by Russia's FSB security service as implements of pure assassination. Clever design and specialized silent ammunition rendered the weapons virtually soundless when fired. They were the ideal tools for Dog and his comrades.

A low electronic tone sounded from the other room and Cat entered, carrying a silver digital tablet connected to a heavy black brick of military-grade communications gear. "She's making contact," said the woman.

Dog indicated the low table in the middle of the room with a jut of his chin, and Cat placed the devices there. He sat in a chair and hunched forward so he could look into the tiny black circle of the tablet's camera. Cat delicately tapped in a numerical code on the screen and an image unfolded.

Dog saw a darkened room of bare concrete walls and shadows that fell deep and black. He made out the shapes of gray pillars and folding tables laden with computer equipment, but there were no signs of life. After a moment, a woman in a rumpled brown leather jacket hove into view and sat down in front of the camera at the other end of the line. Data artifacts occasionally broke across the picture in fragments as encryption software worked to render their communication unreadable, and an oval of blocky, obfuscating pixels tracked with the woman's face as she moved. He could make out the suggestion of ashen skin, outlined with shoulder-length hair in a red-brown shade that seemed very foreign to Dog.

"*Good work*," she began. Her words came in a flat machine monotone rendered by a masking filter, but despite it an American accent was still detectable. Her compliment drew no reply from Dog and he waited for her to continue. "*I would have liked it better if you could have done this with fewer witnesses present.*"

Fox scowled, out of sight of the tablet's video pickup. "He was in danger of getting away," explained Dog. "I assessed the risk and we proceeded. That is what we were sent to do."

"*Sure,*" the woman allowed. "*I'm not second-guessing you here. I'm saying it could have been cleaner.*"

"I will take that on board," Dog replied, deliberately maintaining a blank mien. The mask-face focused on him through the screen and for a moment he felt like she was searching his expression for some indicator of his true feelings. Dog did nothing to betray the thoughts in the back of his mind, the distaste he felt at being ordered to follow the woman's directives. He decided to proceed with his report. "We are in the process of extraction. Now the target has been successfully terminated, the unit will depart before nightfall. We have no indications that local law enforcement are aware of us. The mission was a success."

She looked away for a moment, the image flickering as she stared into the empty darkness around her. "*Lex . . . His resolve turned out to be weaker than I expected. It's disappointing.*" She sighed.

Again, Dog said nothing. He, along with Fox and Cat, had little personal investment in the woman or her people, errant or not. They simply followed their orders, as good soldiers always did.

Some fraction of his uninterest must have slipped through his sullen expression, because the woman brushed a length of her hair away from her face, the blocks of color shifting, and renewed her focus on him. Her tone hardened. "*We're proceeding to the next stage. The test in Taipei performed better than we expected. There won't be any more distractions from now on. Let your people know we're on track. But in the meantime, make sure you're available to me for rapid deployment. Some clean-up will be required, I'm sure of it. This business with Lex has encouraged me to move up my timetable . . .*"

"As you wish. When you have a new target, we will be waiting." He reached toward the tablet to cut the feed, but she continued.

"*One final point. I don't doubt your thoroughness, but what about the materials you recovered? Lex's computer, his gear? Where is it?*"

Dog gave Cat a look that brought her into range of the camera. "A secure package is already on its way to you," said Cat, hovering at his shoulder. "As requested."

"*You didn't find anything else in his hotel room?*" she pressed.

Cat shook her head. "He appeared to have only one copy on him."

"*Good. That's good. But we can't assume that he didn't make another. He had enough time. Did you set up the monitor like I asked?*"

"Yes," said Dog tersely, wanting to end the conversation. "Is there anything else?"

"*I will let you know.*" The woman reached off-camera and the tablet darkened.

The active lights on the communications brick winked out and Cat disconnected the device, unable to prevent a sneer from crossing her lips.

Predictably, it was Fox who gave voice to what they were all thinking. "She talks to us as if she thinks we are only fit to deal with her mistakes. Unable to do anything without being told to." He gave a grunt of displeasure and went back to work, finishing up his cleaning regimen.

"Arrogance," agreed Cat. "That is what it is."

"It is not required that we like her," Dog broke in, before the conversation could proceed. "We have our orders to aid her. We will do as she says, but never forget she is not our commander." He laid his hand on one of the pistols in the case. "Her continued existence is only predicated on how useful she is."

"I distrust her," said Fox.

"Of course you do," said Dog firmly. "She isn't one of us. That makes her the enemy. But one that is, for the moment, of use."

Nestor Kyrkos's modest yacht was not hard to locate. It was standing at the end of a jetty with a line of blue-and-white warning tape acting as a cordon around the mooring cleats. Marc walked past it without making a big deal about scoping it out, catching sight of a large square sticker with a police badge on it adhering to the hull. The text on the sticker explained the boat had been impounded by the Maltese coastguard.

He considered and then discarded the idea of trying to sneak on board. It was broad daylight and there were too many other yachts clustered around, the risk that he would be seen by someone was too great. The police headquarters building Kara had mentioned was only a couple of streets away, so it was doubtful that he would have much opportunity to escape if the cops were called. Waiting until nightfall was an option, but still a risk.

The situation called for a different approach. Marc walked the length of the marina, blending in as best he could with the other boat owners until he found the dock supervisor's office. He straightened his jacket and pulled up a false front of confidence, pushing open the door.

A swarthy, middle-aged man with the look of someone over-worked and underpaid met him as he entered, moving to block his path. "Can I help you, sir?"

"Hey, how are you?" Marc offered him a handshake, and he took it. "You're in charge here, right?" Marc looked down and found a nametag on the guy's uniform shirt. "Stefan?"

"Yes." The man gave him a wary look. "You're not one of our guests . . ."

"Nope." Marc quickly took in the office, seeing neat piles of pa-perwork beneath a high-detail pilot's map of the bay around Valetta. There were a few personal touches—a pennant from the Naxxar Lions football club, some family photos and a peace lily in a pot—but largely the place was all business. Marc mentally sifted it all in an instant and found an approach he could use. He pointed at the Lions flag. "And you're not a Valetta FC fan. That's unusual."

Stefan pulled a face. Clearly this was a sore point. "I come from up the coast in Naxxar. The other men here, they give me a hard time about it, you know?"

"I can imagine." The question served as a perfect ice-breaker, and Marc followed it up with a smile. He'd wrong-footed the man and now he had to quickly take advantage of it. "Look, I wonder if you could help me out? I'm not a guest, you're right. My name's Marcus Dale and I work for the *New York Times* as local stringer."

"Oh." Stefan couldn't stop himself from shooting a look out toward Kyrkos's yacht.

"A man was killed in Mdina yesterday. An American. I'm sure you heard about it on the news. My editor has me reporting on the story for the paper."

"It's very sad," said Stefan, and he took a step toward Marc, clearly trying to get him to move back toward the door.

He stood his ground. "The man who died, he met with one of your guests. Mr. Kyrkos, berthed at slip sixteen. And it turned out badly for him too, I've heard."

"I wouldn't know anything about that." Stefan glanced down at the phone on his desk, and Marc could guess at the thought forming in his mind. *Call the cops. Call security. Call someone to get rid of this reporter.*

He pressed the point. "Look, mate, I don't want to get you into trouble. I know how it is. You have to respect the privacy of your guests."

"Talk to the police," Stefan insisted, with a flash of irritation. "They've already been here twice, throwing their weight around."

Marc saw the opportunity and acted on it, turning Stefan's annoyance into a moment of shared experience. "I know, same thing happened to me," he lied. "I got nothing from them, that's why I'm here." He took a breath. "The bloke who was shot, his family . . ." He made a point of looking at one of the framed photos of Stefan, which showed him hoisting a little girl on his shoulders. She had a sweet face, grinning from ear to ear. "They want to know what really happened to their son, yeah?" Marc felt a distant sting of guilt as he built up the shape of the lie that was going to get him what he wanted.

When the man didn't reply, he went for the last push and pointed at the photo. "That your daughter? She's pretty." Off Stefan's nod, Marc slipped a hundred-euro note between his fingers and rested his hand on the windowsill. "How old is she, eight or nine? Probably has a birthday coming up soon, I imagine."

Stefan saw the note and understood. "Yes. I have to work hard for my family. Long hours, you know?"

"I bet you don't get well compensated for it, either." Marc lifted his hand, leaving the note where it was and gestured at the boats around them. "In my experience, rich folks don't tend to tip much."

He glanced away and when he looked back the money had gone.

"Mr. Kyrkos wasn't a friendly sort," Stefan offered. "But he has . . . He had a lot of influence."

Marc met the other man's gaze. "I bet there are stories about how he came by it."

Stefan studied the picture. "I also have a son. He's eleven. We're going to get him a BMX bike for Christmas."

Marc showed him a friendly smile and another couple of banknotes. "Why wait till then?"

# — FOUR —

Marc found a café near the Lido Fortina that offered free Wi-Fi and approached a table at the back, deep beneath the shades keeping the hard sunshine off the customers. The waiter gave him an odd look, as the tables fronting the bay were usually the most requested, and Marc pulled at the bill of his baseball cap, muttering about having skin that tanned poorly. He took a seat with his back to the wall and ordered an ice-cold Kinnie. The local brand of bitter orange soft drink was an acquired taste, but the sharp flavor gave him focus as he logged on to the café's network.

The Rubicon-issue spyPhone snapped open along its longest axis, part of the casing sliding down to reveal a tiny pad of configurable touch-keys. As a matter of course, Marc activated a security layer to protect him from any dubious malware that might be lurking on the public Wi-Fi net and searched for a video that the marina supervisor had told him about.

He found it on a "live leaks" site where raw, uncensored footage captured by cell phones and digital cameras across the globe could be anonymously uploaded. *Grisly Malta Murder Caught on Camera* read the banner at the top the video window, with a block of ghoulish text providing trigger warnings for anyone who might be thinking about watching it. The film was a twenty-second loop of juddering images from someone's hand-held, starting with a panning shot of two grinning teenage girls in one of Mdina's terrace restaurants. The footage veered as the camera operator turned to take in the view from the battlements of the old city, and captured Lex Wetherby as he scrambled up the slope toward the sheer drop below. He had a micro-chute canister strapped to his back, and Marc guessed what he had been attempting to do when he was shot. Someone saw Wetherby moving and called out in alarm. People thought the hacker had been trying to commit suicide.

Then the guy made a panicked dash for the edge, as if he had caught sight of his killer. Marc paused and rolled back the footage, trying to see what the dead man had seen, but the angle was wrong. He let the rest of the video play out to the end.

Wetherby popped the chute and leaped off, causing a ripple of shock through the onlookers. One of the cameraman's friends started to speak as the hacker was momentarily propelled up by a gust of wind, but then a bloody spurt of crimson erupted from Lex's chest and everyone started screaming. The camera's eye fell to show only a blur of flagstones as the owner panicked and fled. Describing the video as "grisly" had been an understatement.

Whoever had taken the footage wasn't the person who uploaded it. The version he watched had a Ukrainian web address attached to it, doubtless where some enterprising net dweller had copied the original from a cloud server and served it up to garner page-clicks for the ad revenue. It had already been viewed over two million times, and the uploader had added a little stinger by cutting in slow-motion replays and grainy blow-ups of the moment the kill-shot hit.

Marc checked the few seconds before Wetherby had been struck by the bullet, listening to the background noise on the video through his earpiece. He couldn't pick out any sounds of a weapon discharging.

He sat back and nursed his drink, fitting in this evidence with what else Stefan had told him. Once the man had started talking, he had made it clear how little regard anyone working at the Laguna Marina had for Nestor Kyrkos. Stefan described the Greek as a braggart, with a mile-wide mean streak and a reputation for slapping around his women. No one at the marina had been surprised to hear that Kyrkos had been killed, Stefan said. He had ties to criminal gangs here in Malta, along with connections to the Sicilian mafia and racketeers back home in his native Athens. It started to make sense when the marina supervisor made an offhand comment: *Kyrkos was the sort of man you called when you wanted to get away, no questions asked.*

Wetherby had met Kyrkos in Mdina to broker an exit plan. But to where, and why?

Marc stared into the middle distance. Without more information, there was nothing to lay the hacker's killing at the Combine's door. Had he worked for them? The gaps in his timeline made it clear that he had been working for someone off the grid. Was there something he knew, something he had stolen? The possibilities went around and around, going nowhere.

Marc typed in a new command string on the little keyboard, tapping at it with his index fingers. An agile Tor router program built into the phone activated a virtual private network link, which he could use to contact Rubicon's secure cloud servers. Marc composed and encrypted an email request to Delancort for any information the Special Conditions Division had on Nestor Kyrkos, hoping that a clue in the Greek's background might provide a new approach. As an addendum, he attached the URL for the video and suggested that Rubicon's imaging lab in Palo Alto soak it for any clues. But when he sent the message, it returned an *undeliverable* warning tag.

"What the hell?" The words had barely left his mouth before the phone rang. Kara Wei's identity icon blinked at him on the screen and he tapped it. "Yeah?"

"*You're unsecured,*" she told him, without preamble. "*Sorry. Should have told you. Call backs to Rubicon are being routed through my machine right now.*"

"Is that usual procedure?" He stared at the phone, imagining Kara on the other end of the line, sitting cross-legged on her bed at the Hotel Nova with a halo of electronic equipment spread out around her.

"*Delancort put a red code on this. Confidence is high that the Combine are doing deep channel monitoring of everything going in and out of the Maltese comms grid, so we need to compartmentalize. I'm gating everything, is that a problem?*"

"You should have told me." He paused, weighing her words. "Seems like a lot of effort for one dead guy."

Marc was going to say more, but Kara went on as if he had not spoken. "*Okay, so, I broke into the police database. Forwarding you a copy of the case file right now.*" The phone chimed and he found a new digital dossier in the memory, pages of machine-translated Maltese from the initial police report and the medical examiner's preliminary look at the hacker's corpse. *"Long story short, the cops from the Criminal Investigation Division are already tying Lex to Kyrkos and his links with organized crime. They're following the assumption that this is a deal that turned sour."* She made a snorting noise. *"The obvious explanation."*

"But not the actual one?" Marc replied, finding the file pages from the morgue. "I mean, there's a chance this could be what it looks like. Black hat hacker gets in over his head with a smuggler, and—"

*"No."* She shut him down firmly. *"It's not that."*

"Okay." He told her what he had learned from Stefan as he skimmed the file, ignoring the bulk of the text to find the summary section. The examining doctor's report on Wetherby's killing was stark and to the point.

*Cause of death: gunshot wound to the chest. Damage pattern consistent with high-velocity rifle round fired from range.*

Marc thought about the video and the grim possibility of a sniper on some nearby rooftop, and was glad he'd chosen to sit somewhere out of sight.

*"I'm working up an ID that you'll be able to use to access the mortuary at Mater Dei, so you can get a look at Lex's body . . ."* He heard the soft clatter of keystrokes through the earpiece. *"It's taking longer than I expected."*

Marc scrolled back through the pages of the report. "Our guy stayed at a hotel in Paceville, a place called the Adagio." He opened up a web browser and found the Adagio's booking site. It was a small, characterless block of self-catering apartments off the main drag of the nightclub district, little different from the hotel where he and Kara were based. "I'll go scope it out," he added.

*"Good call,"* Kara said distractedly. *"Do that."*

But he didn't move from his seat, instead pausing to finish his drink. At length, the hazy sense of suspicion that had been forming in Marc ever since he left France solidified. "You want to tell me what you're not telling me, Kara?"

*"Say what?"*

"I mean, I admit I'm not the same kind of operator as Lucy, I don't have her experience. But I do have an instinct I depend on." It had been that sense that kept Marc Dane alive in the past when he had gone on the run, and over the past few hours it had steadily rung louder and louder.

Kara remained silent for a long time, and once more he thought he had lost her signal completely. But when she spoke again, she sounded vulnerable and afraid. "*You don't trust me.*" He remembered what she had said to him in Chamonix. That same tone in her voice, like she was lost.

"That's not it." Part of him knew that he should have pressed her, but he was in this now, and the mystery of the motive behind Wetherby's murder had its hooks in him. "Be honest with me."

"*I am,*" she said tersely. "*Get back in touch when you've taken a pass over the hotel.*" Her moment of weakness vanished, the line clicking off.

If anything, the Adagio looked even less appealing in real life than it did from its shots on the travel advisor website. Fitted in asymmetrically between two other equally unlovely apartment blocks, it had a half-hearted set of pastel panels painted up the length of the facia in some vain attempt to make the place look cool. But those colors had gone out of fashion in the eighties and no one had cared enough to update it. The hotel and its neighbors formed a wedge of dull concrete blocking out the backstreets behind Paceville, serving as little more than crash pads for the tourists who lived for the neon-drenched clubs and bars that lit up the place after sunset. At this time of day, the hotels were quiet. Most of the residents would be out on the beach or still sleeping off the previous night's over-indulgence.

The front desk was unmanned. Marc scoped out the cheap security camera aimed at the doorway through the gap between the top of his sunglasses and the bottom of his baseball cap's bill. The lens was covered in a layer of dust, which meant that on the off-chance it was still working, his face would be obscured. *So far, so good.*

Past a grumbling ice machine, Marc found a narrow, steep staircase and jogged up to the fourth floor where Wetherby had been staying. The corridor was dingy and unventilated, but he found what he was looking for straight away. Like Kyrkos's yacht, the door to the dead man's room had crime scene tape cordoning it off and another police warning sticker plastered over the spyhole.

The lock popped open easily with a little work from the knife in Marc's folding multi-tool. He could see scuff marks around the mechanism where it had clearly been forced before. As the door opened, he ducked under the tape and inside, halting on the threshold.

The hacker's room looked like a tornado had ripped through it. Every cupboard in the compact kitchenette had been opened. The mattress in the bedroom was folded up in a corner, the bed frame beneath it shoved away from the wall. All the drawers hung slack and the wardrobe gaped along with them. A breeze came in from an open sliding door on the far side of the room, making the blackout curtain shift and move.

Marc picked his way over discarded piles of clothes and looked into the tiny bathroom. There was nothing but a dripping shower and a few cheap men's toiletries along the top of the washbasin. He crouched and found the shredded remains of a leather wash bag on the cracked tile floor. Whoever had turned this room over had looked in every possible place where the dead man might have concealed something.

*The question is, what did Wetherby have to hide?* The most likely answer was *data*, and if he hadn't risked sending it to a cloud server that meant some kind of physical media, probably a USB drive or a microSD card.

It was clear to Marc that the murders of the hacker and the smuggler were nothing to do with turf wars or criminal payback, as the police were assuming. His gut told him that Wetherby was a thief, and he had died because of it. Marc poked at the torn bag with the blade of the multi-tool. Had the people who killed him actually *found* what they were looking for?

He wandered back into the room and made a slow orbit of it, checking through the mess, coming up empty.

There were too many *if*s and not enough certainties. *If* Wetherby had stolen from the Combine, *if* he was trying to leverage Kyrkos to get him to safety with it, *if* he had been killed for robbing them . . . Marc knew from personal experience that those who double-crossed the Combine's power-players ended up dead.

He thought about Dima Novakovich, a middleman who had worked with the group as a black-book accountant and a broker before turning informant to MI6. A man shot down right in front of him by a Combine kill-team for daring to go against them. And remembering Dima threatened to release a rising tide of other, more acidic recollections.

Marc stifled the anger before it came, but it had already started to distract him. Enough that he had missed the little electronic device sitting beneath the dresser, aiming its unblinking eye into the hotel room.

It wasn't a camera, but a wireless ultraviolet sensor unit, the kind that would be connected to a cheap home-security system. The invisible beam it projected reflected back into a tiny detector, and Marc had broken the line by passing in front of it. *Silent alarm*, he told himself, hesitating at the open window, looking out at the dilapidated sundeck beyond that connected the Adagio's fourth-floor balconies.

He retreated back into the shadows, annoyed at his inattention. If someone had planted the sensor here, it meant they were watching the place to observe anyone who might come looking into the hacker's death—and Marc had blundered right into that. If he was quick, if he ran *right this second*, he might be able to get away before whomever the alarm summoned arrived.

But then another thought occurred to him. This was an opportunity to get a look at Wetherby's killers face to face. He could stake out the room and wait to see who came looking, turning the trap around on those who had set it.

He started for the door, and had it open when a high-pitched whining tone reached his ears. The noise came from outside, a whirring, nasal buzz that sounded like a Formula 1 racing car on helium. Marc made a choice and ducked into the shadowy bathroom, pressing himself into a corner. He felt for the drawstring bag on his back and drew the Glock, pulling back the slide to make sure a round was in the chamber.

The buzzing grew louder. It was in the hotel room now. Marc squinted into the mirror over the washbasin, the angle of it acute enough for him to be able to see a sliver of the bedroom and kitchen alcove. A shadow flickered over the walls and an odd, spindly shape floated into view.

A small quadrotor drone, not much larger than a hardback book, hovered in the air. Four arms ending in the blur of fast-spinning propeller blades suspended the skinny fuselage of the insect-like machine. It had a skeletal, unfinished look to it, the workings of the drone's mechanisms clearly visible as it pivoted in place. Marc saw the stubby mast of a Bluetooth antenna poking up from the middle of the device and the glitter of a mono-eye camera in its "nose." The drone executed a slow turn, taking in the room with its unblinking lens. It bobbed in the air toward the front of the room, coming closer.

Marc shrank back, out of its line of sight. He could sense a human hand on the controls of the thing from the way it moved, and wondered who might be on the far end of its radio circuit. A clever idea, he reflected. Leaving the drone concealed nearby was a good way to keep a watchful eye on Wetherby's room without actually exposing a human asset to discovery.

But the drone could still provide some vital clues, if he could get his hands on it. Marc snatched a damp towel from the drying rack near the bath and made ready to throw it over the little machine.

When he looked up, it was right there in the doorway, rotors spinning in an angry blur. He couldn't help but flinch in surprise, and the drone did the same, jerking away as the operator flicked the controls to back off. With a screech of power, it retreated across the room toward the open window.

"Shit!" Marc dropped the towel and ran after the fleeing machine, hurdling the rusted metal rails of the balcony to land flat-footed on the sundeck. The drone powered upward in a vertical rise, and he brought the pistol to bear, aiming after it. But the target was small and fast, and he knew there was a less-than-likely chance of him hitting it. He kept cursing and stuffed the gun in his belt, grabbing at a series of artfully protruding bricks on the far wall. They gave him the handholds he needed to scramble up past the fifth floor and on to the roof of the Adagio, in time to see the drone buzz away in the direction of the beach. It flew lazily over the crown of the next apartment block along, weaving around a cluster of satellite TV dishes.

Marc sprinted across the tarpaper-covered roof and over a low wall that demarcated the line between the two buildings. If he was actually going to try to shoot the thing out of the sky, he needed to be close enough to make sure he would not miss, because filling the air with bullets in a vain attempt to bring down the drone would have police swarming the area in minutes.

As the little machine dipped over the far gable, he saw it make a yawing motion, turning into a backward-flying attitude to aim its camera eye at him. Whomever controlled the device most likely ran it through a first-person view rig, using video goggles to give them a simulated outlook that would mimic that of a pilot's cockpit. They were trying to get a good shot of him, a clean capture of the face of their pursuer.

Marc slid over the edge in front of him and into a half-meter blind drop down to the top of the next building. He landed hard with a grunt, and a shock of pain lanced up through his shins as the baseball cap on his head flicked off in the rush of air. The drone flipped over and pitched forward to gain speed and distance, zipping over the mildewed tiles around a dusty, waterless rooftop swimming pool.

Cutting off the corner, Marc ran across the shallow end of the drained pool, slipping on a drift of crumbly leaves that had blown into the corners. He skidded and almost fell, losing precious momentum, and saw the drone extend away.

For a moment, he thought he had lost his chance. But then the machine swung back around and bobbed closer, side-slipping through the air.

"You are taking the piss, aren't you, mate?" Marc called out, wondering if it had audio as well as video surveillance capability. The drone's pilot was toying with him. Had they wanted to get out of there and leave Marc standing, it would have been easy enough to power upward in a steep climb, or drop quickly down to the streets below. Instead, they were playing games.

Marc raised his right hand and offered the drone a universal gesture that would communicate his temperament to anyone who saw it, his middle finger aimed upward. The drone bounced playfully through the warm air, circling him just high enough to be out of arm's reach, and as it came around, the operator might have seen where Marc's other hand was resting—atop the grimy haft of an old pool sweeper half-hidden beneath the leaves and windblown rubbish.

He moved in a fast spin, flicking up the length of the sweeper so that the ragged mesh basket at the far end hit the drone square-on, swatting it like a fly. The little quadrotor spun down against the floor of the pool and clattered noisily off the grimy blue tiles, spinning to a halt in the deep end.

"Gotcha, you little sod!" Marc dropped the sweeper and ran down the incline to where the drone lay on its back. The rotors juddered, whined and stopped, fragments of plastic littering the area around it.

If he could tear it apart, get into the control circuitry and radio gear, dismantle it . . . Marc grabbed at the frame of the machine. Taking a good look at it, he could see it was built on a carbon-fiber mount, with high-end components.

This was a custom racer-grade machine, not some gadget store plaything. He turned it over in his hands, and without warning the digital motors at the ends of the frame burst back into life. Razor-sharp polymer propellers slashed at his hands, slicing into skin.

"Damn it!" He let go by reflex and the drone leaped from his grip, and into the air, the high hornet's snarl of its rotors setting his teeth on edge.

Damaged and wobbling, but still airworthy, the drone fled as fast as it could, vanishing over the edge of the pool. Ignoring the pain from the lacerations across his hands, Marc went after it. He scrambled along the roof and over the edge on to a series of staggered concrete sun shades. From there, he made a jump over a meter-wide gap to the next building, a series of older terraced apartments with roofs of red tile. Even as he chased after it, a part of Marc knew there was no way he would be able to catch the drone now. The machine ignored him and flew at full throttle, down the line of the road that ended in the blue-green waters of St. George's Bay.

Each sloping roof brought him one story closer to street level, and from below he heard tourists calling up at him as he ran, ducking under low-hanging antennas or over the humming forms of air conditioner units. The last roof ended in a sheer drop above the entrance to a bar and he used an open awning to break his fall, sliding down off it and on to the road.

The drone sped out over the sand, over the heads of surprised sunbathers who called out in alarm. Marc jumped a low-slung barrier bordering the beach and ran down to the water's edge, the waves swamping his trainers as the drone kept on flying and left him behind, arrowing out over the blue toward nothing. For a moment, he thought it might be homing back on a boat out there, possibly the place from which it was being flown, but there were only empty dinghies bobbing on the water. The drone became a dot, the buzz of its rotors fading as it reached the mouth of the bay where the shallows fell away. Marc shaded his eyes to stare after it, and saw a brief blink of sunshine off the shiny black frame as its battery charge finally gave out and it fell. A white splash of foam marked the place where the drone hit the water, and then it was gone.

Glaring into the distance, Marc retreated back from the tide line and sat heavily on the coarse yellow sand. He did his best to clean the stinging, shallow cuts on his hands with clean water from his pack.

He hung his head and stared at the ground. "I fucking hate drones," he said to himself, wincing as his hands tightened into fists.

After a while, he looked back in the direction he had come, scanning the rooftops of Paceville and considering the situation. The drone's remote pilot had dumped it into the sea to prevent anyone from getting information from it, and with the currents out in the bay there would be no chance of finding the thing in the water. Marc's first thought was that the operator had to be close, no more than a thousand meters away from the drone itself, but then he remembered the high-density antenna he had seen on the machine's casing. With the right kind of on-board communication hardware, the drone's command signal could have been coming from any wireless network within range. That meant the pilot could have been as close as the guy with a smartphone sitting on the patio of the nearest bar, or a world away down some fast-traffic internet connection.

*And they saw my face.*


The day had turned out to be a fine one in the end, and the warmth still lingered as the sun set behind the downtown towers of San Francisco. Now darkness was falling, but the streets were bright with street lamps and loud with the constant ebb and flow of traffic through the grid of avenues and boulevards.

Lucy and Malte had left their car hidden in an alleyway off Folsom Street and worked their way into an empty construction site that faced the corner with 1st Street. The SoMa district—so named because it was South of Market Street—had been the hub of a dozen new builds over the last decade, as foreign investors planted their stakes in the ground to take advantage of the city's fortunes. Their view was filled by the golden glass facia of a newly built office block that was still a couple of months away from opening, the target address that Special Agent Rowan had given them in the diner. They stood in the angular skeleton of a neighboring building, the frame of a high-end hotel that would be finished in a year or so. For now, it was a collection of flat concrete floors arranged around the gray pillars of elevator shafts and utility trunks.

Keeping low, the two operators moved to the open edge of the fourth floor and took up positions behind sheets of plastic fencing that flexed in the wind off the bay. As Malte set up two compact tripods next to her, Lucy pulled a pair of Steiner military binoculars from her backpack and swept the front of the office block for threats. She picked out the wide marble atrium of the new building through a roof made of triangular glass panels, the frontage walled off behind safety barriers.

She immediately spotted two men carrying small machine pistols, and by the way they clustered up too close together, she could tell they were weekend warrior types. They looked nervy.

Still, the Soldier-Saints were not to be underestimated. They had been responsible for the torching of abortion clinics in the South

West and attacks on mosques around the Great Lakes. In the past, they would have been ringing alarm bells up and down the domestic terror watch list for those kind of hate crimes, but in the current political climate they were getting a free pass.

Lucy continued her sweep, picking out a handful of other men on the lower floors and a couple more walking the office block's perimeter. Hard-earned instinct made her skin prickle and she studied the patterns of their deployment, trying to read through the positions of the guards to guess at what was going on in there.

"Something's up," she told the Finn. "I think Rowan's on the money. These creeps are edgy as hell."

Malte took that in with a nod, and plugged a pair of cables into the tube-shaped device on the first tripod mount. It resembled a child's telescope made of black anodised metal, capable of projecting an ultraviolet laser beam for a distance of several miles. On the second tripod was another device, this one a silver box with a wide lens filling one face. Inside it, a detector array capable of picking up the reflections of the UV laser from whatever it was shone at. If the laser beam hit a window or some other surface that conducted vibrations, sound passing through the air nearby could be registered and digitally recovered. The laser acted like a long-range microphone and did away with the need to be in close physical proximity to a surveillance target. Malte ran the equipment through a calibration program as Lucy kept watch.

"Ready," he told her, and activated the laser. He panned it around to find the first pair of guards and they listened in on a discussion that turned out to be a play-by-play narrative of the two men's most recent sexual exploits.

Lucy rolled her eyes. "I've seen this show already. What else is on?" She unzipped her backpack and removed the pieces of a Remington Defense CSR long arm, a magazine of 7.62mm rounds and a compact sound suppressor.

As she assembled and ranged-in the sniper rifle, Malte checked the data from the laser. Over the next half-hour they used the microphone to pluck out conversations from each group of Soldier-Saints visible inside the building. Most of them had little of value to say, but when one man dropped the mention of "an arrival" Lucy exchanged a sharp look with the Finn.

"So they're waiting for somebody. This is feeling more and more like they're staging for an operation."

"Agreed." Malte adjusted a dial on the laser. "You trust Rowan." He made it a statement, not a question.

Lucy remembered a simple tattoo in black ink on the arm of the Secret Service agent, the silhouette of a dagger and the Latin phrase *De oppresso liber*. "He was Delta. He kept his word to me before. Yeah, I trust him." She took a breath and went on. "If he wanted me in cuffs, he had his chance to take me back at the diner. Why give us this lead?"

"There are many reasons," offered Malte.

She shrugged and put her eye to the scope of the CSR. "Guess we'll find out . . ." The rest of the sentence fell away as she sighted a vehicle slowing to a halt in front of the mesh gates closing off the darkened office building. "Action," she said. "I see an ambulance pulling up to the back of the building. No lights or sirens. Can't see who is inside."

Malte tilted the laser and the receptor to bounce a beam off the flat side of the vehicle, but the return they got back was dirty with vibrations from the ambulance's idling engine and it was impossible to pick out anything intelligible. As Lucy watched, the gates were opened enough to let the ambulance through, and then the guards quickly closed them again, casting wary looks up and down the street to make sure they hadn't been observed.

From their high angle, Lucy could see the ambulance turn and drop on to the ramp that led to the office's underground car park. It thudded over the lip of the ramp, rolling on its shocks. Light briefly spilled out from inside as it passed through the gate, and then it was gone.

"An emergency vehicle is good cover," she thought aloud. "It's riding low on the shocks, so now I really wanna know what they have in there."

"Hospital is a soft target," offered Malte, the grim outcome of any such attack giving them both pause.

Lucy drew back from the rifle and checked an area map on her phone. The UCSF Medical Center in Mission Bay and St. Francis

Memorial to the north were a few minutes' drive away, and both would be easy marks for men with guns and hate in their hearts. She wondered about that, and reached deep for a colder, more detached part of her psyche, trying to put herself in the mindset of the Soldier-Saints.

They had clearly invested a lot of time and effort to set up their operation. The free run they had of the office block told her that they must have infiltrated the construction firm charged with completing it, plus the ambulance and the guns on display spoke to careful forward planning. This was more than some opportunistic drive-by shooting.

"How do we proceed?" Malte watched her carefully. She was senior field agent, and the call was hers to make.

Options lined up in her head as she weighed them for viability. An anonymous call to the San Francisco Police Department about men with guns would bring the cops in loaded for bear, but that could have serious blowback and it upped the risk of casualties. If she started picking off the Soldier-Saint guards from range, the whole pack could get wind and make a run for it. That left one more unpleasant alternative; they needed to get closer, and see for sure what was going on in there.

"Another vehicle," said Malte, shifting forward to get a better look. "At the front this time."

Lucy swung the rifle around to find the silver shape of a BMW rolling to a stop by the sidewalk. An androgynous figure in a long leather coat climbed out of the back seat, carrying a black briefcase. Lucy flicked the scope's setting to full magnification and the face leaped closer. The new arrival had dark, slick hair and East Asian features, and stood in stark comparison to the stout white men who came out to meet the car. The BMW pulled away and vanished around the corner, leaving the figure in the coat alone to face the glowering Soldier-Saints.

"Looks like someone is at the wrong party," muttered Lucy, as the two guards patted down the new arrival and then marched them through a gate, into the darkened entrance atrium. "Get the mic on them."

Malte aimed the beam at the glass. Lucy zoomed out a couple of notches and tracked the figure in the leather coat. Other armed men were coming to meet the group, led by a shaven-headed guy who walked with a cowboy swagger and a big revolver in a hip-holster.

"Well, hello, Hop-Along." Lucy took in the bald man, gauging his attitude from the way he moved among the others. This was somebody in charge. The group passed out of sight into the depths of the shadows and she lost sight of them. "Shit. No visual."

"I can still get audio," said Malte, adjusting the laser. The pickup from the decoder crackled.

"*You're it?*" The voice was male and it had a hard, Midwestern edge. He didn't sound impressed, and Lucy surmised she was listening to the man with the revolver. "*After all the goddamn money we're payin,' I expected something . . . I guess, more impressive? Not one little slope. But then again, you guys are supposed to be real smart with the computers, right?*"

She heard a clicking sound—maybe the case opening—and then another voice, strangely low but with a cadence that told her it was a woman's. "*Good evening,*" came the reply. "*You must be Mr. Crossman.*" The words were mechanically bland, a robotic kind of American accent that keyed to no single geographic region.

"*Well, shit,*" Crossman chuckled. "*What the hell is this?*"

"*A courier, nothing more. We can speak freely.*"

Lucy tried to visualize what was going on in the darkness, keeping her sights on the shadows. The CSR didn't have a low-light function, and she regretted that she hadn't packed a thermographic scope.

"*If you're fucking with us,*" began Crossman, and there was the distinctive oiled snap of a pistol being cocked, "*I swear you will be punished for it.*"

"*Please be careful,*" said the woman. "*If it is damaged, we will be unable to provide you with any assistance to your venture.*"

Lucy wondered what the woman was referring to, but then she saw movement as Crossman wandered to the edges of the shadows and back into her sights. He gestured with the nickel-plated revolver in one hand. "*You made a lot of promises, Madrigal. And now here we are, at the moment of truth. Are you gonna disappoint me?*"

"Madrigal." Malte repeated the name. "That's an unknown."

*"Absolutely not,"* said the woman's voice. *"My word is my bond, Mr. Crossman. We're ready to begin at your discretion."*

Crossman smirked and put the gun away, pausing to look at his watch. *"Well, then. It's time we showed this blighted Gomorrah the price of its sins."* He walked off across the atrium, followed by the courier and the rest of the armed men, disappearing down a stairwell toward the lower levels.

"Pack up the kit," said Lucy, after a moment.

"We're going in?"

She gave a slight nod, her eye never leaving the sniper rifle's scope. "No doubt."

# — FIVE —

ade desperately wanted a cigarette, but he had been told by
Bullock in no uncertain terms they were to do nothing to draw
attention to the perimeter, even as insignificant an action as
lighting up a smoke. Wade kept his face blank all the while as the
man snarled and spat, but the fact was, Crossman's heavily tattooed
lieutenant scared the crap out of him.

Rufus, who had driven them down to the coast from the assembly
point in Stockton, had a whole lot of stories about Bullock and none
of them were good. He'd done terrible things before he went to jail
and found the Lord, and more after escaping, or so the driver had
said. Wade saw that type a lot in the Soldier-Saints; guys who figured
that because the cause was righteous, it excused any kind of behavior.
He didn't like that. Their war was about making sure the rules in the
Bible were adhered to, not hurting folks for the fun of it. Wade had
joined up after he lost his factory job to some outsourcing purge that
saw the work sent to India or some other shit, and he was in for the
*right* reasons. To make America clean again, proud again. To kick in
the heads of those liberal assholes who were ripping on the little man
and letting the fags, the women and the Jews run everything. That
was what this fight was about. It was serious business.

At least Crossman saw it the same way. Wade liked the man. He
was inspirational. Smart. And he didn't take any shit from anyone.
Crossman had a way of making you feel like you were the only one in
the room that he talked to, and sometimes Wade thought that if he had
known his real father, that the man might have been the same kind
of guy.

Crossman used the word *payback* a lot. Wade could get behind that. His whole life, he'd felt like someone was short-changing him, and it was only when he started to get woke that he realized he wasn't imagining it.

He rocked off his heels and walked up the line he'd been given, manning the post out by the south side of the street, beneath the shiny glass walls of the office block. He fingered the grip of the TEC-9 submachine gun dangling from a harness over his shoulder, a jury-rigged suppressor made from an oil filter bouncing off his thigh with each footstep. He itched to use the gun, and part of him was afraid that the night's work would go off without that happening. Crossman had told him not to worry, and for the moment that would have to be enough.

From behind him, Wade heard a tinkle of breaking glass and one of the portable work lamp rigs went out. He spun on his heel, fumbling the TEC-9 up to aim in the direction he had come. The work lamp's power generator hummed, but the reflectors on top of the rig were dark. Wade approached cautiously and his boots crunched on broken glass and pieces of still-hot lighting filament.

The bulbs had blown out. Did that kind of thing happen with these rigs? Wade had no idea. He reached for the walkie-talkie clipped to his belt and hesitated, remembering. Bullock had prodded him in the chest and told him not to break radio silence unless there was, in his words, *a shit-storm of jackboots kicking down the gates*. If he called in for a blown light, the big man would take it out of his hide.

Wade was weighing it up when he heard another crash of glass, this time from further down the fence line. A second work lamp guttered out and died, plunging the pathway along this part of the perimeter into darkness. Wade froze, straining to listen, but all he could hear was the rush of traffic out on 1st Street. His jaw hardening, he drew up his determination and raised the SMG, gripping the extended ammo magazine beneath the barrel to hold it steady. He stamped on the urge to call out a challenge. *Who the fuck ever did that, anyhow, except in the movies?* The oil filter silencer bobbed as he walked, moving this way and that in search of a target. *Because if someone is here, if someone is fucking around with the lights, I'll send them straight to Hell—*

Glass crunched out in the shadows and Wade's head flicked to the right. A piece of the blackness detached itself from the rest of the gloom and he saw a blond man with hard eyes come rocketing toward him.

Wade jerked the TEC-9's trigger even though the gun was way off the target, and swept about, firing off a burst of rounds into the air at waist height. The silencer reduced the sound of the discharge to a metallic chatter, but the blond man didn't seem to care.

With one hand, he caught Wade's gun-arm before it could reach him and pushed it away. The other was balled into a fist that hit Wade hard in the throat, hard enough to make the cartilage in his neck crackle as it broke.

Pain shocked through Wade as he abandoned his weapon, clutching at his collar. He couldn't breathe. His lungs emptied but no air came in to fill them again.

He staggered backward and the intruder snaked an arm around his neck to finish the job. Desperately, panicking, he clawed at his assailant. Wade was terrified of dying, terrified of what kind of judgment would be waiting for him on the other side of the shadows filling his vision.

He tried again to draw a frantic breath, but then there was only blackness.


"*You get him?*"

Malte didn't answer as he dragged the guard's body into the lee of the power generator. He put a finger on the young man's neck and felt a thready pulse there. He'd survive, if he was strong.

"*Malte, copy? You're out of pocket there, I don't see you.*"

The Finn began to uncoil the lanyard keeping the guard's gun on his shoulder and threw a look toward the building site across the street. "He is down," he said, pressing the radio bead in his ear.

"Wade?" The voice came from close by, rising up along the nearby ramp that led into the silent building's underground garage. "Where the fuck are you, dickless?"

"*You have company coming,*" reported Lucy. "*I don't have a good angle from up here. You're gonna have to deal.*"

"Understood," Malte replied, sparing the TEC-9 a wary look. The gun was dented and worn, and he felt unwilling to risk his life on any weapon that he wasn't 100 percent certain about. He set it down on the ground and dropped into a crouch as the second guard came into view. This one was stocky and bearded, cradling an identical SMG close to his chest, his weapon also sporting a makeshift silencer.

"Wade!" The guard's tone turned angry as he groped in the pocket of his jacket, finally producing a flashlight as he wandered into the pool of darkness around the smashed lamps. "If you are jerkin' off out here, I swear I will strip you naked and feed you to them feral queers they got in this town—"

"Hey." Malte spoke quietly as he slipped behind him. The second guard had not waited for his eyes to adjust to the darkness, so he didn't see him in the shadows until it was too late. Malte jabbed his fist into the small of the man's back, hitting him hard before he could react. The guard gave a strangled moan and stumbled into the Finn's grip. Malte repeated the sleeper hold he had used on the younger man, and it was over in a few moments. By the time he stripped the second guard of his weapon and stowed his unconscious form out of sight, Lucy had emerged from the shadows.

"I guess I should have known you didn't need my help," she offered, taking one of the SMGs and checking it over.

Malte said nothing and shrugged.

"So where's the party?" She glanced around, back in the direction of the parking garage.

"How do you want to do this?" he asked.

"Quietly," she replied, then paused, thinking it over. "Or as close as we can get."

Lucy flipped her Rubicon-issue smartphone to camera mode and slipped it into the breast pocket of her jacket with the lens peeking out. The device could digitally record hours of sound and video, and with a single tap it was possible to dump that data to a cloud server, so anything she captured from here on would survive even if she didn't. Lucy put that cheery thought out of her mind and led the way with the stolen TEC-9, picking her way down the vehicle ramp and into the parking space.

The empty concrete hall had low ceilings strung with lines of white fluorescent tubes, but only a few were connected up and illuminated. Gathered beneath the stark pools of light were a trio of minivans more suited to soccer moms than domestic terrorists, and the ambulance she had seen earlier. Folding camping tables piled with weapons, bullet-proof vests and radio gear were set before them, and a group of Soldier-Saints were busy kitting themselves up for whatever was coming. All of them were male, white and bristling with unspent anger.

Lucy and Malte kept to the shadows as they approached, moving in low darting motions from behind one thick support pillar to another. The place made her gut clench. There was precious little cover down here, and all it would take was one yahoo with his head screwed on right to pick out the intruders and start shooting.

At her side, Malte jerked his chin toward the back of the ambu-lance and Lucy caught sight of Crossman in close conversation with a big guy covered in prison tatts. They shared a harsh chuckle and then Crossman walked to the front of the vehicle, where the Asian in the long coat stood off to one side, facing away from Lucy and Malte. None of the Soldier-Saints seemed to want to come near the courier.

"Okay, so you have the rest of your money," began Crossman. "Now how about you do your trick for us, huh?"

"*If you'll give me a moment . . .*" Lucy's eyes narrowed as she heard Madrigal's odd voice. Something was off. It wasn't the courier speak-ing, as she had assumed earlier. "*Yes, there we are. The bank registers the transfer is complete. So we're ready to proceed.*"

"I'm going to get closer," Lucy whispered to Malte. "Try to scope out the back of the ambulance."

"Copy," said Malte, and he broke away from her. In turn, Lucy went low, hugging the edges of the shadows as she circled around toward the nearest of the minivans.

"I make a promise before God, I keep it," Crossman crowed. He had a shiny object in his hand, and now she was closer, Lucy could see it was a big silver crucifix on a chain. As she watched, he put the loop of it over his head and kissed the cross. "Tonight we're gonna make good on a whole bunch of them." He turned to face his men and gave them a fatherly nod. "We're doing the Lord's work, boys."

Lucy paused to adjust the camera and when she looked back the courier had moved. "*Let me tell you what your money has bought you,*" Madrigal went on. "*Think of it as your only personal version of Genesis 1:3. The reverse of 'let there be light,' as it were . . .*"

"She's not here." The words slipped out of Lucy's mouth as she had her first good look at the courier. The androgynous Asian hadn't spoken once. The courier held a silver tablet in one hand, connected to a compact sat-comm unit in the other. On the tablet's screen, Lucy could make out the head and shoulders of a white woman with henna-red hair. Her face was a mass of colored squares, veiled by the same kind of gross pixilation that TV interviews used when showing folks on camera that didn't want to be identified.

"*You'll need to keep this with you,*" Madrigal continued. "*My people will monitor the situation and send you a live feed via the tablet, so you and your men can find a clear route out of the city.*"

"Oh yeah?" Crossman didn't seem convinced. "What makes you think we're gonna run when we're done? We're not in this for the glory, lady. This is for the War."

"*Of course.*"

Lucy's thoughts raced. If this meeting wasn't in person, then what the hell was it about?

Madrigal's next words answered that question, and Lucy's gut filled with ice. "*While we have been talking, my team have inserted a digital firmware update into the smart electricity meters that monitor the power for this building. That update is now in the process of communicating itself wirelessly to the meters in the buildings around you. It will keep spreading, hopping from device to device, until every smart meter in the downtown area is affected. It won't take long.*"

"That's it? A fucking computer virus?" Crossman's lip curled. "You promised me a spectacular!"

"*The update contains malware code that gives me direct control of the power supply of everything for miles around,*" Madrigal continued, like she was explaining it to a child. "*You can thank City Hall for that detail. If they hadn't insisted on upgrading their infrastructure, this vulnerability would never have existed.*" She paused. "*Give the word, Mr. Crossman, and I will bring San Francisco to its knees. The city will be in disarray, and you and your men will be free to do as you wish.*"

Finally, a hateful grin broke across Crossman's face. "Well. That's more like it." He raised his voice. "You hear that, soldiers? Today we'll ride right into the middle of those godless freaks out there and burn them down! We will remind them whose nation this is! We will teach them!"

"Teach them! Teach them!" Crossman's men took up the words as chant, their voices echoing off the walls and the ceiling.

Lucy shrank back and spotted Malte coming around to her. The look on his face told her that whatever news he had, it was going to make things worse. "What?"

"Look." Malte had been using his smartphone like a body-camera as Lucy had, but now he handed it to her and spooled back the footage. She saw the side of the ambulance from his point of view as it lurched closer on the tiny screen. Then slowly, the camera revealed what was inside the vehicle.

She saw four pressurized bottles on a makeshift metal frame, arranged around the guts of what could only be an improvised explosive device. The bottles were fire-engine red, the identifying color for industrial-grade hydrogen gas.

"It looks like a two-stage charge," Malte whispered. "You know what that means."

"Oh yeah." Lucy was looking at a jury-rigged thermobaric weapon, a so-called fuel-air explosive device.

Far more lethal than a conventional bomb, FAEs were particularly destructive devices that worked first by igniting a charge that would disperse a vapor of explosive material into the air. The aerosolized fuel mixed with oxygen into a diffuse, fast-spreading cloud, and then a second charge would turn that mass into a huge high-temperature detonation, accompanied by a powerful blast-wave effect. The Russian and American militaries had used them in Afghanistan against hardened targets, and terrorists had been building home-brew versions like the one on the phone screen for decades. The last time a thermobaric bomb had been triggered on US soil, in 1993, it had almost destroyed the World Trade Center in New York City. What sat in the back of the ambulance was a close cousin to that weapon. If it went off somewhere heavily populated—the Financial District, Union Square, Chinatown—the death toll would be catastrophic.

"When we're done today," Crossman told his men, "these degenerates are gonna look at the hole we put in this rotting abortion of a city and they will weep!"

"Time to show the faithful their target, boss," said the tattooed man, pressing a leaflet into Crossman's hand.

The leader of the Soldier-Saints nodded to himself and offered up the sheet of paper. Lucy saw the words YERBA BUENA TOLERANCE FESTIVAL written across the top of the leaflet and her heart sank. Yerba Buena Gardens was only a few blocks away, close to a Jewish museum and a Catholic church, a popular gathering spot for people from all of San Francisco's diverse populace. Crossman produced a Zippo lighter from his pocket and set the leaflet burning, drawing hoots of approval from his men. "They will know that we are the hand of God," he declared, "come down to smite them for their sins!" Crossman flicked the ashy remains of the paper aside and called out to the men to open the gate leading to the exit ramp on the far side of the parking bay. The others strapped on head-mounted torches and readied their weapons.

"If that device detonates in here," Malte said quietly, "it could bring this whole tower down." He knew Lucy well enough to already know what was going through her mind. Rowan and his FBI buddy had stumbled on something far worse than any of them had expected. The Soldier-Saints had to be stopped, and it had to be right now.

Crossman strode over to the courier and snatched away the tablet. "Time for you to do what you do," he said to the woman on the screen, his mouth pulling into a savage sneer. "Let there be dark!"

"*Lights out,*" said Madrigal, and as the words left her lips, the parking garage was instantly plunged into blackness.

Mater Dei's namesake had been rendered in an iron statue in front of the modern hospital campus, the statue of Mary and a young Jesus marking a cluster of sandy-colored blocks that contained Malta's most modern medical center.

There were few vehicles along the campus's service roads, so Marc deposited the jeep as far as he could from the nearest light pole, reversing it into the shadows so he could race for the exit if he had to leave in a hurry. He shrugged on a dark jacket and gloves, then looped a thin gray shemagh around his neck to obscure his face. Staying well away from the hospital's main entrance, he headed toward the low, one-story building on the northern side of the complex where the mortuary was located.

Long past midnight, the air had cooled. The night sky was empty of clouds and the day's heat had faded away, but the flow of inpatients hadn't slowed after sunset. It was the weekend, and that meant that a regular train of tourists who had overindulged passed through the doors. An ambulance sped past him, making for the accident and emergency department, and Marc gave it a wide berth.

He pulled out his phone and a small metal tube the size of his thumb as he approached the entrance to the outbuilding. At this time of night, the door beneath the sign for *Mortwarja* was secured with a touch-key lock and intercom for calling the front desk, but Marc wasn't going to waste time with that. He pointed the tube at the eye of the security camera above the entrance and it projected a powerful blue-green laser into its CCD circuits. The powerful beam dazzled the digital camera for a few moments, enough for Marc to get to the door before it reset. He placed his phone against the sensor pad for the key and it transmitted a wireless ping into the lock, mimicking a digital ID Kara had sourced for him from the database of the Maltese Divisional Police. It fooled the lock into thinking he was a detective-rank officer with clearance to enter the building, and the door clicked open.

Marc edged through and inside, looking around, alert for any kind of confrontation. The morgue's reception area was empty, and he quietly approached the front desk, using the dazzler a second time on another camera mounted above it. A sign on the desk in Maltese and English explained that the mortuary was closed until tomorrow, but the sounds of a television were issuing out from a half-open door on the far side of the desk. Marc heard tinny reports of gunfire and the screeching of tires. Whoever was on night duty appeared to be more interested in watching some action-packed movie than keeping an eye on the desk.

*Fine by me*, he thought, and moved to the next security door, this one leading into a hallway and the rooms beyond. The fake ID programmed into the phone worked a second time and the magnetic locks snapped open. Marc slipped into the unlit corridor and advanced slowly and carefully, reading the bilingual signs on the walls. The preliminary medical report Kara had pulled from the police server told him where to find the body of Lex Wetherby, and he moved from door to door, searching for the right one.

In the quiet and the dimness, Marc had to fight off a nagging uneasiness collecting at the base of his thoughts. He didn't like hospitals. There was something about them that always made his skin crawl, even in one as new and as airy as this. In a more fanciful moment, he wondered if it was possible for all the pain and suffering that had occurred in such a place to be somehow concentrated in the walls, lingering there like an invisible psychic stain. A morgue was even worse, built to service the dead and nothing else.

The bleak thought brought a flash of recall, a moment of sense-memory from a grimy, hot basement in a ruined orphanage in Turkey. He could almost smell the stale blood and rust in the air. Marc dismissed it with a shake of the head and found the room he was looking for.

Inside, he switched on a lamp and angled it toward the hatch of the roll-out freezer storing Wetherby's corpse. Grimly, he opened it and eased out the tray, revealing a translucent white body-bag and the pallid corpse within it. A computer-printed label with the dead hacker's name and personal information was slotted into a pocket on the bag, along with a barcode that Marc couldn't interpret.

Taking a deep breath, he unzipped the bag and found himself looking at Wetherby's pale, bloodless face. Below, the dead man's chest had been torn to shreds where a sniper's bullet had struck him.

"Shit." Marc wasn't a stranger to death, but the sallow, pasty cast to the corpse was particularly grotesque. It seemed unreal, like a prop created in a Hollywood film studio. Breathing through his mouth, he still tasted cleaning chemicals on his tongue as he continued his investigation. He saw no Y-shaped incision down the dead man's torso to indicate that a full autopsy had taken place.

"Cause of death is pretty damn clear," Marc said aloud. Still, he noted scarring on the hacker's forearm and hands, and poked gently at it, seeing evidence of old damage there from a fire or a chemical burn. The right arm was less marked than the left and he found a tattoo there, ringing the wrist in a blue-ink bracelet. Had Wetherby been wearing a wristwatch, it would have been obscured.

At first, he thought the design was an abstract one, a collection of lines and circles, but looking closer he found three numbers arranged in a line: *57 46 53.* They looked like decimal map coordinates, but there were too few figures for that. He checked the other wrist and found nothing.

Marc moved down the body, figuring that perhaps there might be more numbers hidden in another tattoo elsewhere, but he blinked and halted when he found something else—or rather, the *lack* of it.

Wetherby was missing his right leg from the knee joint down. By the texture of the skin there, he had lost it a long time ago, and the lines of hardening in the epidermis made it clear he used a prosthetic of some kind. Where that was now, Marc had no idea.

He plucked the comms earpiece from his pocket and tapped it to go active. "Kara? Are you on?"

The woman responded after a brief silence. *"What? You're at the morgue, right? Is he . . . I mean, the body, is it there?"* Her voice was muffled for a moment, then it came back clearer. *"What have you got?"* He told her about the numbers on the tattoo and she dismissed it. *"That's not relevant. What else?"*

"That report on our dead friend neglected to mention that he's short half a leg. He should have a prosthetic here." Marc spoke quietly, so his voice wouldn't carry. "According to that uploaded video, he very clearly had it when he took a dive off the ramparts at Mdina."

*"The cops don't have anything like that in evidence with his personal effects,"* Kara confirmed. *"So he either lost it on the way down, or—"*

"Or someone found his body before the police did." Marc had

already filled Kara in on his chase after the drone and the state of Wetherby's hotel room, and it didn't take much of a leap to connect the events. "We know the killers were searching for something. My money's on data, so if he stowed it somewhere safe . . ."

"*He hid it inside the prosthetic. Which they now have.*" Kara cut her mic for a moment.

In the silence, he went to his smartphone and toggled a reader app to scan the barcode on the body bag's label. The data keyed to a notation from the hospital's main server that the corpse was scheduled for cremation. *Too soon*, considered Marc. *Somebody is trying to cover their tracks.*

But then his train of thought broke when the handset vibrated and a message bubble appeared on the screen. The smartphone's built-in sensors were detecting a radio frequency ID chip close by.

Marc tapped the screen and studied the read-out. "Kara? I'm getting an RFID ping here . . ." The display showed the signal's proximity, clearly tagging Wetherby's body. "Oh hell, did he swallow it?"

"*What's the ping read as?*" she demanded, her voice muffled and throaty.

The tag returned a series of six familiar digits. *564653.* "The same numbers as the tattoo."

"*He . . . He was sending a message.*"

"Yeah, but to who?" Dialing up the sensor's acuity, Marc began to run the handset over the body, searching for the tag's exact location and trying not to think about the worst places it might be concealed. In a few moments, he had narrowed down the RFID signal location to the fire-scarred hand.

Marc put down the phone and explored the cold flesh of the dead man's fingers and palm. He found a lump in the webbing between Wetherby's thumb and forefinger, a tiny capsule of circuitry no larger than a grain of rice. A chip that size could only hold a couple of kilobytes of data at the most.

"This is a marker," he said, pressing his gloved fingers into the scarification until he came across what he suspected was there. In the heel of the dead man's hand, buried beneath the skin, was a flat, regular object. The old scarring hid the fact that the flesh had recently been cut open and had healed closed again. "I have something," he added, searching a nearby drawer for a disposable scalpel.

"*What is it?*" snapped Kara.

"Give me a second." Grimacing, Marc took the blade and made a deep incision around the foreign object, cutting into the sallow meat of the corpse and peeling it back. Dark, coagulated blood oozed out of the opening, and the light from the lamp glittered on a black sliver of plastic embedded in the layers of Wetherby's epidermis. Marc used a pair of long-nosed forceps to snag the object, but it resisted removal more than he expected. Gently applying force, it slowly came free and he saw the reason why. The plastic shard wasn't all he'd found. A web of metal threads came with it, and Marc realized that he was looking at a "distributed" flash drive built around the core of a microSD connector. The hacker had deliberately implanted it in his hand to keep it concealed.

"You're gonna love this," he told Kara, snapping a picture of the bloodstained circuit with the phone. "Sending you an image now . . ."

"*I want more than that,*" she shot back, recognizing the tiny device. "*There's a data slot in your spyPhone. Upload the drive's contents to me.*"

Marc hesitated. "You sure that's a good idea? There's no way to know what's on it."

"*For safety,*" Kara added. "*You can walk back the original while I start work on the contents.*"

"All right. Here we go." Warily, Marc wiped the card clean and inserted it into the Rubicon-issue handset. Built-in isolation software put a firewall around it in case a virus lurked inside the data, but what came up in the streaming window was only a cascade of information—text and pixelated images that flashed past too quickly for Marc to make head or tail of. "Wetherby had a backup," he thought aloud, "in case he lost what he hid in his prosthetic. Smart bloke, taking the belt-and-braces approach."

"*Not smart enough,*" Kara said bitterly. "*He still got himself murdered. Stupid . . .*"

Her words had an edge that made everything snap into hard focus. The unspoken truth that had been hiding right in front of him abruptly became clear, and he said it without thinking. "You knew this guy . . ." He looked again at Wetherby's slack face. "You were *close* to him, yeah?"

"*It's complicated.*"

"Why didn't you say anything?"

Kara made an odd noise over the open channel that could have been a stifled groan. "*I'm sorry, Marc. I'm really sorry.*" The data upload concluded and the phone's screen went dark. "*About everything—*" Her voice cut out suddenly.

The phone was not just blank, but totally *dead*. The signal through the earpiece ceased at the same instant and Marc stood in the harsh silence that fell in its wake. "Kara? *Kara!*" He tapped at the comm unit ineffectually. "What the hell—?"

The words died in his throat as a blob of white torchlight flicked off the walls of the corridor outside, flashing toward the window in the doorway across the room. Marc quickly shoved the corpse back into the storage locker, his eyes darting around to find somewhere to conceal himself.

He could hear voices now. Two men. He caught the word *pulizija* and the low grunt of a reply. It seemed that the guy on the front desk had not been as inattentive as Marc had hoped, and he pulled the shemagh up around his face, looking around for anything he could use as a distraction. He drew the Glock pistol from his pack and weighed it in his hand. He had only brought it along as a last resort.

The light from the torch came closer and Marc ducked out of sight, behind a metal cabinet near the door, pressing himself into the shadows.

The handle rattled and the door opened. Marc heard the crackle of a police radio. If he didn't act quickly, this would get called in and the alarm would be raised.

Two figures entered. The first was a weary-looking cop in the blue shirt of the local force, a middle-aged guy with a thick mustache, who carried a heavy flashlight. Following him was a shorter, younger man in a white lab coat, waving his hands and talking animatedly in Maltese.

Marc rushed out from behind the cabinet and snatched at a handful of the morgue technician's collar, wrenching him backward and

pressing the Glock into the side of his head. The man let out a strangled yelp of shock and struggled.

The police officer twisted, getting over his surprise in a blink,
whipping out his extendable baton. Maltese police didn't carry firearms as a matter of course, which meant Marc could use his as an
advantage. But he had no desire to turn this into a lethal engagement.
The cop was just a guy doing his job, but Marc couldn't allow the
man to waylay him. Kara's silence could only mean that something
had gone very wrong, and police entanglement was the last thing he
needed.

Keeping the morgue technician between himself and the police
officer, he gestured with the gun and made it clear what he wanted.
The cop reluctantly dropped the baton and the flashlight. "Cuffs!"
snarled Marc, shoving the technician toward a nearby examination
table. The cop glared back at him, then snapped one ring of his
handcuffs around his own wrist. Marc forced him to loop the frame
of the restraints around a stainless-steel pull-bar on the metal table,
and then fasten the other ring around the technician's wrist.

Once they were secured to each other, Marc tore off the radio
handset clipped to the man's shirtfront. It was already spitting out
agitated voices, so he dropped it on the tiled floor and smashed it
under his heel. "Skużani," he offered, as a belated apology.

With the cop's shouted curses trailing after him, Marc gave up on
stealth and fled the morgue at a run. Part of him knew that he should
have got into the security console behind the reception, maybe pulled
the hard drives from the system, but every second he wasted here was
a moment longer that Kara was offline.

He sprinted to the Maruti jeep and leaped in, gunning the engine.
The car bounced through a sharp turn and out on to the highway as
a couple of local police cruisers flashed past in the opposite direction.
Marc kept right on the point of the speed limit during the ten-minute
drive back to the Hotel Nova, threading through the backstreets
of Gzira until the building rose up before him. Along the way, he
ran the comms gear through a hard reset, the smartphone too, but
nothing worked. Somehow, the Rubicon-issue equipment had been

deactivated remotely, and that suggested a whole lot of possibilities. None of them were good.

Kara's words ran around in his thoughts. *He was sending a message.* At first she had dismissed his mention of the numbers on Wetherby's wrist tattoo, but they had been important after all.

"Was the message for her?" He asked the question out loud as he brought the jeep to a halt a few doors down from the Nova.

There were no new vehicles parked outside, nothing that seemed amiss, but Marc wasn't willing to take any risks.

He kept the Glock out of sight under his jacket as he entered the building. The night porter on the front desk snored loudly with his feet up on a chair, and Marc eased past, letting him slumber on.

Instead of riding the lift, he took the stairs, pausing every other level to listen out for any signs of danger. Reaching the fifth floor, music and noise issued out of a few of the rooms, where clubbers had staggered back to the hotel intent on continuing their partying until sunrise. A fast, bassy dance track thudded through the door of room 56, enough that it would cover the sounds of whatever was going on in there.

Marc hesitated on the threshold. What would he see inside? Kara Wei, laid out on the bed with a bullet through her eye? He shook off the unpleasant image. *One corpse is enough for tonight,* he told himself.

He planted a firm heel-kick in the lock mechanism and the whole thing popped right off the latch, swinging the door wide. Marc surged in, the pistol high and close to his chest, and shouted her name.

The twenty-something surfer he had seen earlier that day came storming into the room from the balcony with a beer bottle gripped in his fist, his face like thunder. Then the guy saw the pistol in Marc's hand and the fury dropped out of him in an instant. "Whoa! What the hell?" He had a rough Scottish accent and his cheeks were flushed red.

"Back up!" Marc aimed the gun at him and took a quick look through a side door into the small, dingy bathroom. There was no sign of Kara in there, or anywhere else for that matter. It all seemed wrong.

He advanced, holding the pistol steady. "Where is she?"

"What? Where's who?"

"*Kara!*" Marc spat her name. "Don't fuck with me, mate! She picked you up at the airport, today! Brought you here! What have you done with her?"

The surfer kept his hands raised, still gripping the beer. "What?" he repeated, shaking his head, blinking nervously. "No. I don't know any Kara, pal. I wasn't at the airport! I've been here a week already!"

Marc's gut sense told him he was hearing the truth, but he was still uncertain. "Get on your knees."

"No, please—"

"*Get on your bloody knees!*" he bellowed at the other man with enough force to make him drop the bottle and obey. "Are you in on this shit?" Marc demanded. "You know about Wetherby?"

The surfer shook his head, trembling as the muzzle of the Glock moved closer. "Look. You have issues, okay? But it's nothing to do with me!" The man was clearly terrified. "I've been in this room all week! I came on my own! No girls here, right?" He took a deep breath and nodded toward the table. "That's not what I'm into, you get it?"

Marc glanced down and saw a laptop computer sitting open, the dance music issuing out of its speakers. A very prominent rainbow-flag sticker had been plastered across the corner of the casing. He paused, and his eye was drawn to the pinhole camera atop the laptop's screen. "Have you . . . had that switched on all the time you've been here?"

The surfer's head bobbed. "I Skype with my maw, every day." He gulped audibly, panic making his eyes wide and fearful. "Listen, take whatever you want. Money, passport, the computer . . . I won't stop you . . ."

But Marc wasn't hearing him. Instead, all the comments Kara had made before came back to him in a rush.

*We're running this op under isolated protocol.*

*I figured he'd be good cover.*

*Call backs to Rubicon are being routed through my machine.*

He let the gun drop and looked at the computer, then his hand angrily whipped out and slammed the laptop closed. The music ceased. "She's not here."

"That's what I've been telling you, pal!"

"No," Marc turned away, shaking his head. "She was *never* here." He felt like a fool.

Since he had separated from her in France, Kara Wei had only ever been a voice in his ear, but she could have been sending that comm signal to him from anywhere. What proof did he have that she had actually gone to Turin and then flown out to Malta as he did? *None.* She could have monitored him through the spyPhone and he would never have known it.

In his mind's eye, he put together the shape of the deception. Kara was an accomplished hacker, and it would have been child's play for her to co-opt the laptop of some unlucky traveler. She probably picked the surfer's details out of the Hotel Nova's booking records, snaked her way into his computer through the building's unsecured Wi-Fi network to monitor him. This poor guy had unknowingly become her cover story, little more than a prop to fool Marc into thinking that Kara was close by.

On the breeze, the sound of police sirens filtered up through the open balcony window, getting nearer.

"Th-that for you, is it?" said the surfer.

"Yeah," Marc replied, and left at a run.


He recovered his gear from the hotel room down the hall and found the service elevator to the ground floor, exiting the building through the back via narrow corridors stacked with boxes of toilet paper and cleaning supplies. Marc knew he couldn't risk going back to the rented Maruti. It was likely the Maltese police had tracked it from the hospital to the Hotel Nova, so he helped himself to a Peugeot XR6 that had been left unsecured in the back alley, and took the motorcycle out into the backstreets of Sliema.

Getting well clear of the tourist district, Marc found a hillside layby at the edge of the highway where he could stop and catch his breath.

The wind coming in from the sea pulled at him. He sat on the stolen bike's saddle, glaring at the pre-dawn glow on the horizon. He was trying to make some sense of what had happened when a chiming ringtone sounded from inside his pack. Marc dug through the contents and found the Rubicon phone. The black slab of glass and metal came alive once again. On the screen, a harsh crimson message flashed up warning of an *Incoming Priority Call*.

Warily, he tapped the answer key and held it to his ear. "Kara?"

"*Mr. Dane.*" Ekko Solomon's steady, firm tones had a hard edge to them that he had not encountered before. "*At last. Are you alone?*"

"It's just me," he replied, frowning at the question. "Okay, can someone please tell me what the hell is going on?"

"*Listen carefully,*" said Solomon. "*We have now reacquired your location. Exfiltration arrangements are being made as we speak. You are to cease whatever activity you are involved in and fully disengage. Abandon everything and return to the office at once. This order supersedes all others. Do you understand me, Mr. Dane?*"

"Yes," he began, his confusion deepening. "But where's Kara? What's the—?"

Solomon cut him off before he could finish his sentence. "*You are not participating in a sanctioned operation. Observe silent protocol. Proceed to the airport and extract immediately.*" Then as an afterthought, he added: "*I will explain in person. Until then, continue as ordered.*"

The call ended and Marc stared at the black screen, wary and uncertain.

# — SIX —

The blackout effect blossomed across downtown San Francisco in a soundless wave. It spread across the buildings and down the streets, as if a giant hand had poured a torrent of dark ink across the map. The radius grew to engulf ten blocks, then twenty, then a hundred, two hundred, and kept on expanding. Power failed along the line of the bay up toward Telegraph Hill and down past Mission and Haight. The city's famous Cable Cars were unceremoniously halted in their tracks, and traffic lights winked out, causing dozens of accidents as drivers reacted too slowly to the unexpected darkness.

Nowhere was spared the abrupt fall of night. Every building connected to the electrical grid instantly darkened. Office blocks and hotels become gloomy, tomb-like spaces. Elevators halted in their shafts, trapping their passengers inside, and in the absence of light a flood of panic spread as fast as the power had died.

Back-up generators and emergency batteries, programmed to recognize when the city's mains supply dropped offline, failed to activate. The complex, insidious code that replicated through the smart-meter system fed out a stream of fake data to replicate the normal running of the grid, and the back-ups stayed resolutely inactive. Other command and control signals went back into the Californian power network, confusing the feed and preventing any kind of automated reset.

Out on the streets, the avenues began to choke themselves as vehicles came to a halt, and others collided or shunted. People poured out of the buildings, waving their smartphones to cast what little light they could, even as the cell towers in the city fell dead and cut them off from the rest of the world.

San Francisco was a city of the prepared—you couldn't live in an earthquake zone and not be ready for disaster to strike—but there had been no tremor, no warning of an imminent shock, and the people milled in the streets, nursing the cold fear of the ground shifting beneath their feet.


In the basement of the unopened hotel, brilliant white spars of light stabbed on from every direction as the assembled Soldier-Saints activated their head-mounted flashlights. Lucy recoiled, pulling Malte with her toward the safety of the deeper shadows behind one of the support pillars.

"The power . . ." Malte whispered. "The whole city . . . ?"

"I don't know," she muttered.

Crossman's harsh laughter echoed off the concrete walls of the underground parking garage. "Listen! Can you hear that?" Lucy caught sight of him moving back toward the ambulance. As he walked, he shrugged on a paramedic's jacket. "Oh, they know judgment is coming!"

Lucy heard it, all right. Outside on the streets, a rising, atonal chorus of honking car horns, shouting and screaming filled the air. The disorder Crossman and his men wanted had sparked, catching alight in the first embers of a fire that could engulf the city unless it was stopped.

"Saddle up!" Crossman shouted, and beckoned to another of the men. Lucy saw the tattooed thug briefly illuminated in the torchlight. "Bullock, you take a team, go give a little absolution!"

The other man nodded. "Time to fill some graves," he spat, rocking off his heels in anticipation of imminent violence.

"I'm going for the ambulance," hissed Lucy, brandishing her stolen SMG. "We shoot out the tires, the engine, it won't be going anywhere . . ."

"The bomb—" Malte began.

"I haven't forgotten," she said, knowing full well what kind of horrific damage the improvised thermobaric device could do. "Back me up!"

Lucy bolted out from behind the concrete pillar and broke into a run, but as she closed in on the boxy black shadow of the ambulance, the vehicle's emergency strobes flashed into life. An infernal, blood-crimson light illuminated everything. Flickering color turned the Soldier-Saints into jerky shadow-marionettes, and Lucy was revealed to them. She stood out of cover and in the open.

"Intruder!" shouted someone, and all guns came around in her direction.

She reacted without thinking. Lucy turned into the TEC-9 and let off a blast of full-auto fire from the hip, the shots clattering through the improvised silencer on the weapon's muzzle.

Out in the dark, Malte's gun joined the fray and the Soldier-Saints came in a heartbeat later, most of them firing wildly in her direction. She heard a cry of pain and glimpsed a figure in a long coat jerk and spin. Caught in a fatal crossfire, the courier went down in a heap, body torn open by blind shots with no regard for who might be in the way.

Lucy threw herself at the ground, hitting the floor with a grunt as she tumbled into a shoulder roll. Bullets hummed over her head as she scrambled back to her feet and into a loping run. Behind her, she heard the rattle of Malte's TEC-9 as it cut across the red-lit space, heard the dull spanking impacts of the rounds as they cored through the doors of the parked minivans.

"Get that bitch!" bellowed Crossman.

"Go, go!" Bullock, the guy with the prison tatts, shouted back. "I got this!"

The strobes shifted as the ambulance started moving, and Lucy fired toward it, aiming for the tires—but the TEC-9's slide gave a dull clack and locked in place.

"Shit!" She yanked at the cocking lever to clear a jammed casing from the ejector port, but then a heavy shadow fell across her and Bullock slammed into Lucy with a brutal body-check that sent her staggering. She lost the useless SMG in the impact and brought up her hands to block the blows she knew would be coming.

White light from Bullock's head-torch dazzled her and for a second she thought he was going to shoot her, but instead the ex-con enveloped her in a reversed bear hug and pulled tight. Dense, prison-hardened muscle constrained her. He roared with effort, and Lucy's feet left the ground as he lifted her up.

She distantly registered the exchange of fire between the other Soldier-Saints and a blurry shape somewhere near the pillar where she had left Malte, but the air gushed out of her lungs in a ragged whoop as Bullock's grip tightened and forced her to exhale.

Lucy's hand flailed as she grabbed for a soft spot, but she had hardly any room to maneuver, tearing at Bullock's shirt, punching ineffectively at his gut. She heard him laughing, his breath hot on her bare neck. The angle felt all wrong for her to land a crippling blow in his crotch and he mocked Lucy as he squeezed the life out of her.

Then her long fingers skipped across the top of a snub-nosed revolver holstered on his hip and she grabbed at it, tugging the gun free.

"Oh no, you ain't getting that!" Bullock growled, shifting his grip to wrestle the weapon away, and they struggled against one another. Lucy couldn't bring the gun up, couldn't shift it by more than a degree or two. He had her hand trapped in his, his vise-like grip threatening to crush it. The muzzle stayed pointing at the ground, unable to find a target.

Lucy gritted her teeth and made her play. She stamped down on Bullock's shin, getting a wet hiss of pain from him and a split-second of recoil in his inexorable grip. It was enough for her to point the pistol's muzzle back at his leg and pull the trigger. A round went off with a flat, heavy bang of discharge and blew through the toe of Bullock's boot, blasting blood and bone out across the floor.

He screamed and let go of her, cursing a blue streak. Lucy spun around in a swift pirouette and cracked him across the face with the butt of the revolver, breaking his nose in a wet crunch of splintered cartilage. The ex-con fell on his ass and howled, clutching at his ruined foot.

She took a breath as one of the minivans lurched forward, the headlights coming on in a blaze that lit up the parking garage. Dead or wounded Soldier-Saints lay scattered about as evidence of Malte's brutal but efficient skills. The rest of them had fled, vanishing into the darkened streets in the wake of the ambulance.

The Finn looked out at her from behind the minivan's steering wheel. "Come on," he called.

"Right . . ." She threw Bullock a look, then jumped into the vehicle as Malte jammed the van into gear with a screech of spinning wheels, and they rocketed forward, out through the open gate, up the ramp and on to Fremont Street. Lucy was pissed off at leaving that asshole and his playmates behind, but they were not the priority.

Stuffing the revolver in her jacket pocket, she grabbed her smartphone and glared at the *No Cellular Signal* message blinking on the display. She wanted to get a message to Gonzalez, but without any operational network there was no way to reach him.

"There." Malte pointed up ahead and Lucy glimpsed the red strobes diminishing as the ambulance raced away from them. He stood on the accelerator, but the minivan wasn't built for performance and it felt like they were churning through mud to get after the other vehicle.

Frightened faces and stalled cars flashed past them as they committed to the pursuit, and in her mind's eye Lucy tried to remember the layout of the city streets. The distance to the open-air square that the Soldier-Saints had targeted was less than ten blocks. Were they planning a suicide run, into the middle of the crowds out there to detonate the device? Crossman didn't seem like the type to kill himself for his cause, but her gut twisted. The thought of what damage the fuel-air bomb could wreak on unprotected bodies horrified her.

"Hold on," warned Malte, as they flashed across an intersection clogged with stalled traffic. He swerved the minivan around a halted truck and slammed a town car out of the way, drawing a shower of fat yellow sparks off the vehicle's fender.

Lucy rocked in her seat and glanced around, finding the TEC-9 that Malte had been using. She checked the magazine—a third of the rounds left, maybe enough for a couple of bursts—and detached the oil-filter silencer, tossing it into the back seat. "I need to take them out before they make their target. Nothing else is gonna work."

"Agreed." Malte's unblinking gaze fixed on the dark street ahead and the splash of light from the minivan's headlamps. The white flank of the ambulance ghosted across the avenue before them, long and agonizing seconds passing as the distance between them narrowed.

She hauled herself out of the passenger seat and back into the minivan's middle row, wrenching open the side door with a jerk of her shoulders. The panel slid back, and the wind rushed in as they thundered through the confines of an underpass. Malte leaned constantly on the horn, sending frightened pedestrians scattering before them as he kept up the pace.

Lucy leaned into the van's frame to steady herself and brought up the TEC-9, bracing it to her shoulder. They were coming up on the intersection with Mission Street, and from there it would be a straight shot all the way down to Yerba Buena Gardens. She couldn't wait for the ideal opportunity to present itself. She had to do this *now*.

The SMG jerked in her hand as she squeezed the trigger, and she saw bullets spark across the back end of the ambulance, blowing out the tail lights and chewing into the left rear tire. The vehicle twitched but maintained its pace, and then pivoted into a skidding motion to the right before it hit the crossing at Mission. The ambulance darted across her firing arc and she strafed it again, but as the TEC-9 ran dry the reason for the early turn was revealed.

The long silver shape of a MUNI electric trolley bus blocked the road directly in front of them, stalled across the intersection when the power had failed. Malte wrenched the minivan's steering wheel hard over and Lucy pitched backward into the passenger cabin as it rolled on its suspension. For a heart-stopping second, she thought the high-sided vehicle was going to tilt too far and flip over, but Malte snaked the van through the ugly turn and they made it through—but not before clipping the side of the bus with enough force to rip the open side door off its mountings and toss it to the street.

The ambulance was still moving, but hobbled by the blown tire, throwing bits of black rubber behind it as the wheel cover disintegrated. Malte brought the minivan into the fleeing vehicle's slipstream and gave it a shunt, but that did nothing to slow it. Shots fired from the cab cracked back through the air, shattering the van's windscreen into a spiderweb. The ambulance veered off as it approached an intersection jammed tight with cars, and mounted the curb. The van followed and they swept through the turmoil and back on to the road.

Coming up was 2nd Street, and that meant they were only moments away from the gardens. Lucy hauled herself toward the open doorway and shouted at Malte. "Get us alongside!"

She didn't wait for him to acknowledge her. Lucy grabbed the edge of the roof and hauled herself up and out, the wind buffeting her as she pivoted on to the top of the minivan and swung her legs around. She moved like a gymnast, making the motions fast and fluid, ignoring the tension in her arm muscles.

The ambulance fell in alongside the van and the two vehicles connected, trading paint and fragments of plastic. The flare of a muzzle discharge blinked yellow-white as someone in the cab tried to shoot back at Malte. Lucy took it as the go-sign and coiled her legs under her, before launching herself across and on to the flat roof of the emergency vehicle.

The metal beneath her distorted with an audible crunch and she grabbed the flashing red-and-white light bar to drag herself forward. Ahead, she saw the passenger-side door flap open and a figure in a paramedic's jacket rise up, standing on the seat and twisting backward to take a shot at her. *Crossman.*

He cursed her to hell and back, aiming his big six-gun with one hand, hanging on to the seat with the other. The pistol bellowed and she felt a sting of pain as a hot round creased her leg.

Without warning, the vehicle slowed as the driver pumped the brakes, and Lucy almost lost purchase. She slipped forward over the slick roof and straight at Crossman. He reacted too slowly, jolting against the open passenger door, and she struck out on reflex, landing a clumsy punch in the side of his head. He hit her across the ribs with the big revolver, but Lucy caught his arm before he could draw it back. There was a split second of giddy equilibrium, when the only thing keeping the two of them in check was the mass of the other. Then she yanked at him and let the man lose his balance.

Crossman shouted in fury as he fell out the door and slammed

face-first into the road. Lucy glimpsed his arm and shoulder vanishing under the right rear wheel of the ambulance, the vehicle bouncing as it rolled over him. She felt them slowing, the driver uncertain
how to proceed with his leader torn away, possibly dead.

Lucy did not hesitate. She scrambled around the crown of the ambulance's cab and came in through the open door feet-first. She connected with the startled Soldier-Saint in the driver's seat and planted
her foot in his face, slamming his head against the window. The ambulance staggered to a stop and for good measure, Lucy kicked the
driver again, before pitching him out on to the street.

Malte brought the minivan to a halt nearby and shouted to her.
"Are you all right?"

"Forget me," she called back. "The payload . . ." Shaky with adrenaline, Lucy leaned over the back of the seat to look into the rear compartment. The hydrogen cylinders and the cobbled-together FAE
bomb were still intact, and she saw a glow of green light from what
had to be a triggering mechanism. There was nothing that looked
like a countdown timer, and only a complex nest of wires threading from the electronics into the trigger. The hardware was alien
to her, and her heart sank. Lucy was a shooter, a door-kicker and
a trigger-puller. She wasn't a bomb disposal specialist, she wasn't a
tech. "Shit, Marc," she said under her breath. "Where's your limey
ass when I need it?"

She spotted something lying in the foot well and grabbed at it. The
silver digital tablet the courier had brought to the terrorists was damaged, the screen smashed into a varicolored mess, but there might be
data on it they could salvage.

"Take this!" Lucy leaned out of the window and tossed the tablet
into the passenger seat of the minivan. "I'm going to . . ."

She trailed off. Ten seconds or ten minutes. There was no way to
know how long she had before the device would detonate. All she
could be sure of was that the Soldier-Saints had not built it for show.
It would explode, and countless people would die.

"No," she growled. "Not today." Lucy clambered in behind the
wheel and slammed the ambulance into gear, stepping on the gas.
The vehicle's wheels spun and it jerked into reverse, fishtailing around

to face the way they had come. She rammed the gearstick into drive and accelerated back down Mission Street. Lights flashing a storm of white and red, sirens screaming a banshee chorus, Lucy turned the ambulance into a guided missile. She pushed the pedal into the firewall and leaned forward over the steering wheel. The darkened apartment buildings and office blocks either side of her loomed large, as if she were at the bottom of a canyon cut from hard-edged towers of obsidian.

The rotten-egg stink of hydrogen and the chemical tang of explosives stung her nostrils. Lucy tried not to think about the monstrous destructive power contained in the improvised bomb, instead keeping her eyes focused on the road ahead. In the distance, she could see where Mission Street terminated, and beyond the glitter of a low moon off the waters of the San Francisco Bay.

The stalled trolley bus rose up to fill the windscreen and she navigated around it in a whipping, arrow-fast motion, but the ambulance was heavy and unbalanced with that damaged rear tire, and it fought her. Control began to slip away and the vehicle skidded into a long line of parked scooters, bulling its way through them, flipping the enameled two-wheelers across the lanes of the avenue.

Lucy battled grimly through the skid and kept the ambulance on true. *Almost there.*

There wasn't a plan in her head, not really. It was more like a wild instinct, a last-second piece of improvised action fueled by barely concealed panic. *The kind of insane risk that Dane would take, not me,* she told herself. Lucy didn't want to perish because of the reckless Brit's bad influence on her. *But here I go . . .*

The ambulance burst from the mouth of Mission Street and careened over the Embarcadero intersection, scattering terrified pedestrians before it. Lucy pointed the lumbering vehicle toward a gangway close to Pier 14 and crashed through a chain-link gate. She was rapidly running out of road.

Kicking open the driver's door, Lucy saw a blur of decking and threw herself out toward it. The impact knocked the wind from her and she rolled, feeling her jacket snag and tear, feeling blood wet her face. Behind her, the ambulance's engine gave a dying roar as the vehicle smashed through a wooden barrier at the end of the jetty and crashed into the waters of the bay.

Time blurred and she lost a few moments. Seconds or minutes, she couldn't tell.

People were running to help her. No. *No*. They had to get clear. It wasn't over yet.

Lucy dragged herself to her feet and pulled out the revolver that had been jammed in her pocket, aiming it into the sky. She fired at nothing, the reports of the shots driving the would-be Good Samaritans back the way they had come.

Limping, forcing herself to run-stumble, Lucy put as much distance as she could between herself and the sinking ambulance. A thermobaric weapon worked only when it could disperse a deadly aerosol of explosive material for its secondary detonation, and drowning it in seawater would hopefully be enough to neutralize that lethal effect. But the primary charge could still go off, could still claim lives—

That thought was forming in Lucy's head when a wall of air pressure and heat rammed into her back and threw her forward. The blast lit up the pier like a flash of summer lightning and she stumbled against a low wall.

Lucy turned and saw a bolus of dense black smoke rising from the shallows, framed by the lights coming on again along the distant Bay Bridge. Fat droplets of water and splinters of the wooden wharf cascaded down around her. At length, Lucy allowed herself to slump against the wall and gulp down some air. The ringing in her ears made it hard to concentrate, and it was only when a shadow fell across her line of sight that she realized Malte was standing over her.

*Are you hurt?* His mouth moved but she didn't hear the words.

"Deafened," she managed, tapping her earlobe. Then she broke into a jag of rough-throated laughter. "That was reckless."

Malte gave her a sardonic nod in return and helped her up, guiding her toward the idling minivan. More strobes, blue ones this time, and the searching pillars of spotlights beneath Coast Guard helicopters were converging on the pier.

"We wait?" Malte jerked his chin toward the distant police cars. She saw he had the damaged tablet computer in his other hand, and Lucy guessed the question he hadn't uttered. *Do we turn this over to Rowan and Gonzalez?*

Straightening, she took the tablet from him and levered off the broken back cover. "Knife?" she asked, holding out her hand. He handed over a folding blade, and in quick order Lucy found and cut out the tablet's battery pack, to ensure no kill-code wiper program could be run to blank its contents. "We don't wait," Lucy told him, getting into the van. "These fanatic pricks had help. I want to know who gave it to them."

Marc's route out of Malta took in a blind stop in Tunis and then back across the Mediterranean Sea to Nice, doubling back on the route to make certain that the local authorities had not tracked him leaving the island. The Dutch passport he used went into a burn bag as soon as he left the arrivals lounge, but Marc was barely a few strides into France before two men emerged from of the edges of his vision and surrounded him.

He didn't know their names, and no one at Rubicon had ever thought to tell him. They were part of Ekko Solomon's personal security detail, both muscular men in black Brioni suits and dark glasses, both shaven-headed and utterly humorless. *They could have been pressed out of the same mold in a factory that made tough guys*, he reflected, the only thing that differentiated them being the tone of their skin. One of them had the ruddy tan of a farmhand, the other was dark brass. They moved with careful, economical motions, and with slow alarm Marc realized that they were treating him like he was a potential threat.

"You going to tell me what's going on?" He directed the question toward both of them as they flanked him out into the afternoon sunshine.

"Alert procedure is in effect," said the Farmhand.

"You'll be debriefed at the office," added Brass. And those were the

last words either of them spoke to him. Marc climbed into the back of
a waiting Mercedes GLS and Farmhand drove while the other man
sat next to him, silent and impassive.

Belatedly, Marc fell into a much-needed doze that lasted all the
way to Monaco, and by then the sun had dipped toward the horizon.
He had snatched a few hours of sleep on the flights, but it didn't feel
like it was anywhere near enough. Each time Marc had started to
sink toward real rest, his mind pulled him back out with the dread
about what had happened in Malta, and where Kara Wei had vanished to.

The boulevards of the most expensive city-state on the planet
crowded in on them, and the GLS wove quickly through the traffic
toward the business district and the office buildings on the Avenue
de Grande Bretagne. The Rubicon Group's headquarters in Europe
was a modernist pillar of steel and glass, rising out of the masses of
old-money red tile and nouveau riche stucco lining Monaco's hill-
sides. Most of the lower floors were turned over to offices managing
Rubicon's main corporate interests—mining and construction, bio-
technology and aviation, as well as a more visible private military
contractor branch. The upper tiers were reserved for Ekko Solomon's private suites and a compact operations center for the Special
Conditions Division.

Marc expected his escorts to take him there, but the elevator from
the basement car park descended instead of rising, depositing him on
a level that he hadn't even known the building possessed.

The corridor was all harshly lit concrete and steel panels, and Marc
tensed once more as the two men walked him to a secure room. The
door opened to reveal Henri Delancort seated at a metal table, with
one empty chair opposite him. The room and the set-up screamed
*interrogation*, and Marc stopped dead on the threshold.

"What the fuck is this?" he demanded. A rough mix of fatigue
and irritation curdled inside him and he glared at Solomon's assistant. "You expecting trouble?"

Delancort gave a theatrical sigh and removed his rimless spectacles, pausing to rub the bridge of his Gallic nose. "We already have
more than enough of that to be dealing with."

His tone rang a warning bell in Marc's thoughts. "Where's Lucy? Malte? Has something happened to them?"

"Yes," Delancort said firmly. "But it has been dealt with and they are both on their way here. And it has nothing to do with the conversation we need to have." When Marc still didn't move, Delancort gave him a dark look and replaced his glasses. "Please. Take a seat so we can make some sense of this, *oui*? Do not be difficult."

Brass put a heavy hand on Marc's shoulder and used the other to point the way to the chair. The intimation was obvious. *Sit down before you are made to.*

He shrugged off the bodyguard and dropped heavily into the vacant chair. Brass followed him in, while the Farmhand waited outside in the corridor. "I don't take well to being treated like a criminal," he told Delancort firmly. Marc had too many bad memories from rooms like this one, memories of accusations and threats from his own government, from his former comrades at MI6. Part of the reason he had come to work for Solomon and the SCD was to get away from that. And here it was, happening again.

Delancort fiddled with the cuffs of his silver-gray suit jacket. "Let us get straight to the point." The French Canadian was slender in frame and rakish in the way he dressed, but there was always a manner about him that Marc didn't like. He had a calculating edge underneath all that carefully engineered casualness that Marc found false. "Do you know where Kara Wei is?"

"I thought I did . . ." He took in the bare room and found the mirrored bubble of a monitor unit in the far corner. "I thought she was on Malta with me. Seems not, though."

"There is no evidence of her arriving on the island within the last two days," Delancort confirmed. "She dropped off the tactical grid in France at the same time you did and she has not resurfaced."

"I didn't drop off the grid," Marc insisted. "I was following orders. From *you*."

"Were you?" said Delancort, without weight. "Did you speak to me? Did you speak to anyone other than Kara?"

Marc stiffened. "No."

"Explain it," said the other man. "We lost contact with the two of you after the data upload came in from the Toussaint woman's GPS logs. Good work on that, by the way. You secured a very useful take for us."

"Okay." Marc was silent for a moment as he marshalled his thoughts, getting the facts in order. He talked for the next fifteen minutes and Delancort listened in silence as he went through what had happened. The unexpected call for redeployment, the time-sensitive investigation into the Wetherby killing, chasing the drone, the data-mesh hidden in the dead man's flesh, all of it.

When Marc was done, Delancort looked up at the monitor as if he was waiting for something, and then turned back to face him across the table. "If you were lying about any of that, we would know it."

Marc spread his hands. "So can we stop pissing about now?"

"Yes, let us do that," Delancort said flatly. "You have been duped. I think we all have. Kara Wei has gone rogue, and she used you to get what she wanted." He paused, his tone softening. "I thought you might be in on it with her. I will not lie, I have harbored my doubts about your performance—"

"Really?" Marc couldn't stop the acerbic interruption from coming out. "I hadn't noticed."

Delancort's eyes narrowed. "I have questioned your competence. Let us not forget that Khadir and Glovkonin are still at large."

Marc tensed at the mention of the two names. Khadir, a top cell leader for Al Sayf, had been instrumental in constructing the terror threat that first brought Marc into Rubicon's orbit, and the Russian oligarch Pytor Glovkonin had been running the traitor in MI6 responsible for ruining Marc's life. Both had yet to pay for what they had done.

"You're laying that at my door?" Marc growled. "There's not a day goes by I don't think about them. And what they took from me."

Delancort went on as if Dane hadn't spoken, content to get a reaction from him. "But if I were uncertain of your loyalties, this conversation would be going in a different direction."

Marc's teeth set on edge at the unspoken threat in those words, but he didn't rise to it, waiting for the other man to continue.

"So, to summarize. From what we can determine, Kara received an automated, encoded email from a private server during the operation in Chamonix. Moments after that message arrived, she severed communications with Rubicon and began active efforts to impede our tracking of you both. Two hundred thousand euros were siphoned from an SCD black fund shortly afterward by an unknown source, and we believe this was also Kara's doing." He waved vaguely at the air. "This operation you have been telling me about, this Malta investigation? It would appear that Kara instigated the entire mission on her own and presented it to you as a legitimate Rubicon tasking . . ."

"So I would help her," Marc broke in, color rising in his cheeks. "She set me up?" He could hardly believe it, and he stared at the floor, confused and dismayed. "I knew things were off . . . She kept asking me if I trusted her."

"You did." Delancort cocked his head. "And now here we are. Rubicon's network has gone into siege mode while we make sure that Kara has not tried to gain access elsewhere, or steal any materials from our servers."

"Why would she do that?" Marc shook his head. "You think she's attacking us? That doesn't make any sense!"

The door opened and whatever reply Delancort might have had faded in the presence of the man who entered. Both he and Marc rose as Ekko Solomon filled the doorway with his presence.

In his early fifties but trim with it, the owner-founder of the Rubicon Group looked like he was carved from dark, weathered teak. He wore a sharp-edged suit and his eyes were hard and searching, his brow creased. "I wish I could be sure you are right, Mr. Dane." Solomon gestured for them both to sit, but Marc remained on his feet, wound tight once again.

"Kara let me think this was to do with the Combine," he said. "Led me to that, pushed my buttons . . ." He shook his head, angry at himself. "She did that because she knew I would bite on it, and not look too hard at the mission in front of me."

"I regret that Kara may have manipulated all of our biases," said Solomon. He nodded toward the monitor. "I heard what you said. It is likely that she never intended to go to Malta. We think she headed deeper into Europe, but that is open to question. She is a most accomplished hacker.

She left a number of false trails that we are still in the process of running down."

"If you think this is some kind of play for money, you're wrong." Marc spoke without thinking, instinct finding the words. "The way she acted . . . I think this is something more than that, something *personal*."

"Your insight is correct," Solomon said grimly. "Kara Wei and Alexander Wetherby knew each other. She was alerted to his murder and chose to pursue it using my company's resources . . . And you, Mr. Dane."

Marc recovered the data-mesh from his pack and showed it to them. "She cut me dead once she uploaded whatever was on this. She used me to get it."

"There are certain facts about Kara Wei that you are not aware of," noted Delancort. "To begin with, that is not her real name."

Marc glanced at Solomon, his concern deepening. "What facts?"

"*Ghost5*. You know of that group." The African met his gaze. "Given your particular skillset in the digital realm, Mr. Dane, I imagine you know exactly who they are."

A chill ran through him. "I've heard of them," admitted Marc. The name belonged to a collection of mercenary hackers who held a top slot on the most-wanted lists of US Cyber-Command, GCHQ, the FSB and the National Security Agency. "Like Anonymous, minus the righteousness, with a taste for blood money."

Their name was a play on words. *Ghost5* because it was gamer-geek leetspeak for "Ghosts," the scariest of the phantoms that lurked in the haunted corners of the dark web—and also because rumors suggested there had originally been five members of the group at its inception. There were stories that the hacker collective had worked data intercepts in South America against the enemies of the La Noche cartel, leading to the murders of dozens of Drug Enforcement Agency operatives and informants, and chilling suggestions that they had been behind the downing of a passenger jet in Ghana, as part of an extortion plot against a major airline.

"Alexander Wetherby was a member of Ghost5," said Solomon. "He may have been trying to double-cross them, or perhaps he was taking part in one of their operations in Malta. Either way, information we secured from Kara's workstation makes his status as one of them undeniable."

"Where was the data?" asked Marc.

"A hidden partition on her hard drive," noted Delancort. "She neglected to secure it fully . . . Perhaps because this all took place with such haste. It suggests she was not adequately prepared."

The chill he felt bedded in, and Marc knew what would come next. "She was one of them too, wasn't she? Before Rubicon?" said Marc.

Delancort nodded briskly and he adjusted his glasses. "She had quit the group by the time she came across our radar. We caught her operating on her own, attempting to penetrate one of our corporate mainframes in Senegal."

"When exactly did you know she worked with one of the most dangerous hacker groups on the planet?" Marc could barely believe it. If even half the rumors about them were true, Ghost5 had as much blood on their hands as any conventional terrorist group.

"From the start." Delancort nodded again. "Why do you think we hired her?"

"I built Rubicon on many principles," Solomon continued, before Marc could retort. "Key among them is the promise of redemption." Unconsciously, his hand moved to his throat. It wasn't visible, but Marc knew that on a chain around Solomon's neck hung the trigger of a gun, one that he had used to take a life when he had been a much younger man. "Everyone I have brought into the Special Conditions Division has been somebody deserving of a second chance. You understand that as well as any of us, Mr. Dane." A cloud passed over the other man's face. "Kara . . . She told me she wanted to be free of her previous life. At the time I chose to believe her."

"And now?"

Solomon looked away, letting Marc's question hang in the air. Ekko exchanged a glance with Delancort, and Marc saw a silent communication pass between them. "I have to confer with the head of Rubicon's overt military and security contracts division. The lockdown is causing problems for us . . . Henri, you will restore all of Mr. Dane's privileges and clearances. I want him working on an analysis of that device." He pointed at the mesh. "It is the only lead we have."

"Sir, are you quite sure—?"

Solomon did not allow Delancort to finish. "I am sure," he said firmly. "Both of you know your jobs. Get to work." He hesitated before putting a hand on Marc's shoulder as he walked away. "But first, get some sleep. I need you at your best."

Marc wanted to argue the point, but he was tired and the fight in him was fading. At length, he nodded wearily and picked up his backpack.

After Solomon left, Delancort gave him a tight, forced smile across the table. "I hope you understand, my earlier concerns about you were nothing personal."

"Sod off," Marc said with feeling, and stalked away.

## — SEVEN —

W elcome back," said Delancort.
"Say that like you mean it," retorted Lucy as she strode out of the elevator. She limped a little from the bullet-kiss on her leg, the bandage across the shallow wound tight and uncomfortable. Malte followed close behind, and offered no comment.

Solomon's aide fell in alongside them as they crossed the wide wooden deck that formed the atrium of Rubicon's crisis center. "I sent one of the jets for you," Delancort replied. "What more do you want?"

"That's a question with a long-ass answer," she told him. Malte threw her a nod and broke away, heading off to the residential quarters. "But it's good we had the plane. Otherwise we'd still be back there."

Solomon's personal pilot, an ex-Israeli Air Force flyer named Ari Silber, had leveraged the Rubicon's influence in California to get them out of the US and back to Europe, much to the chagrin of Special Agent Gonzalez of the FBI, who wanted Lucy and Malte to submit to a full debriefing about what happened with the Soldier-Saints.

In the end, they'd found a compromise. Ari agreed to make a stop in Washington D.C. and Gonzalez had flown with them, getting the debrief in the air along the way. By the time they landed at Dulles to refuel for the transatlantic leg, the FBI agent had everything he and Agent Rowan at the Secret Service needed to demand a full-court press on the home-grown terror group.

The plans of the Soldier-Saints to kill hundreds of people and grab headlines for their twisted cause had been stopped dead, but the horrible reality was that they had almost succeeded. Luck had played too great a role in stopping the detonation of their makeshift thermobaric bomb, and that burned at Lucy like acid. Someone had been paid to help the terrorists advance their cause, and she wanted to know who.

*The Combine*, she thought. This was exactly their kind of operation, mass-killing attacks run through proxies, strikes that would hike up the global climate of fear so that they could profit from it. *Was that Madrigal woman one of their agents?*

But that didn't seem right. It was the easy answer. Lucy Keyes trusted her instincts, and they were telling her that more was going on here. The Soldier-Saints were small-timers, little better than a ragged backwoods militia long on rhetoric and short on action. Someone had given them a step up in lethality, and had it succeeded, the San Francisco attack would have been blunt and brutal.

The Combine were more sophisticated than that. For them, it was never just about the bloodshed, never violence for violence's sake. There was always another agenda.

Lucy showed Delancort the evidence bag that contained the tablet computer she had recovered from the ambulance. "I need the techs to give this the full work-over. There's more going on here than some redneck yahoos with a jury-rigged bomb. They don't have the skills to orchestrate the blackout we saw there, and this is the only lead to whoever did." She glanced around. "Marc and Kara are back, right? I could use their eyes on this—"

Delancort held up his hand to silence her. "We have brought in Assim to pick up Kara's workload." He turned his gesture into a beckoning motion and she turned to see the tall Saudi kid with an anxious smile and big glasses coming their way.

Lucy only knew Assim Kader in passing as Kara Wei's reluctant understudy. Young and nervous with it, he usually stayed quiet and hovered on the margins, and he didn't look happy being pushed into the spotlight. "Here, I brought you a gift," she told him.

"Oh. Thanks." Assim took the damaged tablet from her and turned it over in his long-fingered hands. He had a lilting accent that betrayed an expensive education in an English public school. "Someone took a dislike to this device, it appears."

"It's gonna be booby-trapped," she warned. "Digitally *and* physically, so be careful."

"Right-o . . ." Assim held the device at arm's length as he carried it away toward the data lab.

Lucy watched him go. "What am I missing here, Henri?" She didn't often address the French Canadian by his first name, but she did so now.

"We have a security problem," he offered.

"Tell me," she demanded, hearing the cautionary tone in the man's voice. On the flight across the Atlantic, Ari talked about a temporary lockdown protocol in effect across Rubicon's systems, frustrating Lucy when she was unable to log in to the company network. At the time, she hadn't thought too much about it, her mind occupied with fatigue, but now Delancort's words brought her up sharp. "What the hell is wrong? Is Marc all right? Is Kara?"

He frowned. "Kara is . . ." Delancort paused, and started again, leading her toward one of the glassed-in conference rooms so they could talk privately. "While you were in America, there was an incident. You are not going to like it."


Madrigal walked out across the tarpaper roof and lit a Gitanes, holding up a hand to act as a windbreak for her lighter. The air had cooled now the sun had set, and the breeze that seemed agreeable during the day turned chilly, gusts of it rattling through the exposed triangular spars of the ragged geodesic sphere that dominated the top of the derelict building.

Flaps of polymerized cloth waved where they hung from the lower frame of the gigantic golf ball shape. Further up the sides of the construction, the panels were undamaged but weather-stained and grimy from the rain. Complex layers of graffiti covered every surface as high as human hands could reach, giving the sphere the look of a strange paper sculpture rotting from the bottom.

She liked it up here. The giant orb was one of a trio, a smaller sister off to one side on its own blockhouse and another atop a phallic tower nearby. When the Cold War had been raging, the domes contained state-of-the-art listening equipment aimed into the dark territory of enemy nations, sampling and interpreting every last radio signal for signs of aggressive intent or actionable intelligence. But now the entire site was an empty husk, lost and overgrown among a rambling woodland. Its echoing spaces and vacant halls had been repurposed, first by the rogue creatives who had turned it into a ghost-town installation for anti-establishment street art, and now by her people. Madrigal's troupe were artists and rebels too, in their own way, but they worked from a very different palette.

She liked the symbolism of taking this place and occupying it. A complex that had once housed the silent weapons of information warfare did so again. But not in service to faceless nation-states and gray men in the corridors of power. Today, the war was in the hands of the disenfranchised and the betrayed.

Something about this place brought a long-buried memory to the surface. Other people would have walked these disused, decaying corridors and only seen the patina of paint and change on them, but Madrigal looked through that. The familiar, institutional design of the buildings reminded her of the places where she had grown up.

*A seemingly endless parade of blockhouse-built military bases. Schools and gym halls, post exchanges and prefabricated homes for the families of soldiers. She remembered running through those corridors, laughing and playing. Identical spaces, built from the same kit of parts, never too different. Always familiar and safe.*

*The skies overhead and the weather would change. Cold and snowy in one place. Then sandy and dry somewhere else. Warm and humid in another.*

*The faces of the teachers in the schoolrooms and the other children would change as well. So would the people outside of the wire, and the languages they spoke, the signs on their buildings turning from letters she knew to strange squiggles and pictograms. All of it a great adventure for a little girl.*

*And with her every time, her father in his crisp and perfect uniform, a sharply defined image bright like the illustration from a storybook. Her mother, though, more faded with time, a washed-out watercolor.*

Madrigal felt the weight of the memory starting to turn toward darker shades and tried to arrest that shift before she lost control of it. Only hurt, heartbreak and anger lay past that point.

*Her pale mother weeping, beginning her slow process of breaking apart. Her destruction would take years, and she would almost drag her daughter down too. It would take courage, in the end, to break away and let her disintegrate alone.*

*And then the casket draped with the flag that they refused to open, stopping her from saying goodbye. Her father lost in the dark of one clammy, rain-whispered night. The unanswered question that would kindle a cold, slow burn.*

"No." Madrigal shut down those thoughts with a physical effort, refusing to indulge them anymore. This was not the time.

She drew hard on the cigarette and the tip glowed cherry-red. *Events will start moving quickly now,* she thought. After so long, after so many years of small, incremental motions toward her goal, it would happen in a matter of days if everything went to plan.

There were regrets, of course. Matters that had to be dealt with. So many choices made over those years. Lines crossed and unnecessary principles discarded.

She thought about Lex. Poor, weak Lex. How sad it had made her to learn of his duplicity. He was always too inquisitive for his own good, and he had discovered more than he was meant to know about her plans for Ghost5. Without context, without understanding, he had reacted poorly.

*If he had come to me,* Madrigal assured herself, *we could have worked it out.* She would have made it clear, if only he had not failed her by running. His death had been close, close enough to pierce her brittle armor of aloofness. Distantly, she reflected on the thought of his blood on her hands, examining the notion as if she were observing from outside herself. Madrigal could not count the number of lives her actions had ruined, but they were small things, faraway things. They didn't connect to her. They were not, in the sense of her personal reality, *tangible.* But she had known Lex personally, she had invested in him. That made the regret bothersome.

Madrigal took another pull on the cigarette and brushed a thread of copper-colored hair out of her eyes, losing herself in the view over the dark woods. She dismissed the thought with purposeful finality.

Lex wasn't the first she had been forced to leave behind. He would not be the last.

Boots clanked on the rusted metal stairs behind her, and she glanced over her shoulder as Erik approached, carrying a tablet and a comms rig. His hard, eternally glaring eyes locked on to her like gunsights, the dark umber of his face lost in the shadows. Madrigal was in her late forties, which meant Erik was young enough to be her son, although that hadn't prevented them from sleeping together a few times over the last year. He had an athlete's physique and the stamina to match, but it had been a machine-like process, all function and no joy to it. More recently, there simply hadn't been the opportunity. They had too much to do, too many other diversions that were far more engaging than mere sex.

"Is it time?" she asked, but of course it was. Erik was German and he was flawlessly precise, utterly unaware of what a cliché that made him. She wandered inside the sphere and out of the breeze as he set up the gear, unfolding a thick satellite antenna to aim it at the cloudless sky.

"We have word from Andre," he told her as he worked. "Lex's gear has arrived by courier from Malta. They took everything of note from the hotel room and the corpse. He will bring it up later tonight."

"What are the others saying about Lex's disappearance?"

He shrugged. "Some are confused. Most don't care. But Pyne talks about it a lot. She doesn't understand why he ran."

"Don't let them focus on it," Madrigal said firmly. "Keep them occupied. Pyne's skills are useful but she's easily distracted. There could be complications if people start pulling at loose threads." She sat down on a steel box in the middle of the empty space. "As for Lex's gear . . . Is the flash drive there?"

Erik nodded once. "Our new friends will have made a clone image of the drive's contents before they sent it to us," he noted.

"They will," echoed Madrigal. "Bureau 121 and their cohorts in the Lazarus Group are good, but they won't be able to make use of that data on their own." She smiled briefly. "Otherwise, why would they need us?"

He paused. "Why do *we* need *them*?"

She shot him a warning look. "You know the answer to that question. The partnership grants me access to resources that I can't get on my own."

"Not true," said Erik, eyeing her. "We could do this without them. Agreed, it would take longer, but—"

"I've waited long enough!" she spat, crushing the cigarette against the floor in a flurry of annoyance. "It's taken too long." Madrigal shook her head and the moment faded. "I'm sick of walking the slow road."

He didn't press the point. The tablet came to life in Erik's hands, and he set it on a section of the dome's frame at eye level. "Ready to begin. I'll leave."

"No," she ordered, covering her flash of anger with this small allowance of trust. "You stay this time. Just listen."

He knew enough to stand beyond the range of the tablet's camera, and he loitered in the shadows as the complex electronics in the comms brick analyzed the incoming satellite transmission and set up the masking filter.

Presently, an image blinked into being on the tablet screen. Before a blank backdrop sat a round-faced Asian man with olive skin and receding hair, in the same poorly tailored suit he always wore. Undoubtedly a soldier of some high rank, she surmised that he didn't enjoy being out of uniform for these conversations. He had protruding ears that always put Madrigal in mind of a cartoon character, but the sullen glower he sported put paid to any sense of levity about him.

"*My officers have communicated with me,*" he said, without preamble. "*They tell me your stray has been put down before he could compromise the project.*" His voice came tinny and harsh through the tablet's speakers, his words tight and over-enunciated.

"I'm grateful," she said, with a turn of the head. "They are as good as you said they were."

"*Of course,*" replied the man. "*It is not their efficiency that concerns me. It is yours, Madrigal. The deployment in America failed!*"

She held up a finger. "I beg to differ. We did our part perfectly. The mistakes were made by the Soldier-Saints, and I can't be held responsible for their poor operational security." Madrigal glanced briefly at

Erik. The full details of what had happened in California were still unclear, and nearly a day later San Francisco's power grid was only partly functional. But the plan of the far-right radicals to detonate an explosive device in the city had not come to pass. "The third phase worked," she went on. "We paralyzed a major city. With the initial test in Germany and then the Taiwan hack, we've had nothing but successes." She eyed the man on the screen. "Are you having second thoughts?"

Predictably, he bristled at her suggestion. *"When you brought us this project, you agreed that if we entered into a collaboration, certain criteria would be met. We remain . . . unsatisfied."*

Madrigal's tone hardened. "How many people lost their lives in Taipei?" She was willing to play the role of inferior from time to time, but the man's tone grated on her. She needed to remind him where the talent lay in this association. "Your people could not have made that happen. We did. And when this is over, we will have given you what you have been craving for decades. *Respect.*" She leaned closer to the tablet screen. "I think that will satisfy you."

He chewed on that for a moment, and when he spoke again his tone was more moderated. *"When will you initiate the main operation? The timetable is vague."*

She sensed his impatience. It was a mirror of her own. "We're ready for the main event, don't fret. Your, uh, officers may have some more work, depending on how we progress from here. But soon. Very soon."

*"There must be no further distractions,"* insisted the man on the screen.

"I could not agree more," she told him, reaching for the tab to cut the connection. "I'll be in touch shortly."

The image winked out and Erik stepped in to dismantle the gear. "More work," he said, picking up on her comment. "More loose ends like Lex?"

She sighed, tapping another Gitanes out of the packet and into her palm. "He was a problem that I didn't see coming."

"It was dealt with before it got out of control."

"Yes," she allowed, "but now we are a man short and I'm thinking about other people outside the circle who could be an issue. It might be prudent not to wait for the next problem to occur."

"You are talking about Dart." He gave her a level look. "You think he's a liability? He has everything he wants. Our deal with him is over and done."

Madrigal shrugged, flicking on a wavering flame from her lighter. "Is it?" She lit and took a drag on the fresh cigarette. "Then call this *being prepared.*"

"Kara left Marc twisting in the wind? In the middle of a goddamn mission?" Unconsciously, Lucy's hands contracted into fists. "He could have been killed out there!" She stood up from the conference room table and walked to the frosted-glass window, glaring out over the Monaco skyline and the bay beyond.

"Quite," said Delancort. "Fortunately for him, Dane managed to make his escape, and after Kara cut off communication with him, we were able to re-establish a link and set up an extraction. It is unclear if her intentions were to leave him to fall into the hands of the Maltese police, or to the mercies of Wetherby's killers."

Lucy shot Delancort a look. "You think she'd deliberately do that?"

"I have learned that the world we move through seldom has any firm truths in it. People change to fit their circumstances, or they are eventually forced to reveal the reality of themselves. I think we have seen Kara's mask fall from her face."

Lucy found she didn't have a reply to that. Kara Wei had always been difficult for her to get a handle on, even though she had considered her a friend. Lucy suspected that the dry, petite Chinese American woman was on the autism spectrum somewhere, better at handling the rigid structures of computer code and technical hardware than parsing social cues and dealing with human beings. But still, she found it hard to believe that Kara had so vague a connection with other people that she could intentionally cut someone off and leave them in harm's way. Marc was capable of looking after himself, sure, she knew that. But Kara's actions set Lucy's teeth on edge.

"We are attempting to track her movements," Delancort went on, "but as of now, we have no firm leads and no sense of her ultimate purpose. In light of this, I have advised Solomon to keep Rubicon at secure status, until we can be sure Kara's actions are not part of a concerted move against the company."

Lucy gave a grim nod. "Given the access she's had . . . Damn, she could have got into any of the company servers, downloaded files or uploaded a virus . . ." The more she considered the possibilities, the worse they were. "Kara betrayed us . . ." When Lucy finally said the words out loud, it made the notion permanent and real. The last embers of sympathy she held for the other woman faded as her sniper's mindset reasserted itself. "What can I do?"

"Solomon is talking to the board of directors. He'll want to brief you privately when that's over."

There was an unspoken inference in Delancort's words, but neither of them acknowledged it. "I'll be ready," she said, after a moment.

A blurry figure formed behind the glass door before it abruptly slid open. Carrying his laptop under one arm, Marc peered into the room and found Delancort at the table. "Good, you're here . . ." He took a step in, ignoring any protocol, and then caught sight of her. A brief but honest smile crossed his face. "Lucy . . . You okay? I saw the news about San Francisco, was that—?"

"That was," she said with a wan nod. "Malte and me had a little trouble." Then she shook that off, feeling the slow burn of her previous anger return. "Delancort filled me in on this shit with Kara."

"Yeah." Marc seemed to remember why he had arrived. "About that." Without preamble, he took a seat and opened up the computer, his fingers clattering across the keyboard.

"We were in the middle of a conversation," Delancort began, but Marc paid no attention to him.

Panels appeared on the opaque walls, displays opening like windows into streams of text and computer code as Marc sent information through the table's wireless pickups to screen circuits concealed in the glass. "So, long story short, I broke the encryption on the mesh drive from Wetherby's body," he told them. He glanced at Delancort. "She knows who that is, right?"

"I brought her up to speed on your unauthorized jaunt to Malta, *oui*." Delancort's brow furrowed. "How did you crack the protection so quickly?"

"I've been working on it for the last ten hours straight." Marc eyed him. "Probably drunk my own body weight in coffee and Red Bull. Plus, I still have a server full of GCHQ icebreaker programs from my days at Six and I *am* really good at this," he said, as if it was obvious. He took a breath. "Anyway. I found something serious on the drive. It's not just data, it's a piece of software. An executable attack program." Marc spoke quickly, falling over his words to get the information out. "Don't worry, it's dormant. Like a gun that's not loaded. At first I wasn't sure what I had here, I mean, it's *very* high-spec. Not the kind of code some Lulzsec wannabe could put together, more advanced even than a hacker team like Ghost5 could build. I'm talking about a nation-state level of sophistication. But when I took a look into the base code I started seeing elements I recognized . . ."

"Wetherby was gonna traffic a digital weapon?" Lucy was vaguely familiar with cyberwarfare protocols from her time in Special Forces, but only in the places where they had crossed over with her own, more kinetic brand of havoc.

"He put up some good firewalls on the drive but it was a quick and dirty job," Marc explained, the explanation tumbling from him in a rush. "Formidable, but not impregnable. I mean, his Interpol jacket said his expertise was as a red team raider, all about the act of penetrating digital security. A wall-*breaker*, not a wall-*maker*, yeah?" He took a breath. "But anyway. I got in. I got in and I found . . ." She saw him lose momentum, like a runner faltering in their steps. "I know what it is, Lucy. I know it because they stole it out from under us! And now here it is, years later, right in front of me!"

"Slow down, hoss," she said, walking back to look down at the screen in front of him. "You're skipping whole chapters, I have no idea what you're talking about."

Marc made a physical effort to reel it in and re-frame his thoughts. "What I'm talking about is Arquebus. I mean, I never thought I'd see it again . . ."

"*Arquebus*," repeated Delancort. "A sixteenth-century matchlock rifle. Like a musket."

"That's the code name," Marc explained, "for a multi-vector worm program designed to act against compromised systems, enemy networks, embedded infrastructure targets, the works."

Lucy watched a pane of dense command text scrolling down the wall-screen. "I don't want to ask how you know what that is."

Marc let his hands drop off the keyboard. "I know because I helped to write it. Back when I was working for British Intelligence."

She eyed him. "I thought you were tech-ops at MI6. Field support and that kinda thing."

"I was. See, Arquebus was part of a cross-agency initiative involving all the UK actives. Six and Five, GCHQ, Defense Intelligence, even SO15 were read in on it . . . I was part of a group from K Section at Six, brought in to assist on the design. We were going to build the software tool equivalent of a Special Forces operative. Configurable for any threat environment. Highly adaptable . . ." He paused, letting out a sigh. "Shamoon. Crash Override. Stuxnet. Any of those names mean anything to you?"

"I heard of that last one," said Lucy. "Computer virus. Used in an attack on Iranian nuke enrichment plants, back in 2010. Screwed with their systems."

"Basically, yeah. But it's more complex than that." Marc gestured at the screen. "So, Stuxnet was—*allegedly*—developed by the US and Israel to throw a spanner in the works of Iran's nuclear weapons program. They wanted to stop them refining bomb-grade uranium in violation of UN treaties, but putting airstrikes on the labs wasn't a viable option. Mostly because no one knew for sure where all the Iranian facilities actually were."

"They deployed this virus instead?" said Delancort.

Marc nodded. "Yeah. It could attack not only the sites that were known to exist, but the ones that were hidden as well. Stuxnet penetrated the industrial command systems of the nuke plants and broke them from the inside out. It was clever. It used multiple zero-day exploits to get in and do damage subtly. If it hadn't been for some computer security nerds catching on, it would never have been found.

Iran had their own version, Shamoon. They used it on the Saudis to mess with petrochem plants and bank servers—"

"I would appreciate it if you were less free with the technical jargon," Delancort broke in. "What is this 'zero day'?"

"It's a critical software vulnerability," Marc noted. "Deep in the code, a bug that the original programmers missed. It's like finding a loose brick in the wall that only you know is there. Marry that to an agile malware program and you have a way to get in and kill an entire computer network, if you apply it correctly. Stuxnet worked like that, and Arquebus was designed to do the same. You could plug in a zero day the same way you'd load a warhead on the tip of a missile. Aim it at the target, and . . ." He trailed off. "The British government saw what happened to the Iranians and they wanted the same offensive capability."

"Which begs another question," said Delancort. "Why did Wetherby have a copy of it?"

Lucy watched Marc's expression harden as he framed his reply. "Because I think . . . I think that Ghost5 stole it."


Project Arquebus had been, in the end, a bloody mess.

A few months before the *Palomino* incident, the horrific explosion on board the freighter in a French harbor that had killed the rest of OpTeam Nomad, Marc Dane had been seconded from his unit to the Arquebus programming and evaluation group. In a blandly modernist office block in Cambridge, concealed behind the false front of mobile app developer, a covert software design lab operated under the aegis of GCHQ. Marc was there to provide a field technician's point of view on the final stages of the software's development, evaluating and refining the program that MI6 and the other agencies had collaborated on.

Marc recalled that he didn't rate the idea that much. Arquebus was meant to be a jack-of-all-trades, capable of pure digital espionage, directed attack or subtle sabotage as the mission demanded. But it was master of none of those theaters, in danger of becoming a cobbled-together compromise instead of the sleek do-everything weapon desired by the gray men on the Joint Intelligence Committee. He contributed where he could, but the project wavered on the verge of cancelation.

Until one rainy night, when a massive digital attack came out of the depths of the dark web and hammered down the lab's firewalls.

Marc saw it happen. He remembered the raw panic in the room as the security team watched the spikes of malware blow through their defenses and commence a vicious "wiper" assault on every database in the building. It was the virtual version of a scorched-earth raid, a critical mauling of the lab's network that erased the contents of each hard drive it touched.

When it was over, Arquebus was in pieces. Backups of earlier prototypes still existed on GCHQ servers, but they were incomplete and only partly functional. The lab's security had been thought impregnable. To reconstruct the software would take months, but in the wake of the penetration of the network, the focus moved to fixing the blame rather than any meaningful recovery of the project.

Spurred into action, MI5 uncovered evidence that one of the cover company's software engineers had a connection to a known cut-out for the Chinese Ministry of State Security, and the situation quickly escalated. GCHQ's vetting procedures were called into question and cooperation between the British intelligence agencies faltered. Within weeks, responsibility fell at the feet of a group known as Unit 61398, the cyberwarfare division of the People's Liberation Army.

Marc went back to Nomad, and while the Arquebus project group struggled to rebuild, the hawks in the JIC demanded a direct and forceful response to what they now believed was a preemptive digital strike by China against the United Kingdom.

The rest of the story had come to Marc in pieces, through hearsay and dark rumor. One of 61398's top hackers died in the toilet of a Singapore casino from a bullet though his right eye; in return, MI6's Op-Team Javelin lost half their number during a mission in Hong Kong when they were ambushed by a trio of PLA shooters. Eventually, the trail of tit-for-tat attacks between the Chinese and the British were stalled by clearer heads before the conflict could intensify. Both sides reluctantly declared the scales balanced, and backed off.

The ceasefire also sounded the death knell for Arquebus. The program was shut down, the funding behind it diverted elsewhere. Forever tainted by the fallout of the attack and the deaths that had followed it, the unfinished project was buried. GCHQ went back to the cheaper option of collaborating with the Americans on building their digital espionage tools.

But no one had ever really believed the men in Beijing who swore that the wiper attack was not their doing.

"The fact about Ghost5," Marc said bleakly, as he concluded his story, "is that they have a track record for this kind of operation. The clue's in the name, right? *Ghosts*. They move around without leaving a trace, except when they want to. And if they don't want to be known for whatever they did, they find a way to point the finger at somebody else. They did it with the FSB a while back, leading the Russians down a blind alley after a bunch of Chechen separatists . . ."

"You reckon Ghost5 did the same to the Brits with this Arquebus hack?" said Lucy.

"Yeah." He glanced at Delancort. "That could be it. They left false leads for MI5 to follow. You said Kara used to be with them, right? So she had to have been there when the Cambridge lab was attacked. She's got the skills—enough to have concealed Ghost5 duplicating the Arquebus software under cover of wiping the network." Marc scowled at his own conclusion. "I dunno, maybe someone paid them to do it, or maybe Ghost5 were acting on their own. But it fits the circumstances."

"She never said a word about it." Marc watched Lucy turn a glare on Delancort. "And you kept that part of her past hidden from the rest of us."

"Kara's contract with Rubicon has—*had*—a number of very specific clauses," noted Delancort. "Her new identity was one of them. The concealment of her previous exploits was another." He met Lucy's gaze. "We all have history that we would rather leave behind, *n'est-ce pas?*"

The hard truth settled on Marc as his thoughts drifted away from the moment. Kara was someone he had put his trust in, not only during the operation in Chamonix but many times before. If not for her being part of the Rubicon team, the Special Conditions Division might not have stopped the bombing in Washington, the plans of a pirate warlord to set off a nuclear device in the heart of Europe, or any one of the other threats the SCD had quietly neutralized.

But he had been burned before, in his time at MI6, when traitors within his own team had revealed themselves. Perhaps it had been naive to believe that couldn't happen again within Rubicon's close-knit ranks.

Delancort was right. Everyone in the SCD had come from somewhere else, dragging the legacy of past misdeeds and mistakes behind them. But as Solomon promised, it was a place for second chances. Now that sentiment seemed hollow.

"Dane." He looked up as Delancort addressed him. "Some of the data we found on Kara's secret partition shows evidence of incoming email messages from a blind server, the same one Wetherby used to reach out to the smuggler, Kyrkos. But she deleted them all and never responded."

"She blanked him?" Lucy considered that. "Why? She didn't want contact from someone in her old life, or . . . what?"

Marc remembered the look on Kara's face when he had returned to the staging point in France. She had to have known then. Right at that moment, Kara had been putting together the pieces of the lie she needed to get Marc to help her.

*Why didn't she just* ask *me?* The question pushed to the surface of his thoughts. Kara had spoken about trust. That was the point around which all of this orbited. *She couldn't trust me with the truth about Ghost5 because she knew how I would react.*

"All we can be certain of is that Wetherby was killed for the data you found," Delancort said, nodding toward Marc's laptop. "If he met with Kyrkos, it is because he had something to trade."

"You said Arquebus was incomplete when it was taken." Lucy looked to Marc for the answer. "So what value would it have?"

He shook his head and tapped the screen in front of him. "Here's the thing: the software on Wetherby's drive isn't what was copied from the Cambridge lab. It's more than that. This is like, *Arquebus 2.0*. It's a finished version. Shit, it's *better* than the original design!"

"So all this time Ghost5 have been . . . improving it?"

"Yeah," Marc said grimly. "There's code in the program config-uration for targets, internet IP addresses that would act as the vir-tual front door of whatever they wanted to attack." He worked the keyboard, highlighting a section of data. Strings of numbers scrolled down the wall-screen, blinking blue. "There's a bunch here that cor-respond with physical locations in Germany. Dusseldorf, Cologne, Berlin. Another cluster halfway around the world in Taipei. And here, San Francisco."

Lucy became very still. "There was a massive power outage when we were in San Francisco. The terrorists we were tracking had out-side help. Are we assuming this is part of the same thing?"

"Assim has the tablet computer Lucy brought back from Califor-nia," Delancort explained. "I think you will need to compare notes with him."

"Yeah," Marc said, with a nod. "Taking down a power grid is exactly the type of mission Arquebus was designed for."

"You mentioned Taipei." Delancort stared at the table in front of him, thinking. "There was a major train collision in Taiwan a few days ago."

Marc nodded again, remembering the radio report he had over-heard in France. "Yeah, that tracks. Again, we're talking about a soft target for an infrastructure attack by digital means. What do you want to bet that we'll find similar incidents if we dig in to news re-ports from those German cities?"

"I heard a woman," said Lucy. "Talking online with the Soldier-Saints before the lights went out. From the way it happened, I guessed she was running the tech side."

"Madrigal." Marc dredged the name up from the depths of his memory, from an old MI6 security briefing.

Lucy reacted with a jerk and jabbed a finger into his shoulder. "White, forties-fifties maybe. Redhead. American."

"You *saw* her?" Marc's eyebrows rose. "She's the only one of the original members of Ghost5 still alive."

"I didn't exactly *see* her," Lucy admitted. "The image had a digital mask."

"In my experience, people who live in the shadows only venture from them when they are motivated by fear or by greed," offered Delancort. "Go on. What do you know about her?"

Marc shrugged. "There's a lot of rumors and half-truths in the black hat community. Oftentimes, it's deliberate. To muddy the waters, yeah? I mean, back in the day when they first appeared, Ghost5 were pure hacktivists. They had an anti-globalization, pro-freedom agenda, and all that. But somewhere along the line they became darker and more destructive. Madrigal is the handle for a hacker from the bad old days of dial-up and acoustic modems—she's the original ghost. No one knows who she is or where she came from."

Lucy sneered. "But now she's showing her face, more or less. That's not good tradecraft."

"Yeah," Marc admitted, "but that's only useful if there's a name to go with it. I guarantee you this, if Madrigal had a past, it's gone. All that's left is the legend." He reeled off a list of possibilities. "She's an anarchist, she's ex-KGB, she's former CIA, a teenage computer prodigy, she's the daughter of old-skool phone phreakers from the sixties . . . Take your pick. If she was legit, she'd be up there with Gates or Jobs, that's the tale."

"At first I thought this was those Combine assholes resurfacing," said Lucy. "But this doesn't have their stink on it. If these Ghost5 hackers are selling their skills to any nut-bar with an AK and an axe to grind, these could just be the opening shots."

"Bespoke terror attacks," said Delancort, framing the horror of it in a single sentence. He eyed Marc. "You know the capabilities of this software weapon. How bad could it get?"

"Theoretically . . . if they have the right exploits to weaponize . . ." He swallowed hard as the full scope of it became clear. "Anything connected to the internet becomes vulnerable. From the phones in people's pockets to air traffic control systems, nuclear reactors, power grids, financial servers. Aim it at the right place, and you could knock out a dozen vital utilities at once. Plunge a whole country into chaos overnight. The disaster would pretty much write itself."

"You always bring *such* good news," said the other man dryly.

"We may be the only ones who know about Ghost5's part in this," added Lucy. "The FBI and the Secret Service had no intel on them being part of the Soldier-Saints plot. If they'd have known, Gonzalez would have told us."

"That's how Madrigal likes to work," said Marc. "Fade away and let someone else take the blame."

"We cannot reveal this to the American authorities, not for the moment," Delancort said firmly, preempting Lucy's next words. "Otherwise there will be unpleasant questions about why Rubicon employees removed a piece of evidence from a federal crime scene."

"And then there's the whole *fugitive-from-justice* thing," added Marc.

"So we wait for these nerds to drop an airliner out of the sky or do something equally shitty?" Lucy's tone rose.

"No," said Marc, folding the laptop shut. "We have a smoking gun here, and no one else knows that we do." The next move formed in his mind's eye. "I know Arquebus. I can pick it apart. And maybe we can get a line on what Madrigal is planning."

# — EIGHT —

The rain rattled against the window of the S-Bahn carriage as the train left Tiergarten and headed west over the canal. Kara watched the patterns formed by the droplets, unfocusing her eyes until the streets and buildings of Berlin on the other side of the glass became a blur of boxy concrete forms. She had no reflection in the window, her face hidden beneath the cowl of the dark-green hoodie she wore under her leather jacket. The clothing swamped her skinny and angular form.

People moved around her as the train pulled into the next stop, and she ignored them. Perhaps she should have been acting with more care and attention to her surroundings, observing the travelers in the other seats in case one of them was a watcher. But she trusted in her own skills. She had done enough in her escape from France to make certain that no one from Rubicon could track her. Every device she carried had been scrubbed clean or digitally neutered, every place that a locator could have been hidden ruthlessly searched a dozen times over. She had sanitized herself with the singular, machine-like focus of an obsessive-compulsive, and so she knew she was free.

In a way.

It was much harder to escape what followed Kara inside her head. The alien sense of guilt that lay in her chest. She imagined it as an egg made of cold, gray-white stone, pressing down on her lungs with a force that was almost physical. It accreted there as she ran, fleeing Chamonix to here, into a constant drizzle that she could not get free of.

She thought about Marc Dane's voice crackling down the encrypted satellite feed to her earpiece, and picked apart their last conversation for the twentieth time. There had been a distinct tone in his words, just before she told him she was sorry and severed the connection. A note of knowing. The imminent understanding that she was about to abandon him.

But it couldn't be helped. Kara had committed herself to this course. This was how it had to be. Dane was resilient and adaptable. She imagined he would be able to get to safety. If not . . . she would remember to be sad about it later.

A sense of inevitability fell over her and Kara closed her eyes, letting herself slip into memory. Like the train, her life was moving on a set of rails, one of countless hard-coded pathways inexorably leading her back to where she had begun. A loop line, doubling over on itself. It didn't matter what she wanted; the route had already been marked out, back into Madrigal's orbit.

To who Kara Wei really was.

"There's a good chance that you're gonna be charged as an adult," said the man from the group home. "You know what that means? They ain't gonna wait until you turn eighteen!" She'd never bothered to learn his name. He existed in the same way as the other adults in her life, as random forces of nature more than actual people. They would blow through, a tornado tearing at her, ripping up her shit, then dissipating and leaving pieces to be picked up in their wake. "You listening to me?"

She nodded, doing the absolute minimum needed to register attention and not be considered "disrespectful."

"Shit," he went on, looking down at the papers in his hand, the arrest record that the cops had given to him. He pulled at the collar of his sweat-stained shirt and blinked. "I don't know what half of this crap means . . ." She thought he looked sick and fearful, his chubby face robbed of the usual ruddy color it showed when he ranted at the kids. He was worried about how her exploits were going to reflect on him.

She'd been at the group home for six months before they figured out she had a brand-new laptop computer hidden in the crawlspace above the communal bathroom. Naturally, they thought she had stolen it. And she had, but not in the way these morons understood.

First, by co-opting the aging PCs at the local library, she'd hacked the Savings & Loan in town, faked herself a modest bank account and used the money to mail-order the laptop. Then, it had been easy enough to arrange for the old lady in the house next door to the group home to get "free" cable TV—in fact paid for by an anonymous benefactor—and a home entertainment package that included a decent Wi-Fi router. The couple running the group home didn't believe in computers. There was nothing in the house smarter than a decade-old flip-phone.

So while the old lady enjoyed dozens of channels of soap opera faff and Lifetime movies, the router silently worked as a partner in crime. Once the set-up was in place, it was easy to roam the web and look for trouble to make.

In the group home, the other kids were numb or dumb. At seventeen, she had nothing in common with any of them besides the broken wreckage of a childhood, and she wanted as little to do with them as possible.

She found her tribe out on the net, working her way into hacker circles by crunching code and breaking encryptions for shits and giggles. It was what she was best at, and it didn't take long for her skills to draw the attention of some big guns out on the lawless digital frontier.

They tested her. Gave her targets and applauded when she took down protected servers or single-handedly ran fierce denial-of-service attacks.

She wasn't stupid. She knew they were grooming her for better, bigger things. And this wasn't some old pervert angling to get her panties off on a webcam. It was people like her, who saw how the internet could be both playground and goldmine, if you worked it right.

But then one day the police were at the group home, talking about how the old lady's son had come visiting and found something he didn't like the look of. And pretty soon after that, the laptop had been discovered. Then there was a cop car and a cell and now this conversation.

People, of course, had ruined it for her. People, with their unpredictability and clumsy behavior, and their failure to follow the paths she wanted them to.

The cops called her exploits *wire fraud*. Real jail time came attached to that sort of crime. Some bright spark in an office somewhere had tracked a line of misdeeds back to a certain IP address, and that was all she wrote.

The consequences were supposed to be frightening to her, but what really cut deep was the thought that she would lose her lifeline to that other place. The meat-space of the real world was such a grinding, empty void and the net was her oxygen. Isolated from it, she would curl up and die. It was the closest she had ever been to really *feeling*, and now it would be taken away.

The others, her friends behind their ghost identities and virtual phantoms, would learn what happened to her and she would become a cautionary tale. She would never see their world again.

The door to the cramped meeting room opened suddenly, and in came a severe-looking woman with shoulder-length hair the color of coal, and dark eyes that glared out from behind a pair of glasses with heavy frames. She wore a gray pantsuit with an FBI badge hanging out of the breast pocket.

The woman introduced herself as Special Agent Trecento and told the man from the group home that wire fraud wasn't all that was going on here. The question had been raised about federal crimes taking place, the invasion of government and military networks. Crimes that veered into acts of treason.

It took less than ten minutes for him to sign off on surrendering her to the FBI agent's custody, and with her wrists cuffed at her back, the last she saw of the man was as the door closed on his angry, judgmental glare.

Trecento took her to a black rental car waiting in the parking lot outside the police station. A male agent in dark sunglasses sat in the driver's seat, and he didn't wait for her to get comfortable before they peeled out on to the highway.

The female agent watched her from the front passenger seat. "You've been clever," she said. "Broken a lot of laws. Did you think that no one would notice?"

"I'd give you the finger if I could show you my hands," she replied, affecting a defiant air.

Trecento started laughing, like it was the funniest joke she'd ever heard. She pulled a packet of French cigarettes from her jacket pocket and lit one. "We noticed," she went on, after a moment. "We were impressed." With her free hand, she reached up to the nape of her neck and tugged. Her black hair came away in one pull, revealing rust-red tresses beneath. She tossed the wig into the back seat and then fished a small key out of another pocket. "That doesn't happen often. Not many pass the audition," said the woman, leaning in to unlock the handcuffs.

"You're not the Feds," the younger woman said, as everything caught up with her.

The woman with the red hair smiled and blew out a thin streamer of smoke.

Kara blinked back to the present as the train rocked over a set of points in the track, and for a second she could still smell the bitter perfume of Madrigal's cigarette.

The stone egg in her chest shifted, grew smaller, but it did not melt away. The real guilt, the weight at the core of it, was made from her feelings for Lex.

He liked his riddles and his games. The one he left for her on the subdermal flash drive had been easy to see through, opening up a hidden partition that only she would have known to look for. It wasn't up to Lex's usual standards, and she imagined that was because he had programmed it in a hurry. And what the partition contained, what it told her about the rest of the files on the drive . . .

Sitting alone in the silence, poring over the data Dane had uploaded from Malta, Kara understood far too late what Lex had been trying to tell her.

*Poor, stupid, funny Lex.* With his jokes and his smiles and his idiocy that made her so angry. He had always been the puzzle she could never solve.

He knew why she had broken away, back when everything went wrong. What right did he have to come after her years later? That had been part of the deal that Kara had made with herself. She had left that life behind and become someone else. But the past had come looking for her. Uninvited. *Unwanted.*

Lex reached out, again and again. Bombarding her with anxious messages. Each time Kara had reflected them back into the digital void, hoping that he would understand and leave her alone. But then one day he was dead and the stone in her chest appeared. Absently, her finger went to the strap of the smartwatch around her wrist and she pulled at it. Kara caught herself in the action and shook it off, irritated by the impulse.

She hated this. The awful, human mess of these emotions. They were part of why she had wanted to leave, back then. When Kara was small, there were doctors who explained that her mind was not a typical one, that it followed patterns some might find unusual, even abnormal. She craved order and clarity. What was so strange about that? She hated the random and the chaotic. At times, those things were almost physically painful for her.

And when she grew up, she found ways to deal with that. Boxes, inside her mind. Boxes for memories. Boxes for skills. Boxes in which she could put away the untidy and haphazard bits of reality and concentrate on what was vital.

But Lex opened them all up. Even after he was dead, he was still doing it.

Kara closed her eyes as the train clattered through another elevated station and she placed a hand on her chest. In the dark behind her eyelids, with the rain ticking against glass by her head, she reached in and closed her fingers around the stone. She imagined carrying it to a box and dropping it inside.

*Closing the lid. Sealing it tight.*

This was how it had to be, if she was to survive. She could not take anything extraneous with her where she was going. This was the plan.

Like everything else in her life, Kara had a strategy for what was happening now. She had a million of them, stacked in the boxes of her mind, one for every possible outcome.

Other people—ordinary, typical people—would daydream or zone out, but Kara's mind never went adrift. Instead, in those blank moments she built plans in her head for every eventuality, from things as trivial as choosing the colors of the clothes she wore to the path of her life from hour to hour. That way she was never blindsided by anything. If something could happen to her, she had already thought about it. Made a strategy to deal with it.

Lex's death had been in those possibilities, one more computed variable among countless others, and the plan she had to react to that event was now in play. Seamless and clear.

Back in Chamonix, when the monitor program she'd set up told Kara that Lex had been killed, she didn't even hesitate. The plan was already in place, and she was executing it. Events were turning full circle, and Kara was heading back to where she had started.

To do that, she needed to reboot herself. Re-format her emotional state as if it were a fragmented hard drive. And then she would be ready.

She opened her eyes again and watched the rain streak the window, the runnels of water curving downward.


Lucy blinked to clear her vision and tilted her head slightly to look back through the Nightforce scope atop her weapon. The warm wind had been gusting for a while, but now it was starting to drop. She watched the motion of pennants of steam rising from vents on the rooftops of buildings around the Rubicon tower to gauge the strength of the breeze, and adjusted her aim.

The cylindrical suppressor on the barrel of the Vanquish sniper rifle moved to point northwest, and Lucy lined up on the target she had picked out, a penthouse apartment in the complex off Kraemer Square, on the French side of Monaco. The range set in at around 300 meters, which for somebody with her level of training was as good as having the mark in her hip pocket.

She found the target. A woman in her mid-thirties in a flowy silk dress, wandering around the penthouse's open-plan kitchen with a phone pressed to her ear. The target was getting ready to leave for a night out on the town. Lucy could see the bright-blue high-heeled shoes she carried in one hand, waving them about as she spoke animatedly to her caller.

The woman described the same path. To the window, and back. To the window, back again. Lucy gauged where to lay the .308 round, accounting for the possibility of some deflection through the window glass. It didn't look armored, but she wasn't taking any chances. The shot would go into the woman's chest, above her left breast. The kill would be instant.

Sound and muzzle flash from the Vanquish's report wouldn't reach the street several stories below, and even if someone happened to be looking directly at Lucy's sniper nest, the thin light-dampening drapes that covered the rooftop would hide her.

The woman stopped walking and waved as a small boy wandered into the sight picture. She covered the phone with one hand and spoke sternly to him. His shoulders slumped. He wasn't happy.

Lucy willed herself to ignore the presence of the child. She blotted out how much he reminded her of her kid brother and focused on the target. The green dot above the scope's range gradient settled on the woman's chest.

The safety catch off, Lucy moved her finger to the trigger and applied gentle pressure, keeping her breath in check. Everything else fell away in the moment, every nagging concern from the outside world, every resentment and uncertainty. Lucy found clarity in the simplicity of her actions.

"Please do not kill anyone," said a resonant voice from behind her. "Rubicon must deal with many objections to our presence in Monaco as it is."

She drew back and pulled out the rifle's magazine, tilting it so Solomon could see the inert metal training rounds it held. "Practice," Lucy explained. She reloaded and moved to her second target, mentally logging the first "kill." "It helps me relax."

The next mark was in an apartment block off Avenue Marquet, and the sight picture was cluttered. Closer to the shoreline also meant she would have to reassess windage to be sure of making the hit.

Solomon sat down on an air conditioning unit and surveyed her. In his immaculate cotton Kiton suit, he looked utterly out of place among the dusty machinery, but his manner was unfazed. "I am sure there are other ways you could ensure your skills remain sharp."

"Build me that shooting range in the basement I keep asking for," she replied, reaching up to adjust a dial on the side of the scope. "If I could burn off a few hundred rounds, that might help." Lucy found the window she had picked out, one with a jolly little flag hanging off the frame. The shape of a heavyset man on a home exercise bike jumped into focus inside the apartment, twice as far away as the woman in the dress had been. She estimated the bullet drop at that distance and refocused.

"I spoke with the board," Solomon told her. His tone indicated that it had not gone well. "Kara has presented us with a myriad of concerns, even at the most conservative estimate of the situation."

Lucy touched her finger to the rifle's trigger and "killed" the man on the exercise bike. She released what remained of the breath she had been holding in and drew back from the weapon. "And then some." She shifted into a cross-legged position and started dismantling the Vanquish, piece by piece returning it to a plastic case packed out with foam inserts. "If she cut and run, that's one thing. But if this is part of a longer game . . ." Lucy let the sentence hang. The simmering annoyance that the work of the shoot had shrouded revealed itself again, and it pushed in on her thoughts.

Solomon broke eye contact. "It is difficult for me to admit, but I may have made a serious mistake bringing Kara into our fold. I believed I could trust her. Now it appears that conviction was misplaced."

"You knew where she came from." Lucy's reproach was open but there was little malice in it. "Who was she, before she became Kara Wei?"

"I did not know her real name," he replied. "There were a variety of aliases . . ." Solomon paused and then went on. "If she is acting against us, we are vulnerable. She knows much about the operations of Rubicon and the Special Conditions Division. If that knowledge is used, everything I have struggled to create is put at risk."

Lucy gave a slow nod. Rubicon was not without its enemies, both in the realm of overt corporate competition and the more shadowy spaces where the SCD operated. The Combine were out there, biding their time and rebuilding after what happened in Washington and Naples, along with other groups like Al Sayf and Russian Intelligence, all of whom had axes to grind with Solomon's organization. "If Kara's going to sell us out, she's not lacking for people who'd want some of that action."

"We may need to take steps," Solomon went on. "I have to ask you. If an extreme sanction is required, will you attend to it?"

Lucy didn't hesitate. "Say the word and it's done."

"The others may be reluctant to go that far."

"You're not asking them," she replied, closing the lid on the rifle case. "You're asking me. And frankly I don't find it that hard to see someone who broke my trust through a gunsight."

Solomon stood up and brushed dust from his suit. "Be prepared for the eventuality," he told her. "We have to protect Rubicon. The ideal. The people. All of it. One rogue operative cannot be allowed to threaten that."


The train pulled into the stop at Heerstrasse and the doors chimed for arrival.

Kara waited until the last possible second to get off, bolting through the doors as they started to slide shut. No one in the carriage was following her, but if they had been, she would have left them stranded inside as the train pulled away. Kara watched the train shrink in the direction of the Olympic Stadium. When she was sure of herself, she walked briskly away. First she followed the road, before veering on to the leafy, damp paths that wound their way up the shallow, forested mountain which overlooked Berlin.

Teufelsberg; *Devil's Mountain*. Beneath the dark green canopy rose a man-made hill born from the rubble of homes obliterated by the bombings in the Second World War, dumped there to smother the remains of a Nazi military training facility that defied all attempts to destroy it. In the Cold War that followed, Teufelsberg became the site for an Anglo-American listening post to spy on Communist East Germany, eventually falling into disrepair as that conflict also crumbled and faltered. She saw the ruin of it as she progressed up the incline. The drab spheres of the old radomes peeked over the tops of the trees. Their skeletal, strange forms made Kara think of the shed husks of giant insects.

The rain blurred their shapes and she hesitated, lost for a moment.

When she had tried to explain it to him, Lex had laughed.

"It's not easy for me to process being *present*," she said. "I mean, I see how emotions work on other people. I can observe them like an outsider looking in."

"You going to tell me next you don't feel it?" Lex rolled over under the sleeping bag and the floorboard beneath them creaked. He ran a hand through his unkempt bob of brown hair and peered at her. "You felt *this*."

Under the thermal layer, they were both naked, surrounded by a halo of body heat trapped by the covering. Lex was the warmest person she had ever met, in the literal sense. Some people were cool or tepid when they touched you, but he was a furnace. Beyond them, the cold brought by the rain pattering on the roof of the abandoned farmhouse seemed a far-off and unimportant thing.

"It's like a strange kind of gravity," she went on, and there was a smile trying to pull at her lips. "Love and hate, fear and joy. Exerting a push and pull on the people around me." The smile faded. "Sometimes I think the connection that makes those feelings real is missing."

"You fake it well enough to pass," he said, still grinning at her. "I appreciate you making all that effort for me."

"I don't have to for you," she told him. "You bridge that gap for me." She gave him a quizzical look. "How do you do that, exactly?"

"I don't know," he admitted. "Do you want to find out?"

"We could do that," she breathed, and leaned into his warmth.

She wiped the rain from her face. The walk was long, and by the time Kara reached the top, the steady rainfall had soaked through and darkened the shoulders and crown of her hoodie. As she got closer, there were moments when she thought she saw someone in the trees. Off the path. Watching. She didn't react, allowing them to think that she didn't see or didn't care.

Gales of vivid, profane graffiti covered the derelict buildings. The paintings had been left behind by street artists from the Berlin scene who had made the place their open-air gallery, or at least they had until the new tenants arrived. Now the dreamers with the spray cans kept their distance, or so the anonymous posters on the dark web shadow boards had told her.

Kara found some of the artworks unsettling. Monstrous faces and deformed figures vomiting abstract floods of words. They were meaningless to her. Others—geometric shapes, animals and colored forms—attracted her eye. She crossed over to one that seemed to emerge from the overgrowth and reached out to touch the painted bricks.

Behind her, someone stepped on a loose stone and it clattered against the cracked and broken asphalt.

"*Geh weg!*" shouted a male voice, the intonation thick with the implied threat of violence. "*Hey! Hast du mich gehört?*"

She turned around slowly and faced the pair of figures who had emerged from the shadows. Both male. One of them had the hatchet-faced look of a street punk, heavily tattooed, wired with too much energy and not enough places to spend it. The other was thickset, with a moon face framed by a ragged leather trapper hat. The punk had a crowbar in his paw and he looked familiar, but she couldn't place him.

Kara rolled down her hood and let everyone get a good look at her. Not only the two men, but those watching from behind whatever cameras were hidden in the corners of the derelict buildings. She looked around, searching for the best vantage point, finding a tatty tower and a dull white sphere next to it atop a nearby roof.

"You know who I am?" She directed the question at the man with the crowbar. Kara saw his brow crease as he studied her. He was thinking the same as she had. Faint recognition glimmered there.

These jokers had been shadowing her since she left the main road, and now it was time for them to know who they had been watching. Time for her to shed the identity she wore and regress a few steps. Roll back to an older iteration of herself, to one closer to the truth.

"Do this for me," she told the man. "Go tell Madrigal that *Song* is here."

"Song is in prison," said the one in the hat, switching from German to heavily accented English. "Or dead."

She spread her hands and presented them with an approximation of a smile. "Beg to differ."

"There's enough similarities in the code for me to call it, right now," said Assim. He took a deep breath, steeling himself. "I see the same quirks in the encryption on the San Francisco tablet as in the barrier code you pulled out of the software weapon." He pointed at the gutted device on the tech lab's workbench and then at the air-gapped forensic system Marc had been using. "Whoever worked on *this*, worked on *that*."

"Confirmation," agreed Marc. After the conversation with Lucy and Delancort, he had thought about taking a break but sleep eluded him. Instead, he went to the only place he knew would center him. The data lab was set up in one of the rooms off the crisis hub, and he got back to work on his analysis of the data-mesh from Wetherby's body.

Marc had uploaded a custom suite of digital cracking tools from his personal laptop and set to it, with Assim hovering nervously in the background. The tech gave Marc the run of the machines and did his best to stay out of the way.

Marc felt sorry for the younger man. Kara's disappearing act had both forced Assim into the front rank at Rubicon and placed him under suspicion as a possible co-conspirator, a situation not unlike the one that Marc had experienced at MI6 when his own circumstances had been compromised. In Marc's case, that had ended his career with British Intelligence and brought him into Rubicon's orbit. Assim wasn't handling it as well as Marc had, though, and he watched him drink cup after cup of tarry Turkish coffee and fret over every line of code he uncovered.

After a while, Marc noted Assim staring into the middle distance, lost in thought. "You all right?"

Assim jolted back to awareness and colored slightly. "I'm sorry. Miles away." He took a breath. "Look, I have to say this. It's chewing on me and I have to say it to someone." Marc raised an eyebrow at the outburst, letting the technician find his way. "Why is everyone assuming that Kara has turned on us? I mean, how do we know that?"

"She cut me dead in the middle of a live operation." Marc failed to keep a flash of irritation from his reply, even as the same question echoed in his own thoughts. "Lied to me. Hacked Rubicon systems. Stole money. It doesn't look good."

"What if she had a reason? One we don't know about?" His brow furrowed. "Did anyone consider the possibility?"

"I'd like that to be true," Marc offered. "What do you know that the rest of us don't?"

Assim shrank back from the suggestion of an accusation in the question. "Nothing," he said quickly. "This doesn't feel right . . ."

Marc looked for a reply, but he came up empty. After a moment, he turned back to his monitor and focused on the work.

Time blurred into the continuous rattle of keyboards and the phosphor glow of data screens. Marc's mind detached. His body fell away as the contents of the mesh expanded to fill his attention. He lost himself in the structure of the modified Arquebus program, dismantling it into its component modules.

Piece by piece, he backtracked the virus program from the targets it had been aimed at, as a coroner would pick traces of gunpowder or bullet fragments from the corpse of a shooting victim to identify a killer's weapon. The mental image brought back thoughts of Wetherby's body lying in the hospital morgue and Marc involuntarily grimaced.

Isolating elements of the software's "warhead," he used a custom decompiler program to search the threads of data for commonalities, and slowly lines of green began to pop up where code from the zero-day information had been implanted.

Marc tapped the screen with his finger. "What do you make of this?" He highlighted a few text strings for the other man. "I'm seeing this reference over and over."

"*HIOS Sigma.*" Assim read the text aloud. "That rings a bell."

"Yeah, it does . . ." Marc moved to a network-enabled machine and ran the term though a search engine. He got a hit immediately. "Here we go. It's a software suite for industrial control systems, yeah? Programmable logic controllers and so on. The new and improved Arquebus has a half-dozen exploits grouped around the core code of it." He leaned back from the monitor, thinking it through. "How the hell did Ghost5 get their hands on those?"

"That's very alarming," said Assim, blinking behind his glasses. "Breaking through ICS software vulnerabilities is how Stuxnet got in."

"And this is aimed at the same kind of targets." Marc scrolled down a page of data on the capabilities of the program. "With a much larger capacity for mayhem."

The Sigma software was a next-generation operating system common to internet-connected machinery on an industrial scale. Factories used it to run production lines, cities used it for traffic control, nations used it on power utilities. If it was susceptible to covert attack, the potential risk to infrastructure and human lives was huge.

Assim worked at another keyboard, following Marc's chain of thought. "I've found a press release from eight months ago. SoCal Electric announcing the completion of a modernization initiative in San Francisco. It mentions HIOS Sigma being used in the power monitoring subsystem."

Marc felt a chill crawl over his skin. He looked back into news feeds from earlier in the week, finding reports about the train crash in Taiwan. A metro express had collided with a commuter service at the height of the local rush hour, causing many fatalities and leaving dozens more critically injured. There was a lot of static about the Taipei police stonewalling relatives of the dead over confirmation of their losses, but digging deep he soon found what he feared would be there.

The previous year, HIOS Sigma had been installed in the control network for the Taipei MRT, governing the movements of trains carrying over two million passengers a day. "Those German IP addresses I found," he said quickly, turning to meet Assim's gaze. "Cross-reference them with this Sigma info. Look for reports of unexplained malfunctions, accidents . . ."

"You have a lead." Lucy stood in the doorway, leaning against the glass partition. He hadn't heard her approach. "I know that look."

*And I know yours.* The thought formed as he studied the woman and recognized the expression on her face. Behind those eyes was a dark mood at odds with Lucy's usual dry humor. Flint-hard and uncompromising, Marc had seen it before, but only when the shooting started.

He let it pass unmentioned for now, and gave her a quick runthrough on what he had learned about the exploit code and the Sigma connection. "It's published by a commercial software developer in Australia called Horizon Integral." Marc brought up the corporate website, a slickly minimalist affair of the kind sported by companies who were rich enough that they didn't need to advertise. "They're in the Fortune 500, with clients all over the world, although that list isn't circulated publicly."

Lucy's lip curled. "They might be more willing to spill it, if they know that everyone who buys their programs is open to a catastrophic hack." She pointed at the monitor. "What are the odds that they would already be aware of it, given the train crash and the blackout?"

"And the cars," Assim spoke up. He gestured at his screen. "I've found a correlation in the German links. A series of highway crashes, all in vehicles with an on-board digital control system."

"Another soft target," said Marc. He had hacked similar technology in Celeste Toussaint's limousine, but without taking it to the same extremes. Assim mirrored the information to Marc's screen and he scanned it, grim-faced. The crashes in Dusseldorf and elsewhere had claimed the lives of everyone in the vehicles that been targeted.

"I think we may be looking at tests," Assim continued, carried along by the idea. "Look at the pattern of events. First, small and isolated incidents with the cars. Attacks that could be replicated to fine-tune the details. Then a more complex deployment with the metro trains. And then a bigger hit with the power grid. The initiator has been refining the hack, scaling it up each time."

"And no one's caught it?" asked Lucy.

Assim shook his head. "No one has been looking for it. But with 20/20 hindsight, it's suggestive of a larger intent."

"So this means Horizon Integral are involved, knowingly or un-knowingly," Marc added. "If we can access their client list, we'll have an idea of possible targets for Ghost5."

"They're not going to give up that information to anyone—" Lucy fell silent as Delancort hove into view at the door, with Solomon's bodyguards flanking him. He gripped a small data tablet tightly in one hand.

"Step away from the keyboards," said Brass, glaring at Mark and Assim. The Farmhand stepped in around him, moving to hover menacingly over the technician.

"You know how to knock, right?" snapped Marc, irritated at the unexplained intrusion.

"Do it," Brass added, and Assim raised his hands as if he had a gun aimed at him.

Delancort gave Marc a searching look. "Why are you digging into information about Horizon Integral?"

Marc's eyes narrowed and he glanced around the lab, answering the question with one of his own. "Are you . . . Are you *monitoring* us?" He fixed on the tablet in Delancort's hand.

"Of course we are," the other man said crossly. "Or did you forget that there has just been a major breach of our digital security? So please, clarify the situation." Delancort turned an acidic glare on Assim, who faltered beneath it.

"W-we believe they're linked to the incident in San Francisco," began the technician.

"What does that matter to you?" Marc pressed the point. He rose from his chair and took a step toward Delancort. The man's attitude grated on him, and he was too tired to mask it anymore. The Farmhand heard the shift in Marc's tone and moved to block his path.

Delancort folded his arms across his chest. "It matters to me because Horizon Integral is a corporate partner of the Rubicon Group, and it is my job to protect Solomon's interests."

"A partner?" repeated Marc. "How, exactly?"

"We do business. If there's an issue with them, I need to know about it right away."

"Please tell me you're not using their software for anything essential," said Lucy. "Or dangerous. 'Cause you are not gonna be happy you asked."

Marc watched the color drain from Delancort's face as Assim explained what they had discovered. When he had finished, the French Canadian's arrogance had dialed down a few notches.

"We . . . have a pilot program using HIOS Sigma at two aluminum plants in Nigeria," Delancort explained. "There's a deal in place to roll out the system to a dozen other sites in Rubicon's industrial sector portfolio over the next few years . . ." His accusatory mood crumbled and he rubbed a hand across his face. "*Mon dieu.* I have to deal with this immediately. Solomon needs to be informed, we have to take the plants offline—"

"You do that and it'll send up a red flag," Lucy countered. "If Horizon Integral is compromised, if Ghost5 have an insider, that's as good as telling them someone knows about the software weapon."

"Maybe you could do it another way," said Assim, mulling it over. "Call it a spot-check safety inspection?"

A crooked smile pulled at the corner of Marc's lip as a new thought occurred to him. "Exactly how much money does Solomon have in the deal with these people?"

"Let us say it is a notable amount, and leave it at that," Delancort deflected. "Not enough to get them to spill their deepest corporate secrets, of that you can be sure."

"Oh yeah?" Marc nodded to himself. A plan started to form. "You know what? I think Solomon has just decided he wants to review his investment with Horizon Integral. *In person.*"

"Their corporate headquarters is in Sydney," Assim offered helpfully.

"And that's where their central data server will be," said Marc. He glanced at Lucy. "You see where I'm going with this?"

Delancort snorted. "You appear to be suggesting that we collude to use the CEO of Rubicon to facilitate an act of international corporate espionage."

"That's exactly right." Marc smiled thinly. "I'm glad we're on the same page."

"*T'es ouf!* And of course, I am sure you have an airtight strategy to protect this company from any blowback that might be incurred?" Delancort glared at him over his spectacles, daring him to disagree.

"How long does it take to fly from Nice to Sydney?" said Lucy.

"Twenty-two hours, give or take," Marc replied.

She showed a sly grin. "Plenty of time to figure it out."


A massive metal sign that bore the words *Entritt Verboten* had been hung upside down and repurposed as a partition wall inside the central blockhouse of the old Teufelsberg field station. Portable lights threw hard illumination to all corners of the room, drawing power from heavy-duty batteries salvaged from electric cars. Other humming generators suppled juice to a long workbench lined with communications and server hardware. Cables were everywhere, bunches of them snaking back and forth across the dusty concrete floor, but Kara negotiated them deftly, silently gauging the gear by sight and guessing at what it was being used for.

The "work space" went quiet when she entered, flanked by the man in the trapper hat and his companion. Faces turned to look at her. Some of them dismissed Kara without another glance, but others lit up with recognition.

Someone came toward her at speed. A skinny Polish girl in her early twenties with bleached-blonde cornrows stalked up with a glare on her face, the expression half-shock and half-fury. She punched

Kara hard in the shoulder. "You bitch," the girl said hotly. "Damn it, I thought you were in the gulag." She glared at the guy in the hat. "Back off, Billy!" He wisely stepped away to give the two of them some space.

"Hey, Pyne. I suppose that means you missed me?" Kara winced at the impact.

"Fuck off," she shot back. "Where the hell did you go? You just fucking left without a word, you left . . ." Her voice dropped. "You left me here on my own."

Kara fumbled for an explanation. "I didn't mean for it to go that way. I knew you'd be okay. You're resilient."

Pyne blinked, letting the comment pass. "You came back. I knew you would, one day. Andre said you never would, but I said fuck him, *fuck you* I said, *she*—"

"Yes," Kara said firmly. "Things have changed."

"Yuh." Pyne's head bobbed and she shot a sneer at Billy and the guy with the tattoos as they hovered closer again. "Get lost."

"Don't give me orders—" began the punk, but Pyne cut him off.

"Eat shit, Null. You know who this is, right? You are fucking skiddies compared to this one." Pyne prodded her where she had landed her punch, with a long finger lined with rings. "This is the *Song*."

"And it's a tune we haven't heard for a long time." The voice came out of the darkness, cool and metered. It made Kara tense, and a long-closed part of herself unlocked, emerging whole and full as if it had been waiting for this moment. A want, a kind of belonging that Kara had convinced herself was gone, came back in a rush—but this time corroded by raw anger. The emotions were too swift, too strong, and she felt giddy as she dragged them back under her control.

"Madrigal," she managed. The woman walked into the light and smiled, in a way that someone who didn't know her might have called maternal. It was all part of her performance. A step behind her came a dark-skinned guy with a storm-cloud face, all clenched and sullen.

"Wong Fei Song," said the older woman, sounding out the name like a line of poetry. "Here you are."

"That's not who I am anymore," she corrected. "Call me Kara."

"Kar-ah." Madrigal tried it out. "I like it. It suits you." She glanced at the man with her, who advanced, brandishing a security detector wand as if it were a short sword. "No offense, but Erik here is the suspicious sort."

Erik took the bag off Kara's shoulder and gave it to the trapper-hat guy to paw through while he ran the wand over her. She allowed it, surrendering the two smartphones she had in her pockets. Erik carried them to a gutted microwave oven and deposited the phones inside, where the appliance's shielded interior would block any incoming or outgoing signals.

"This is interesting timing," Madrigal said lightly, looking her up and down. "After everything we went through, you show up here, out of the blue. How did you know where to find us?"

Kara faked a smile. "You did teach me a lot."

"Everything you know," she returned. "But not everything *I* know." Madrigal cast around the room, and from the looks Kara was getting, she had the sense that she'd become a cautionary tale for those among the Ghost5 crew.

*Wong Fei Song, the one that broke faith*, she imagined them saying. *The one who couldn't cut it. The self-starter outcast, lost and forgotten.*

Madrigal gave her a familiar, easy smile, and it was tempting to slip right back to where she had been a few years ago. Like she'd never left. Kara hated that part of her actually wanted to.

Madrigal's expression became one of sadness, of motherly disappointment. "As delightful as it is to see you, we went our separate ways for a reason," she said. "Why have you come to Berlin?"

"Answer the question," Erik grated, when Kara didn't reply right away. He returned her bag, and she saw the butt of a pistol peeking out from under the MA-1 jacket he wore. It was a deliberate show, to remind her of her place.

She ignored him and spoke to Madrigal. "Can we talk privately?" Kara made sure the inference was clear: *only you and me.*

Madrigal drifted toward the shadows again. "Let's take a walk."

She led Kara to the roof beneath one of the hollow domes, and in the shade it cast the air had turned night-cold. In the distance, light glittered off the stainless-steel tiles that formed the silver orb of the Berlin TV Tower, as the sun dropped toward the horizon. The spire was signaling her, telling Kara that she was past the point of no return and still falling.

*Falling back into the darkness. Becoming a ghost again.*

Madrigal reached up and brushed a thread of dyed-dark hair from Kara's eyes. "You haven't smiled in a long time," she said. "I can tell."

"Not much," Kara admitted. Madrigal had always been too good at seeing into her, when others had rebounded off her walls of brisk sarcasm and indifference. It was a struggle to keep anything from Madrigal. It always had been. She decided not to give the other woman the time to dig deeper. "I want to come back in."

Madrigal gave a chuckle and set to work lighting a cigarette. "Just like that? No explanation, no apology. You ask, I open the door?"

"You don't need my skills?"

"It's not about that," Madrigal arched an eyebrow. "Where have you been, Song—?" She stopped, catching herself. "Sorry. *Kara.* What have you been doing all this time?"

"I stayed sharp. I'll be of use." She hated how desperate she sounded.

"Do you remember what you said when you left?" Madrigal aimed the lit tip of the cigarette at her like a weapon. "You told me you couldn't be part of us anymore. You said we were on the wrong side. That *I* was on the wrong side."

"I remember," she said tersely.

"So why come back now, at this moment?" Madrigal demanded, her tone hardening. She advanced on Kara. "What do you really want? Who are you working for?"

Kara glimpsed movement at the edge of the dome and she realized that Erik stood in the gloom with that gun of his drawn and ready. One wrong word, and he would use it.

"*I want to come back,*" Kara repeated. "I'm not working with anyone. I'm alone and I don't like it." She looked at the ground and found a truth to tell her. "With Ghost5 I knew who I was. I've never had that anywhere else."

"Why now?" Madrigal pressed.

She met her gaze. "Because I realized you were right all along, okay? When I left, you said I was naive. Because I thought the world could be black and white. But that isn't how it goes, out there. There's nothing but gray. There's no good guys or bad guys, no wrong or right. There's just the place—"

"The place where you're standing." Madrigal's tone softened and she turned away. "Oh, girl. I want this to be what it seems. I really do." She eyed her. "I've missed not having you around. But the timing raises questions. And you did burn through a lot of trust when you abandoned us."

Kara carefully selected another truth and cut it to length. "You're a man short. I heard about Lex."

"Ah." Madrigal's head drooped. "Tragic. I blame myself. I should have looked out for him more. But we have a lot of enemies and some of them found him . . ."

"I want to know who did it," Kara told her. "I'll help you find them. Punish them."

"Yes." Madrigal took a long draw on the cigarette. "We have that in hand. We think we know who murdered him. Everyone in the group wants to see Lex get his measure of justice."

"So do I," Kara said flatly. "He was my friend too."

Madrigal studied her. "I didn't think you were that close to him. You were never really close to anyone."

"It's not about that," Kara went on. "He was one of us. So there's a price for someone to pay."

"Did he ever try to contact you, after you left us?"

"No." Kara shook her head and sold the lie. "But I heard about the shooting. I want to do something about it. It can be my way to prove you can trust me."

Madrigal sighed. "I'm sorry. But I need more than that." From the corner of her eye, Kara saw the shape in the gloom move again. The older woman's voice thickened with emotion, real and sorrowful. "And I don't think you can give it to me. I'm close to the end of a venture I started a long time ago and I can't . . . I can't let anyone distract me. Not even you."

"You'll change your mind when you hear what I have to say." Kara reached for the last truth she had, and played it. "I know who's tracking you."

Madrigal stopped dead. "What did you say?"

"The guy in Malta. The one you caught searching Lex's hotel room. I can tell you who's running him. They'll be closing in. You must have an inkling, right? Spider in the web, feeling the tremors?" A flicker of concern crossed Madrigal's face and Kara knew she was right.

"How could you know about any of that?" Madrigal's face turned stony.

"They're called Rubicon," said Kara, the words coming easily. "And I can tell you a lot about them."

## NINE

Two minutes out," Lucy reported, flicking open the thin pocket mirror built into the lid of her lipstick case. She'd chosen a rose-pink shade to complement the ochre of her face and the dark navy of her outfit. She gave herself a quick once-over and pulled gently at the material. The asymmetric bodycon dress rolled off her right shoulder and ended just above her knees, the figure-hugging form of it flattering her athletic silhouette. She had a black clutch bag on her lap that resembled a Chanel, but the faux-leather exterior was actually cover for ballistic nylon with a special weave that fogged the scans of metal detectors.

*"Roger that."* Marc's voice whispered to her from the skin-colored radio bead in her right ear. *"We're setting up now. Should be green for go by the time you're on site."*

Lucy looked across the interior of the limousine at the other passengers. As always, Ekko Solomon appeared to be in his element, elegant in some Savile Row suit worth as much as a new midsize car. At his side, Delancort appeared decidedly less at ease, alternately adjusting the silk tie around his neck or fiddling with his cufflinks. Solomon's aide had insisted on coming along, and Lucy had agreed to it only because it would have raised questions about their cover not to have the man around.

They were here on an impromptu "fact-finding" visit, after all, in the guise of allowing the Rubicon CEO to meet his opposite number at Horizon Integral in order to cement future collaboration between the two companies. But all through the flight to Australia, Delancort had been pushing his dislike of this operation. It was only now they were on the way in that he had let it drop. Still, Lucy could tell he would demand they pull the plug at the first hint of danger.

For his part, Solomon had accepted Dane's scheme and the subterfuge that came with it without question. It was easy to forget that the African billionaire's fortune had grown out of a life of ashes, blood and bullets. Solomon was no stranger to personal risk. He had been a soldier once. He understood the needs of the mission.

Lights flashed past outside as the limo turned on to Bridge Street and headed east across Sydney's central business district, a skyscape of modern glass and steel office towers rising around them. In the day, it would have been thrumming with activity, but it was early evening here—although Lucy's body clock tried to convince her it should be morning. She still hadn't got her sleep pattern synched back from California time, and she stifled the urge to yawn by downing a caffeine tablet from a pack in the clutch.

"*Okay, I have your car in sight,*" Marc reported. "*Here we go. Comm check.*"

"Good to go," said Lucy.

"*Copy,*" repeated Malte. The Finn's reply was terse, as usual.

"*Base copies,*" said Assim. The technician was back on Solomon's private airliner out at the airport in Mascot, running overwatch for the operation from the on-board conference room.

"Do we get radios?" Delancort eyed her.

"You have your spyPhone." Lucy nodded at his jacket pocket. "It'll buzz you, three short bursts if there's a problem. That happens, you make your excuses and leave immediately. Got it?"

"*Oui.*" Delancort shifted uncomfortably. He didn't like being on the back foot in this, but even he was smart enough to know when to get out of the way and let the professionals do their job.

The limo slowed as it approached their destination. "I do not need to remind you what will happen if this evening's events do not proceed smoothly," Solomon offered, pausing to brush a speck of lint from his lapel. "So I will not." He met Lucy's gaze. "After what has happened, it would be easy to slip into second-guessing every choice we are making." He shook his head. "I will not. Do what you are best at."

The vehicle rolled to a halt and a valet leaned in to open the door. "Count on it," Lucy told him, and stepped out on to a green carpet leading to the entrance of Horizon Integral's head office. She gave the valet a dazzling smile and took in the surroundings. Well-dressed young women and men in sharp suits were walking in through a wide-open atrium of tinted glass, and a cluster of photographers behind a velvet rope were in the process of snapping shots of a tanned, muscular guy in a tailored Armani ensemble. She didn't recognize him, but she knew the type; he had *professional sportsman* written all over him. He played to the paparazzi, grinning wildly as he posed in front of a three-meter-high model of a racing yacht in black and green livery. Horizon Integral's corporate logo featured prominently on the boat's sails, and Lucy remembered that this was the reason for the evening's gala reception. The company had inked a major sponsorship deal for a big-ticket race taking place in the summer, and the yacht crew were here to be feted and take part in a charity auction.

Solomon climbed out of the limo, with Delancort following on behind, and offered his hand to Lucy. "Shall we, Ms. Keyes?"

"Absolutely, Mr. Solomon."

*"Well, don't you three look nice,"* said Marc. *"Drink some champers for me, will you?"*

"Don't pout," Lucy replied. "Next time, you can be Henri's date."

*"Can't wait."*

"Fascinating . . ." Solomon's gaze ranged along the length of the building as they walked up the stairs. "One might think it had been grown rather than built."

"Yeah . . ." Lucy followed his line of sight. Horizon Integral's headquarters was an unusual fusion of emerald glass, white concrete and a mass of living greenery. Tropical creepers formed patches of leaves that clothed the tower, rising from the base toward the upper stories nearly thirty floors above street level. She could see the edges of another cavernous atrium toward the top third of the tower, the open space lined with trees shifting in the evening breeze coming up from Circular Quay.

"It's amazing, isn't it?" An aboriginal woman with jet-black hair and a welcoming smile approached them. She wore an orange sportsuit ensemble and what Lucy thought at first was some kind of fingerless glove. "Our building hosts a living ecosystem as part of its structure. As well as the plants, we have insect colonies, even birds nesting up there. It's a trailblazer in green design." She gave a little bow. "I'm Orani! I'm Mr. Wehmeyer's personal assistant. He asked me to escort you in."

"Delighted." Solomon shook Orani's hand, before introducing Delancort as his aide and Lucy as his "companion."

Lucy smiled back and the woman led them inside, beckoning over a waiter to provide them with flutes of Bollinger.

As they crossed the threshold, Orani's glove emitted a digital chime and she raised her wrist to her mouth and spoke into it. "Mr. Solomon. Mr. Delancort. Ms. Keyes." The glove chimed again and, looking closer, Lucy could see it had a curved screen fitted to the back of the hand.

"What is that?"

Orani smiled. "As well as being a *green* building, this is also a *smart* one. We have a computer system that regulates all functions of the tower, from the lights and the power to the elevator. Even down to the food stocks in the employee break rooms. It automatically manages heat and light to make sure we're not burning electricity in empty rooms. It's helped us to be one of the top five most efficient companies in the country."

"It runs off the HIOS software?" said Delancort.

"That's right, yes!" She nodded. "With a more advanced voice-recognition system built in . . ." The woman paused and spoke to the device on her wrist again. "Isn't that right, Sigma?"

"*Yes, Orani,*" replied a synthetic, slightly stilted female voice. "*I have logged in the arrival of our guests. Mr. Solomon. Mr. Delancort. Ms. Keyes. Do you require anything else?*"

"No, we're fine." Orani grinned at them. "We're very proud of our products."

Lucy eyed Delancort, silently warning him to say nothing more.

Within, the building's motif of merging of hi-tech with raw nature repeated itself. Weeping willow trees grew out of an ornamental pool in the middle of the atrium, and pillars of steel and concrete wreathed in vines ranged upward, supporting the floors above them. Glass elevator tubes, under-lit by warm yellow lights, vanished up into the shadows.

Lucy sipped at her champagne and continued her survey of the area, casting a tactical eye over the layout, noting exit routes, potential cover and the like. She immediately spotted a handful of men and women in dark suits wearing radio earpieces, each of them carefully minding their posts.

"Good deployment," she noted quietly. "Horizon Integral is certainly serious about their security."

"We have a lot of guests here tonight," said Orani. "It's wonderful that you were able to join us. We do love to have our investors come visit."

"I'm looking forward to seeing more of what you do here," replied Solomon.

They crossed the atrium, through knots of well-heeled company types and the great and the good of Sydney's rich set, finding their way to an older white man in a tan suit holding court with a group of Chinese investors. He had a wide, smiling face and thinning brown hair. Lucy recognized Horizon Integral's CEO, Martin Wehmeyer, from the images she'd seen on the company website. The man had a reputation for instilling loyalty in his employees and dealing harshly with his rivals, but right now he projected an avuncular persona, laughing as he cracked a joke about the prospects of the yachting crew. His gaze found Solomon's and he excused himself, walking over to offer warm handshakes to the group from Rubicon. Another man, tanned and square of face, disengaged from the other group and trailed after Wehmeyer, as Orani melted into the background.

"Good man, glad to have you here tonight!" He clapped Solomon on the back and then made a show of taking Lucy's hand like that of a newly arrived courtier in a king's castle—which in a way she was. "Welcome, welcome. We have a lot to talk about. I hope you're pleased with the Nigeria thing."

"As you say, we have some matters to discuss," began Delancort.

"Later," Solomon cut in. "We are here for a few days. We will see what develops."

"Sure!" Wehmeyer nodded. He seemed to remember the other man standing nearby and gestured to him. "This is Bob Crowne, my head of security. Keeper of my secrets, you know?" Wehmeyer laughed and Lucy smiled politely.

"Good to meet you," said Crowne, revealing an East-Coast American accent. Lucy immediately ran a silent evaluation of the man. *Ex-CIA*, she decided. He had the look of a former spook about him. "Welcome to Australia."

"I hear the fishing is real good out here," said Lucy, tossing out a lure of her own.

"It is," Crowne replied, and that was all she got. The man leaned in to Wehmeyer's shoulder and spoke to him quietly. "Sir. The guests are all here now. We should start."

"Oh. Of course." Wehmeyer unconsciously raised his hand and Lucy took a good look at the gold signet ring hanging loosely on his little finger. It had a flat onyx insert the size of a nickel, but beneath the ornamental surface it concealed a suite of microelectronics. She knew this because of the all-too-thorough briefing Dane had given her on the flight over.

Wehmeyer was about to tap the ring with his other finger when a voice cut through the air like the whine of a police siren. "Dad. Dad? *Dad*." A girl in her late teens, with shoulder-length hair as chestnut as her father's, drifted through the crowd and pulled Wehmeyer into a kind of half-hug, burying her face in his chest. He gave Solomon and the others a knowing *what-can-you-do* shrug and disengaged himself. "Sunny, sweetheart, Dad's working. Can you give me a minute?"

Sunny Wehmeyer, one of the current darlings of Sydney's gossip pages, gave a regretful smirk and let go. "Okay." Her attention snagged on Lucy's dress and her eyes widened. "Now that is lit. I want one. But in red, though. Do they make them in red? Where'd you get it?"

"Sunny," her father continued gently, "I thought you were chatting with Charles." He nodded across the room, in the direction of a younger guy with shaggy hair, wearing a suit jacket over a designer T-shirt emblazoned with an ironic design that Lucy didn't get.

*Charles Hite*, she guessed, recalling his name from the briefing. *Horizon Integral's chief technology officer and their top gun-systems programmer.* Hite looked their way, adjusting his thick-rimmed glasses before continuing his conversation with some of the yacht crew.

"Chuck is such a—" Sunny caught herself before she said something insulting and tried again. "We don't have a lot in common, really." Before Lucy could stop her, Sunny took her wrist and started leading her away toward the bar near the ornamental pond. "But you and I, we have to talk fashion."

"I guess we do . . ." Lucy surrendered to the inevitable and allowed Sunny to steer her.

*"How's it going?"* Dane's voice sounded in her ear. *"Talk if you can."*

"I'm getting a refill," she said to the air, depositing her empty glass on the tray of a passing server.

"Damn right we are," Sunny said firmly.

Behind them, Wehmeyer stepped on to a low stage. Lucy saw him tap the ring and the lights came up. The man cleared his throat and told another joke, riding a wave of chuckles before launching into a speech.

*"Take your time,"* said Marc dryly. *"No pressure."*


"Remember," he went on, "if you don't get what we need, this will be over before it even starts." Lucy didn't reply, and Marc's lip curled.

"All secure up here," said Malte, crossing the rooftop toward him. Like Marc, Malte was dressed in a black tactical coverall beneath a gear vest, with gloves on his hands and a watch cap on his head. Marc joked that they couldn't have looked more like criminals if they'd been toting around a bag with the word *SWAG* written on it, but the Finn didn't seem to get the reference. "You are sure about this?"

"No," Marc admitted, snapping open the latches on a hard-shell gear case hidden in the lee of an air conditioning unit. He removed a custom-made compound bow from inside, the curve of dense plastic fitted with cross-strung cables, rotating cams and a polymerized string that quadrupled the release force of the weapon. Putting on a wrist guard and a finger tab, Marc gave the bow a test pull, checking the resistance.

"If you miss . . ." Malte began.

"I won't," Marc insisted. "Been practicing." The offices of the Browder Insurance Agency were a couple of floors taller than the Horizon Integral building, and from their roof he had a good sight-line down into the upper atrium and the highest levels of the software developer's headquarters. Marc had already picked out a good target; a recessed section where an automated window-washing cradle rested when it wasn't in operation. He flicked on the laser-assisted sight ring attached to the side of the bow and adjusted it. Point to point, the distance between the two buildings covered less than twenty meters, but it was the thirty-plus stories of sheer drop down to the street that gave him pause.

The carbon-fiber arrow he prepared was feather-light, and with care he connected a fine cable to a clasp behind the mushroom-shaped head at the end of the shaft. The arrowhead had a frangible structure, filled with powerful adhesive gel that would stick instantly to practically anything. Marc tugged at the cable spool he had strapped to the roof ledge, making sure it freely paid out the line.

He and Lucy had used a similar device on a rainy night above the Port of New Jersey, the graphene spider-wire acting as a descender to drop them in on a target from a great height. This was an upgraded version, capable of supporting the weight of a small car, or so the tech specs promised.

"Keep back," Marc warned. "If this snaps and whips back on us, it'll cut through you like cheese wire." He nocked the arrow, and took a breath before drawing back the string and pushing away the bow. The cams turned and the bow limbs creaked as he waited for the wind to drop. The muscles in his arms and across his back stiffened.

This wasn't like shooting a pistol. A whole different set of physics was involved in the act, but Marc found he liked it. Plus, the fusion of archery's low-tech marksmanship with the hi-tech next-generation bow kit appealed to his hardware-geek side. A rope gun-line launcher could do the same job, but it was louder and far more likely to be noticed than what Lucy had nicknamed "the Hawkeye option."

The breeze momentarily faded, and Marc put the ring-sight where he wanted the arrow to land. *Release.* The shot was gone before he was fully aware of it happening, the bowstring giving a low twang. The spider-wire went fizzing out after the arrow, glistening as it caught the light from the street below.

The arrowhead landed a little off the mark, but close enough for what he needed. Marc put down the bow and tugged experimentally on the graphene cable, making sure only to touch it using the ceramic pads on the fingers of his tactical gloves. It held firm.

"Ready?" said Malte, offering him a slide-wire rig made of the same diamond-hard material.

Marc eyed him, intuiting what the other man wasn't saying. "I know you want to go in my place. But you don't have this." He showed Malte his ruggedized tablet computer before slipping it into a protective pocket in his gear vest. "And honestly? You're not nerd enough for what's gotta happen."

Malte gave a reluctant nod. "Agreed. I don't want to repeat what we did at Strefa G." The Finn referred to a black-site prison in Poland, when Marc had been forced to work Malte like a game avatar, so they could extract a high-value target. "I cannot help you from over here."

"I'm sure it'll go fine," Marc replied, snapping the rig into place and threading his hands through its safety loops to seize the grip bar. "Piece of cake." He slid his legs over the edge of the roof.

"Don't look down," Malte told him, then shoved him hard in the small of the back.

Marc's stomach fell through a giddy swoop as he went off the ledge, and for a split second he thought the cable had snapped and he was plummeting to his death; but then the tension equalized and he was rocketing through open space.

Ahead, the leafy cladding of the Horizon Integral building rushed to meet him and he swung up his legs to take the impact. Marc hit it square on, and grunted as the shock of deceleration passed through him. Scrambling into the cradle dock, he disconnected himself from the rig and climbed up. Pushing through to maintenance space past that, he very definitely did not look back over his shoulder at the yawning gap he had traversed.

Adrenaline prickled in his fingertips and he flexed his hands. "Okay, I'm in." He tapped the radio pickup pressed to his throat. "I had my *oh shit* moment, but we're good."

*"Welcome to the party, pal,"* said Lucy.

"Yeah, thanks for that." The door that led from the maintenance room to the corridor beyond had a digital magnetic lock, and Marc made short work of it, using a non-conductive knife to slice through the wiring. No alarms sounded as he stepped out into the gloomy, unlit floor.

He dropped into a crouch and booted up the rugged tablet, double-checking the layout against the floorplans taken from architectural blueprints of the tower. The database server was located eight levels below him, in a secure section of the building with triple layers of security. One layer Marc knew he could defeat, but the others . . . they would require Lucy's assistance.

Marc tapped into the building's wireless network and uploaded a variant of the GCHQ Optic Nerve driver-control software, using the intrusion program to spoof the motion sensors in his immediate surroundings so that no lights would come on and no warnings would be sent to the security desk. That done, he moved fast toward the main elevator bank.

"I'm on my way to the server," he said into the throat mic. "Do your thing."


Sunny was telling a story that she seemed to think was pretty engaging, about a guy who drove a white Lamborghini and had a tendency to get a little too "handsy" after a few drinks. Lucy nodded and smiled like she was actually interested, but her goal was to work her way back through the partygoers in the atrium and find Sunny's dad. Without him, the mission would stall.

Sunny was already on her second Piña Colada but Lucy had only pretended to drink hers, and the younger woman trailed after her, going on about the dress again. "C'mon, spill. Where'd you buy it? Paris? Tokyo?"

"Custom-made," she admitted. "Cut-Tex anti-slash fabric. Mil-spec."

"Anti-what?" Sunny didn't catch all of it. "Milan, you said? Yeah, I get that. Those Italians know how to bring the look."

"And then some." Lucy opened her clutch and retrieved her spy-Phone, activating the device's high-acuity camera as she returned to Solomon's side. "Darling?" she purred.

Solomon offered her a sardonic smile. "Lucille, my dear. I was telling Mr. Wehmeyer about our facility in Switzerland."

"Oh, yes!" Lucy slipped into the part easily, shifting her accent northward from New York to New England. "Yes, you must come! Fantastic skiing!"

"I love skiing!" Sunny chipped in. She gave her father a hug. "We should go!"

"We should!" Lucy echoed, and grinned as she saw her opportunity. "Look at you two! So cute!" she chirped. "*Selfie!*" Before Wehmeyer could disengage, she slipped in next to him and snaked her arm around his waist, cupping his hand. She brought up the spyPhone and it snapped three fast shots of father, daughter and her.

The flash was dazzling, a tiny starburst that made all of them blink in surprise. Lucy used the moment to slip Wehmeyer's ring off his finger and palm it, and it was gone before he noticed.

"Oh, that was bright," he muttered. "I'm seeing stars!"

"Charmer!" Lucy planted a kiss on Wehmeyer's cheek with a theatrical *mwah* sound and disengaged. Her gaze caught Solomon's and she gave him the tiniest of nods. "I'm gonna go powder my nose," she told him. "Don't talk business all night, Ekko."

The men went back to their conversation, chuckling at her comments, and as Lucy stepped away, she let the act drop off her like a discarded item of clothing.

She stopped momentarily and pivoted back to Sunny, leaning in to offer the girl a thought before leaving her behind. "Hey. About Lamborghini Boy? Next time he tries to grope you, take one of these . . ." She handed her the tiny cocktail umbrella from her drink. "Put it in the heel of your hand. Then jam the pointy end under his thumbnail. After that, I guarantee he'll leave you the fuck alone."

Sunny twirled the umbrella in her fingers as Lucy walked off, abruptly at a loss for words.

*"Image uploads are coming in now,"* said Assim over the radio channel. *"This is a good take. Give me a few minutes to enhance it."*

"I'm heading to the elevators now," Lucy replied. "How's that going?"

*"Almost done,"* said Marc.

He tapped the call button for the lift, but the illuminated control remained dark.

An automated voice issued out of a speaker above the frosted glass doors. *"We're sorry. All lifts are currently out of service above the tenth floor. If you need to access this system, please contact security. Would you like me to do that for you now?"*

"No thanks," Marc muttered, cuing up a digital sound-synthesis program on his tablet.

*"I'm sorry, I didn't catch that. Can you repeat, please?"*

Marc typed a short sentence into the tablet and held it up to the speaker grille. *"Sig-ma. This is. Martin Wehmeyer."* The speech sounded stiff and full of pauses in the wrong places, but Marc counted on it being enough to fool the smart building's voice recognition software. *"Unlock the. Lifts."* He pushed the call button again.

Horizon Integral's CEO liked being in the media spotlight, and that meant that Wehmeyer left a considerable digital footprint behind him, data that Rubicon had been able to mine in order to assemble a passable digital impersonation of the man. Constructed from corporate promotional videos, news reports and so on, the data gave the tablet enough sound elements to make Wehmeyer say whatever Marc needed him to. The quality wasn't good enough to dupe a human, but a computer was a different story.

*"Recognize: Martin Wehmeyer, Chief Executive Officer. Good evening, sir,"* came the reply. *"All lifts are now unlocked."*

The irony of using a fake human to hoodwink another fake

human made him smirk. Presently, an empty car slid smoothly to a
stop and the doors opened to present Marc with a glass-walled elevator giving a view down the core of the office tower. He pulled the
watch cap tight over his hair and kept his back to the camera dome in
the corner of the car.

Far below, he could make out the glow of the gathering on the
ground floor. He stepped inside and tapped the keypad to take him
to the server level. *"Going down,"* said the building's synthetic voice.

"Lucy, you read me?"

*"Ears on,"* she replied. She sounded tinny and distant, her voice
flattened by the comm gear's built-in encryption protocols. *"Where's
my ride at?"*

"Should be ready now," he said. "Meet me on floor twenty."

*"Copy."*

The doors hissed shut and the lift began a rapid descent. The tablet pinged and Marc booted up an image package that Assim had
sent to him. He smiled. *Two down, one to go.* Once he met up with
Lucy and she handed him the smart-ring, he would have everything
they needed to enter the company's secure server. It all was going according to plan.

The lift slowed to a halt and Marc turned back to the doors. As
they started to open, he noticed the level indicator read *22* and not *20*.

Directly outside stood a Samoan guy in the uniform of a security guard. The man had a rugby player's build, all broad neck and
glower. He and Marc both reacted in surprise to see the other, but
the guard was faster off his feet and he barrelled into the lift, body-
checking Marc into the control panel. He slammed up against the
buttons and the elevator car dropped once more.

*"Going down,"* said the computer voice. *"Express to ground floor."*


*"Going up."*

Lucy made sure no one saw her slip into the waiting elevator,
and she crouched low as it rose, in case someone happened to be
looking up the glass shaft as it ascended. When she was sure she

was out of sight, she started re-configuring her evening wear, as the level indicator climbed into double digits. First, the folds across the shoulder of the dress opened along hidden lines of Velcro so she could wrap it over and mask her silhouette. Next, the ornamental sections around the skirt were turned into figure-hugging shorts for ease of motion. Lastly, she pulled her clutch bag inside out and uncoiled concealed straps to make it into a cross-belt holster for the flat, slab-like ML-12 pistol secreted inside. Lucy drew the gun and cracked it open along the width to check it. The two-shot weapon was loaded with a pair of non-lethal 12-gauge bean-bag rounds. Solomon had been adamant about that. No bloodshed . . . and ideally, no traces.

As the floor indicator passed 18, Lucy glimpsed motion through the clear dome above her and caught sight of another elevator coming down the neighboring shaft. She barely had time to register what she saw inside as the other glass-walled car flashed past; Marc Dane and a guy about twice his size going back and forth like two boxers trapped in a phone booth.

"Oh shit!" She went to the glass, craning her head to follow the other elevator's descent.


The first punch the Samoan guard landed rang a church bell through Marc's head and hit him hard enough to knock the radio bead out of his ear. He heard it crunch under his boot as he staggered back to avoid the one-two follow-on, ducking as best he could to avoid a meaty haymaker that whooshed through the air where his face had been a split second earlier.

He went for a Krav Maga strike, hitting by reflex at the guard's gut, hoping to get a lucky shot in his opponent's solar plexus, but the blows landed and appeared to do nothing. The guard tried to grab him, and they both pivoted in the tiny space of the lift car. Marc kicked out and made contact with the bigger man's shin, getting a growl of pain in return and briefly putting the Samoan off-balance.

Marc had dropped the computer tablet, but with his hands free he was able to snatch at the security guard's belt. The man's holstered pistol was on the wrong side, but Marc could still get a grip on the nightstick dangling from a belt loop, and he snagged it.

He was holding it wrong, but that didn't matter. With all his might, Marc used the weapon like a hammer and cracked it against the guard's bull-neck. Breath gusted out of the man in a choked cough, and Marc kept up the attack, this time going low to smack him in the back of the knees.

"Motherfu—" The guard swallowed the half-formed curse and struck out blindly, getting a good hit in Marc's belly that made him double over. The two of them connected again and lurched back.

The floor indicator was on 12 and falling. Marc had no desire to reach ground level and have the two of them come tumbling out into the middle of the well-heeled party-goers in the atrium. He pushed off the wall and slapped the heel of his hand against the keypad, and the lift stopped on the tenth, doors parting to reveal an expanse of open-plan office cubicles.

The guard snarled and charged at Marc, reaching out, intent on grabbing him in a bear hug, but Marc dropped and struck out with the nightstick, hitting that same spot on the man's injured shin. The big Samoan tripped and couldn't overcome his own momentum. He stumbled, cracking his head against a fire extinguisher mounted on the wall. He swayed for a long moment, his eyes misting, before he finally went down like a ton of bricks.

"Shit," Marc said to the air.

"*I'm sorry, I didn't catch that,*" began a synthetic voice.

"Oh, piss off!" he shot back.

It took longer than he wanted to drag the unconscious man into the nearest restroom. He used the guard's handcuffs to secure him to the pipes behind a toilet cistern before dumping the guard's gun, his keys and his walkie-talkie in a nearby waste bin.

Marc swore again under his breath. The operation had always been on a clock, but now that timeline had contracted to *as long as Sleeping Beauty here stayed out cold.*

\* \* \*

Lucy shot a look at the elegant Cartier watch on her wrist and tapped the comm bead in her ear. "Dane? Are you on?" When he didn't reply, she tensed, anticipating a chorus of alarm sirens.

"*Do we abort?*" Assim said nervously. "*I think we should abort.*"

"Wait one." The elevator was coming back up, and the indicator above the doors flashed and chimed to announce the arrival. Lucy pulled the ML-12 and moved to the side, taking aim so she could put a round in the chest of whomever got off.

But then Marc stepped out and he recoiled in shock at the sight of the weapon. "Fucking hell!" He pushed the muzzle away. "Watch where you point that!"

"You're giving me shit?" she retorted, jerking her thumb at the elevator. "What the hell was that?"

His jaw worked. "An unexpected variable," Marc offered.

"Uh-huh?" She holstered the pistol. "And where is Mr. Unexpected right now?"

"Sleeping it off in the men's room." He walked past her, and she noted the beginnings of a nasty bruise starting to form on his face. "So, we better make this quick."

"Nice trophy," she noted.

"Yeah," he allowed, wincing. Marc looked at the display on the tablet in his hand. "The server's this way."

Through another set of tinted glass panels, they arrived in front of a large compartment that the rest of the floor had been built around. It had only one entrance, a thick brushed-steel door set flush with the walls. Lucy put her hand on the edge and felt for a seam. It was a perfect fit, airtight with no visible hinges or mechanism.

Marc moved to a digital panel mounted next to the door and tapped it with a finger. A glowing blue display lit up, and a tiny plate slid back to reveal a sensing grid.

Lucy rapped twice on the metal door with her knuckle. It made the same noise as tank armor. "This is some serious protection."

Marc nodded. "Top-end kit. Tempest barrier materials, hardened against electromagnetic pulse, fire-safe, even flood-proof. This whole tower could collapse and you'd be able to dig this compartment intact out of the rubble."

She stepped back to study the door. "I guess Horizon Integral really like their secrets."

"Here we go." Marc typed a string of text into his tablet and held it up to the panel. A slightly off-kilter rendition of Martin Wehmeyer's voice spoke from the device, identifying itself as the company's CEO. A glowing green tab illuminated on the locking screen.

*"Recognize: Martin Wehmeyer, Chief Executive Officer. Tier one authorized."*

"It worked." Lucy made a face. "All right."

Marc looked her way. "Yeah, but this isn't a low-priority system like the lifts. You have the ring?"

She tossed the golden signet to him and he snatched it out of the air. "The king's royal seal," Lucy added airily.

"Something like that . . ." Marc pressed the ring to the sensor panel and the building's computer spoke again.

*"Tier two authorized. Proceed to retina scan."*

"And the last one. Here we go." His fingers danced over the tablet's touch-sensitive surface, bringing up a video window showing a disc of complex lines—the pattern of veins inside Wehmeyer's right eye, captured by the gigapixel digital camera fitted to Lucy's spyPhone. Back on the plane, Assim had run the images she had taken through an animation program that would simulate the appearance of a real human retina. Like the voice synthesizer, the idea was that the building's security software wouldn't be able to tell the difference.

Marc blew out a breath and held the tablet up to the scanner. "If this doesn't work, we drop everything and run."

The scan seemed to last forever, but finally the voice spoke once more.

*"Final security tier authorized. Thank you, Mr. Wehmeyer. Please proceed."*

The tension across Lucy's shoulders lessened a little. Hidden magnetic bolts retracted with a series of hollow thuds, and the metal door slid out of its frame, yawning open. Cold, dry air wafted out into the anteroom, and inside she could see stacks of black computer hardware, their surfaces covered with lines of blinking green-red LEDs. "It's a

SCIF," she said to herself, pronouncing the name as "skiff," like the rowing boat.

Lucy was familiar with concept of a so-called Secure Compartmentalized Information Facility, having often been briefed inside one during her time with Special Forces. SCIFs were usually deployed to manage the transfer or storage of highly secret information, but this was the first time she had seen one being used by a civilian group. It was Horizon Integral's information vault, isolated from the office's internal network and the global internet beyond, accessible only to staff with the right clearance.

*Or so they hoped.* To one side sat a workstation, already booted up and ready for use. Another thought crossed her mind. *Does Solomon have a place like this back in the Monaco office?*

Marc glanced at his watch. "All right, this shouldn't take me long. Keep an eye out, yeah?" He pushed past her and dropped into the seat by the workstation, quickly threading a cable from his tablet to the waiting computer. "Radio won't work inside here," he called over his shoulder. "I'm downloading the files now."

"Copy." Lucy left him there and wandered back out across the office floor, keeping her pistol handy. "Assim? We're through the door. Marc's doing his thing. What's your status?"

*"I'm monitoring the New South Wales Police Force channels,"* he explained. *"No alerts at this time."*

"That's good . . ." she began, but then her words trailed off as one of the elevators closed its doors and dropped away, falling back down toward the ground floor. She walked back across, eyes narrowing as the level numbers spiraled down until the indicator display showed a letter "L."

Lucy held her breath. Maybe it was the system resetting itself. Maybe it was—

The numbers began to climb again. *5. 10. 15.* The elevator was coming up fast.

She sprinted back to the anteroom and stuck her head through the open door to the SCIF. "Dane! Are you sure you nailed all the security layers? Someone's coming up here in a tear-ass hurry."

He gave her an affronted look. "Unless someone added a completely new protocol to the system in the last twenty-four hours, there's no way . . ." The expression on his face froze. "Well, I mean, unless it was set up covertly . . ."

"Like, by someone working at the company who's actually in bed with a bunch of rogue hackers?"

"That is possible," he said.

On the far side of the office floor, the elevator bank chimed to announce a new arrival.

## — TEN —

Hite pulled at the collar of his designer T-shirt and glared at the two security guards sharing the confines of the elevator with him. "Back off," he told them. "You don't get paid enough to crowd me."

The pair, a man and a woman whose names he couldn't be bothered to learn, shared a look and stepped away, or at least as far as they could inside the glass lift car. Hite dug in a jacket pocket and pulled out a small-frame Beretta Nano semi-automatic, checking for a round in the chamber.

The male guard raised an eyebrow. "Sir . . . should you be carrying that? Perhaps we should—"

"Don't fucking tell me what you should be doing," Hite broke in. He jabbed a finger at the holsters on their belts. "Get them out. I'm giving you an order."

Reluctantly, the guards drew their firearms. "Mr. Hite," began the woman, "we haven't had any alarms from the upper floors."

"You told me one of your men hadn't reported in!" He glared at her.

"That could be a radio down," offered the other guard. "Like, a dud battery. He won't be overdue for another ten minutes."

"Trust me, it isn't!" Hite said firmly. "We have intruders. They're up here." He looked out as they passed the fifteenth floor. "Assume they are armed and dangerous."

The female guard sniffed. "If that's the case, we should notify the police, sir. Those are the regulations."

"No," Hite insisted. "You work for this company! You do as I say! Cops stay out of this until we have the situation under control, is that clear?"

"Yes, sir," said the other one, giving his partner a warning look. That was good. It meant these people remembered where their wages came from each month. Hite never liked having to be around the security team. He always got the sense that they were looking down their noses at him, the computer geek in the expensive jacket. But Hite could have them fired on the spot, and he made sure they knew it.

He glanced down at the warning message on his smartphone. Someone had accessed the isolated server on the twentieth floor, and apparently used the CEO's authority to do it. He smiled thinly. The software patch he secretly uploaded to the building's secure net only a few hours ago had done its job, adding an extra hidden monitor program to the existing security layers.

Earlier that day, when Wehmeyer had told him that a delegation from the Rubicon Group were coming to the reception, Hite had almost choked on his chai tea latte. His first instinct had been to cut and run, but he had squashed that cowardly impulse immediately. No one could be allowed to interfere with his plans, and he wasn't ready to pull the ejector switch with Horizon Integral yet. This was a problem that he would have to handle. In fact, it might work to his advantage.

Exposing these Rubicon idiots and their industrial espionage would strengthen Hite's position with the company board and make the CEO look like a fool into the bargain. That would all help Hite's ultimate plan to enrich himself and pave the way to getting out from under Wehmeyer's shadow.

He pocketed the smartphone, exchanging it for the cheap, commonplace burner handset that had arrived on his desk in a courier package the day before. Hite knew where it had come from the moment he opened the padded envelope. There was only one number stored in the memory. This was how Madrigal and her Ghost5 rabble liked to communicate, through links on untraceable devices to covert voice-over-internet protocols. That was fine with him. Hite would play their little spy games as long as it got him the money and the power he needed.

He gripped the metallic phone in his hand and hit the speed-dial key, pressing it to his ear. The answer came after a single ring, the familiar, not-quite-female tone of Madrigal's disguised voice. *"Hello, Dart,"* she said, using the agreed-upon codename. *"So tell me. Was I right to warn you about potential visitors?"*

"Yes. Rubicon's here." Hite spoke quietly, covering his mouth and facing away from the guards so they couldn't hear him. "They're poking their noses in where they shouldn't."

*"I told you they might be coming,"* she said, a hint of a smile almost audible in her voice. *"Aren't you going to thank me?"*

He glared out at nothing. Until Wehmeyer's announcement that morning, he hadn't believed what Madrigal had said. "How'd you even know about it?"

*"A little bird sang me a song. Now, the big question. Can you deal with them?"*

Hite weighed the pistol in his hand. "That's already happening. I'm on it."

*"Good. Use the burner to contact me when it's dealt with."* Madrigal cut the line and he jammed the phone back in his pocket as the lift slowed.

"This is it," said the female guard.

"Yeah." Hite waved irritably at the doors as they started to open. "Get in there and sort these pricks out!"

"How much longer is this gonna take?" Lucy demanded.

At the workstation inside the secure chamber, Marc stared at the ruggedized tablet computer in his hand, watching a status bar on the screen slowly march toward the 100 percent mark. "I need two more minutes."

"I'll get them for you." Lucy turned and strode back across the anteroom as the elevator doors opened, and a pair of figures in Horizon Integral security uniforms fanned out, SIG Sauer pistols in their hands raised and ready. Charles Hite came after them, cautious and wide-eyed.

Lucy kept her own weapon held down. "Well, this is awkward," she offered, keeping her tone conversational. "Would you believe I got lost on the way to the ladies' room?"

"Gun!" The closest of the guards, a white woman with an austere blonde bob and a narrow face, spotted her pistol. She took aim at Lucy. "Drop it!"

The other guard, a big guy carrying a little more paunch than he needed to, cast around, looking toward the server chamber. "You alone up here?"

"The men she came in with are downstairs," snapped Hite. He had a weapon of his own, a boxy little hold-out pistol that he held like an amateur.

"Take it easy," Lucy said reasonably, and she dropped the beanbag gun to the floor. "I can explain everything."

"Kick that to me," said the woman. Lucy complied, deliberately taking her time over it.

"You're on company property, so we can shoot you," Hite insisted. "Try something!"

"Hands on your head," said the blonde. "Turn around and get on your knees."

Lucy obeyed, moving to face the wall. The other guard headed toward the SCIF's open door. She knew she had to slow this down. "Does Mr. Wehmeyer approve of what you're up to, Chuck?" She deliberately used the diminutive name, counting on the fact that it would piss Hite off. "He already knows you're creeping on his daughter. But this? I would guess not."

"Shut up," said Hite. "Make her shut up!"

"I mean, why else would you come up here personally?" Lucy added, making eye contact with the male guard. "And bring a gun too? You wouldn't do that unless you had something to protect." She allowed a grin into her words. "You have a dirty little secret, don't you, Chuck?"

"You are a criminal," Hite snarled. "Keep running your bloody mouth and we'll see where that takes you!"

She heard the clicking of the female guard's handcuffs coming open, near to her head. One metal band went around her right wrist and snapped shut. She tensed for what would happen next.

*   *   *

The guard stepped cautiously over the threshold of the security compartment, shifting his aim to look inside. His gaze passed over the server tower and the workstation, catching sight of the out-of-place tablet computer wired into the set-up.

Even as his mind registered that, he saw movement from the corner of his eye and swung his gun arm around to bear.

Waiting until the last second, Marc had flattened himself against the wall of the SCIF and held his breath. Now he lunged at the control pad that operated the thick security door and slammed the button with his fist.

The door hissed into motion and the guard reacted, too slow to get out of the way, crying out in shock. The thick, heavy panel slammed into his chest and shoved him back into the doorframe. His arm flailed, his trigger finger jerking.

The gun in his hand went off, the sound of the discharge like a thunderbolt within the SCIF's close confines. Marc recoiled as the bullet ricocheted off the wall and the floor before embedding itself in one of the stacks of computer hardware with a flash of sparks.

The door didn't crush the guard—there was a built-in safety mechanism that sensed resistance, and it juddered to a halt before retracting again—but it struck the man with enough force to batter him against the wall and leave him dazed and reeling.

Marc scrambled to tear the man's weapon from his hand, as more shots cracked through the air out in the anteroom.

The echo of the first shot inside the SCIF made everyone jump, but Lucy was fast enough to make the surprise work for her.

She twisted around in the female security guard's grip, the woman still holding on to her with the open ring of the handcuffs around Lucy's wrist, and yanked her off-balance. Springing back to her feet, Lucy spun the woman around, even as she tried to dig her heels in and claw back some momentum.

"Shit!" Hite flinched backward, raising his hold-out pistol in the same motion.

He fired without aiming, putting two wild rounds in Lucy's general direction. One bullet missed widely and cratered a video screen on the wall, but the second hit the security guard below her clavicle and the woman howled in pain, sagging back against Lucy with the shock of the impact.

Hite's eyes widened behind his glasses and he panicked, breaking into a run, dashing back toward the elevator bank.

Lucy felt the guard's warm blood on her cheek as the woman's weight descended on her, legs buckling. From behind, she heard the sound of movement inside the security room, but Lucy ignored it. Carefully, she lowered the injured guard to the floor and held the woman's hand over her bullet wound. "Keep pressure on that," she told her.

Crimson blossomed wetly across the gray of the guard's uniform shirt. "He fucking shot me!" gasped the woman.

"It's a through and through," Lucy told her, surveying the injury with the cold certainty of hard-earned field experience. "Didn't hit anything major. You'll be okay . . ."

The guard made a rough, animal cry of agony, and shivered. Lucy's initial instinct was to find an emergency medical kit, but expedience had to come first. She quickly disarmed the woman, took her radio and the keys to the cuffs, disengaging the restraints with bloody fingers. Off across the floor, she heard the elevator chime and the doors hiss shut. Hite was getting away, but she couldn't leave someone to bleed out.

"Whoa, what the hell?" Marc was at her side, eyes widening at the sight of the blood. "Who did—?"

"None of it is mine. This is Hite playing the goddamn cowboy," she hissed, answering him before he could finish. Lucy looked over his shoulder and saw the other guard lying slumped against the SCIF's door.

"So he's our rat in the nest," said Marc. "Makes sense. Hite's the CTO. That means he has top-level access to all the software developed here. If anyone knew about zero days in their code, it'd be him."

She nodded. "Now we just have to catch the son of a bitch."

\* \* \*

Hite's hands were shaking as he rode the elevator down to the executive offices. He had fired the Nano dozens of times on the range and got pretty good with his groupings, but when the moment had come to open up on a human, that had left him. He cursed himself for botching the chance to kill the Rubicon agent. Now he would need to find another way out of this escalating mess before it overtook him.

He fiddled with the signet smart-ring on his finger. Everyone on the top tier of Horizon Integral's management got one, but he hated the thing. It looked ugly, too retro and clunky for Hite's tastes. Now it might save his life.

The ring glowed blue when he tapped it on the lift's intercom panel. *"Recognize: Charles Hite, Chief Technology Officer,"* said the building's control system. *"How can I assist you this evening?"*

"Emergency executive override!" He barked out the words as the lift came to a halt. There could still be a way for him to come through this and maintain control of the narrative. But he had to be ruthless about it. "Access systems on floor twenty! Close safety doors and activate fire suppression systems on that level! Do it now!"

*"Mr. Hite, that operation conflicts with a number of safety protocols."*

"Emergency override," he said, louder this time. "You heard me! Do it!"

*"Override accepted. Proceeding."*

"Ha!" Hite gave a savage grunt of defiance and pushed out of the lift, past the planters full of cacti and toward his wide corner office.

The fire alarms sounded across the entire level in a keening refrain, emergency strobes flashing in time with the wailing chorus.

Marc rushed to the nearest exit door, and his heart sank as he put his weight on the push-bar to no avail. "It won't budge. The magnetic locks are engaged."

"Did Hite do that?" Lucy called out.

"Reckon," managed Marc, but the word caught in his throat as he tasted a rough chemical tang in the air. In the next second, concealed nozzles mounted in the hung ceiling above his head began dispersing jets of white vapor. He coughed, catching a tainted breath. "That's $CO_2$! Ah hell!"

"We've got to . . . get out . . ." The female guard gasped through her pain, and tried to raise a hand to point.

"She's right, this gas is used to smother fires," said Marc. "We'll suffocate in here."

"Not if I can help it." Lucy stooped to gather up the guards' SIG Sauer pistols, and took one in each hand. She squinted through the falling columns of mist and fired a salvo of shots from both weapons at the nearest window. The glass fractured and split, but it didn't break. "What the fuck?" Angrily, she discarded the guns and went at the damaged window with an office chair, smashing at it over and over.

"Won't work," said the guard, her eyes losing focus. "Polymerized. Unbreakable."

"Forget that!" Marc bent down to gather up the insensible guard in the SCIF and beckoned Lucy to follow him. "Bring her!"

He half-dragged, half-shoved the semi-conscious man to the elevator bank and dumped him there, before grabbing the gold signet ring Lucy had stolen. Slipping it on, he jammed it into the sensor pad by the call button.

"*Recognize: Martin Wehmeyer, Chief Executive Officer,*" said the building computer. "*How can I assist you this evening?*"

"Elevators," Marc almost choked as he blurted out the word. It was getting hard to breathe.

"*I'm sorry, I didn't catch that. Can you please repeat it?*"

"Open the elevators on twenty!" Marc bellowed, and he hoped that a low-priority system like this one wouldn't need the CEO's voice print or optic scan that the SCIF's doors had required.

The smart-ring seemed to be enough. The synthetic voice told him to "*Wait a moment,*" and then the doors to a lift car obediently opened. Marc shoved his semi-conscious charge in, as Lucy followed right behind with the wounded guard supported on her shoulder. The elevator doors shut again and they gratefully gulped in air that wasn't fogged with fire retardants.

"Hite," said Marc, eyeing the injured woman. "Where's his office?"

The guard hesitated, instead pushing away from Lucy to crouch next to her comrade.

Lucy glared at her. "He shot you. Are you really gonna look out for him?"

The guard hung her head and pointed downward. "Floor sixteen. The forest atrium."

Marc stabbed the number into the keypad and the lift descended. "You have to get medical attention," he told her. "And you may want to stop on ten. There's a mate of yours in the men's, cuffed to a toilet."

"Who *are* you people?" demanded the guard.

"Concerned shareholders," offered Lucy, and then she halted, placing a finger to her ear, listening to a voice that only she could hear.

Marc belatedly remembered that he had lost his own ear-bead communicator in the fight with the Samoan, and he gave her a questioning look.

"Assim," she said, by way of explanation. "He had a call from Delancort. Apparently, the fire alarms are going off down on the ground floor. The reception's being evacuated. Emergency services are on the way."

"Good." Marc nodded, pulling the tablet and manipulating the screen. "We still have a chance to isolate Hite, but we have to do it fast. If he gets out of the building, we'll lose him."

"Open to suggestions," said Lucy.

"We flip it around." Using Wehmeyer's stolen authorization, he tapped back into the building's wireless network and brought up the subroutines controlling the door locks on level sixteen. "He tried to trap us . . . so we trap *him*."

Hite had a vintage one-sheet from *Top Gun*, complete with Don Simpson's autograph, hanging on the wall of his office, and behind it was a small safe locked with a thumbprint reader. He tore the framed poster off its hook in his haste to get into the secure box, and hastily pulled out everything inside. Papers, passports and identity papers in more than one name, a bag of uncut conflict diamonds and some wads of US dollars; all of it went into a shoulder bag. But what he wanted the most, what he had really stopped here to get, was a simple brass key on a metal chain. He looped that over his neck and tucked the key down the front of his T-shirt, then ran back out into the hall, pointing the way with the Nano pistol.

He ducked around another of the oversized planters that were home to a dozen painstakingly cultivated miniature palm trees decorating this part of the floor. Green was everywhere on this level. It was like working in a fucking rainforest, and Hite quietly loathed it—just one more reason why he wanted to make his own mark and get himself shot of Horizon Integral as soon as bloody possible.

He was halfway down the corridor, heading back toward the closest elevator bank, when every closed door around him let out a metallic clack. Hite knew the sound; the magnetic locks had been activated. That could only have been done by someone inside the building's command system.

Light spilled out of an elevator as it slowed to a halt and the arrival bell chimed. He didn't wait to see who was inside. Hite spun around and started running as the doors opened. He threw a passing glance over his shoulder and fired the Beretta, cracking off two shots to discourage pursuit.

His thoughts raced. Rounding a corner, he skidded to a halt and pulled at the handle of a fire exit door, but it remained resolutely shut. He slammed his fist uselessly against it. These pricks were using his own tactics on him!

There were other banks of elevators he could try for, but they were on the far side of the faux-forest atrium in the middle of this level, and it was likely they too had been locked off. It was exactly what he would have done.

Hite jammed his smart-ring signet up against the nearest intercom pad. "Emergency override! Open this door!"

"*I'm sorry,*" said the nannying synthetic voice. "*That function has been taken offline by a higher operational clearance. Would you like me to contact reception for you?*"

Footsteps were coming closer, moving at a runner's pace. Hite's face twisted in annoyance and he rushed away. They were trying to trap him. He patted his chest where the key was hanging, making sure it was still there. It was his lifeline. His insurance. But it was meaningless if he couldn't get *out*.

Hite sprinted through a series of elegant glass arches and into the open, elevated space of the sixteenth floor's forest atrium. It resembled a square of woodland that had been transplanted from some idyllic countryside landscape, but the reality was an engineered stream and a swath of force-cultivated dwarf grass, carpeting a space between carefully neutered trees. Hite disliked it as much as he did the rest of the falsely "green" environments in the building. They were expensive wastes of time, more of Wehmeyer's ridiculous eco-friendly pet projects.

But he could still make use of it. Hite knocked a wooden chair out of his way as he crossed a clearing set aside for recreation and outdoor brainstorming, finding a control podium hidden in a stubby steel bollard. His signet clacked against the glassy surface of the display. "Access atrium settings," he demanded. "Uh . . . water management!"

*"Accessed,"* came the reply, and he grinned. This was good. It meant that whoever Rubicon was using to screw around with the building's systems didn't have them all under lockdown. They didn't know the tower as well as Hite did, and that would be how he would escape them. *There are other ways out,* he told himself, *you just have to be willing to take the risk.*

He leaned over the screen. If the gas nozzles hadn't slowed his pursuers down, then maybe this would. "Emergency dump," he commanded. "Vent atrium water tanks."

*"That operation conflicts with a number of—"*

"Just fucking do what I tell you!" bellowed Hite, jabbing at the keypad.

*"Override accepted. Proceeding."* As the voice spoke, the first fat drops of artificial rain began to fall from sprinkler arrays on the ceiling twenty meters overhead. In a few seconds, it became a drizzle, then a shower, and finally a torrential, hissing deluge.

Hite ran toward the edge of the atrium in big, splashing steps. Behind him, he heard voices. They were closing in.

He turned in the direction of the sound and saw ghostly shapes outlined in the hard rain. He aimed the Nano and squeezed the trigger, firing off the remaining rounds in the clip.

They sent the elevator carrying the two guards down and continued their pursuit of Hite. Lucy caught sight of the man as he fled into the fake woodland in the center of the office tower.

She pulled the ML-12 pistol and stayed on his heels, wishing that she had kept hold of one of the SIGs.

One shot and she could have put this asshole down—but they needed him alive and chatty. Charles Hite was the best chance they had to close the net on Ghost5, and in the back of her mind Lucy thought of the ways she could make him talk. The digital take Dane had secured for them was good, but there was no substitute for old-school human intelligence. And having someone try to choke her to death always brought out the worst in her.

"Out here," said Marc, indicating the arches that led into the atrium. "They got their own park . . ."

"And a storm, too . . ." Lucy squinted through the rainfall, trying to find their target.

"Shit! Get down!" Out of nowhere, Marc crashed into her and shoved Lucy to the ground as bullets sizzled through the wet air where she had been standing. They skidded behind a stone bench as the deluge sluiced down around them.

"Thanks." Lucy shrugged Marc off and peeked over the edge of the bench, irritated that she had almost taken a hit. Her reactions were still slow from breathing in the $CO_2$. "Where'd he go?"

"He was heading toward the edge." Marc moved out of cover and pointed. "There." He blinked. "We're halfway up a skyscraper. You think he jumped?"

She shook her head. "He's not gonna kill himself."

The two of them ran to the edge, scrambling over chest-high safety barriers of toughened glass and through the waterlogged foliage bordering the atrium space. The downpour became a flood, with streams of muddy fluid gushing over the verge and into the air. Behind them, the lower quad in the middle of the atrium was already awash, ankle-deep with the overflow from the overhead tanks.

Marc risked a look over, bracing to jerk back if Hite waited below them. "I don't see him. But there are open windows."

"*He's on the next level down*," Malte's voice muttered in Lucy's ear. Her head jerked up and found the office block across the street, where Dane had crossed over. She saw a figure in black on the roof-top, waving a hand. "*I saw him climb out.*"

"Got it," she replied. "You need to get out of there. This op is falling apart fast and we need to be ready to extract."

"*Copy that*," said the Finn, and the figure in black vanished. "*See you on the ground.*"

"Hopefully not the quick way down," Lucy said, under her breath.

Marc pulled on a bunch of twisted vines that grew through a polymer net cladding on the outside of the building, trying it for strength. "This webbing can support our weight. So we keep on him, right?" He nodded out at the long drop.

"Can't stay here," she agreed. "You ever done free-climbing?"

"A couple of times, yeah," Marc replied.

"This won't be anything like that," said Lucy.

"Great." He took a deep breath and swung out over the ledge, into the evening air.


There had been a moment when he almost lost his grip and ended it all, but then Hite tumbled through the window he had opened on the fifteenth floor and landed in a heap, twisting his ankle as he face-planted on the carpet.

Now, limping and cursing with each painful step he took, he ejected the Beretta's ammunition magazine and discarded it, slamming a fresh one into place and cocking the gun. Enough was enough. If anyone else tried to get in his way, he was going to put a bullet in them and worry about the consequences later. He was rich and he was smart, and he was going to sail through this unscathed. Hite kept repeating that to himself like a mantra.

*The only obstacle is this fucking building.* He had to get out. Get away. Hite entertained the fantasy of setting the place alight on his way out, grinning at the image in his mind's eye. *Drown it and burn it*, he thought. *Poor old Marty would have a heart seizure.*

Hite found what he was looking for. Floor fifteen was one of the levels where the executive express elevator stopped off, a discreet shaft built into the tower's central structure for anyone who wanted to avoid the public eye and bypass the big atrium to the street. He cracked his signet ring to the authorization panel with enough force to splinter the plastic, but still it lit up. The express lift would take him straight down to Horizon Integral's underground car park.

He fell through the open doors and against the far wall, and felt relief wash over him as the lift started a rapid descent. Soft New Age music, all tinkling wind chimes and soothing pan pipes, serenaded him as the level numbers dropped. The elevator worked independently of the rest of the tower's subsystems, so even the fire alarms and the CEO's personal authority would not be enough to take control of it.

*Change of plans*, he told himself. *Get out now, deal with this shit later.* Hite was close now, close to freedom. A burst of elation swept through him. *Screw them*, he thought. *Marty and his bleeding heart. That snotty bitch daughter of his. Screw them, screw the board, and screw this company.*

"I'm out!" he spat, wet and shivering in the chill of the lift's air-conditioned interior. Hite reached inside the damp confines of his jacket and brushed his fingers over the chain and the key once more, before pulling out the Ghost5 burner phone.

He turned it over in his hand, thinking. Madrigal had promised him that her group would honor their agreement, that they would cover for him, even get him out of the country if the situation warranted it.

There were plenty of places he could go. Hite had money hidden in the Caymans, in London and Zurich. He'd been quietly sewing his parachute for a long while now, waiting for the right moment.

Now was the time to call in that favor.

\* \* \*

The vine-laced webbing sheathing the building shifted alarmingly every time Marc moved his weight, and he had to get himself into a kind of sway-drop-grab rhythm to scramble down to the floor below. The task wasn't helped by the water gushing over the ledge above his head. Doing it more by feel than sight, he faced the wall rather than risking a look down.

Hand over hand, he moved closer to the gaping windows Hite must have opened using some other subroutine in the building's complex matrix of automated systems. Another of the robot window-washer rigs hung nearby, and Marc realized the man had found the same kind of entry point that he had exploited on the upper levels.

His boots touched the edge of the glass panel and it creaked. Marc took a breath and let himself drop the last bit of distance, trying his damnedest to pretend that if he slipped or missed, the fall wouldn't be a few seconds of cursing himself and then a red mess on the pavement.

Marc tucked his legs in and slid through the open window, shaking off the moment of ice-cold fear with a gasp. Lucy came after him a moment later. Behind her, water sluiced down the window frames, drooling through the open gap and pooling on the expensive carpet.

Lucy recovered, panning around with her pistol. This floor was another sparsely decorated one, mostly conference rooms and open-plan meeting spaces. "I don't see him," she said quietly. "Where did he go?"

"I've had enough pissing about," Marc told her. "Let's *ask*." He found one of the building's ubiquitous smart-intercoms and tapped it into life with Wehmeyer's signet ring. "Hey, uh, Sigma."

"*Hello,*" replied the computer. "*How can I help? Please be advised that this building is currently experiencing some technical issues, so automated options may be limited.*"

"Can you locate an employee for me?"

"*Yes.*"

"Charles Hite," Lucy demanded, stepping up to the panel.

A light blinked on the display. "*Mr. Hite is currently on Parking Level B-1.*"

"Sub-basement . . ." said Lucy. "Shit, he's going for a vehicle!" She took a step back toward the window. "We're gonna lose him!"

"No." Marc shook his head, pulling his tablet computer from the pocket on his tactical vest. "We can still get this guy." He tapped out a string of commands on the screen, and a set of doors on the nearest elevator bank hissed open, revealing an empty space beyond. The walls of the concrete shaft were wet and glistening with floodwater cascading from the floor above.

"You wanna do what, fast-rope down there?" Lucy made a face.

"No," he repeated. Marc queued up another command and a metallic platform extended out of a hidden alcove in the shaft, snapping into place like a closing lid. "Maintenance rig," he explained, stepping over the gap and on to the open-sided unit. The decking was a metal mesh grid, and looking down he could see right through it, all the way into the black pit of the subbasement far below.

Lucy followed him on to the platform and it shuddered under their combined weight. Anticipating what would come next, she grabbed a safety rail painted in yellow-and-black hazard stripes. "How quick is this thing?"

"Fast enough," Marc replied, crouching by the platform's automated controls. "As soon as I bypass the safety limiters." He took a breath, stripping through the warning code, running a brute-force hack. "Hold on."

Then the decking dropped like a stone and they fell with it, the rush of hot and stale air inside the shaft buffeting them, sparks flashing from the gear wheels as the platform shook like it might break apart at any second.


Hite hobbled across the underground garage to his smoke-gray Audi TT roadster and wrenched open the door, dropping hard into the driver's seat. Down here, the fire alarms were still hooting, the strobes still flashing, the lights and the noise beating at him.

He thumbed the starter and reversed out in a screech of tires. The main exit on to Bridge Street would be shuttered, but he knew that the secondary discreet exit on the other side of the basement would answer the command from his signet ring, and let him out through a concealed passage to Pitt Street. From there it would be a matter of getting clear of downtown Sydney as fast as possible.

Hite allowed himself a sly grin. By the time the emergency services had gone through the building and things had calmed down, he would be back at his house in Vaucluse, picking up the rest of his gear. There was something freeing about the thought of it. All the contingencies were in place. Maybe it was better this way, pulling the trigger now instead of later.

He pressed the speed-dial button on the burner phone and waited, bringing the car around in a half-circle. Madrigal answered on the first ring, that familiar digitally masked, barely human voice in his ear. *"Hello, Dart. Still alive?"*

"I'm on my way out," he said quickly. "And I'm calling in my marker. I have my departure planned, but I need help to execute it!"

*"I asked you to deal with Rubicon. This is making me think you didn't do that."*

"I trapped them inside the building," he retorted, dismissing her words. "They're not going anywhere . . ." Hite's voice faltered as he accelerated past the elevator bank on the far side of the underground car park, and saw two figures come sprinting out into the red glow of the alarm strobes. "Aw, shit!"

*"Is there a problem?"* Madrigal's tone was frustratingly calm.

Hite jammed the burner phone between his shoulder and his ear so he could put both hands on the Audi's steering wheel, and slewed toward the two Rubicon agents, hoping to clip one of them on his way out.

They split apart, diving away in different directions, and he missed them, instead coming around in a skidding turn to aim the car in the direction of a curved exit ramp.

*"You've let me down, Dart,"* Madrigal purred. *"And now you want my help?"*

"Yes!" Hite stood on the accelerator and the Audi jolted forward. From the corner of his eye, he saw the woman aiming a gun, saw it jerk twice as she fired. But the windscreen didn't break, the expanding stun-shot rounds only cracking the glass as they deflected off it. "You owe me!" he shouted.

"*I do,*" Madrigal admitted. "*Look at the phone.*"

Hite pulled it from his ear and held it up in front of him as the Audi bumped up the ramp. "What—?"

"*So long,*" said Madrigal. An instant later, the battery inside the modified burner phone released a powerful high-ampere discharge through the device's metal frame, triggered by the end of the call.

Every muscle in Hite's body contracted at once and his heart seized in his chest. Unable to release his grip on the phone, draw his foot off the gas pedal or shift the steering wheel, he drove the roadster into the wall of the exit ramp with such velocity that the rear half of the car left the ground and slammed back down again.

Gasoline trickled down the ramp from the car's ruptured tank as Lucy jogged up to the creaking, steaming wreck. A horrible stench of burned hair and scorched fabric wafted out of the vehicle where the driver's side door had deformed and fallen open.

Charles Hite lay back in his seat, the airbag uselessly deployed across his agonized, frozen features. His eyes were a mess of blown capillaries, and blood streamed from his nostrils.

"The fucker's dead," she pronounced.

Marc hissed through his teeth. "So much for getting some human intel."

"Help me get the door," said Lucy, and together they forced it further open. Hite's body lolled out of the seat, only held in placed by his seatbelt, and his hand fell off his lap. Blackened and bruised with more burst blood vessels and the after-effect of violent muscle damage, it gripped a grimy, scorched object.

Marc leaned back. "Wasn't the impact that did him in. Looks like he was volted."

Lucy pulled open Hite's fingers and peeled the cooked remains of a burner phone from his palm, sticky fluid and melted skin coming with it.

She tossed it to Marc, and his sickened look deepened. "What is this . . . ?"

Lucy quickly went through Hite's jacket, finding another cell phone. She noticed an odd pattern of searing on the dead man's chest, visible through his T-shirt. Looking closer, she hooked out a chain with her finger. A blackened brass key dangled on the end of it. "He kept this close," Lucy said, thinking aloud. "Safe." On an impulse, she jerked the chain and tore it off the corpse.

Marc looked over her shoulder. "Could be from a strongbox. That's pretty crude tech for a guy like him, though."

"Could be that's the point," she noted. "If the enemy expects crude, go technical. If they expect technical, go crude."

"Where does it fit, though?" Marc looked away.

Up at the end of the exit ramp, firefighters were coming into sight, calling out to attract the attention of anyone still trapped inside the building.

"That's the question. Hite wanted to protect this," Lucy replied. "Come on, let's get out of here."

## ─ ELEVEN ─

Erik rapped on the rusted steel of a girder to announce himself, and Madrigal stirred awake on a collapsible pallet in the middle of the derelict office. She blinked at him, for a moment chastely pulling the sleeping bag up to cover her bare chest. When she realized he was alone, she let it fall away and swung her feet out and on to the dusty floor.

"So," she said, "it's time?"

"The trucks are outside," Erik explained, as she stood up and crossed to a pile of clothes on a folding chair. "The last of our equipment is being loaded. Andre says the jet will be fully fueled by the time we reach the cargo terminal."

"Mmm." She paused, watching him. He said nothing, allowing his gaze to slip off her naked skin. She wanted to draw a reaction from him, but he saw no reason to provide one. After a moment, Madrigal began to dress. "Then we're ready. I don't want to leave anything behind." Her tone shifted toward commanding. "Make sure everyone double-checks the building before we go. Nothing can remain to trace us."

"It's been done."

"Do it again," she ordered, then more lightly, *"please."* An implied dismissal lurked in the word, but when Erik didn't leave, she gave him a hard look. "Was there something else?"

"What are we going to do with Song?"

Madrigal shrugged on a surplus Bundeswehr uniform shirt and buttoned it up. "Her name is Kara now."

"I don't care what she calls herself," Erik retorted, heat showing through. "I don't trust her. We need to get rid of her."

"Like we did with poor Lex?" Madrigal looked away, her gaze finding the nylon bag Andre had brought up the previous day. Inside was the dead man's laptop, his personal effects, and a flash drive containing gigabytes of data on their current operation. She seemed to consider it, then dismiss what it represented. "A shameful waste of potential. And if we do the same with Kara . . ." She paused. "No. We can make use of her."

He took a step closer, his jaw stiffening. "Did it occur to you that *she* may be making use of *you*?"

"Don't ever talk to me like I am stupid," Madrigal said coldly. "I know exactly what I am doing."

"Then explain it to me," he demanded. "We don't keep things from each other. That is how I have helped you maintain control of the group. But now this, now her . . . You're acting out of character and it concerns me."

She smiled without humor. "How arrogant of you to think you know me that well, Erik." She shook her head, the smile fading.

He folded his arms across his chest. "I will state a fact that you do not want to acknowledge. You have a blind spot where that woman is concerned. When she left, you should have dealt with it, yes, as we did with Lex. If I had been here then, I would have insisted. But you let her abandon the group. You let her go because you hoped one day she would come back."

"Song—Kara—she abandoned *me*." Madrigal continued to dress, reaching for her leather jacket. "How I deal with that is my concern."

"No." Erik glanced back toward the door, to be sure no one was listening in on their conversation. "You *want* to believe she has returned to the fold, because that pleases you. You like to be right. So you ignore everything else."

She eyed him. "You are making a lot of assumptions about me, Erik. Be careful." Madrigal walked toward him. "You're in a position of trust because you are competent. Don't give me cause to doubt that."

"Do you hear yourself?" he shot back. "That was almost a threat." He advanced toward her, closing the gap between them. Erik stood a good head taller than the woman, and he used that

height to deliberately impose on her personal space. "If it were anyone else, what would you say? This is too convenient. Days away from
our most ambitious operation, days after Lex was dealt with, and she
appears out of nowhere. With a gift of information. And you believe
in it without question—"

Madrigal's hand came up in a blur and slapped him hard across
the face. "You really do not know me at all, do you?" She turned
and stalked away from him, gathering up her gear for the departure.
"Don't second-guess me, Erik. *Of course* I am suspicious. *Of course* I
am being careful. I'm not a fool."

He wanted to say more, but held his tongue. He tasted blood in his
mouth from a fresh cut on his lip.

"Kara ran away because she was immature. She believed we were
on the wrong side," Madrigal went on, "but now she understands
the truth I told her back then, that there are no sides. There's only us
and them. These people, this Rubicon group. They're pulling at the
edges of our operation, interfering. But the intelligence Kara gave me
is bearing out. You've seen it yourself. The man in Malta we caught
on the drone's camera. She *named* him. She's already proving of use."

Erik remained silent. Off the lead Kara had given them, Ghost5
had drawn a sketch of the Englishman from data scoured from several military and security databases. Marc Dane was former Royal
Navy, recruited into Britain's MI6 external spy agency for undisclosed
operations, but the intelligence on him was frustratingly disjointed.
Two years previously, an Interpol arrest warrant had been issued in
his name, only to be rescinded less than a week later with no explanation. The CIA had him on a watch list. And if Kara was to be
believed, he was now in the employ of a private military contractor
whose agents were in the process of tracking Ghost5.

"Your problem, Erik, is that you see everything in such binary
terms." Madrigal's tone softened. "You miss the opportunity that
blossoms in the subtle shades of gray. Everything Kara has said so far
has proven correct. And if we *use* this information instead of reacting
to it, we can make Rubicon work for us."

"So far," he echoed. "She knew this man, yes? And then she betrays him, for what? For you?"

Madrigal paused, her back to him as she folded up the sleeping pallet. "She came back because of Lex's death. She wants to know who was responsible."

"And what happens when she finds out?"

"I won't let that happen." She picked up her bag, and walked back across the room. "I won't be disappointed again."

Erik gathered up the pallet and followed her into the corridor, down the creaking metallic stairs. Pressing the point would only anger Madrigal further. Instead, he changed tack. "You said we should leave no clues. What about Dart?"

"He's dead, or were you not paying attention?"

"We need to make sure he didn't leave anything behind that could implicate us," Erik insisted. "Rubicon were clever enough to find him. They'll be looking for his connections to us."

Madrigal nodded. "That's already in hand. I've reached out to our partners. They're going to deal with it."

At the foot of the stairs, some of the group had gathered, waiting for the word to proceed. Erik saw Pyne and Kara halt in mid-conversation as they approached. Kara's gaze crossed his, and she didn't hold it.

"It's time to move on," Madrigal said brightly, addressing the group. She put a hand on Kara's shoulder and smiled. "All of us."


"I really don't think this is a good idea," Marc said quietly, rocking on his heels as the elevator rose.

"We don't get a vote," Lucy replied, out of the side of her mouth. She was back in her more usual outfit this morning, an ensemble of lightweight cargo trousers and a black bolero jacket over a teal blouse, and somehow she wore it with the same kind of dash that she'd shown in the ten-grand dress from the night before.

Marc hunched forward in his khaki field jacket and jeans, patently aware of the Samoan security guard's searing gaze boring into him from across the lift car. He looked up and met the man's eyes directly. A nasty gash below the guard's hairline had been taped up, and his seething expression made it clear exactly what he wanted to do to Dane, if the two of them had been alone.

"How's the head?" Marc asked.

"Fine," growled the guard. "Yours?"

Marc involuntarily touched the fresh bruise on his face and winced a little. "Terrific." He looked away, through the glass walls of the lift as it climbed toward the upper levels of the Horizon Integral building. In the daytime, the greened tower stood out among the plain concrete and steel of its neighbors. Splashes of emerald color flashed past them on each floor they passed, and here and there Marc spotted work crews in high-visibility vests already engaged in cleaning up the mess caused by the flooding of the forest atrium.

"Relax," Lucy went on. "We're not gonna walk out of here in cuffs."

"Don't count on it," said the Samoan.

The elevator reached its destination and the door pinged open. Waiting for them in the reception area was the young Aborigine woman, wearing a professional smile completely devoid of warmth. "Hello again," she said to Lucy. Her gaze shifted to Marc and she looked him up and down. "I see your associate chose to enter the building by more conventional means today."

"Hello, Orani," Lucy smiled back at her. "No hard feelings?"

Orani didn't answer that. "The boardroom is this way." She walked on, not waiting to see if they followed. "I hope you brought your lawyer's phone number."

The conference area she led them to filled a whole corner of the building, treating the space to a spectacular view overlooking the surrounding streets, the Royal Botanic Gardens and Farm Cove. Marc could make out the sweeping white curves of Sydney Opera House peeking out from behind the skyline, but then he was torn away from the sight by the sounds of a full-throated argument in mid-flow.

On one side of a heavy wooden table, Martin Wehmeyer, his head of security and what were probably the cream of his legal team were ranged against Ekko Solomon and Henri Delancort on the other. Wehmeyer was flushed and angry, jabbing a finger at Delancort and snarling about "illegal intent." But he was momentarily shocked into silence by Marc and Lucy's arrival.

Crowne, the security executive, recovered first. "This man is one of *your* people," he accused Solomon, pointing at Marc. "He's guilty of breaking and entering, assault, industrial espionage, hacking . . . I have a list of criminal charges a mile long!" He looked at Wehmeyer. "Sir, that's the guy who broke into our secure unit and accessed our isolated server."

"You cannot prove that," said Delancort. Which was partly true, because on Marc's way out of the company network the night before, he had left behind a worm program that had deleted the majority of the building's internal security camera footage.

"We have witnesses," Crowne replied, gesturing toward the guard. "A member of our staff was shot!"

"By one of your own executives," Lucy said mildly. "Who is now dead himself. Awkward."

Crowne glowered at her flippant response. "What happened to Mr. Hite will be thoroughly investigated."

"What is going on here, Solomon?" Wehmeyer turned stony. Any suggestion of the jovial persona he had shown at the reception was a distant memory. "Do you have any idea how many laws your employees have broken? I want them arrested, and I want it done right now—"

"Stop talking." Solomon's voice cracked across the room with the force of a gunshot. "You would do well to consider your own guilt before you begin assigning blame to others." He leaned forward in his chair and eyed the members of the legal team. "I think you should have them leave before we take this any further."

"We have nothing to hide!" retorted Crowne.

"Are you quite sure about that?" Delancort raised an eyebrow.

Wehmeyer ran a hand through his thinning hair, and then waved at the lawyers. "Wait in the reception." He looked at Orani and the guard. "You too."

"Sir—?" Orani began, but Wehmeyer shook his head.

When they were alone, Solomon stood up and gestured for Marc and Lucy to take a seat.

Solomon advanced on Wehmeyer and Crowne, and Marc saw what in the past he had only caught in glimpses: a hard-eyed soldier's aspect, and a veiled threat in every move the man made. "You think you understand this situation. You are wrong." The African nodded toward the other end of the table. "Ms. Keyes and Mr. Dane are my Red Team. I use operatives like them to test the integrity of any company that Rubicon is interested in acquiring."

"Acquiring?" Wehmeyer blinked. "You don't own enough shares to do that . . ."

Solomon went on without comment. "They confirmed for me what I already know to be true." He glared at the other man, and when he spoke again, he truly showed his fangs. "Horizon Integral's executives are in collusion with violent extremists. Your company has facilitated terrorist attacks in Germany, the United States of America and Taiwan, and more may be on the way. Your man Hite's death was a consequence of this. We have proof."

Delancort slid a data slate across the desk toward the stunned men. "The HIOS Sigma industrial automation software has been deliberately co-opted. Critical vulnerabilities in its central codebase were not only concealed by members of your staff, Mr. Wehmeyer, but actively traded for financial gain to a known terror group."

Marc watched the blood drain from Wehmeyer's face as he scanned the pages of the digital file. He resembled a man reading his own death warrant.

"I have prepared a copy of that information to send to the governments of the nations that were targeted, and to the Australian Secret Intelligence Service," added Delancort.

"You're threatening us?" snapped Crowne.

"My aide is making clear the reality of the situation," Solomon replied.

"I had no knowledge of any of this!" insisted Wehmeyer, pressing the data slate into Crowne's hands. "I mean . . . I read about that train crash . . . I even assigned a team to look into it, to make sure there was nothing connected to our systems . . ." He swallowed hard. "I told Charles to run point on the investigation."

The man crumbled before Marc's eyes. He could imagine what was going through the CEO's mind. One whiff of this to the media, even the slightest possibility of such a grave lapse, and Horizon Integral's share price would be in freefall by the time the financial markets closed. And that was before considering the potential for legal ramifications, corporate responsibility, and countless lawsuits from angry victims.

"Hite. That arrogant piece of shit." Crowne read the text and put down the tablet. "He did this!"

"Perhaps Charles Hite acted alone, exploiting his high-level access," said Solomon, offering up a lifeline. "It would be hard to prove."

Wehmeyer's hands gripped one other tightly. Marc felt sorry for the man. A moment ago, he had been the king of the castle. Now he was in danger of losing everything.

Visibly keeping his emotions in check, the CEO spoke. "Charles . . . He was difficult to manage, you know? A very gifted programmer, a genius in fact." He blinked, then stared blankly out of the window. "But an egotist with it. That was the trade-off. I wanted his skills, so we tolerated his bullshit. Then about two years ago, he started dropping hints about jumping ship. Setting up his own company, after all we'd invested in him!" Wehmeyer shook his head. "I couldn't let that happen! I have too many people to be responsible for!"

Crowne nodded in agreement. "We convinced Hite to remain with us. But he wanted concessions, and not just a bigger office and more money. I had to approve a higher security clearance and a greater degree of autonomy for his work."

"He played you," said Marc, seeing the shape of the man's great lie in the wake of it. "Hite was marking time until he quit. He could sell off Sigma's zero-day exploits and when the time came, make it look like Horizon Integral were liable."

"That's a stone-cold plan," offered Lucy. "If Hite wanted to go it alone, undermining his former employers, who happen to be big potential rivals, would get him off to a good start."

"I had Mr. Dane infiltrate your server because I wanted to see who else may be vulnerable to these attacks," Solomon explained. "But also because I was sure it would flush out whoever inside your organization was working with these terrorists. It appears we know now."

"We think Ghost5 killed Hite to silence him," said Marc. "And with the number of HIOS Sigma installs on that list I pulled from your database, there's a lot of potential targets out there for them."

"Oh dear God." Wehmeyer put his head in his hands. "We rolled out the newest version of the software last month! It was smooth as glass . . . Your factories in Nigeria. Airport traffic control in Abu Dhabi. A steelworks in Pakistan. City management in Seoul, refineries in Bolivia and Peru, even a bloody children's hospital up in Norway! And now you tell me, if some psycho decides to press a button . . . ?" He fell silent as the enormity of it struck home. "How did we let this happen?" Wehmeyer shouted, but the accusation was aimed at himself.

Crowne scanned their faces, ending with Solomon. "You wouldn't have brought this to us unless you had a next move in mind. What is it?" He stared daggers at them. "What do you want?"

"We want to neutralize Ghost5," said Solomon. He reached out and drew back the data slate. "And you want this information to remain unseen."

"Charles Hite is our only hard lead on tracking down the hackers," Marc continued.

"Bob," began Wehmeyer, shooting Crowne a defeated look. "Give Solomon's team full access to Hite's office and whatever they need." The other man started to protest, but his boss spoke over him. His moment of raw panic faded away and he was back in command again. "You work with them, and you keep this business under lock and fucking key, right? We don't get out in front of this, dead or not, that conceited little bastard will end up taking us down with him!"

Crowne gave a tight nod and stood up, straightening his jacket. "Come with me," he said.


Lucy listened with half an ear as the security guy explained how Horizon Integral's lawyers were stonewalling the local cops, picking up on the one significant point. There was a very small window of opportunity to search for connections between the programmer and his pals in Ghost5.

Crowne hovered over Marc's shoulder as the Brit took a look at the dead man's desktop computer, while Lucy surveyed the rest of the room. Hite had done well out of coercing Wehmeyer to keep him on the payroll, getting a nice corner workplace with a sweet view. She took in the decor and her lip curled in a sneer.

The whole place had been furnished in that *asshole feng shui* style enjoyed by male executives on a power trip. Everything in the room was designed to make the man who worked there look important and those who visited feel small. The desk was big and deliberately retro, fashioned out of part of an aircraft fuselage. The chair behind it looked like a high-tech mini-throne, while the seats on the visitor's side of the room were minimalist, low to the floor and uncomfortable-looking. Hite had an ego wall behind his seat, the space crowded with framed diplomas showcasing his doctorates, sitting side by side with cheesy posed photos of him shaking hands with other toothsome white men of similar stripe. The only one she recognized was that bald guy who owned Amazon, and from that Lucy surmised the others were all similar tech-industry royalty.

Hite also seemed to have had a liking for aeronautical junk. One of the walls had a display of antique items, a few small replica aircraft cast out of chrome and a polished wooden propeller. She spotted an obvious dull spot where a framed picture, now lying discarded on the floor, had hidden a wall safe. Lucy used a pen to push open the safe door, which had been left unsecured. She tapped around inside, searching for any hidden compartments, and came up empty.

In her pocket, she had the tarnished brass key taken from the chain around Hite's neck. It didn't look like it fitted anything in here, and she decided to keep quiet about it for the moment.

Her phone buzzed and she pulled it out. Assim was calling on an encrypted line from the ops room on Solomon's jet. "Go for Keyes," she said, pressing the handset to her ear.

"*I spoke to Delancort,*" said the tech. "*He told me to pass this on to you. We received a call from our contact in the German Federal Police. Someone matching Kara Wei's description was seen getting off a train at Berlin Hauptbahnhof thirty-six hours ago.*"

"Berlin . . ." Lucy repeated, thinking about the first wave of digital attacks that had taken place in Germany.

Assim had made the same connection. "*We believe that Ghost5 have a safe house in that city.*" He gave a resigned sigh. "*Unfortunately, SCD don't have any other operatives to spare, so we can't send anybody to in-vestigate. But if Kara went there . . ."*

"Then she's working with them." Lucy ended the thought for him with brisk finality. "She probably always was."

Assim's silence spoke volumes. He had known Kara as well as any of them, and the technician was undoubtedly dwelling on the same cutting truth that burned in Lucy's thoughts. *We trusted her, and she tore that up.*

"Contact me if you get anything else." She ended the call and re-sumed her survey of Hite's office.

"Problem?" said Marc, looking over the top of the monitor at her.

"We got confirmation. Little red leather jacket has gone back to her friends, the big bad wolves."

He understood the inference and looked away. Lucy knew that deep down, more than anyone, Marc had wanted to believe that Ka-ra's actions had some kind of reasoning behind them. An explanation that clarified her betrayal, even justified it.

If she had ever shared that hope, it faded, and in its place a flinty resolve hardened in Lucy's chest. It didn't matter if Kara Wei was out for herself, or acting on behalf of Ghost5. She had aligned against Rubicon, and that turned her into a threat. *A target.*

"There's no evidence here of any communications outside of proper company channels," said Crowne, as he glared at Hite's computer.

"No hidden partitions on the hard drive or anything like that," agreed Marc. "But let's be realistic. Hite wasn't an idiot. He wouldn't have used his office system to send coded messages to a renegade hacktivist collective." He paused. "Some interesting logs from his search history of the company intranet, though. Hite was keeping a very close eye on the software patches being written for HIOS Sigma. That's a job way below his pay grade."

"Looking to see if anyone found the zero-day exploits he sold to Ghost5," said Lucy. "Couldn't let that happen."

"Yeah," said Marc. "But wherever he did his initial dive into the core code, it wasn't on this machine."

Lucy studied an odd-looking model aircraft on a glass display stand. At first she thought it was a prop from a sci-fi movie, a sleek and angular shape like a wingless stealth fighter with matte black rotor blades at the four corners of the fuselage. "Is this a drone?"

Marc's head snapped up. "What?"

Crowne gave an offhand nod. "Hite was into it as a hobby. Drone racing, if you can believe it." He made a wafting motion with his hand, briskly dismissing the idea. "He had a side business building custom models. It's the new sporting trend for rich nerds, apparently."

Lucy brought over the remote-control flyer and handed it to Marc. "Look familiar? Anything like the one you saw in Malta?"

His eyes narrowed. "Yeah, I reckon so."

"Hite made this himself?" Lucy said to Crowne.

The man nodded. "There's a workshop set up in his house. He's got . . ." Crowne halted and rephrased. "I mean, he *had* a big place in Vaucluse. It's one of the more upmarket districts around Sydney. He lived out there like he thought he was in the Hollywood Hills."

"Show us," said Marc.


They met in the rooms that Fox had rented, above a noisy convenience store in a district that Sydney locals called "Koreatown," but to Cat's eyes it was an inauthentic simulation. It looked like a Westerner's idea of the reality, a mocking and gaudy version that allowed them to both deride and indulge the foreign at the same time. She had no respect for these Australians. They were like the Americans and the Europeans; over-fed, over-privileged and full of thuggish swagger. And the exiles who lived here, they were worse. She thought even less of them.

Cat could not let that show, however. The team were hiding in plain sight, and it would only take one error for them to blow their cover.

In the center of the narrow living room, Fox systematically dismantled and cleaned their guns. The near-silent OTs-38 pistols had been delivered that morning by a loyal patriot, along with a vehicle and a few days' worth of food supplies. But they were not planning to stay long. Through the open door to the apartment's small kitchen, she heard Dog finish his conversation with the woman whose face was always ghost-masked.

She stood as he entered the room, anticipation tingling in her feet. "What does she want us to do?"

Dog gave her a neutral look. "A man was killed last night," he explained. "Madrigal had her people commit the act. We are to ensure there is no fallout."

Fox clicked shut the chamber on one of the silenced revolvers. "We are soldiers, not janitors."

"We are whatever we are told to be," Dog replied evenly.

Cat licked her lips. "Why bring us all the way here if not to use us?"

Dog considered that question for a moment. "I think . . . the woman wanted to do it herself. Perhaps for the thrill."

Fox snorted. "Self-indulgence is a path to self-destruction. She should leave the wet-work to us."

"There will be enough for us to do," Dog said firmly. "Make preparations. Madrigal has requested assistance in sanitizing a location. She is sending one of her people to accompany us."

"We do not require an escort," grumbled Fox.

Dog gave him a nod of agreement. "Regrettably, we are required to indulge the American."

"How many more of her messes must we clean up?" Cat let the complaint slip out. She felt fatigued and normally she wouldn't have voiced it so easily. But it had been said, and now the words could not be called back.

"Orders," said Dog. "Remember?"

Cat bowed her head. He had given her an out, and a chance to stop herself from speaking words she might regret, an utterance that might border on an actual criticism of their commanders. "I never forget," she insisted.

Fox, however, was less cautious. "Cat has a point," he noted. "We have done much for this woman."

Dog nodded. "This is true. So be pleased. When we complete this assignment, we will move into the final phase."

"The target?" Cat almost grinned with anticipation. "At last?"

"This will be worth it in the end," Dog told them. "These small deeds and minor deaths. All of it lays the way toward a greater victory. We are going to be part of it."

She allowed herself to smile. "Then we will do all we can to speed the course."

"Deploy at sunset," he told them. "A day from now, this will be behind us. And a new dawn will be breaking."


The company provided them with an SUV and the group drove in sullen silence, out toward Charles Hite's home.

Marc watched Sydney's environs fall away as they left them behind and entered the prosperous suburbia of Vaucluse on the South Head peninsula, out across the bay from the city. Dense green hedges and stands of close-planted trees screened expensive modernist homes from the road, their entrances hidden behind artfully sculpted walls and security gates. In the more affluent ends of the district, Marc saw the same kinds of "stealth mansions" that he had glimpsed in places like Monaco and Beverly Hills, where the rich kept their homes under cover of clever landscaping to deter criminals, the media and everyone else from seeing too much.

He looked away from the window and noticed Crowne, sat up front in the passenger seat, watching him in the rearview mirror. At Marc's side, Lucy seemed not to be aware of it, affecting a sleepy aspect that he knew was pure theater.

"We'll be there soon," began the security chief. "And to be clear. You're both here as observers, okay? Look but don't touch."

"Observers," Lucy echoed. "What does that make you? I'm pretty sure all of us are on dubious legal ground right now, if you wanna get technical about it."

Crowne ignored her and glanced over his shoulder at Marc. "You know, I reached out to some old friends of mine in the agency. Asked around about Solomon and Rubicon. I heard some interesting stories."

"He's an interesting man," Marc replied.

"That why you quit MI6 to go work for him?" Crowne smiled, like he had scored a point, and then quickly corrected himself. "Oh, but you didn't quit, right? I'm told you were kicked out. Why was that?"

*All my friends were killed.* The reply came to him and it was so strong, so immediate that for a moment Marc thought he had actually said it out loud. "That's a thread you don't want to pull on, mate." He met Crowne's gaze and held it. "Let's stay professional, yeah?"

Crowne blinked first and gave the driver, the Samoan security guard who Marc had crossed paths with the night before, an arch look. He clearly didn't want to let it lie. "How about you?" he asked, switching targets to Lucy. "There are a few stories floating around about the woman who works as a consultant for the Rubicon PMC. Some even say she might be ex-Delta Force. What do you think about that?"

Lucy shrugged. "Delta don't have any female operatives. Strictly boys only, or haven't you heard?" She graced Crowne with a brief look. "Anyone who says otherwise watches too many movies."

Marc suppressed a smile. The black-ops urban legend about the US Army's covert troop of female soldiers was more truth than lie, but it didn't hurt to muddy the waters a little.

"You want to know what I think?" Crowne went on, as the vehicle turned off the main road and down an even-more exclusive avenue.

"Not at all," Marc told him, and finally the man got the message.

Up ahead, a collection of artfully angled concrete cubes, steel verandas and blue panoramic windows formed the elements of Hite's home that were visible from the street. Barriers of brushed metal sat across the end of the drive, serving as the modern portcullis to the dead man's castle.

Marc climbed out as the SUV rolled to a stop, dragging a battle-worn Swissgear backpack over one shoulder and squinting in the sunshine. The house stood atop a curve of rust-colored cliffs, directly overlooking a sheer drop into breakers of white foam, where the waters of the bay crashed against the rocks. Even from outside the house, the view back toward the city was an impressive one, with Sydney Harbor Bridge clearly framed against the sky and the white arcs of the Opera House resembling a distant bird about to take flight.

"Good enough optics, and Hite could be looking right into his own office from here," said Lucy, walking up to Marc's side. She pointed out the distant nub of the Horizon Integral office tower among the other buildings of the city skyline. "Looks like maybe six klicks and change, as the crow flies."

Marc crossed to the gate, eyeing the security system. A magnetic card reader was mounted at the pedestrian doorway. He unzipped his pack. "I have icebreaker software on my tablet and an RFID spoofer. I can probably get this open—"

"Or I could get Hite's staff to let us in," Crowne told him, pushing past. He buzzed the intercom and waited. "They work for the company. They're not going to give us any shit about being here."

The gate retracted and the Samoan drove the SUV in through the widening gap. Marc gathered up his pack as Lucy followed the vehicle on to the property. She paused to give Marc a pat on the shoulder. "Don't worry. You're gonna get your chance to impress everyone."

Crowne's prediction turned out to be dead on. By the wary expressions on their faces, the maid and the two guards who met them at the entrance clearly knew the security executive, and his presence was enough to make them give the group a wide berth from then on.

Stepping inside, Marc craned his neck to take in the entrance hall of Hite's house, a cylindrical space that extended down a set of shallow steps into a wide reception, and up three floors to a clear dome roof. Hanging directly below the dome, suspended on cables, hovered an abstract winged sculpture; a half-naked angel with line and form that veered more toward eroticism than virtue. To Marc's eye, it resembled an illustration off the cover of some low-grade heavy metal album.

"True what they say," Lucy sniffed, giving the piece a cursory glance. "Money can't buy good taste."

Her pronouncement proved accurate as they moved through the rest of Hite's home. There was a lot of gold and marble, except where there was leather and steel, and if the place had a room that didn't have a gargantuan television screen, Marc didn't see it.

"I expected a rich nerd to have more books," said Lucy. She glanced around. "Any books, in fact."

Marc shook his head. "Hite is what you call a *bro-grammer*. All the usual macho alpha-male crap with a high-tech gloss."

"Charming."

A shiny, polished object on the mantelpiece caught Marc's eye and he wandered over to look. A stylized cloud made of glass, it appeared to be a trophy of some kind. Etching on the surface read *DroneSpeed Tokyo Invitational 2016: Hottest Lap Winner—DART.* Next to the award was a framed picture showing Hite standing at the number one spot on a racing podium, caught in the middle of spraying a fan of champagne from an open bottle. He had a wild grin on his face, and the polo shirt he wore in the image had the same word embroidered over his breast. "Dart," Marc read it aloud. "Must be his racer handle."

"He have a study or a home office?" said Lucy.

"Before, you mentioned a workshop?" Marc added. "Hite doesn't strike me as the type to go for the obvious choice."

"There's the garage out back," Crowne explained. "Where he kept his playthings."


It turned out to be a well-appointed work space the size of a small barn, stocked with hardware and tools worth hundreds of thousands of dollars. Marc saw computer-controlled lathes, platforms for plating custom circuit boards, and more. In one corner, a high-specification 3D printer worked slowly through a lengthy production cycle, and he peeked in through a window in the machine's hatch, watching as it assembled a complex honeycombed shape out of resin.

Drones and unmanned aerial vehicles of all shapes and sizes hung from racks on the walls. The smallest of them were tiny flyers that could fit in the palm of a hand, or toy-like replicas of real-world helicopters. The larger ones were futuristic blended-wing designs with meter-wide spans, and spidery airborne camera rigs clustered under sets of six rotor units.

One entire workbench had been given over to racing drones, similar to the display model that Lucy had examined in Hite's office. Marc crossed over to it, his gaze taking in banks of lithium-ion batteries docked to slow trickle chargers, bins of spare propeller blades, motors, cables and other components. Hite's workshop had the same geometric precision as his office layout, everything there for a reason, and nothing on display that didn't have a function.

A gutted quadrotor drone lay in the middle of the bench, half-finished in a halo of unsoldered wire. It reminded Marc of a science lesson dissection experiment, and the shape of the small UAV triggered a moment of muscle memory in him. His hand clenched, the still-healing scars on his palm and his fingers tingling.

He picked up a triple-bladed plastic rotor and ran his thumb lightly along the razor-sharp edge of the blade. "This *is* the same gear they used in Malta. I wasn't certain before, but I am now." Marc examined the quadrotor. It was a twin to the skeletal machine he had swatted out of the air on the roof of the hotel. He turned it over and studied the cyclops-eye camera mounted on the front of the device.

"How does it work?" Lucy held a bulky remote control unit in her hand, moving the metal joysticks with her thumbs. "My brother had an RC car with one of these when we were kids." A prop-less drone on the rack in front of her buzzed angrily as its motors spun in response to each push of the stick.

"You wear these." Marc showed her a set of blank-faced virtual reality goggles and held them up to his eyes. "Got monitors inside, they give you a direct live feed from the drone's camera. It's called FPV . . . First Person View."

Behind them, Crowne folded his arms across his chest. "Hite was off doing this shit at tournaments around the world every other month," he said sourly. "Don't see the appeal, myself."

Lucy shrugged, looking up at the other machines. "They're not exactly Predators or Reapers." She glanced at Marc and they shared a silent communication, both of them remembering a moment on the rooftop of an abandoned orphanage in Turkey, when the bigger brother of these sport drones had rained Hellfire missiles down on them. "But any tech can be weaponized, if you're motivated." Lucy took in the workshop with a sweep of the hand. "A swarm of them, loaded with explosive charges or toxins? That's a goddamn nightmare."

Crowne snorted. "Now you're telling me Hite built drones for terrorists?"

Marc moved to a desktop computer in the corner of the workspace. "Maybe." He jerked his thumb at the 3D printer. "Anybody with one of those and a soldering gun could assemble a working quadrotor with components you can buy off the web. I reckon Hite traded his drone designs to Ghost5, probably as a side-deal along with selling them the zero-day exploits." He pulled out his hardened tablet and connected it to the desktop's USB socket. "Let's have a look-see what else Chuck was working on . . ."

Marc's intrusion programs went to work bombarding the firewalls Hite had set up on his system, and the barriers were as formidable as he had expected. The dead man knew his stuff, placing layers of redundant protective code around the password protection and input protocols. Marc waved away Crowne's impatient demands to see immediate results and let himself be drawn into the business of navigating the firewall code, looking into the heart of it for a weakness.

He hardly noticed when Lucy and Crowne left to search the rest of the house for anything else that could incriminate Hite. In the back of his mind, he guessed that Wehmeyer was probably halfway toward constructing a plausible narrative that would hang responsibility for any wrong-doing around Hite's neck, and keep Horizon Integral clean of any blowback. But the fate of the software company was only collateral damage when weighed against the potential horrors that Ghost5 could wreak with a fully functional Arquebus digital weapon. With hundreds of industrial systems out there in the world running vulnerable code, there would be no way to protect them all from potential attack without causing panic and ruining Wehmeyer's company.

Time passed, and the software barriers were slowly eroded until Marc's army of digital scouts began their forced assault on the workshop's mainframe. Once he was in, he set a search macro running for anything that could connect Hite to the rogue hackers, sifting petabytes of information and data mining files.

But the dive into the database turned up nothing of use. It appeared that the workshop mainframe was exactly what it appeared to be, a system used only for operating the printer and the computer-controlled tools, a place where Hite had stored volumes of performance data harvested from thousands of test flights for his prototype racers. On the surface, it seemed like the ideal place for Hite to have concealed any data he didn't want to show up on his office system or personal laptop—after all, the best place to hide a tree was in a forest. But there were no detectable phantom partitions on the mainframe's drives, nothing that resembled one kind of data masquerading as another.

Marc found countless logs that stored battery charging rates and discharge times, motor efficiency ratings, GPS records and statistical information for every aspect of racer drone operation. There were endless FPV videos where Hite had saved the footage shot by the cameras in his UAVs. For a while, Marc searched those files, wondering if the drone on Malta had sent its images here, but he came up empty.

He pored over folders of digital recordings from race meets, kinetic action sequences where Hite flew his custom-made machine against other drone pilots, through obstacle courses set up in abandoned warehouses and disused factories. Other files contained endless repeats of test flights in the national park across the bay, or down along nearby Shark Beach, Camp Cove and around the lighthouse at Hornby. Marc picked some videos at random and fast-forwarded through them, seeing Hite film himself as the drone circled his goggle-wearing form. It would take months to sift through all of this, to be sure that nothing was buried there.

Marc stood up and stretched for the first time in hours, abruptly realizing how thirsty he was and that it was now late afternoon. He walked around the workshop to kill the lethargy, draining the aluminum water bottle from his pack to the last drop, and his gaze snagged on a calendar hanging from the door. Hite had marked off flight days for his drones, and something in the numbers needled at Marc's thoughts.

Going back to the database, Marc found the current month's log of the drone calibration flights and ran down the list. There was only one day when Hite hadn't sent up his racer for its practice run, logging the reason as "bad weather." Marc flipped back to the month before, and the one before that. Each time, a single test day had the same no-fly tag, but cross-checking it against the battery use log showed a charge-and-drain cycle no different from any of Hite's other practice sorties.

Marc knew for sure he had a lead when he looked up the local weather report for the missing days and found clear skies for all of them. A slow smile crossed his face as he pulled the GPS logs. If nothing had gone up, there would have been a blank entry, but Marc's scout software showed him the ghostly fragments of a deleted file instead. Hite *had* been flying a drone, but he hadn't wanted anyone to know about it, and erased the data after the fact.

"Gotcha, you little sod . . ." Marc said to the air, and he began to sift through the digital ashes of the trashed GPS data, slowly reassembling what Charles Hite had tried to hide.

# — TWELVE —

This is you working?" said Crowne, curling his lip.

"Can you be quiet?" Marc told him, tilting his head behind the big video headset. "You keep distracting me and I'll crash it." His hands were clasped around the RC controller Lucy had fiddled with earlier, his thumbs making tiny course corrections to the left and right with the stubby joysticks.

Lucy looked away. A monitor screen on a nearby bench showed a repeater view from the nose camera of the quadrotor drone that the Brit was piloting, and she watched trees part and give way to a sheer drop over the edge of the cliffs. "Where are you taking it?"

"Following the virtual trail," Marc replied. "I reconstructed the GPS path of the missing test flight. I want to see why Hite was so determined to delete it."

Crowne made a disgusted noise. "This is a waste of time."

"I have to do it now," insisted Marc. "We're losing the light out here. Can't fly in the dark."

"I'm starting to think that this shit about Hite and these ghost-hackers is a smokescreen." Crowne turned his gaze on Lucy. "You could be covering up for Rubicon and your boss. You're the ones who broke in, after all. I only have your word that Hite was dirty."

"That's fair," Lucy allowed, and Crowne raised an eyebrow. It wasn't the answer he had been expecting. "I mean, he wasn't the only one with top-level access to the HIOS Sigma codebase, am I right? Wehmeyer had it too. You have it." She let that sink in. "We have proof that the exploit data found its way to Ghost5. Maybe I'll get our guys to look into your financials like we did with Hite, see if the same indicators are there?" She didn't tell him that Assim had already done that, of course. Hite's banking transactions were the only ones that flashed up enough red flags to be suspicious, but Lucy guessed that Crowne might have some cash of his own that he didn't want any outsiders knowing about.

"That sounds like a threat," he said.

"Call it an *observation*," Lucy countered.

On the video screen, the drone's point of view dropped until it was halfway down the sheer cliff wall, staring out at the bay. "This is where the route ends," said Marc. "I don't see anything."

"Was the tide out when he made the flights?" Lucy wondered. "Did he land it?"

Marc sighed. "I don't know. There's a magnetic gripper rig on the belly of the drone, but I can't see anything here that could be picked up . . ."

"Turn it around," said Crowne, forgetting his impatience for a moment.

Marc pivoted the drone around 180 degrees and the cliff face came into view. There was a small cleft visible as a black shadow, a hole punched into the rock. "Hello . . ." With care, he guided the little machine into the gloom and the video camera adjusted to the blackness.

A slimline steel attaché case was wedged at the back of the fissure, tucked out of the way in a place where no one was ever going to stumble upon it. Lucy could see the handle had been modified with a magnetic clamp. "Please tell me we haven't found Chuck's porn stash."

Marc snorted and pushed the drone in closer. The point-of-view video juddered and then began a slow retreat. Previously the movement had been fast and smooth, but now it was leaden and sluggish. "Feeling the extra weight," said Marc. "I have the case."

"Bring it on home," Lucy said, turning back to Crowne. "What was that you were saying before?"

"Could be anything in there," said Crowne. Then he shifted slightly, mulling it over. "Whatever that case represents, it's best if Horizon Integral take custody of it. I'll return to the office, we'll have our people open it up and—"

"No," Marc spoke over him. "I can drop this into the sea in a second, pal."

"Besides," said Lucy, fishing the brass key from her pocket. "You don't have *this*."

They gathered in the games room on the ground floor of the house, beneath another massive television and a cabinet packed with media players and consoles. Marc repurposed the regulation size pool table in the middle of the space as a work area. Getting the hang of the drone had been easy enough once he called on the twitch-action reflexes he'd honed playing videogames, and he piloted the compact UAV down through a skylight in the roof to deposit its payload on the blue baize.

Putting aside the goggles, he disconnected the magnetic clamp and took the case in his hands, studying it. A single lock held it secure, and as Lucy had predicted, the key that Hite had died with fit it exactly.

"You think he booby-trapped it?" Lucy said quietly.

Marc held his breath and turned the key. The lock opened with a metallic whisper and the lid rose automatically. No explosive blast followed, and he let out his breath in a low whistle. "Let's see what he was hiding."

USB sticks or a hard drive, a pack of data discs, these were what Marc had expected to find inside the case. Instead, he drew out a grubby, dog-eared cardboard folder, thick with yellowing sheets of paper and news clippings. Beneath it was a flat brick of black plastic, and it took him a second to realize he was looking at an actual vintage VHS video tape cassette. Along with that, a dusty manila envelope contained a loose wad of faded photographs, the rubber band holding them together having long since degraded.

"What the fuck?" Crowne snatched the video tape from his hand and held it up in front of his face, examining the tape like it was some artifact from some ancient civilization. "Haven't seen one of these for years."

Marc opened the folder and carefully laid out each item inside it on the pool table. He glanced over the first few articles: pages torn from an American high school yearbook circa 1978, a photocopy of a heavily redacted document bearing CIA code references, and a Chicago Police Department arrest report for a "Jane Doe."

Lucy flipped through the photos, sorting them into piles, pausing to study an image shot on some long-ago beachside holiday.

Crowne leaned in for a look, then glanced at the file pages. "That's the same face." He pressed a finger on the police mugshot and then indicated the photo in Lucy's hand. Both were of a skinny teenage girl with short, copper-red hair.

Marc stepped back to take in the content of Hite's secret stash. "All of this . . . it's one person." He nodded to himself as the understanding hit him. "We've got pieces of someone's life here."

Lucy picked up the police report. "Arrested for breaking into an AT&T telephone switching facility. Estimated age suggests a birthdate in the early 1960s."

Marc nodded. "That'd make her, what? In her mid- or late fifties now?"

"Yeah." She stared at the page, and Marc saw a realization wash over her expression. "The redhead. This is *her*. Shit! I think this is *Madrigal*."

"No . . ." Crowne's first reaction was skepticism. He had heard the stories about the notorious hacker and seemed doubtful.

Marc blinked, taking in Lucy's discovery, reframing the material in a new context. "Madrigal's a phantom. Her identity has never been confirmed. Hacker legend says she deleted her past from every database on the planet."

"You can't erase a piece of paper with a mouse and a keyboard," said Crowne, examining one of the news clippings, slowly coming around to the idea. "This is whatever she missed."

"Low tech," Marc thought aloud. "Like the brass key. Hite knew he couldn't get anything on Madrigal through digital methods, so he went old school. Probably been gathering this material on the quiet as an insurance policy."

"Too late for that," said Lucy. She looked at the security exec. "So, you on board with us now?"

Crowne gave her a sideways glance. "I don't know. Some of this . . . It's not about her. See?" He handed Lucy the CIA document. "Look at the date. *1971.* If this woman is who you say she is, she would have been a kid then."

"*Marie Stone.*" Marc found the name scratched on the back of one of the photos, and sounded it out as he said it. "Same surname here." He pointed to a piece of still-visible text in the redacted document. "This could be about someone in her family, then?"

"I see more agency pages," said Lucy, continuing to go through the papers, offering up a sheaf of blurry typewritten sheets. "Looks like an after-action report. References to an operation in South Korea." She glanced at Crowne. "Am I right?"

"Why are you asking me?"

She glared at him. "Don't play dumb. I could tell you were an ex-Virginia farm boy by the haircut and the suit."

He sighed and took the papers from her, looking them over. "This is from way before my time. But it looks legit. I don't even want to speculate how a dickhead like Charles Hite got his hands on these."

"Money opens a lot of doors," Marc noted. "Right now, I want to see what's on *this.*" He tapped the video tape. "It has to be significant, right? Hite wouldn't have kept it otherwise."

Lucy eyed the cassette. "So how do we do that? Call the local thrift stores and hope someone has a VCR that can play it?"

Marc shook his head, and started searching the cabinets around the walls of the games room and beneath the big TV. "Hite was a crook and an asshole, but he was a techie. And so am I. And we hoard obsolete hardware like other people collect stamps."

Crowne sneered. "He's not just gonna have one lying around—"

Marc opened the third bureau along and smiled, running his hand down a set of carefully preserved electronic gear. "Laser Disc. Betamax. U-Matic . . ." He stopped as he found a compatible player. "*VCR!* Here we go."

"You're kidding me." Lucy eyed him. "Should I get the maid to make some popcorn?"

His smile faded as he studied the label on the tape: *Evidence*

*Item #34A. Dade County Sheriff's Office Case File #93–37 (Cooper Homicide).*

Marc slid the cassette into the machine and pressed the play button.


Time has worked on the cheap magnetic coating of the video tape, and the playback is full of static. A title card shows the case file numbers and the location where the assembled footage was shot. Bright Palms is the upbeat name of a Florida retirement complex in Hialeah. Twenty years ago, it was home to dozens of elderly men and women looking for someplace warm to see out their twilight years.

A civilian auxiliary working in the Sheriff's office assembled this recording from other tapes, and the cuts are workmanlike and clumsy. Grainy black-and-white images show the exterior of the gated community on a stormy August night. Lightning flashes in the distance.

A black sedan that had been stolen earlier that night, according to the notes accompanying the tape, cruises past and melts into the shadows. The figure that climbs out is impossible to identify, lost under a sweatshirt and baseball cap, hands in dark gloves.

Then different footage, from a security camera looking across the gated community's swimming pool. Palm leaves are drifting on the surface of the rain-lashed water, and there are a few lights still on in the windows of the motel-style apartments. The time code in the corner of the frame reads *3:23 a.m.*

Something moves; a dark shape coming over the top of the exterior wall. The figure in the cap drops down and navigates across the open space, careful to stay in the dark as much as possible. The intruder knows where the cameras are mounted, and has planned their entry accordingly.

The video jumps jarringly to a few seconds of footage shot during the daytime, from a bulky hand-held camera. The view shows the outside of a laundry room, peeking in at the ranks of aging washers and tumble dryers through a reinforced window that has been forced open. The gap is small, too narrow for a grown man to fit through.

The edit flashes snow-static again and returns to the night in question. A camera at the end of a corridor looks down past dozens of apartment doors. If not for the slow tick of the time code in the corner of the frame, it might appear to be a static image. Then a door halfway up the corridor opens and one of the residents leaves his room. The notes say that this man is Calvin Cooper, age eighty-six. He's wearing baggy tracksuit trousers, slippers and a housecoat.

He walks with a metal stick, away down the corridor, disappearing around the corner with a newspaper tucked under one arm.

The screen flicks to a grimy point of view over the day room. It's dark in there. The chairs are empty, the rest of the residents asleep in their apartments. Calvin goes to a table in the corner where he can sit with his back to the wall. Lightning illuminates him briefly as he moves. He's thin and stiff.

The long corridor again. The figure in the cap enters the frame. The intruder moves carefully, never once looking in the camera's direction. They stop outside Calvin's room and force the lock. The resident rooms maintain their privacy, so there is no video of what happens inside during the minute that elapses. The notes say Calvin's room was searched.

But the intruder isn't here as a thief. They have come to find someone. The figure emerges again and there's a moment of hesitation before they move off, following in the old man's footsteps.

The remainder of the video plays out from the perspective of the day-room camera. Calvin reads his paper, lit by a small lamp. He doesn't seem to realize that he isn't alone until the intruder is almost upon him—but then he moves faster than someone of his age might be expected to. He strikes out with the stick. The action isn't random, but an attack someone who has been trained to fight would employ. It's only age that betrays him.

The intruder blocks the blow and disarms the old man, tossing the stick away. For a split second, the face beneath the cap is visible. A woman? It's unclear.

The figure sits down across from Calvin and stares at him over the small table. And they talk.

There's no audio in any of the footage, so everything unfolds in silence. But it isn't hard to imagine the quality of their voices, if not the actual words. Their postures suggest a terse interchange made in low, hissed tones. It goes on for some time.

Slowly, their body language changes. Calvin becomes stoic as an invisible weight descends upon him. The expression on his face looks a lot like sorrow. Like *guilt*. He seems defeated.

Seen from the back, the intruder hardens. It's anger there, cold rage that builds as the minutes pass. Finally, the figure in the cap pushes a notepad and a pen across the table to Calvin, and reluctantly the old man begins to write. It is impossible to see what he scribbles on the pages.

When he is done, the intruder puts the pad away and takes back the pen. Calvin looks as if he is about to speak.

There is a blur of motion and the figure jams the pen into the old man's throat. He rocks back in shock, and the intruder springs up to smother his cries with one gloved hand. Calvin's killer tears the pen free and stabs him again, and again. The assault is violent, furious. The notes state dispassionately that there were six separate entry wounds.

Blood, rendered ink-dark by the video recording, gushes down the front of Calvin's housecoat and he pitches on to the table, shuddering. His killer doesn't leave, not straight away. The intruder stands over him, watching until there is no question that the man is dead.

Lightning flashes again as the bloodied figure moves to the exit. The camera catches their face, and it is clear, recognizable.

A woman in her thirties with ash-pale skin and henna-red hair, her eyes hollow and predatory.


With Assim working backup from the jet, Marc dove into a search across the US Department of Justice database and records from Florida law enforcement that were two decades old.

Behind him, while Crowne stood by silently, Lucy removed the video tape from the VCR and weighed it in her hand. "If we get this to the techs in Palo Alto, we might be able to have the images enhanced . . ." She trailed off, looking down at the scattered photographs. "Ah, hell. It was her. No question about it. Younger, but definitely Madrigal. She murdered that poor bastard in cold blood."

"Not *cold* blood," Marc corrected. "You saw what she did to him. That was hate letting go. She didn't just kill Cooper, she wanted to brutalize him, she wanted—" He stopped himself. Marc knew he was right, because he recognized that ghastly moment of violent rage. He had experienced the exact same impulse himself when loss had driven him to kill. *Like knows like*, he thought.

Lucy seemed to understand what was passing through his mind and gave him a nod. "What else have we got on this?"

He showed her. The first hits had come up straight away, from public records, newspaper articles and the like talking about the brutal attack and the police manhunt that followed. No one had ever been arrested for the crime, but the black sedan had been found in a ditch off the Florida Turnpike a week later. The vehicle had been torched, and the body of a woman the State Troopers recovered from the driver's seat had no identity that they could find. No dental records, no fingerprints. Nothing that could have indicated who she was existed in county, state or national records.

"Madrigal covering her tracks," Lucy said quietly. "Someone else died in her place."

But where things took a turn for the unusual was when Calvin Cooper's life went under the microscope. Information about the old man was sparse, in that very engineered way that only those who worked in the shadow realm of intelligence warranted. Marc knew the telltale signs when he saw them. Vague references to a past career as a "government consultant" and "embassy staff" stood out like red flags. "That's code for a non-official cover if ever I saw it," he noted. "What do you want to bet this bloke was a former spook?"

"He was," said Crowne, his manner abruptly muted.

Marc turned to look at him and saw recognition in the other man's eyes. "You knew him?"

Crowne shook his head. "Not really. I knew *of* him. I wasn't sure at first. Didn't think it was the same guy. But now . . ." He glanced at

Lucy, then reluctantly pressed on. "At Langley. There was a Cal Cooper who served as an instructor out at the Farm, for a while. Old guy, probably taught hundreds of trainees over the years." He indicated the video tape. "That could be him."

"The Farm" was Central Intelligence Agency shorthand for the organization's training facility at Camp Peary, in the woodlands near Williamsburg. Within the base's walls, trainees were subjected to a regimen of intensive physical and mental challenges designed to hone their skills for eventual deployment in the field, and the CIA often seconded veteran field agents to teaching duties there. Marc had gone through the MI6 equivalent of the program at Fort Monckton in Hampshire, after his recruitment into the British intelligence service. "Go on," he prompted.

"All I know is, the man was a case officer in the '70s. Far East specialist. Word around the agency said he'd been pulled off active duty after an op went south in a bad way, and never allowed to go back." Crowne looked down.

"How does that connect to Madrigal?" said Lucy. "Did he know about her past?" She turned to Marc. "Whatever information he had, she was willing to kill for it."

"The notepad." Marc nodded. "Cooper gave her what she needed and then she disposed of him. But that wasn't a loose end getting tied off."

"It was a revenge kill," agreed Lucy.

A message window pinged open on Marc's tablet and Assim's face filled the small panel. "*Okay, I ran the file codes from that redacted document,*" he said quickly, launching in without preamble. "*They appear to be legitimate, part of the paperwork from an operation code-named Overtone that ran in the winter of 1971. Details are scarce, but the paper trail connects the CIA and the US Army to an office of, get this, the Korean Central Intelligence Agency.*"

"As in South Korea?" said Marc.

Assim's head bobbed in assent. "*Whatever Overtone was, all primary materials on it have been thoroughly scrubbed from any databases that Rubicon can access. That only happens when someone at a senior government level wants something buried deep and forgotten.*"

"Rubicon has offices in South Korea," Lucy noted. "We got any assets there we can deploy, find out more about this?"

Assim shook his head. *"I don't believe so. The KCIA doesn't even exist in that form anymore, largely because the head of the agency assassinated the country's sitting president in 1979 . . ."* He paused. *"Long story. Not relevant. The bottom line is, South Korean Intelligence has a very checkred past that nobody wants to dredge up."*

"No doubt." Lucy looked at Crowne. "So, backing up, if we put two and two together, Overtone could have been Cooper's failed operation. The time period, the location. The facts line up."

Crowne folded his arms across his chest. "You're making a lot of assumptions."

*"Respectfully,"* said Assim, *"this isn't the first time Korea has come up in recent days. We know that Ghost5 hacked a metro in Taipei to deliberately cause a head-on collision with another train—"*

"Taipei is in Taiwan, not Korea," interrupted Crowne.

Assim kept talking. *"Yes, I know, but there are rumors emerging that one of the victims of the crash was a prominent dissident from the North with a price on his head."*

"They caused a rail disaster to kill one man?" Marc was disgusted by the callous possibility.

*"There's also the fact that Horizon Integral do a lot of business in the South . . ."* Assim paused, losing momentum. *"It's another connection."*

Marc leaned over the pool table, staring at the papers. "All right. Keep digging, get back to us if you find anything else." He tapped the video window on the tablet and it folded closed. Marc released a breath and pinched the bridge of his nose. "Shit, for every piece of intel we find, we get a dozen more unanswered questions!"

"Then we need to step back and refocus," said Lucy. "We're going at this the wrong way. Ever since that bomb in San Francisco, since the dead guy in Malta, we've been running to catch up and failing. Face it, Madrigal is ahead of us! She's a game-player, right?" She looked to Marc for confirmation and received a slow nod in return. "She has that whole chess master *ten-moves-ahead* bullshit down pat. So how about we stop wasting our energy trying to get out in front of her and attack this the other way?"

"Slow her down," said Crowne, following Lucy's reasoning. "How do you propose to do that?"

"The fly likes honey." Lucy gestured toward Marc. "Hite already got us what we need, right?" She laid the tip of a long finger on the pile of old photographs.

He saw where she was heading. "We make Madrigal come to us. She has a serious fixation on keeping her identity concealed. All this stuff would be irresistible for her. If we use it to draw Madrigal out into the open—"

"We can take her," Lucy concluded. "Cut off the head of Ghost5 before they do any more damage."

Marc nodded to himself. "It could work. And odds are good she'd come in person. This isn't the kind of material Madrigal would trust to anyone else."

"To be clear," said Crowne, "it sounds like you're asking me to be party to what amounts to an illegal rendition."

"Your job is to protect the interests of Horizon Integral, yeah?" said Marc. "Madrigal is holding your company hostage as long as she has those zero-day exploits in her possession. It's only a matter of time before someone figures out that the Sigma software is the common denominator in all the attacks. When that happens, the company stocks will tank. So your window of opportunity to deal with this problem is swiftly closing."

"Unless, of course, you wanna wait to see what she'll do?" Lucy went in for the coup de grace. "Those other hacks were the warm-up. I guarantee you whatever comes next will be a show-stopper."

Crowne was silent for a long moment before he finally replied. "I'll need to talk to Wehmeyer."

Lucy waved him away. "Do what you have to." She watched him walk to a windowed door that opened out on to a sun deck, and step through, dialing a number on his smartphone. When the door clicked shut behind him, she turned back to Marc. "Before you say anything, *I know*. I know this play is a gamble."

"No argument there," he agreed. "But our other options are thin on the ground. And you know me, I like to roll the dice." Marc considered the most expedient approach. "I can put out a message to a few trading hubs on the dark web. Drop some hints. We get Crowne to front it. Pretend he was Hite's partner. Ask for a load of money and threaten to go public. She'll bite."

Lucy gave a harsh snort of derision. "Laughing boy out there is never gonna go for that." Then a darker mood clouded her expression. "But suppose he does. Let's say we do get our hands on Madrigal. What has to come next, you sure you're up for that?"

"Madrigal's a pragmatist," said Marc. He knew exactly what Lucy was suggesting. "She'll make a deal."

Lucy raised an eyebrow. "Think so? In my experience, the ones who think they have their emotions in check are really just burying them deeper than the rest of us. When that comes to the surface . . ." She frowned. "You said it yourself. We saw what she did to Cooper. You have to know that wasn't the action of a rational person. Even with all the years that have passed, someone who stabbed an old man a half-dozen times isn't likely to go easy."

Marc found he didn't have an answer for that.

The door creaked open again, letting in the early evening breeze. Outside, the sun had set and the sky above the garden darkened toward magenta-blue. Crowne stepped back across the threshold. "All right," he began, "Mr. Wehmeyer says I am——"

The front of the man's head erupted in a mess of bone and blood as a high-velocity bullet entered the back of his neck and ripped through his skull. The horrendous crater where his face had been emitted a whine of escaping air from his lungs, and Crowne's body crashed to the floor.

*"Fucking hell!"* Marc jerked back from the grisly sight and Lucy collided with him.

She caught the familiar stink of death drifting up from the dead man's ruined body and a trigger pulled in her mind, an automatic artifact of her military training. She moved into a different means of thinking, shifting instantly to soldier-mode.

"Stay back," she hissed, pushing Marc toward the wall and out of the line of any potential follow-up shots. Lucy flattened herself against the frame of the door and dropped low, calculating that any aggressor lurking outside would be aiming at chest height. She jerked her head out across the open doorway, taking a fast mental snapshot of the gardens behind Hite's house before pulling quickly back into cover. The image was a jumble of impressions. Blackness and long shadows in the fading evening light. Had she imagined that brief instance of motion in the trees, the glitter of reflected light off a targeting scope?

"Anything?" Marc whispered.

"We got at least one shooter with a high-powered rifle. And if there's one, there's more than one."

Marc grimly dragged Crowne's corpse toward him, and patted him down. "He doesn't have a weapon."

Lucy swallowed a curse. Wehmeyer had insisted that no Rubicon representatives could be armed while working with his people on Australian soil, even with non-lethal weapons, and Solomon had agreed to the restriction. She was now regretting her decision to obey that order.

"We need to—" Marc started speaking again, and as he did every light in the house abruptly went out. The slow-moving fan hanging over the pool table spun to a halt.

"They cut the power." She scrambled over to where a telephone sat on a small side table and snatched up the receiver. The device was silent. "Landline too."

Marc glared at his smartphone. "Nothing here, either. Wireless, cellular, satellite, all negative. They must have a jammer set up nearby."

Both of them fell silent, straining to listen for the sound of an approaching enemy. From the far side of the house, Lucy heard glass breaking and a man's voice call out indistinctly.

"Ten moves ahead . . ." muttered Marc. He jabbed a finger toward the papers on the pool table. "We have to get that out of here!"

Lucy shook her head. "Forget it, we gotta move!"

"We lose those files, we lose our only edge on Ghost5," he shot back. Marc rose and kicked the garden door shut. "Give me a second . . . Keep me covered . . ."

"With what?" Lucy growled. As the Brit scrambled desperately to repack the metal attaché case with Hite's bounty of blackmail, she moved to the far door that led back to the main atrium.

She eased it open a crack and slipped through. A wordless shout from the far end of the corridor reached her. It sounded like the Samoan, the noise strangled and full of pain. More glass broke and there was another cry that echoed through the house.

In the dimness, each shadow potentially concealed an armed assassin. Lucy dashed into the cover of a wide support pillar and looked toward the front door. Through the narrow slit-windows either side of it, she could make out the shape of a large black van parked sideways across the mouth of the driveway. The path was completely blocked, and three men stood between the vehicle and the gate to the house, watching. They were dressed in dark street clothes, but their faces were hidden behind hard-shell masks that only revealed their eyes. Each one had what looked like a submachine gun in their hands, the barrels elongated with a thick sound suppressor.

She watched, waiting for them to move in, but they stood their ground. Belatedly, Lucy realized that the men by the van were there to keep the area contained. If someone broke out of the house and tried to run, their task was to gun them down.

Hite's home had the kind of structural security that someone rich and paranoid would prefer, with few points of entry and high walls around the gardens to keep out the uninvited. But that layout also meant that anyone trying to leave the grounds would be funneled out in a single direction. In this case, right into a hail of bullets.

*Sweep and clear.* Lucy understood how this was going to play out. It was a scenario she herself had frequently participated in as an aggressor, sometimes as the backstop, but more often than not as the attacking element. *Which means they're coming in through the back.*

Down the hall, a door banged open and the terrified woman in the maid's uniform came through, skidding over the tiled floor as she fled. She was gripped by total panic, her eyes wide and lost in terror. The woman caught sight of Lucy and faltered, stumbling against the wall. From her point of view, Lucy would have seemed to be a dark human shape, another threat.

Lucy opened her mouth to call out to her, but the words didn't have time to form. The clattering noise of a silenced weapon echoed and the fleeing woman jerked abruptly as a bullet struck her in the back. She collapsed against an ornamental shelf and dragged a glass lamp down with her to shatter against the tiles.

Her killer came into view, and Lucy saw a slight female figure in tactical gear holding the angular shape of a heavy pistol in both hands, the thread of an under-barrel aiming laser probing the air before it. The shooter's shoulders tensed and Lucy knew in that fraction of a second that she had been spotted.

She wasn't aware of the soldier's equation in her thoughts on a conscious level, the instinctive evaluation of risk versus reward, of one danger traded off against another. It was ingrained in her. Lucy *reacted*.

She broke from her meager cover and sprinted up the curved staircase leading to the first floor, gambling against the chance of drawing this armed killer away from Marc, putting herself in harm's way in order to buy him time to escape.

The rattling report of the silenced pistol sounded again and a large caliber round embedded itself in the wall as she ran. Lucy glimpsed movement down in the hallway as the killer came after her.


Marc heard the disturbance and held his breath, the case half-shut as he tried to close it on the papers jammed inside. Through the gap in the door he saw Lucy vanish in the direction of the stairs, and he almost ventured out after her before his caution hauled him back.

A petite, athletic woman in a black combat rig flashed past, and took the steps two at a time to race up after his partner. He saw the gun in her hands, and Marc's gut twisted.

He knew exactly what Lucy was doing. And he knew he should take full advantage of the moment, grab the case and find a way out of this place, get clear of the range of whatever frequency jammer they were using and call for help.

But the notion of leaving Lucy Keyes behind to an uncertain fate was like a ball of lead in his belly. It didn't matter that she was more than capable of defending herself, it mattered that he would be the one to exchange his safety for hers.

With all that had been taken from Marc in recent times, Lucy was one of the few people he could still count on, one of the diminishing number he considered a trusted friend. A year ago in Somalia, Marc had been torn by guilt after being forced to leave Lucy for dead on the strife-torn streets of Mogadishu. Leaving her now was making the same choice all over again.

*But she knows that*, he told himself. *Because that's the mission.*

Marc reached for the attaché case and as his fingers touched the handle, he heard the scrape of a boot on the tiles out in the hall. Someone was out there. *Another shooter.*

The half-open door to the games room began to move, slowly easing wider.

He dropped behind the pool table and held his breath, looking under the supports toward the doorway. From his low angle, Marc couldn't see the figure clearly, but he estimated it was a man, slightly below average height. Each step the intruder took was measured, slowly putting one foot in front of the other and carefully placing the weight so as to be virtually silent.

Marc turned, finding the television screen on the far wall. Reflected in the inert surface of the display, he saw the blurred form of a man in black, one hand holding a gun aimed down toward the floor, the other reaching to touch his throat.

In the near-silence, a faint buzz sounded. It could have been a voice across a radio channel, but there was no way to be sure.

The dark figure grasped the case where it still lay atop the pool table, and metal scraped on the blue baize.

Marc's hand found a cue stick hanging in a rack on the side of the table, and his fingers closed around the maple-wood shaft. The lessons of the Bosniak cop who had schooled him in a few Krav Maga techniques rang in his thoughts. *Use the environment to beat your enemy. If in doubt, use anything you can find as a weapon.* He took a breath and saw the intruder turn away, distracted by the sight of Crowne's body sprawled on the carpet.

Hesitation gave way to action, and Marc burst out of cover, swinging the cue around in a vicious crossing strike. The gunman spun back, trying to block, but the stick smacked him hard across the face and he reeled as the wood splintered.


Lucy went through the first door she saw on the next floor up and kicked it shut behind her, finding herself in a well-appointed bathroom with a big tub just short of the size of a kiddie pool. In the semi-darkness, the tiled marble space was all dull reflections and bronze mirrors, and what light there was came in through misted windows on the far wall.

She shrank into a shady corner and covered her eyes, forcing them to dark-adapt. Lucy heard the soft padding of her pursuer's approach, then an odd whispering with a metallic timbre. *Speaking on a throat mic*, she guessed, but Lucy couldn't place the language. *Asian. Not Cantonese or Mandarin.*

The woman in black kicked open the door and flowed into the room, her gun's red laser thread flickering and rebounding off the mirrors. She pivoted toward the glass door of the shower cubicle and opened it.

Lucy attacked. She bolted out of the shadows, head down and fast into a full-tilt shoulder charge. Slamming into the back of the smaller woman, the blow transferred the full energy of her assault and sent the assassin sprawling into the empty cubicle. Before the woman could recover, Lucy swatted at the shower controls and knocked them into the crimson end of the dial.

A powerful blast of searing hot water gushed from the rainfall head mounted on the ceiling of the cubicle, and the assassin emitted a piercing scream as it scalded her. Lucy fought through the natural urge to recoil from the heat, instead leaning in to put two hard punches through the water and into the other woman's torso.

She thought that would be enough to put the assassin down, but Lucy had underestimated her opponent's toughness. The woman had lost her gun in the shock of the steaming deluge, but not her resolve. She came hurtling out of the cubicle with a howl and barrelled into Lucy, clawing at her face.

Light flashed off the polished steel edges of a dagger as it slipped from a wrist-holster and into the woman's hand. Lucy jerked back as the blade slashed through the air at eye level, feeling a sting of pain as it nicked her cheek and drew blood.

The gunman struck out at Marc blindly, swatting at him with the attaché case. He wasn't fast enough to avoid it and the metal case slammed into his shoulder. The blow was hard enough to pop the latch and the contents spewed out across the floor, the old VHS tape bouncing away over the carpet.

He drew back from the blow, but the other man was already bringing his pistol to bear. Marc had no choice but to close the gap again and try to get inside his reach before he could fire.

They fell into a clumsy wrestle. The gunman had less body mass than Marc, but he was compact and muscular, and a trained killer. It was all Marc could do to keep the bulky pistol from pivoting toward his head. The gunman squeezed the trigger and the weapon bucked, firing uselessly into the ceiling. The muffled discharge of sound from the strange-looking revolver was little more than the metallic *snap-clack* of its moving parts, but he had no time to dwell on how that might have worked.

The two fighters struggled, clawing at one another as they fell against the pool table. The gunman snarled and jolted forward, clipping Marc with the flat of the firearm.

He shook off the impact, but the moment it took to react was enough for the other man to grab at his face. His opponent's gloved hand snatched at him, fingers trying to gouge his eyes, palm smothering his mouth.

Marc reacted and savagely clamped down on the webbing between thumb and forefinger, the bite crushing flesh through the material of the glove. He wrenched at it, and the gunman let out a long yelp of agony, letting go of him, giving him an opening.

Into that gap, Marc sent a series of bullet-fast piston punches, as his instructor had taught him, landing them in the softer tissues around the throat and beneath the jaw. Keeping up the momentum, with his other hand still firm around the man's wrist, he slammed the gun-hand hard against the lip of the pool table until the pistol left his opponent's grip and tumbled to the floor.

The moment the weapon was unseated, Marc gave the gunman one last shove to put him off his balance, and dove for the weapon. At the edge of his awareness, Marc sensed new motion on the far side of the room, somewhere near the door to the sun deck, but he had already committed to what would happen next.

He landed on the pistol, snatching at it as he rolled. The weapon felt dense and off-balance, and he pulled the trigger again and again as he turned toward the gunman. The hammer fell three times, the first round missing as it buried itself in the side of the pool table, the second and third hitting Marc's assailant in the thigh and the belly at close range. As before, each time he fired there was no full-throated roar, instead a smothered, tinny rattle as the heavy recoil shocked through his wrist.

The gunman crumpled with a strangled wheeze, a fatal surge of blood drenching his legs as he went down. The thigh shot had gone through the man's femoral artery, and the life gushed out of him.

Gasping for breath, Marc tried to scramble back to his feet, but there was someone behind him. Another figure in black loomed over Marc, his face craggy and hard, with the long and spear-like silhouette of a sniper rifle in his hand.

The rifle butt came down and struck Marc across the head, lighting black fires across his vision, sending him sprawling.


The fight spilled out of the bathroom and back on to the first-floor landing.

Lucy was on the defensive, drawing back with each advance the other woman made. She was smaller and she didn't have Lucy's reach, but the wicked length of the assassin's combat dagger gave her an edge that Lucy did not want to test.

As they moved through the spin and the dance of it, she caught glimpses of her opponent's face in the shafts of weak illumination that spilled in through the windows. The assassin was East Asian, which connected with the language Lucy had heard her speaking, and she could see the woman's throat-mic comm unit around her slender neck. Her face was reddish-pink down one side where the shower had scalded her, and her hair was cut short enough to suggest someone with a soldier's habits.

The equipment and the angry focus in her eyes seemed to back up that last detail. Lucy wasn't facing some hired hand or local talent gun-thug. This woman was military trained. But that she could exploit.

She was losing room to maneuver, backing toward the bannister around the edge of the landing. A slow ache from the bandage around her leg threatened to put a drag on her speed, and she tried to ignore it.

Lucy faked a stumble and left a small opening to see what it would get her. The assassin swallowed the bait without hesitation, following the line of her training to make a fast, hard kill whenever the opportunity presented itself.

She stabbed forward with the dagger, but the exposed flank the assassin was targeting was abruptly gone.

Lucy stepped into the motion and trapped the woman's arm before she could withdraw, twisting it cleanly below the elbow, tearing the knife out of her hand in the same motion. The joint dislocated with a wet click and the assassin bit back a bitter shriek of pain. Lucy kicked the other woman hard across the knee and sent her sprawling.

Rocking off her heels, she rolled the knife around to get a feel for it, and pitched forward, ready to go in and finish the job.

Behind her, part of the wooden bannister exploded into splinters and she was knocked off-kilter, flinching at this new attack.

Turning, Lucy saw another figure, a man in black tactical gear working the slide of a long rifle to load a fresh round, bringing it to bear on her.

"No!" The shout came from the other side of the atrium. "We need that one alive as well!"

Lucy knew the voice. Her knuckles tightened around the hilt of

the stolen combat dagger as a familiar figure came into view, followed by two of the masked men dragging a semi-conscious Marc
between them. Her heart sank, but then the emotion drowned in a
flood of new fury.

"*Kara*," she spat, turning the woman's name into a curse. "You
fucking bitch."

# — THIRTEEN —

The blur of pain that packed Marc's head pulsed like a living thing as he felt muscular hands drag him into the back of a vehicle and dump him on the metal deck. Sounds muffled by the singing of blood in his ears slowly began to re-form into human voices and he heard the grumble of an engine starting up. There was a strong scent, like gas. *Is that real, or am I imagining it?* He remembered someone once telling him that people who suffered brain damage smelled odors that weren't there. And the man with the rifle had hit him very hard.

The metal pressing against his face vibrated and the vehicle lurched into motion. Dragging himself back to awareness seemed to take forever. The needles of agony in his skull and the sickly pressure in his gut ebbed, but only a little. His hands were heavy and leaden, secured together by a tight plastic band.

He flashed back to the blow that had knocked the sense out of him, back in Hite's games room. *Is this what a concussion feels like?* The thought failed to connect to anything and faded away.

It took all his effort to roll on to his side. The first thing his eyes focused on was the metal attaché case, sitting on its narrow axis between a pair of booted feet. Marc's gaze climbed up the body of the person minding the case and fixed on hate-filled eyes boring back into him. A slight oriental woman in combat gear, with one arm in a makeshift sling, glared at Marc with undisguised animosity. She wanted to kill him; it was written all over her face.

A flash of yellow-orange blinked through the rear windows of the van, making the woman look up. An instant later, the sound of an explosion rumbled over them.

Someone up front gave an order, and the van increased speed, putting more distance between them and the detonation. Marc thought about the smell of gas. Was that how they were covering their tracks? He pictured Hite's expensive clifftop home going up in a ball of flames. It would look like an accident at first, at least until someone examined whatever corpses were dragged out of the building.

That thought jolted him with a flood of cold dread. He looked around, ignoring the sparks of pain the movement generated, searching the van's shadowy interior. He saw masked men with guns, and then relief hit as he spotted Lucy sitting across the way. She bled from an unattended cut on her cheek and her hands were bound with plastic cable ties, the same kind that held Marc's wrists together. The moment didn't last long.

She met his gaze and gave him a rueful nod that communicated a wealth of unspoken information. *We're in the shit all over again*, it said.

"This feels . . . familiar," Marc said thickly.

"They killed everyone else," Lucy replied, breaking eye contact. "Shot them in the back as they tried to run. Executed them."

Belatedly, Marc realized that there was no sign of the Samoan security guard or the house staff in the van with them.

"That's what Ghost5 have become, right?" Lucy asked the question of someone sitting across from her, and Marc shifted so he could see who she was speaking to. "They destroy the lives of innocent people without remorse. And for what?"

Kara Wei leaned out of the shadows and studied him, ignoring Lucy's words. "Sorry, Dane," she said, with a shake of the head. "You should have stayed out of it."

For a moment, the piercing pain in Marc's skull was forgotten, overcome by his surprise at seeing her here. "What have you done?" He blurted out the question. He wanted to know why she had deceived Rubicon, why she had deceived *him*. "I don't understand why you're part of this."

Kara cocked her head and studied him, as if Marc's words were being delivered in some alien language she couldn't decode.

His perception of her changed, like that optical illusion that could be a vase or two faces, the form shifting from one image to another.

Marc knew her face and her name and he thought he had known *her*, but now the young woman in the red leather jacket was a complete stranger to him, and he wondered for a moment if the blow to his head had knocked something loose in there.

Kara's expression was *wrong*, in a way he couldn't put into words. Almost as if she were wearing it as a painted-on mask. It was fake, like the new identity Rubicon had given her.

Then his brain caught up to what he was perceiving. No, it wasn't that Kara Wei had become a different person. She was actually showing Marc who she really was. *This isn't her mask*, he thought, *this is the truth. The mask was who she pretended to be around us.*

"There's nothing I can do for you now," Kara told him. "What happens next will be out of my hands."

"When I get free," said Lucy, her voice loaded with menace. "You're gonna regret it."

Kara looked up at her. "You shouldn't be angry that you trusted me. It's not your fault. It's what I had to do to survive." The words were delivered in a flat monotone, and Marc felt his friend's bland admission of her betrayal like a void in his chest.

"Were you ever one of us?" Lucy demanded.

"I've never been one of anything," Kara said bleakly, her tone hardening as she gestured to one of the masked gunmen. "Get him off the floor."

Hands pulled at Marc's arms and hauled him up on to one of the benches welded to the interior wall of the van. A gunman shoved him into a sitting position across from the woman with the broken arm, who continued to glare hatefully at him.

"What's her problem?" said Marc, with a jut of the chin.

Kara indicated a black body bag lying near the rear doors. "You shot her comrade. I guess she's not real happy about it."

"Oh. Yeah." Marc's throat turned arid as he remembered the weight of the silenced pistol in his hand. "He didn't give me much of a choice."

"No more talking," said Kara, as sirens sounded up ahead of them.

Crimson strobes pulsed through the interior of the van as they passed fire and emergency vehicles racing the other way, and Marc tried to crane his neck for a look out through the cab of the vehicle, but the gunman at his side shoved him back into his seat and prodded him in the chest with a silenced Micro Uzi. "Stay," he grated.

Marc admitted defeat, for the moment, and hung his head. He marked the passage of the drive by mapping where he was bruised or sore, gauging the pain, trying to put it out of his mind.

His jacket had been ripped in places, the lining showing through on the shoulder and around the pockets. When he had been semiconscious, they must have searched him for weapons and kit, swept him for trackers. He couldn't feel the weight of his spyPhone in his pocket, and there was no sign of his computer tablet or backpack.

It was smart operational security for his abductors. The phones, the ear-bead comms, the tablet, anything that had been tagged with a GPS locator that Rubicon could activate, was gone. The only thing still in place was the familiar weight of the careworn dive watch on his wrist. Marc glanced at the luminous hands on the Cabot's face and watched the minutes tick away. He wondered how long it would be before Solomon and Wehmeyer learned about the explosion at Hite's house. *What would they do next?*

The van drove on in silence for almost an hour, before making a sharp turn into an area lit by bright overhead floods. Marc heard the sounds of jet engines and guessed that they were entering the grounds of Sydney Airport. No other airstrips were close enough to reach in so short a time.

He gave Lucy a sideways glance and she silently met his gaze. She had to be thinking the same as him. Out on the eastern side of the runways, Ekko Solomon's private A340 airliner sat parked among the other business jets, having flown the team in from France less than forty-eight hours ago. But surrounded by armed thugs, there was no way Marc and Lucy would be able to get free and make it back to the Rubicon aircraft, and no way to alert Assim and the others on board that they were close at hand.

The van passed through an entry gate without stopping, which boded poorly for the two of them. That meant that Ghost5 had already bypassed airport security, and a chilling possibility rose in his thoughts.

What if Sydney was the next target for the Arquebus software weapon? What if they had taken over the air-traffic control system or hacked the autopilots of a dozen jetliners? The horrifying potential for mass destruction was sobering.

He looked back at Kara, trying once again to reach the woman he thought he had known. "Do you care that innocent people have died because of Madrigal?" He saw a brief flicker of reaction as he used the criminal hacker's alias. "Or are you incapable of that?"

"You don't know anything about me," she replied, her tone even.

"On that point, we agree," he said. "The Kara Wei I knew wouldn't be involved in this."

"That person doesn't exist," said the woman. "She's a phantom you made the mistake of thinking was real."

The van slowed and jolted as it bounced on to a wide ramp, and Marc caught a glimpse of a cavernous metal tunnel yawning open around them. They were driving up into the back of a huge cargo aircraft, the white flanks of the fuselage briefly visible through the windscreen. Once inside, the vehicle halted and behind them heavy pistons ground into motion as massive doors swung slowly shut.

"Out," ordered the gunman, prodding Marc again with the Uzi.

Lucy stepped down on to the deck of the cargo plane in time to see the clamshell doors at the rear of the aircraft come together with a thud. The black van was nestled up against one side of the interior, a space wide enough to incorporate two vehicles side by side and still have room to spare. In the past, she'd ridden on board the USAF's giant C-5 Galaxy transporters, but this was bigger even than those monster jets. The cargo bay extended up and away, the curved walls covered with orange-brown thermal quilting to retain heat and dampen vibrations. Toward the nose, she saw that the interior had been modified with converted cargo containers slotted into place. Complex webs of cables festooned the walls, leading to and from heavy pods of hardware that had a distinctly military look to their design. The air inside here smelled like ozone and jet fuel.

Up ahead, a handful of people—all of them dressed like they

should have been at a rock club or a *World of Warcraft* tournament—
were in the process of setting up portable computers and communications gear.

While he was distracted by removing his combat mask, Lucy
risked taking a step away from the gunman acting as her chaperone,
trying to get a look through a porthole in the fuselage. She saw the
red flashing strobe of a landing light off the end of a broad, high
wing, from which hung a pair of massive jet engines. An AvGas
tanker nestled under one of them, the elephant trunk of a fuel pipe
disappearing up into a service port.

"A *Ruslan*," said Marc, from behind her.

"Say what?"

"This is an An-124," he explained. "Biggest military transport plane
on Earth. I have to wonder how Ghost5 got their hands on one."

"We bought it," said a new voice, the clipped edges of the words
betraying a German accent and a forbidding attitude. Lucy turned to
see a dark-skinned guy with a hard but handsome face and searching eyes approach from the front of the jet. Without the arrogance
that followed him like a cloud of smoke, the man might have actually
been her type, but he could barely speak to them without letting a
sneer into every word. "From the Libyans."

"Let me guess," said Marc. "A day later, you stole the money back
from their Swiss bank accounts."

Lucy heard a woman chuckle. "No. We do have some standards."
The words had the same cadence she'd heard in the parking garage
in San Francisco, only without the digital filtering to mask the voice
beneath. A figure in a rumpled leather jacket over a black hoodie
stepped into view and long-fingered hands came up to roll back
the dark material. Lucy saw henna-red hair and a face that would
have fitted some Hollywood character actress at the top of her game.
It was the same face she had seen on the old video tape, but with
twenty more years of wear and tear written across it. "Here you are,"
she said, looking Lucy over and then giving the same treatment to
Marc. "This is a rare opportunity for me. I don't often get to meet the
people who pursue me in the real world, not face to face." Madrigal
smiled like she knew the win was hers.

Marc mirrored the woman's slow grin. He recognized her too. "Marie Stone," he said, enunciating the words loudly and clearly. "I thought you'd be taller."

Despite all of her self-control, Madrigal couldn't prevent a momentary flash of annoyance from crossing her expression as Marc tossed out her real name. She covered it quickly, but now there was real flint in her eyes. "You've heard that old saying about how a little knowledge can be dangerous?"

"Oh, I know a lot," he went on, determined to twist the knife while he still had the chance. "Especially about you, Marie."

"I doubt that."

"No, really." Marc shook his head. "Your friend Chuck over at Horizon Integral was more paranoid than you gave him credit for, I reckon. He put a lot of time and money into finding out about you. I suppose that alone was a good enough reason for you to have him killed." The last sentence he said loudly, so that some of the other Ghost5 hacker crew heard him. They paused, more of them turning to see how it was going to play out. Marc made a twitching motion, mimicking the effect of being electrocuted. "*Bzzzt.* Nasty way to go."

Madrigal's neutral expression hardened into solidity, and Lucy knew he had scored another point. But as much as she liked that, if Marc kept it up it would get him killed. The Brit never did seem to know when to keep his goddamn mouth shut.

"Speaking of which," Madrigal said, after a moment. She reached out with a hand. One of the shooters from the house, the woman whose arm Lucy had dislocated, approached and passed her Hite's blackmail case before backing off again. The other shooter, the older guy who had most likely put the kill-shot into Crowne, stood nearby and watched in stoic silence. "I want to thank you for finding this for me," Madrigal added. "There are a few things I've missed over the years. This will help to cover some of those gaps."

She opened the case and there was a strange light in her eyes as she fingered the photos and the papers. Lucy couldn't read the expression. It might have been sorrow, anger, happiness, or some conflicted mix of all three.

"I knew someone had been looking into our operations," continued the woman. "Imagine my surprise when I discovered who it was. The Rubicon Group. Ekko Solomon's private vigilante brigade. Luckily for me, I recently reconnected with someone who is very familiar with the—what does he call it? The Special Conditions Division." She inclined her head toward Kara.

Lucy realized she was holding her breath, and her jaw set. As much as she didn't want to admit it, like Marc, she had held on to a thin thread of hope that Kara wasn't the traitor she appeared to be.

That thread was severed. "The Englishman is Marc Dane," said Kara, her tone blunt and matter-of-fact. "He's the one the drone got a shot of."

"Former British Intelligence officer with K Section, MI6," said Madrigal, watching Marc's reaction. "Yes, I've been told a lot about you. Your own side kicked you out when you lost your strike team in a terrorist ambush. You're skilled and you're clever, but you have poor impulse control. It gets you into trouble."

Lucy had no doubt who had supplied that information, and she glared at Kara as her former comrade took her cue from Madrigal. "That one was with US Army Special Forces before they threw her in the stockade for trying to kill her commanding officer. When she escaped from prison, she wound up working for Rubicon. Her name is Lucy Keyes. She's a recon-sniper specialist."

Lucy felt Marc's eyes on her, but she didn't meet his gaze. There were details of her past he didn't know, and this wasn't how she wanted him to find out about them. She stared fixedly at Kara. Any lasting doubts about the woman's intentions were long gone now.

"A spy and an assassin," said Madrigal. She indicated the man standing next to her. "Erik here thinks I should wait until we're up over the ocean and throw you both out, along with this . . ." She held up the attaché case. "I am considering it." Slowly, deliberately, Madrigal reached under her jacket and her hand came back holding a small-frame Taurus semi-automatic. She turned the pistol in her grip so that she was holding the weapon by the barrel, offering it like a gift to the other woman. "Maybe you should do it for me, Song?" She made a face. "Sorry. I keep forgetting. *Kara.*"

"I won't kill anyone," said Kara, after a long moment. Her face betrayed no emotion of any kind.

Madrigal let the words hang for a few beats, before she replied. "Of course not." She smiled again, putting the pistol away. "We have people to do that for us." She nodded at the older shooter and he came forward, grabbing Marc's arm to drag him off.

Lucy felt a gun muzzle jab her in the small of the back. "Move," said Erik, prodding her forward.


Marc had known they were in a lot of trouble when the shooters had dragged him and Lucy out of the house. Keeping them alive opened up a whole raft of nasty possibilities that he didn't want to think too hard about.

Madrigal clearly relished her chance to lord it over the two of them, and that fitted what he knew of the secretive hacker's modus operandi. She liked the feel of control over others, the power of life and death at the push of a button. Charles Hite had fallen victim to that, and now Marc expected a similar fate awaited the Rubicon operatives.

Anyone else would have shot them and left their bodies to burn in the house. Madrigal wanted something from them. If Marc could figure out what it was, use that as an edge . . . He winced from the pain in his skull. The headache made it hard for him to think clearly.

He looked around as the man with the rifle marched him up the plane. The big Antonov cargo carrier had been converted into a kind of mobile hacker hub, and he had to admit it was a smart play. The jet could travel relatively incognito, put down at any major airport, and the Ghost5 crew would only need to patch into the local internet nodes to start making trouble. In fact, with enough fuel on board they could stay airborne for hours at a time and use satellite links to do the same.

He had wary looks from the black hats as he passed them by. They were setting up, bringing their machines on line, booting up laptops and custom computer rigs. Whatever Madrigal planned to do next, he had the sense that it was going to begin soon.

Marc's gaze raked over the computer gear, picking out the elements he could recognize from a distance, and then he spotted the communications hardware racked against the wall of the cargo bay. It was a military kit, but not of Western manufacture. On board a jet built in the Ukraine by way of the Libyan government, he expected to see Russian-made gear, but the equipment retrofitted into the hull was from somewhere else. He struggled to place it, slowing his walk.

"Move along," snapped the man with the rifle, and gave Marc a shove. He spun to glare back at his captor and out of nowhere the answer hit him. He was literally staring it right in the face.

"Korean," said Marc.

"What?" said the man, his hands tightening around the rifle.

Like the woman with the busted arm, like the masked men in the van, the shooter was East Asian. But he wasn't Chinese or Japanese. The more Marc studied him, the more he became certain of it. "From the North," he said firmly, and glared at Madrigal as the woman walked up behind them. "That's how you've been able to float this whole gig. There's only so far you could go as a non-state actor. So you reached out to Pyongyang and did what? Made a deal?" He waved at the communications gear. "They gave you hardware and manpower. And you give them a new weapon for the digital war."

"That's an interesting theory," Madrigal said airily. "But Ghost5 don't work with governments. It isn't who we are." The last few words were addressed not toward Marc, but more for the rest of her team, who watched the confrontation with guarded interest. "Fox and Cat here are with another interested party, one that is aligned with our current aims. That's all."

"Bollocks," Marc retorted.

His mind raced as he tried to mentally rearrange the fragments of information that had bombarded him over the last few days. Assim's mention of the Korean connection to the Taipei train crash, the murder of the old CIA case officer, the redacted file on Operation Overtone, and now the identity of the shooters and the equipment on the jet. It was all pointing in the same direction.

He had nothing to lose, so he threw the only logical possibility in Madrigal's face. "All those other attacks were you field-testing the

Arquebus software and the zero days you bought from Hite." He shook his head. "I thought you were here to hit Sydney, but that's not the mark. You're going to target *Seoul*." Marc's thoughts unspooled as he said them aloud. He remembered what Wehmeyer had said about the South Korean capital. "Half that city's critical infrastructure runs on the HIOS Sigma codebase. What better target is there for the North than that? Tell me I'm wrong."

"What we do," Madrigal said coldly, "is teach the rich and the powerful a lesson. Corporations and governments, we make them fear and respect their citizens, not treat them like cattle. We are justice coming to claim its due. And there are a lot of people that deserve to learn that lesson the hard way."

"Like the passengers on the trains in Taipei?" Marc threw the retort back at her. "The people in those cars in Germany? Or the ones who nearly got blown apart in San Francisco? Did they deserve it?" He shook his head bitterly. "You're lying," Marc told her. He knew it instinctively. Staring into Madrigal's icy gaze, he glimpsed the ghost of the truth and seized upon it. "You're lying to yourself and your own people." He gestured at the other hackers. "And not only about who you've got them into bed with." Marc tried to take a step forward, but the man Madrigal had called Fox grabbed his arm and yanked him back. "Do they know who killed Lex Wetherby? Do they know the real reason you're doing this? It's not about justice, *Marie*. It's about just *you*."

"That's clever," she said. "We'll see how that works out for you." Madrigal shot Erik a look and he gave Lucy another shove.

Marc moved of his own accord, not wanting to invite another blow from the man with the rifle, who eyed him with renewed suspicion. "You talk too much," offered Fox.

"It's been said," Marc replied.

As they reached the front of the aircraft, Marc expected to be sent up the ladder to the Antonov's crew deck above the cavernous cargo bay, but Erik gave a grave shake of the head and gestured to keep moving. "Not up there. You're going in the cooler."

Stepping around thick trunks of power and data cables leading
back to the hacker hub, Marc saw that the forward quarter of the
jet had been modified from its usual design. Most An-124's had a
mechanism that could swing up the entire nose so that cargo could
be loaded from front and back at the same time, but this aircraft was
missing that machinery. Instead, the nose section had been welded
in place and walled off into its own compartment. An airlock-style
hatch was the only way in, and Fox opened it while Erik kept his
weapon trained on Marc and Lucy.

A familiar waft of dry air and ozone smell pricked Marc's nostrils as they were marched though, and he knew what he would find
within.

The forward compartment housed the brain of the Ghost5 operation. Racks of computer servers filled the space, complex function
lights blinking along their faces, and yellow data cables coiled away
into bunches, disappearing back down the fuselage through narrow
access channels in the deck. Each server sat on a vibration-proof dais
within an armored cage, and in turn the entire server "farm" was
behind another metal barrier like a dense chain-link fence. On their
side, a small anteroom area held a monitor panel and security station.

Lucy looked around. "What the hell are we supposed to do in
here?"

Erik produced another set of zip ties. "Get comfortable. This is
your home for the next eleven hours."

Once more, Madrigal's lieutenant kept his gun trained on them
while Fox secured them to the chain-link, looping new ties around
the ones already holding their wrists together.

Marc didn't resist. The uncompromising look in Erik's eyes told
him that the man would shoot them both dead if they tried anything.
*Play for time*, he thought. "You know Madrigal's speech out there was
bullshit," said Marc. It wasn't a question. "So what are you getting
out of it? Money?" He jutted his chin at Fox. "A nice medal from the
Dear Leader? Or does Madrigal have something on you?"

A nerve twitched in Erik's jaw and he knew he'd touched on the
truth. "Is this the moment where you try to make me a better offer?"

He showed his teeth. "Despite what you may think, your patron Solomon cannot throw his money around to make us go away."

"So you're the loyal kind, huh?" said Lucy, backing up Marc's play. "Is that why Wetherby got smoked? Because he wasn't loyal *enough*?" She glared at Fox as he secured her. "And you . . . that was a tough shot, hitting a moving target like that from range. I bet you didn't even break a sweat killing Crowne back at the house."

Fox spared her a look, and then stepped away. "You are the same as him," he said, nodding at Marc. "You talk too much."

"Wetherby is dead because he was weak." Erik offered the comment, ending the conversation as the two armed men went back through the airlock hatch. "He got what he deserved."

The door thudded shut and Marc waited for the hiss of the pressure seal before he turned back to Lucy. "Okay. Once we're off the ground, our options narrow considerably . . ."

"Copy that." Lucy made a face. "Shit, is it getting colder in here?"

"And dry too." Marc nodded toward the server farm, where air ducts in the ceiling of the retrofitted compartment were visible. "There'll be dehumidifiers up there, sucking out all moisture in this room."

"Right. For the computers . . ." She nodded, looking around. "Lot less insulation in here too."

"It's set up to cool the equipment. Servers generate a lot of heat when they're running, and overclocked custom rigs like these even more so." He glanced at her. "They probably have vents to draw in cold outside air when the jet is at altitude, to keep the temperature down."

"Can we mess with that?" As usual, Lucy immediately went for the option that would cause the most trouble.

"Not from here." Marc eyed her. "And not while we're trussed up." He paused. "You know why Madrigal's keeping us around, yeah?"

"She doesn't strike me as the type to miss an opportunity. She wants to know more about Rubicon and the SCD." Lucy's brow furrowed in concentration as she tested the play in the zip ties. "You heard what she said. Most people who go after her don't get as close as we have. She'll want to stop that from happening again. Know what we know."

Marc shook his head and shifted his weight. "There's more to it than that." He tried to lean out in the direction of the control panel on the opposite side of the compartment, but it was way beyond his reach. "Hackers like Madrigal, they look at the world the same way they look at computer code. As a thing they can exploit, re-program or crash."

"Rubicon is on Ghost5's target list," said Lucy, her tone turning acid. "That's a given. She's had her own personal Trojan horse inside our firewalls for years."

There was little he could say that wouldn't fan the fire of Lucy's anger on that front, so Marc let the comment pass. "So now our plan to draw out Madrigal has gone totally and utterly into the shitter, we need to figure out what the hell we do next."

"I'm thinking I wait for them to come interrogate me, and kill whoever the fuck they send," Lucy said flatly. "Then drop this jet into the sea as an encore."

"Or," Marc began, drawing out the word. "We try something with a smaller percentage chance of fatality for both of us."

She gave him a sideways look. "I'm listening."

Assim looked at the jerky video displayed on the monitor screen hanging from the wall of the conference room, and his heart sank. The inferno that ripped through Charles Hite's house was now under control, and the local firefighters visible in the shot were spraying water to damp down the blackened ruin. Framed against the dark sky, blue strobes flashed off cascades of broken glass, the collapsed walls and fallen gates bordering the house. The pattern of destruction matched what eyewitnesses had reported to the emergency services. Hite's home had gone up in a catastrophic gas explosion that had been heard clear across the bay.

The point of view shifted, passing behind the bulky shape of a fire rescue truck liveried in red and yellow checkerboard, to reframe on a group of paramedics dealing with the victims of the fire.

*"Do you see this?"* Malte's voice was low in Assim's earpiece, re-layed over the encrypted network to the Rubicon jet and to Ekko Solomon's private phone. Solomon was still in the city, watching the same footage on a screen in the office of Horizon Integral's CEO. *"They are bringing out the dead."*

One by one, the paramedics loaded an ambulance with five black body bags, before slamming the doors and sending the vehicle on its way. The camera view moved, tracking the ambulance as it pulled out.

"Should we follow?" said Assim.

*"No."* Solomon sounded distant and fatigued. *"There were three staff at the house. Crowne brought his driver with Mr. Dane and Ms. Keyes. Remain close to the site . . . in case others are found. We need to be cer-tain."*

Assim's eyes dropped to the laptop in front of him. The computer's screen showed several data panels, each pertaining to elements of the Special Condition Division's communications network. The indicators for Lucy and Marc's personal tracking devices were dark. The track-ers were resilient, he reflected, but not enough to survive the heart of a firestorm. "It's going to be days before we can get access to any evi-dence gathered by the New South Wales police," he added. "How are we going to proceed?"

*"This was not an accident,"* Malte insisted. *"Someone will have seen them entering or leaving."* At the corner of the image, a police offi-cer started walking in the observer's direction, and the camera view abruptly cut out as Malte palmed his spyPhone and moved away.

*"Investigate,"* said Solomon. *"But be careful."*

*"Affirmative,"* came the Finn's reply, and he disconnected from the group conversation.

*"All other efforts should be applied to the data recovered from the com-puter in Hite's office,"* continued Solomon. *"Contact Henri if you require anything more."*

Assim reached for something to say, something to express his regret, but the words seemed trite and thoughtless. Then Solomon cut the call and he was left there alone, staring at the blank screen.

He minimized the comm display and went back to a subroutine

that had been quietly running in the background. Henri Delancort had made certain that a data image of Hite's office hard drive had been copied to Rubicon's secure cloud servers, and a few hours ago Assim set a complex search program running through the volume of information.

The program was a mesh of heuristic learning algorithms that, given the correct clues to follow, could piece together disparate bits of computer metadata to recover deleted files and work back through blinds to follow hidden email trails. If Hite had ever been complacent enough to use his office machine in his dealings with Ghost5, the search program would sniff it out. But there was nothing Assim could do to help speed it along. It would take as long as it would take.

They nicknamed the software "the bloodhound"; both Marc Dane and Kara Wei had helped to write it. Assim watched the agonizingly slow pace of the program's progress bar and thought of the two of them, both lost now.

A sense of raw, powerful dejection followed, and abruptly Assim wanted very badly to be out of this room and away from the grinding inaction of his role. He let that impulse propel him up and out of his chair, through the door and down the corridors of Solomon's jetliner. Grabbing his jacket, he pushed past the broad-shouldered bodyguard standing sentinel at the aircraft's open hatch and took the steps down the mobile jetway two at a time, until he was standing on the tarmac.

Long past sunset now, the airport was still busy with jets taking off and taxiing past toward the main buildings. Assim saw the bright glow of the terminal across the way, and the aircraft rolling past the apron where the big private jet was parked, without really being aware of them. He was too deep in his own thoughts for anything else.

*I'm not ready for this.* The words kept turning around in his mind, and like he always did, Assim fell back on bad habits when things slipped out of his control. He dug in a pocket for a pack of cigarettes and a lighter. He'd given up twice this year, but every time he needed to steady his nerves, he went back to them.

He had the cigarette between his lips when a shout reached him. "Hey! What the bloody hell do you think you're doing, mate?" One of the airport's safety crew, a woman in a bright-orange visibility vest, marched swiftly over to him and plucked the cigarette out of his mouth before he could react. "*No. Smoking.*" She grated, saying the words slowly and loudly. "Do that indoors or not at all, right?"

"Oh." He nodded profusely. "Sorry. Sorry. I wasn't thinking."

"That smell in the air is jet fuel," she added, prodding him in the chest to underline her point. "You want to end up burned to a crisp, that's your lookout, but don't put the rest of us in danger!"

"Yes. Sorry." Visions of blackened corpses and body bags filled his mind's eye. "I've had a really bad day."

The woman must have seen the truth in his expression and her manner softened a little. "Be careful—"

A deep, echoing drone drowned out the rest of her words, pulling Assim's attention toward the departure runway. He saw two dazzling points of white from the lights along the bottom of a huge cylindrical fuselage, as a massive cargo jet clawed its way off the ground and into the night sky. It was the biggest thing with two wings that he had ever seen, and the aircraft's quartet of engines emitted a steady, metallic howl that briefly rose into a shriek as it passed over them.

Then it was gone, a fading black shadow blending into the darkness.

# — FOURTEEN —

When the Antonov reached cruising altitude and the green light pinged on to indicate they could move freely around the aircraft, Kara wasted no time in shrugging off her seatbelt and making her way down to the cargo plane's lower deck.

Pyne followed closely behind, giving her a distrustful, sideways look. "This is not a good idea," she said, pitching her voice to be heard over the steady rumble of the engines.

"I didn't ask for your opinion," Kara replied. She glanced around, making sure there was no sign of Erik, or anyone who would go running to Madrigal if they saw her.

"But you did ask for my help," Pyne noted, pulling the baggy, shapeless mass of the woolen jumper she wore around her skinny form. "I can just walk away . . ."

They halted in front of the hatch to the server compartment and Kara studied the magnetic lock. "Fine. Then don't give it. I can get this open myself."

"Yeah, but how long would it take you?" The girl played with the closure-ring piercing at the corner of her lip. "Why do you even want to talk to them?" Pyne's nose wrinkled, like she smelled something bad. "After what they did to Lex?"

"What *they* did?" echoed Kara.

"Madrigal said the black woman is the one who shot him."

Kara glanced at her. "Do you believe that?"

Pyne gave Kara a blank look. "Okay. Listen. You've been out for a while, so I'll let that slide. But seriously, Song. You need to get with the program. You gotta deal." She showed her teeth in a grin. "We got the band back together. You know what means? The whole fucking internet should be shitting itself!"

She sighed. "If you know the code, open the door. Otherwise, go away."

"Don't have to be nasty about it," Pyne scowled, and leaned in to tap out a string of numbers. "There. And screw you."

The red light on the mag-lock turned blue and Kara twisted the handles to open the door. Inside, Marc Dane and Lucy Keyes reacted to her appearance with surprise, then annoyance. Kara glanced back at Pyne and held up a hand to make her stay on the threshold. "Keep an eye open. Tell me if anyone comes up here."

Lucy's mouth curled into an ugly snarl. "What do you want?" She shifted against the restraint holding her to the metal barrier across the compartment, and Kara knew that the woman wanted to go for her throat.

Kara's gaze moved to Marc. Where Lucy showed her fury, the Englishman looked back with sorrow. "We trusted you," he said, after a moment. "And you burned all of that . . . for what?" He indicated the plane with a tilt of the head. "For this?"

"I'm here to explain," she began, and doubt crossed the man's face. Kara looked back and saw Pyne watching her, then turned away again. "I am sorry about how this has turned out. I know you won't believe that, but it's true." She took a breath of the compartment's dry, cold air and went on. "I made a mistake. I thought I could work with Rubicon, but it wasn't right." She shook her head, cementing the truth of it in place. "Once a black hat, always a black hat."

"To hell with you, Kara . . . or Song, or whatever your name really is." Lucy spat the words back at her.

"I thought we were friends," said Marc, and the simple honesty of the statement seemed to weigh on him.

Kara gave a slow shake of her head. "I have always had trouble with that."

"So who is Kara Wei?" Marc's jaw hardened. "Someone you invented? Just a cover?"

"A cover," she repeated. "I suppose so. I was trying to be what I'm not. I don't want to do that anymore." She took a step closer, mimicking Marc's nod toward the walls around them. "This is where I fit, I think."

"What about doing the right thing?" said Marc.

Pyne gave a derisive snort, unable to hold her silence. "Hey, asshole, you work for some billionaire's mercenary mega-corporation. Anyone who makes money off other people's conflict isn't doing anything that's *right*!"

Marc eyed Kara. "You agree with that?"

"No," she replied. "The difference is, I realized I don't care. It's actually quite liberating."

The emotion, the coiled anger that had lurked behind Lucy's gaze, faded. "Let me help you with that," she said, a dark and predatory calm falling into place.

Lucy tore her wrists away from one another with a high-pitched crack of breaking plastic, as the zip-tie holding them together snapped in two.

Kara's prediction about the sniper's next act was not an error. Lucy dove at her, revealing a wad of thick black cord hidden in her hand. She snapped it out into a garrotte and looped it around Kara's throat before she could flee the compartment.

Pyne shouted in shock as Lucy drew the cord tight and choked Kara's breath from her lungs. Marc cried out for her to stop, but the dark-skinned woman ignored them both, applying steady force.

Kara tore at the cord, struggling to force air into her chest. Pyne ran from the room, and Lucy dragged Kara toward the doorway. "You fight it," she hissed into her ear, "and it won't end easy."

"Lucy!" Marc roared. "Don't do this!"

"Your boy Erik should have taken my bootlaces," Lucy explained, as the color drained out of everything and gray fog grew at the edges of Kara's vision. "Sawed through those ties in ten minutes."

"Stop," Kara choked desperately. "This is . . . is not . . ."

She heard Marc call out the other woman's name again, but the sound seemed to be coming from far away, echoing down a long, fog-filled tunnel. Then she heard the crackling of electricity and a savage scream.

The murderous tightness around her throat went away, and Kara wheezed, stumbling into the bulkhead as she gulped down painful chugs of air. Each effort was agony, but she could breathe again, and she pawed at her face, wiping away the tears of pain that streamed down her cheeks.

She heard the howling screams again and the buzz of electric discharge.

"*Bastard!*" shouted Marc.

Kara blinked as her vision cleared. Lucy lay on the deck in a quivering heap. Standing over her, Erik held a stun prod in one fist, the metal tines sparking with bright blue light. At his side was his thuggish cohort, the burly Romany German with the metalhead tattoos who called himself Null.

Null had an identical weapon in his hand, and he was generous with his use of it. He hit Lucy again and the woman let out another cry.

"You fucking cowards!" Marc tore at his restraints with all his strength, but only succeeded in shredding the skin around his wrists and drawing blood. Null crossed the compartment and jammed his prod into the Englishman's belly, giving Marc a taste of the same treatment to silence him.

"I warned Madrigal. We should have shot these two and been done with it," said Erik. He glared at Kara. "She didn't kill you. You must be stronger than you look."

Kara could only make a wheezing noise in reply. She caught sight of Pyne on the other side of the hatchway. "I had to get them," said the woman. "That bitch would have strangled you!"

Erik aimed a finger at Null. "You stay here. Watch him." Then he looked back at Kara. "As for you. From now on, keep your distance, understand?"

"What . . ." she had to force out the words, "you going to do . . . with her?"

Erik reached down and hauled Lucy to her feet. "That is not your concern," he said, dragging the stricken woman out of the compartment.

\* \* \*

After a while, the tremors in her muscles subsided and the pain in her joints dropped to a manageable level. Lucy had weathered hits from tasers more than once in her life, and she knew that as long as you could ride out the shock, it wouldn't kill you. That was the theory, anyhow, but then again there was always the outside chance that getting volted by some psycho with a cattle prod would stop your heart. She eyed the German guy as he shoved her into a metal chair bolted to the floor. He still had the stun baton in his hand, warning enough for her to know that he wouldn't hesitate to use it again.

He didn't secure her to the seat. Lucy guessed he was making the assumption she would play nice from now on. If so, then he had seriously misread her.

They were on the upper crew deck of the cargo plane, a narrow space aft of the cockpit curtained off into a handful of bunking areas and common spaces for the aircrew. This section was dimly lit by a lamp fitted to the curved wall, and the only other furniture was a second chair facing the one she was in.

The set-up was obvious. They were going to interrogate her.

Lucy looked at the floor and drew on her pre-game ritual, calling up the training she'd gone through at Camp Mackall back when she was Army Green. The instructors on her SERE course had done their best to prepare her for the worst that any enemy could throw at her, from physical abuse through to psychological torture, but there was no way to know how this situation would unfold until the punches started landing or the thumbscrews came out of the box. She focused on the hum of the Antonov's engines as she waited, clearing her mind.

Madrigal came through the curtained partition and pulled it closed behind her. She had a laptop computer open on the crook of her arm, and she took the seat across from Lucy without speaking.

Lucy watched her prop the portable computer on her knees and type rapidly. "There is data I require," said Madrigal, without looking up from the screen. "Specifically, the scope of the intelligence that Rubicon has on Ghost5's current operation. In case I need to alter any elements going forward." She stopped typing. "That's clear enough, isn't it?"

"We know everything," Lucy said lazily. Her guess about why the woman had kept them alive had been right on the money. "When you land, you're gonna find a strike team waiting for you. Want my advice? Turn this bird south and fly somewhere warm with no extradition treaty." She studied Madrigal's complexion. "Although with that skin, sister, you may want to get some sunblock first."

"If you refuse to give me the information I need, I am going to take steps to punish you for withholding it." Madrigal cocked her head as she manipulated icons on the screen. "I don't have the time to get Erik to beat it out of you. And we're not really set up for chemical interrogations here. I want you to understand that nothing you say is going to change your personal circumstances."

Lucy's lip curled. "Have you, like, not read the manual? Because that's not how threats work."

Madrigal looked up at her for the first time, long enough to deliver a smirk. "Oh, I assure you, my threats will work."

Lucy glanced up at Erik. "I've shit things more frightening than your little clan, sweetheart. You think you can scare me?" She leaned forward in her chair, and Erik stepped closer, hefting the stun baton as a mute threat. She ignored him. "What are you gonna do? Post some swears on my Twitter page? Sign me up to a million *Cat Lady Magazine* subscriptions? Fuck with my credit rating?" She made a mock-scared face.

"You have a social media feed? Huh." Madrigal took the slights in her stride. "Who knew?" She folded her hands across her chest, affecting the manner of a schoolteacher lecturing some disappointing student. "I could, given time, search out every element of your digital existence and completely obliterate it. But you're right, that doesn't matter to a person like you, who already lives on the margins. It only matters to people in the real world. Normal people. People with lives and bank accounts, jobs and mortgages. Like your brother, John."

Externally, Lucy didn't react in the slightest. She refused to give Madrigal the satisfaction of seeing it. But within, a flood of sickly cold ran through her veins and questions bombarded her. *How did she know about Johnny? Was this Kara's doing? What could they do to him?*

"Or should I call him Jasur? That's the name he took after he converted to Islam, am I right?" With a flourish, Madrigal turned the laptop's screen around to show her the scanned image of an Ohio driver's license. Lucy's brother looked back out at her, his plain face staring at nothing.

"Not much of a family resemblance," Madrigal went on. "Does he take after your father?"

"I have no idea who that is." Lucy tossed out the denial like she meant it.

The other woman seemed to consider her words. "Well. Maybe that is so. Maybe this man is some average person who isn't actually related to you in any way. Perhaps it's a coincidence that he has a little girl with a middle name the same as yours. This ordinary man, who works long hours at his ordinary job as a delivery driver so he can provide for his family. It doesn't really matter to me if he's your sibling or not. Unless you tell me what I want to know, I'm going to destroy everything he holds dear. Probably orphan his daughter into the bargain. Brother, stranger, whoever." She slowly turned the screen back around and put her hands back on the keyboard. "You can stop it happening."

"Bullshit," Lucy snapped. "You're gonna have to do better than that, Red."

Madrigal swiped down the laptop's touch-sensitive display, reading aloud. "Hmm. So the human resources file on Jasur's wife says she was passed over for a promotion at her job last month. Apparently she didn't take it well. There's probably a lot of stress in their home, wouldn't you think? And there's kid's cough medicine on their last grocery bill. The little one must be unwell." She made a sad face. "Oh, look here. The people who live in the apartment above them are on vacation for a week, but they have an internet-enabled TV. I wonder what would happen if that started switching on at full volume, at random intervals through the night. Losing sleep makes people irritable and that's a nasty combination with preexisting tension in the mix . . ."

Lucy said nothing. The stun prod hovered close to her cheek. If Erik gave her the opportunity, she would grab for it, or at least try. The muscles in her legs were still weak from the last shock she had taken. It was fifty-fifty that she would even be able to stand under her own power.

"I think a couple of hours of that will make Jasur edgy and short-tempered," continued Madrigal. "That's when a 911 call goes out to the local police department to warn them that a black man, a Muslim man, with a gun at his address, is threatening to shoot his wife and child. And it won't take much to alter the shift rotations, so that the officers on call for the SWAT team response are the ones who have had disciplinary issues, or complaints made about them engaging in racist behavior. When those cops get to Jasur's house, they'll be the kind of men who are predisposed toward shooting first and asking questions later." Madrigal paused, considering the repugnant scenario she was constructing. "We can help that along by using that internet TV to blast out sounds of gunfire when they arrive. I can't guarantee who will end up getting killed, of course, but it's not hard for me to shift the odds in the direction of the outcome I want."

"That man has done nothing to you," Lucy said, forcing herself to remain calm.

"Why are you saying that to me, as if it should matter?" Madrigal shook her head and patted the laptop. "When I'm done with this, I think I might go looking for someone else. Are your parents still alive? I imagine they'll be on some kind of medication, most people that age usually are. It won't take much to hack the prescriptions database at their local pharmacy to dispense a drug that will give them a heart attack, poison them . . ." She met Lucy's look. "All that I can do from here, from this cabin, with this computer. I won't feel a moment's guilt. Because these people are expendable when weighed against the larger goal." Madrigal's eyes glittered. "That's the way the world works. What I am doing is more important than their small lives could ever be. The information you have, that I want, is more important than them." She took a breath, her gaze never wavering. "Family is a weak point. It's an exploit." Then she seemed to realize she was showing more of herself than she wanted to, and the woman leaned back in her chair, looking toward Erik. "Lock her up again. Give her some time to think it over."

He pulled Lucy to her feet as a walkie-talkie clipped to his belt gave a squawk of static. The man snatched up the radio and growled into it. "What?"

"*Tell Madrigal to get down to the hold.*" Lucy tensed as she heard Kara's voice on the other end of the channel. "*The animals are out of their cage.*"

Madrigal took the radio from Erik's hand and spoke into it. "What are you talking about? We have the woman here. She's under control."

"*Not her,*" Kara said roughly. "*The other one.*"


Marc let a minute or two pass after Lucy was taken before he decided to make his move. He let out a groan, more real than he wanted it to be, the ill-effect of the electric shock still churning in his belly. He hunched over, pulling against the zip-tie holding his bloodied wrists to the server compartment's mesh barrier. Fixed securely at waist height, there was little room for him to move, but he could feel it starting to give.

"Oi. *Ugly!*" He glared at the tattooed thug and made a pained face. "Listen, I don't know what you did by belting me, but I think you busted up my gut. Seriously. I feel like I'm going to piss blood."

"I don't care." The thug pulled at the collar of his jacket, revealing more of the dense inking around his neck. The designs were devils, skulls and inverted crosses.

"I need to get to a bathroom." Marc grimaced in pain. "You know what I'm talking about? *Das Klo, ja?*"

"Hold it in," snorted the other man.

"Yeah, that ain't going to happen." Marc turned his back on the man and faced the barrier, with the server stacks beyond. He stretched up, pulling at his belt. "Fine. I'll take a leak over this lot, then. And you can be the one who tells Madrigal why her plane stinks like a backed-up toilet. That's if I don't short-circuit something first."

"*Nein.*" The thug rocked off his feet and came over to stop him.

Marc tucked his head forward, and when he felt the man's hand on his shoulder, he lurched in an unexpected motion. The back of Marc's skull connected with the thug's nose and the German gave a grunt of pain. Striking out blindly, Marc pushed through the cramping from his muscles and fired off a sharp downward kick that connected with the guard's knee. He howled and stumbled to the deck.

*Now or never*, Marc told himself. He jumped back and kicked at the mesh barrier, for one brief moment putting his weight against the restraint holding him up. The move would either break the bones in his wrists or snap the plastic lock on the zip-tie, and fresh jolts of pain lanced through his forearms as his body mass shifted.

The mesh deformed and the zip-tie finally gave way with a high-pitched ping. Marc couldn't arrest his fall, and he collided with the thug as the other man tried to rise, flattening him back on to the metal deck.

Marc drove his elbows into the tattooed man, striking him in the gut and the chest. The thug swore at him and swallowed a choking cough.

The stun baton lay on the deck and the two men scrambled wildly to be the first to grab it. Marc clawed at the thug's face to keep him back, and his other hand snatched up the weapon. Without hesitating, he jammed it into the man's chest and the touch-switch in the metal tines made the connection. A roiling crackle of discharge buzzed loudly in the confined space of the server room and the thug cried out. If it hadn't been for the compartment's heavy door and the constant thrumming of the Antonov's engines, someone might have heard the commotion.

Marc kept hitting him again and again, inflicting payback for the jolts that he had been given, but more for the brutality that Ghost5 had inflicted on Lucy. Finally, panting and twitchy, he relented. But it wasn't over yet.

The thug gasped for air, shivering uncontrollably as his muscles went into spasm. Marc lurched across the deck and trapped the man's throat in the crook of his knee, then pulled tight. His opponent flailed, but the shock hits had drained the resistance from him. Marc's sleeper hold was a clumsy mess, like the rest of the fight had been, but in the end it had the effect he wanted. The thug's convulsing subsided and at length he lay still.

His hands prickling, Marc pushed away from the unconscious thug and tucked the stun prod into his belt. The device's charge was almost spent, but in this situation he was reluctant to give up any kind of weapon. Searching the thug's pockets produced nothing of use, so finally he dragged the man to the door and positioned him so that his body weight would push it shut when he left.

He opened the hatch and slipped through, back into the cargo bay. The engine noise was louder out here, and most of the interior lights were off, leaving the space in patches of blackness. Marc saw a few of the Ghost5 hackers gathered in a group near their workstations. The skinny Polish girl who had been with Kara was there, talking animatedly to her comrades, but of Marc's former colleague there was no sign.

He considered his options. On an aircraft like this one, the cockpit above him would be staffed by a crew of at least three, maybe four people. Getting up there and taking control of the plane, even for a little while, would be nearly impossible. The Antonov's radio was in the same compartment too, so reaching it to call for help presented the same problem. His window of opportunity was going to last exactly as long as the tattooed thug stayed insensible—or as long as Lucy Keyes could hold out against whatever Madrigal and her toy boy were doing.

Marc pushed that unsettling thought aside and dropped into a crouch. Staying out of sight, he kept in the shadows and moved down the length of the plane, heading toward the rear where the black van sat secured to the deck. When the shooters had captured them at Hite's house, all of Marc and Lucy's gear had been taken away. If that kit was still in the van somewhere, if he could get to it, Marc would have a means of communication.

He didn't want to dwell on the slim likelihood of getting out of this situation alive. The odds were colossally, *hysterically* bad. But if he could alert Rubicon, get them to have the authorities ready to intercept the jet when it entered South Korean airspace, then at least there was a chance to stop Madrigal from executing the terminal phase of her operation.

He crawled the last few meters down the narrow gap between the fuselage's interior wall and the side of the van. The hackers were too engaged in their own conversation to see him, and so far there was no sign of the shooters. The cargo plane rocked as it passed through an area of turbulence and Marc moved into position, getting ready. The next time that happened, he would use the rattling of the aircraft's hull to cover the action of getting inside the van.

His mind kept circling back to what Madrigal had said earlier. *Or rather, what she didn't say,* he corrected himself. There were still gaps in the logic of what Madrigal and Ghost5 were doing out here, pieces of the puzzle that Marc didn't have.

The deck beneath his feet shuddered and the fuselage groaned. Marc twisted the handle on the door and vaulted into the back of the van, securing it behind him in less than a second.

To his dismay, he wasn't alone.

"What are you doing, idiot?" At the far end of the van's interior, Kara sat on a gear case with a laptop open over her crossed legs, the glow from the screen painting her face in a bloom of cold, polar blue.

Marc pulled the stun baton and brandished it before him. "Don't you make a sound."

She didn't seem to register the implied threat. "You're jumping the gun," she rasped, rubbing a hand over her reddened throat. She waved a hand in his direction. "Go back to the lock-up before somebody sees you."

He took a step toward her. "Where's my gear?"

Kara guessed what his intentions were. "You're not going to be able to contact Rubicon. Erik trashed your phones before we took off," she said dismissively.

Marc halted, dealing with this new information. "Never mind. Get up. You can be my bullet magnet." Perhaps he could still send out a digital call for help, if he could take control of her computer.

Kara eyed him. "For crying out loud, Dane. *Catch up!* I am not going anywhere with you. You have to trust me. Let me do what I do and we might be able to get through this." She trailed off for a moment. "We can make sure Madrigal pays for what she's done."

"Trust you?" He spat the words in harsh snarl. "Are you out of your fucking mind? *You betrayed us, Kara!* You lied to me and left me in the shit! You gave up Lucy and the rest of Rubicon to your hacker mates. People are *dead* because of what you've done, do you get that?"

She stopped working the laptop and looked up at him. In the weak digital light from the screen, Kara's face seemed strangely empty. "I . . . I think so." Then the moment passed. "But I mean what I say. You can't be here, Marc. You're going to ruin everything."

"Ruining Madrigal's plans is exactly what I want to do," he shot back.

"Not her plan. *Mine*." Kara scowled in clear frustration. "Good grief, you neuro-typicals are so dense! What do you think I'm doing now?" She held up the laptop. "Madrigal's techs have a transient electromagnetic device wired through the plane, to blitz all the hard drives at once in case of an emergency. I'm trying to crack the control protocol. Or I was, before you interrupted me."

"You expect me to believe that?" Marc advanced on her, his temper flaring. "I don't know if you're lying to me now, or if you were lying to me before!"

She stopped again and Kara sighed. "It's my fault. We had a friendship and I broke it. But this is how it is. You can't interfere."

"I want to trust you." The words escaped from his mouth, coming up of their own accord. Marc found that it was the truth. He *did* want to have Kara walk back from what she had done. But the losses and the treacheries of his past told him that was a vain hope, and he said as much to her.

"You need some proof," she said, after a while. "That's it, isn't it? But I only have one thing to offer." Kara got up and walked to him, rolling up her sleeve as she did. She unclipped the smartwatch around her wrist and held out her right arm so he could see. "Here."

He saw a tattoo. A blue-inked bracelet. *An abstract collection of lines and circles.* It was an exact duplicate of the one he had seen on the body of the dead hacker in the Maltese mortuary, and as she turned her arm he could see there were numbers written into the design. But before, where there had been three groups of digits, Kara's tattoo only showed a pair. *41 57.*

"That's the only proof you can have," she concluded. "Is it good enough?"

At first, he didn't answer, and looked away. The meaning behind the tattoos, the resonance they suggested, spoke to him of a deep personal connection. Marc had known of people who had survived great adversity or long periods of separation from someone they cared for, and this kind of ink was often a way to make those connections indelible and real. Kara put her watch back on, concealing it once more.

"If you're telling me the truth," said Marc. "Then you have to level with me, right now. I need to know everything."

When he looked up again, she had a small frame .25 caliber pistol in her hand, aimed at his head. "I don't have time for that." Kara pulled a walkie-talkie from her pocket and keyed the mic.

"*What?*" Erik's voice grated.

"Tell Madrigal to get down to the hold," Kara said into the radio, the gun never wavering. "The animals are out of their cage."

Conflicted, dejected and angry, Marc raised his hands and let the stun baton drop. Kara stared back at him, turning blank and unreadable once again.

"*What are you talking about?*" He heard Madrigal's terse reply. "*We have the woman here. She's under control.*"

"Not her." Kara's eyes were dead and emotionless. "The other one." She released the push-to-talk button so her next words would not be heard by anyone else, and studied him coldly. "I'm sorry, Marc. But I can't have you getting in my way."


They came and dragged him down to the cargo bay, Erik and the older man from the shooting party, the one that Madrigal had called Fox. Marc caught a glimpse of Lucy being shoved back into the server room, this time with double the people guarding her and the other shooter, the woman called Cat, watching her every move. Cat and Fox shared a loaded look as they passed each other, and then Marc was being marched forcefully up the crew ladder to the Antonov's upper deck.

Erik hauled him into a curtained-off area with two metal chairs bolted to the floor and gestured for Marc to sit down.

He dropped heavily into one of the seats and saw a figure in the shadows. "Before you get started," said Marc, squinting into the gloom. "Can I just say one thing? The hot-fixes you used on the Arquebus beta build? Quite good. But I have to tell you, the code is a bit sloppy. You've had it for long enough. I thought you'd have taken more time to streamline it."

Madrigal stepped into the light. "That's how you want to start this? By ragging on my programming skills?" She sniggered. "Poor effort."

"I don't think so," replied Marc. He rubbed at his aching wrists. "I tested you. See, a proper hacker wouldn't let someone take the piss out of their kung fu. Good code is like music. Yours has a lot of bum notes."

A flicker of displeasure flared and died in the curling of her lip. "I'm a pragmatist. I go with what works, not with what's pretty."

"That's abundantly clear." Marc gave a pointed look at Fox, observing from the other side of the compartment. "So, did you go to the DPRK or was it them who recruited you?" The gunman feigned uninterest, and Marc answered his own question. "Yeah. You went to them. Because Ghost5 need the resources of a nation-state to land this nasty little project of yours."

"Careful," warned Madrigal, a mocking playfulness in her manner. "You keep disparaging something I've put a lot of time and energy into, and I might get angry."

"Makes sense." Marc turned his attention to Erik, ignoring her reply. "I mean, Ghost5's profile is solid, isn't it? Fearsome. Your black hats rock up and any network-security nerd will shit themselves. But North Korea? Their rep is a bit inconsistent. All that rubbish about hacking Sony because the Dear Leader was pissed off about some stoner movie. Did Bureau 121 do that? More likely some bored kids from North *Wales*."

Bureau 121, the hermit kingdom's secretive cyberwarfare division, also known as the Lazarus Group or Hidden Cobra, were often held up as one of the key threat vectors in the digital battlespace, and they were keen not to lag behind other actives like China's PLA Unit 61398, Russia's infamous web brigades and the NSA's Tailored

Access Operations division. The North's conventional military forces were antiquated and unreliable, but their cyber-army were making strides in internet warfare, and the offer of an alliance with a group of experienced mercenary hackers like Ghost5 would have been irresistible to the generals in Pyongyang.

"But so much for you lot being the masterless rōnin anarchists of the dark web, eh?" Marc's gaze returned to Madrigal. "You've ruined that reputation forever. When people find out what you've done, Ghost5 will forever be remembered as a bunch of sell-outs."

Madrigal smiled at him. "You say that like it should matter. I was never in this for anything as crude as bragging rights. Our goals align with North Korea's, so we're in partnership. Ideology doesn't play any role in this."

"I refer you to my earlier statement: *bollocks.*" Marc leaned back in his chair. The longer he could keep her talking, the more chance he had to draw out information from Madrigal that he could use. "How much did they give you to crash those trains in Taipei? What's the going rate to kill a few hundred innocent people so that one dissident pain in the arse winds up dead?"

"I considered it a proof of concept," Madrigal replied.

"So you didn't even get paid for it?" Marc snorted in derision. "You're not only sell-outs, you're cheap."

"What does that make you?" The woman's affected amusement started to slip. "Marc Dane. Once the loyal patriot for Queen and country, propping up a corrupt government on its tired, provincial little island. Now a bought and paid-for mercenary for a billionaire with a vigilante complex. You have no high ground to stand on." She folded her arms across her chest. "I know about Solomon and Rubicon, and his crusade. I know more than he's told you, about where that impetus of his comes from. After all, no one understands someone better than their enemy . . . And you've done well making one of the Combine."

Marc said nothing. Madrigal's mention of the shadowy cabal of power brokers was unexpected and troubling.

"Oh, I know them too," Madrigal went on, sensing his interest.

"We've had mutually beneficial associations in the past. It's a shame you won't be around to see what their endgame is." She cocked her head. "I'm sure they'll be pleased to hear you and Keyes have been taken off the board." Madrigal glanced up at Erik. "Remind me to contact them when the operation is complete, will you? They'll owe us for dealing with their problem for them."

"You know, the difference between me and you," Marc said, pacing out his words, "is that I don't pretend to be what I am not. You've gone against everything you ever said you stood for. You don't give a fuck if you bring South East Asia to the brink of war. You whored out yourself and Ghost5—not because you're looking for justice or balance or any shit like that. You want to settle a score." Marc gave a wolfish smile and pointed at her face. "I've seen that look in the mirror. I know where it comes from."

"You're going to tell me what Rubicon knows about our operations," said Madrigal, switching gears. She'd plainly had enough of the small talk. "I'm not going to have Erik here beat you until you break. That would require effort I don't want to expend." He got the impression she'd been through this play more than once. "Instead, we're going to find what family you have, and we're going to bring their lives crashing down on them—"

"No, you won't," Marc broke in. "Someone tried that with me before. Afterward I made sure that anyone I care about is living behind firewalls with encryption so complex, you won't be able to crack the keys before the sun goes out." He glanced at the dive watch on his wrist. "I don't reckon you have that much time to spare."

Madrigal shrugged. "Fair point. Like I said, I believe in expediency. I'll go with my other option instead." She outlined how Ghost5 would remote-hack a series of systems to ensure that a man who might or might not be Lucy Keyes's brother would be shot dead in a botched police raid. "I'd rather not be occupying myself with this. I have other concerns right now. But I'll make the effort if I have to. So by all means, say nothing if you're willing to let more innocent people die."

Marc was quiet for a moment. He'd reached the point where there was no more dissembling he could do, no other opportunity open barring a violent and risky prospect that had as much chance of getting him killed as it did of succeeding.

All he could do now was to give Madrigal exactly what she wanted.

"I'll tell you what I know." He straightened in the chair and consciously made his body language neutral, open and honest. "I know you've been gearing up for this for years. Most of your life, I'd imagine." Marc thought back to the police video from the old folks' home in Florida, the clippings and the papers in Charles Hite's blackmail file. He saw the jigsaw of the truth that they represented and tried to fill in the missing pieces. "Operation Overtone. Decades ago, now. A joint black-ops mission between the Central Intelligence Agency and what was then their South Korean counterpart. Over the border into the North, in violation of UN regulations and international laws. They would have used men already deployed in-country—soldiers from the US Army, trustworthy men with good records. *Patriots*." He leaned on the last word, watching for a reaction. "Most of them would have been selected to have few family ties. But not everyone ticks that box, yeah? One of them had—what?—a wife and a daughter?"

Madrigal's expression turned stony, and Marc knew he was on the right track.

"Nobody expects Overtone to go as utterly, calamitously wrong as it does, though. It's botched so completely that the CIA redact their files to hell and back. The South Koreans pretend it didn't happen. But the men sent to do the job . . . they never come back. Fathers and husbands lost because someone fucked up." He held her gaze, searching for something to tell him how close he was to the truth. "That kind of trauma, it breeds a deep hate, doesn't it? The kind that you nurture for years and years. That doesn't go away. And someone wounded by that starts a life that will always be in the shadow of what she lost."

"Get out," Madrigal ordered.

"You mean—" Erik started to speak, but she silenced him with a throat-cutting gesture.

"Both of you, get out."

Reluctantly, Erik walked from the room, and the gunman trailed after him. Fox hesitated at the curtain partitioning off the space from the rest of the crew deck. "This is not the time to allow your resolve to weaken," he said.

"I won't say it again," Madrigal told him, without looking up. When they were alone, she studied Marc with a new intensity. "You are very perceptive. Keep going. Let's see if you can find your way to the end."

He tried to picture Madrigal as a child, dealing with the loss of a parent under such circumstances. "No father means no more protection. Sent home from an army base in some foreign country, back to a place that's just as alien. How does that work? Things don't hold together. The wife, the mother . . . she can't handle it, can she? What does that mean for the daughter? Foster homes and a childhood in the cogs of a broken system. If you're a smart kid, you turn hard. Put up walls. Your skills get aimed toward the darker places. And off we go. You grow into someone who wants payback."

"Very good." Madrigal studied him coldly. "It's just the details you're missing." She took a breath and carried on, emotion bleeding out of her voice. "They were shot by border guards on the southern side of the Joint Security Area. Killed by their so-called allies. The intelligence was wrong. They were sent in to steal military secrets, but they deployed into a hornet's nest. None of them were prepared for what happened. They fled. But by the time they approached the border, the word was out. They had become politically inconvenient. Operation Overtone had to be erased."

"The old bloke . . . Cooper. He told you?"

She nodded. "His lies and his failure caught up with him."

"But that wasn't enough for you. And now here we are." Marc gestured at the air. "You're not going to be satisfied until you make them pay. The CIA, the South Koreans. And the North is happy to help you rip it all up."

Madrigal rose from her chair. "You don't know what I'm going to do. Rubicon don't know. But you will." That cold smile of hers returned. "You and your lady friend are going to have a ringside seat."

She turned to walk away, and Marc called after her. "What about Kara? What happens to her?"

"She's where she was always supposed to be. If you had ever really known her at all, you'd understand that." Madrigal pushed through the curtain and left him in the gloom.

# — FIFTEEN —

Kara jerked awake as the Antonov rumbled through a pocket of turbulence, the motion of the big aircraft shoving her against the back of her seat. There was no blurry transition between sleep and awareness for her. Adrenaline shock sparked through her veins and she blinked, pawing at the seatbelt across her lap.

Behind her, in the rear sections of the cargo compartment, she could hear the rattle of keyboards and the low mutter of conversation. Kara twisted in her seat and pulled up the blind on the oval window beside her. Dawn was just below the horizon, and through patches of gray storm clouds she could see a craggy, forest-green landscape extending away to the coastline.

She did the math in her head. They were traveling up the Korean peninsula, with the Yellow Sea out there beyond the angle of the jet's portside wing. Soon, the Antonov would start its descent into the pattern for landing at Incheon International, a few kilometers from the South Korean capital. Kara released her seatbelt and stood up, assimilating this new information. She rubbed her throat and swallowed experimentally. It was still uncomfortable, bruised and swollen where Lucy had tried to strangle her. When she reached for any resentment toward the sniper, she found nothing.

What bothered her more was that Madrigal had let her sleep through the majority of the journey, and even now as they were nearing their destination, she hadn't roused her. Had she planned to let Kara sleep all the way to Seoul? That wouldn't do.

Kara made her way down to the work area, drawing sideways looks from Andre and some of the others. They didn't like her, but Kara didn't allow herself to dwell on it. The others only mattered to her if they got in the way or if they could help her reach her goal. Whichever it was, the end result would be the same.

Pyne intercepted Kara, but she pushed right past the skinny hacker to where Madrigal and Erik were working on panels connected to the jet's mobile mainframe. "You didn't wake me?"

Madrigal kept typing and didn't look up. "You needed the rest. And we have this covered."

"Right." Kara turned a laptop screen around so she could see what was written across the display. Panes of digital code were running in multiple instances, aggressor programs that the Arquebus software had deposited in their target systems like cluster bombs strewn from the warhead of an area-denial weapon. In one, she saw a myriad of data intrusions in play against controller area network software, the kind of tech that 80 percent of cars in the South had fitted as standard. Blood-red lines of corruption laced the text, each one signifying a vehicle that had been rendered useless. Arquebus had blown through the firewalls of the interconnected network that linked the city's vehicles to the traffic grid and poisoned them.

"The morning commute is gonna be a bitch from hell," Pyne said, with a callous chuckle. "Pretty much every car in Seoul is gonna have to go into the shop."

"You triggered the vehicle hack already."

Madrigal gave Kara a quick look beneath an arched eyebrow. "We did it a half-hour ago. Anything not on the move has been bricked and won't start without a full software reinstall. As for the ones already on the road . . ." She went back to her work with a shrug.

Pyne had a tablet screen in her hand, and Kara snatched it from her. It showed a live feed from the national YTN news channel, an outside broadcast framing a reporter in a raincoat standing on a footbridge over one of Seoul's main highways. In the rainy, predawn gloom, it was possible to see lines of stalled cars clogging the street, and over the reporter's rapid-fire explanations the screen cut to other scenes from around the city. Jackknifed trucks blocked intersections, and buses had collided with buildings. The camera view swept over traffic cops waving illuminated batons and desperately trying to get a handle on the unfolding disaster.

"How are we on social?" Madrigal threw the question toward Andre, seated nearby at another laptop. "People are getting out of bed and looking at their phones. I want to see the uptick."

"It's happening," he replied. "Better than our projections by about twelve percent." Outwardly a slight, unassuming Frenchman in a bulky parka, Andre was the field marshal for Ghost5's troll army of social-media foot soldiers. Under his command, simple intelligent software "bots" scanned the messaging platforms in use across the city, from basic text through to image- and video-based postings. The bots sought out posts that matched a set of pre-programmed criteria, looking for key phrases containing words like *"panic," "disaster," "attack," "terror,"* and reposted them dozens of times on fake accounts that mimicked those of human users. It turned the feeds into an echo chamber filled with the clamor of frightened people.

The bots were the line infantry of the troll army, cheap and disposable, there to make noise and clog up the system. The next line of attack was a legion of human agent provocateurs. Some of them were junior-league wannabes who jumped at the chance to work with the notorious Ghost5 crew, mostly bored kids or destructive nihilists who liked to create mayhem for the sheer hell of it. Others were low-end workers in illicit click-farms out on the Indian subcontinent, men and women paid in anonymous bitcoin to put up pre-scripted postings on hacked Facebook pages and hijacked Twitter feeds, hundreds of times per hour.

The last part of the social-media strike force was Andre and a few of his top troublemakers, who surfed the tone of the shared information space in real time, watching the rise and fall of hashtags and popular posts, and manipulating them to reflect the reality that Madrigal wanted the world to see.

As she watched, Kara saw Andre loading up an image of the same stretch of highway she had seen in the YTN news video a few moments earlier—but now the picture had been manipulated to show cars on fire and what looked like heavily armed riot police on the march. He fired it out into the net and watched it ricochet from server to server, gaining more page-clicks and re-postings with each passing second.

Existing public dissatisfaction across the country with the current administration and law enforcement propelled the falsified report even further. The presidential impeachments and political chicanery that had tainted the South Korean government in recent years only served to deepen the distrust that Ghost5 were now co-opting for their own ends. Add that to the climate of tension generated by American allies engaged in a dick-measuring contest with the military across the border to the north, and things could only deteriorate. People down there were willing to believe the worst without questioning it too deeply.

An instantaneous, malleable and unstoppable propaganda assault was unfolding right before Kara's eyes, sowing dread and discord. "We are past the point of no return," Andre noted. "This is already feeding itself. Everyone on the ground is buying into it, they're re-blogging for us. And anyone who tries to swim against the tide, the bots are fake-news shit-posting them into oblivion."

He grinned, pleased with his work.

The goal of the "panic attack" was to convince anyone on social media that the city of Seoul was on the verge of imploding, and gradually turn that falsehood into a self-fulfilling prophecy.

Run in isolation, this kind of social engineering hack had a finite lifespan. People would eventually figure out where the truth really lay, given long enough. But with the vehicle network malfunction already happening, the fear was underpinned by something real and tangible. To keep the ball rolling, the imagined dangers had to become actual ones.

"Tags are now in place on the nine primary lines of the subway," reported Erik. "Still working on the others."

"The metro system," Kara gave voice to the thought. "That's the next target." It made a ruthless kind of sense. With a city waking up to roads jammed with stalled vehicles, taking control of the public transport infrastructure would bring Seoul to a grinding halt, at the very least. But she doubted that Madrigal would be so forgiving as to only render the subway network inert. It would be within her power to cause a train crash like the one in Taipei all over again, and not a single collision, but dozens of them.

A green light mounted on the inner wall of the cargo bay blinked three times, and Madrigal's head tilted to look up at it. Kara felt another shudder move through the deck beneath them and the Antonov tilted as it started to descend.

"Everyone secure your gear for landing!" Erik shouted out the order. "We'll pick this up when we're on the ground!"

Pyne, Andre and the others set about switching their computers to standby, and Kara stood among them, watching impassively.

Madrigal met her gaze. "Don't worry," she said. "I have a vital task for you when we're down."

"Are you going to tell me why you've brought us to this?" Kara leaned in, so only Madrigal could hear her. "When I came back, you promised me you'd be truthful with me from now on. But everything about this hack feels like it's moving to someone else's beat." She nodded toward the windows, and the rain-swept gray city they were approaching. "We never take this kind of risk. We never go *on site*. That's the whole point of what we are. Ghost5 has no center. We strike from half a world away and still hit hard. That's how we roll."

"You're right, we don't need to physically be here," replied Madrigal. "But *I* do. Some deeds you can't do at a remove, Song." Her eyes clouded with memory. "Sometimes you have to hold the knife yourself." Then she shook off the brief reverie and smiled again. "I promise I will explain. Trust me. It'll make sense. Justice will be done."

At length, Kara gave a nod, knowing that she would get no more from the woman. "What about Dane and Keyes? What are we going to do with them?"

Madrigal pushed past Kara toward her seat. "Oh, you already know the answer to that."

After the fist fight in the server compartment, Madrigal's people had re-thought the whole idea of keeping Marc and Lucy together, putting her back in the room and taking him all the way to the rear of the cargo bay. They were as far apart as they could be and still be inside the Antonov, and it had been hours since Marc had seen her.

The thug he had hit with the stun prod, the one with the tattoos who called himself Null, took great delight in knocking Marc around before securing him to one of the metal ribs supporting the cargo jet's inner wall. He left him there to huddle up and suffer through the chill soaking through the hull, weathering the polar cold with each sharp breath.

Here and there Marc snatched a few moments of sleep, but for the most part the flight seemed like an endless droning nothing.

He tried to keep his brain active by running over the facts he had to hand. The puzzle of Madrigal's intentions was almost solved, and through the hours he tried to figure it out. There were so many targets in Seoul for someone with a grudge against the government and its American allies, it was hard to narrow it down.

*What is her endgame? To drive a wedge between the South and the USA? Or to cause so much mayhem that the North could roll across the border?*

Every option he gamed out in his thoughts seemed more unpalatable than the last. Born in the early conflicts of the Cold War, the fractious relationship between the two Koreas had balanced on a knife-edge for decades, each side continually posturing against the other. Their shooting war had ceased in a stalemate generations ago, but the battle had never really ended. There was no way to know how much or how *little* would be enough to begin the slide toward open warfare once more. And for all their bluster and threats against Japan and the continental US, the South was the prize that the North really wanted.

Madrigal was callous and driven, and paired with her amoral legion of hackers and operatives from the belligerent DPRK, he doubted any target would be beyond them.

Other questions rose and fell in his thoughts. The interrogation to learn what Rubicon knew, such as it was, had petered out. Madrigal had no reason to keep Marc and Lucy alive, and yet they were still breathing. It wasn't through a reluctance to shed blood. Madrigal's cold-hearted dismissal of the lives she had ruined in the past and those yet to suffer made that clear. There was another motive at work.

Marc's mind drifted back to that anxious night in Cambridge, when the attack to steal the Arquebus prototype was under way. Even then, Madrigal had been playing a game within the game, seeding a lie about who had been behind the hack to conceal the reality of Ghost5's involvement. MI6 had almost walked into a clandestine war with China's spy agency because of the near-flawless misdirection the hacker group had spun, fooling them into thinking the source of the attack was Beijing's cyberwarriors. It was a tactic Madrigal had used time and again, not only in that scenario but in ventures against Russian intelligence, even when she had murdered Cooper on that stormy night in Florida and framed some unknown woman for the crime. It didn't escape Marc that Kara had used a similar ploy back in Malta, with the hapless tourist in the Hotel Nova.

*Madrigal always makes sure she has someone to take the blame.* There was no question in Marc's mind that this was the reason why he and Lucy Keyes were still breathing. Whatever was going down, they would take the fall for it.

The grim certainty threatened to weigh him down. For the moment, there was nothing he could do about that. His only hope was to wait, to watch and be ready to seize on any opportunity that presented itself. He was still alive, and that meant he could resist, he could fight, perhaps even escape.

Marc stared into the middle distance, eyes focused on a string of numbers stencilled on the side of a crate. The figures didn't mean anything to him, but they pulled up recollection of the bracelet tattoos on Kara Wei's arm, and the twin of it on the body of the dead hacker he'd seen in the morgue at Mater Dei.

*41 57* on her wrist, *57 46 53* on the dead man's. Marc dismantled the digits in his head, trying to find a connection, a common element. If they were digital map coordinates, he guessed that would put them somewhere in Eastern Europe. It was hard to be sure, but that didn't feel like the right call.

Each group contained one prime number. He added them together, multiplied them, and rearranged them. It passed the time, one more mystery on top of all the others, until slowly Marc understood he had been looking at it the wrong way.

If Kara and Wetherby shared the tattoos, they must have shared something more. The ink signified that intimate connection, and the numbers were personal. They had to be a secret only they could intuit. *A code that only two computer hackers would understand.*

He straightened, the airframe creaking as the cargo plane made a wide, slow turn. "Not binary, that'd be too obvious," Marc muttered to himself. "So what does that leave? Has to be *hex.*"

Closing his eyes, Marc visualized a hexadecimal grid and counted it out, feeling the kick of discovery as he realized he was on to something. Hex was a Base 6 numeral system that only mathematicians, computer programmers and other high-end nerds tended to use, allowing the representation of long strings of binary ones and zeros in a couple of numbers or letters. It could also be a way to signify alphanumeric text, if correctly converted. And more importantly, it fitted with the kind of geekish, *too-smart-for-you* attitude that hackers loved to adopt.

He lost himself in working through the problem, losing track and starting over more than once. Without pen and paper to work on, it was harder than he expected, but after a while Marc managed to decode the dead man's tattoo into three letters: *W F S.* Kara's duplicate had just two: *A W.* Marc frowned, his initial enthusiasm quickly ebbing. Whatever answer he had expected to leap out at him, didn't. Maybe his whole premise had been wrong from the start. Whatever the numerals meant, for now he was back to square one with them.

Movement further down the cargo bay drew his attention. The Ghost5 team were strapping in and securing their equipment in place. The angle of the deck eased into a shallow tilt and he felt his ears pop as the Antonov began to descend.

They were going to land. Through the metal of the hull, Marc felt the vibrations from hatches opening along the bottom of the plane as the undercarriage deployed, then the buffeting of the thicker air at lower altitude as it raced over the wing flaps. He expected Null or one of the Ghost5 crew to take him back to the seats near the front of the jet, but they ignored him, left him tethered to the wall to ride out the landing.

It wasn't a smooth arrival. Marc heard driving rain clatter hard off the Antonov's fuselage as it fell out of the sky toward the runway, and his stomach swooped in sympathy as the big jet crabbed through power-ful crosswinds. He could only see a sliver of the outside world through a window in the hull a few meters away. Marc caught glimpses of low buildings and bright lights glaring through the downpour, and then the plane touched down with a long, lingering crunch of tortured metal. The massive engines screamed into reverse thrust and gravity tugged him forward as the plane fought to bleed off its speed before it ran out of asphalt.

Eventually the howling chorus from the engines flattened into a throbbing whine and they rolled on across the apron. The rain on the fuselage sounded like handfuls of gravel being thrown at a tin roof.

A shadow fell over him and Null stood there, brandishing a fold-ing survival knife. "Try to be clever again and I will cut you," he hissed, before leaning in to sever the restraint holding Marc's bruised wrist to the support. "Get up," continued the hacker, and pointed with the blade. "That way."

"Whatever you say, mate." Marc massaged his aching forearm, try-ing to get the blood flowing again. He did his best to look tired and beaten—he was halfway there, after all—while keeping his head on a swivel to take in as much as he could. The clock on how long Mad-rigal would keep him alive was running into its last hour, he was certain of it. If he couldn't find a way through this before it hit zero, that would be the end of him.

The jet's engines were still winding down, but already the Ghost5 hackers were back at their computers, reaching into the systems that the repurposed Arquebus software had penetrated. He glanced around, searching for Kara, but once again there was no sign of her or of Madrigal.

Madrigal's toy boy, the muscular German, snapped out orders to the sallow-faced girl hunched over a custom laptop. "Pyne, are you listening to me? Make sure the switching systems are all looped. Keep them out of any critical reset until we're done."

She nodded, her head bobbing like a bird's. "The reverse shell ex-ploit is in play. All good here."

The German jabbed a finger at another one of the hackers and made a throat-cutting gesture. "Hit them."

"What now?" Marc turned to see Lucy being marched up the length of the plane toward him. She jutted her chin in the direction of the computers. "Let me guess. They're doing the San Francisco blackout again?"

"Worse," Marc said grimly. "This time it's everything at once."

On a repeater screen set up by a series of computer towers, a display showing the spidery lines of Seoul's metropolitan subway system turned, in fits and starts, from steady blue and green to a warning orange. Segment by segment, the city's rail network failed, and Marc imagined it like veins in a body clogging with clotted blood. Intersections and crossovers blinked bright crimson, and alert panels filled with strident Korean ideograms popped up all over the screen.

"Those are trains?" said Lucy, aghast at the horrible possibilities the images represented.

"Andre," said the German, glaring at the guy in the parka. "Anything coming up?"

The other hacker nodded. "Getting pictures now." He showed his teeth. "Here. This is a good one." Andre migrated a blurry video clip to the repeater screen. There was no sound, but the view showed the interior of a subway carriage populated by early-morning commuters and hungover revellers heading home after an all-nighter. Marc's gaze caught on a couple of drowsy teenagers propped up against one another, young lovers with their arms interlinked, heads bowed. Without warning, the video spun wildly as the phone shooting the images went flying. When it settled, the people in the carriage were scattered everywhere, doused in broken glass, lit by flickering emergency lights. "That was outside Itaewon station. Ran off the rails at the turn."

"Make sure you put anything with visible fatalities at the top of the churn," ordered the German. "We want people to see the blood."

"You heartless fuckers!" Marc's fists clenched in rage. "No one has to die for this!"

"Yes, they do," Andre replied, eyeing him over the top of his screen. "Otherwise it is for show." He shook his head and returned to his keyboard. "It has to be real."

"Get them out of here," said the German, beckoning to two figures in black combat gear.

Marc saw the M4 carbines in their hands and looked up into the faces of Fox and Cat. Both of them were clad in tactical gear that bore no markings, wearing heavy boots and armored gloves, with the same throat-mic comms rig he had seen on them during the earlier assault.

Cat gestured with the assault rifle. Marc saw that her pupils were dilated and guessed that she was dosed on painkillers to negate the effect of the injury Lucy had inflicted on her.

Lucy, of course, wasn't about to miss the chance to remind her of that. "How's the arm?" The other woman responded by jabbing her in the gut with the M4's barrel, and she coughed and staggered back under the blow.

Fox shoved Marc toward a hatch in the side of the fuselage, and as he approached it thudded open, turning into a short stairway down to the tarmac outside. Marc deplaned first, pulling up the collar of his jacket at he stepped into the rain. Wind whipped around under the high wing of the Antonov and the hangar it was parked in front of, so the downpour seemed to be coming from every direction at once.

Waiting outside were a handful of other armed men and women, all of them dressed in the same kind of black ballistic-cloth oversuits as Fox and Cat. Most wore full-face combat helmets with bulbous low-light vision units set on the brow, but a couple of them went bareheaded. Like the assassins, they were Koreans, and they shared the same hard-eyed, machine-like quality to their expressions.

Marc looked them over as he walked. He knew their kind. Black-ops specialists, operators who worked in the margins with ruthless efficiency and robotic focus. They didn't have the slack, casual braggadocio of most private military contractors or the world-weary and resigned manner of career soldiers. It was unsettling, the way the lenses of their helmets tracked the prisoners as they were marched toward the hangar, the silent tilt of their heads and the small motions of their hands.

As he passed one of them, Marc tried to make eye contact, but the glassy visor remained dark and impenetrable, adding to the alien impression the operators gave off. They were talking to each other, he realized. The helmets had to have built-in radio rigs, but they were sealed so that no sound could be heard by anyone outside. All the more to ensure these killers could operate in stealth and silence.

He looked back over his shoulder at Lucy and she gave him a look that said *be careful*.

Up ahead, the hangar doors were rolling open and weak yellow light spilled out. They were on the very furthest edge of the airport, close to the northerly shore of the artificial island on which it had been built. The cargo hangar was remote enough from the airport proper that Ghost5 and their allies from the DPRK would be able to work without drawing attention from the control tower. In the gloom and the rain, bad visibility would conceal them perfectly.

The yellow glow revealed another aircraft within the cavernous shelter. Like the Antonov, it was a giant among its kind, even if the big jet still dwarfed it. Marc recognized the bullet-shaped nose and twin ducted intakes of a heavyweight transport helicopter, a Russian-made Mil Mi-26 that ran under the NATO reporting name of "Halo." Eight drooping rotor blades hung over the slate-colored fuselage, and aside from an identification number, the Halo had no distinguishing marks of any sort.

Marc surveyed the machine as it was rolled out behind a tow-tractor, looking up to the high cockpit and wondering for a moment what it might be like to fly. His skills with helicopters, earned during service with the Royal Navy's Fleet Air Arm and later as part of MI6, were limited to aircraft of much smaller size. Anything he had flown could have fitted inside the Halo's cargo bay and left room to spare.

"What the hell is this for?" said Lucy, from the side of her mouth.

"No idea," Marc admitted, and he pointed at the hull. The gray shade was new and patchy in places, a sure sign that it had been applied quickly. "See that? Fresh paintjob. They don't want anyone guessing where it's from."

"You have an inkling?"

He nodded. "Only two air forces in this region fly them. Russia—"

"And North Korea?" she said. "Must be a loaner from Kim."

An unmarked truck was parked deeper in the hangar, and there were a few more of the black-clad soldiers standing by the rear, loading weapons and making ready to move out. One of them strode

over, carrying two helmets identical to the others, and handed them
to Fox and Cat. The shooters hooded up, becoming the same faceless
automatons as the rest.

"So what do we do now?" Marc demanded, staring into the blank
masks. "Come on. You brought us in here. Speak up."

"Inside the truck." He turned as someone else entered the hangar
behind them. Kara straightened her blood-red leather jacket and
hefted a sling bag over one shoulder as she came closer. She pointed at
the vehicle. "Get changed."

The silent soldiers parted to allow them to approach, and Lucy
looked into the back of the vehicle. "I don't think so."

"It's that or a bullet," snapped Kara. "Your choice."

"Where's Madrigal?" said Marc. "Curtain up on the finale, and
she's not around?"

"She doesn't tell me everything," said Kara. "The next stage has to
be triggered before we go."

"And what's that going to be?" Marc fixed her with a hard look.
"Drop a few planes out of the sky or some other shit like that?"

"Power grid," offered Lucy. "Kill the electricity across the city and
mass mayhem will set in." She glanced at Kara. "Am I right?"

Kara said nothing, but her expression gave the answer. She looked
away, digging inside the bag. "You better do what I told you."

"And what if we don't?" Marc took a step toward her, and Fox
raised his rifle. "What if we tell you to go fuck yourselves?"

"Lucy's brother." Kara paused. "Madrigal will do what she said
she would. End him."

"*Bitch.*" Lucy ground out the word between her teeth, but at length
she climbed into the back of the truck. Marc followed her, knowing
that neither of them had a choice. Inside they found two sets of tactical gear identical to the outfits worn by the North Korean black-ops
squad.

"Get changed," Kara repeated, watching them from the truck's
open doors. "Quickly." Nearby, Fox and Cat turned their attention
elsewhere, and Marc guessed they were listening to a radio message
over their discreet comms channel.

Lucy stripped down to her T-shirt and underwear, shrugging on the close-fitting tactical gear with the swiftness of an experienced professional. Marc followed suit, tossing aside his jacket and scuffed black jeans, stepping into the scratchy, ballistic-cloth oversuit. The gear's fit was snug, and he stretched experimentally before putting on the boots.

He and Lucy exchanged looks. Whatever happened next, it seemed the two of them were going to be closer to it than either would have liked.

Marc jumped down from the back of the truck and waited for Kara to make the next move. "Hold out your right arm," she ordered. He did as he was told, and from the sling bag Kara produced a device that resembled an electronic ankle tag. She snapped it into place around his wrist and he felt metal contacts on the inside face bite through the sleeve into his skin. "Galvanic induction," explained the woman, her voice carrying. "You try anything—you run, grab a weapon—Madrigal is going to know. That cuff will put out enough charge to drop you."

She moved to Lucy and put a similar device on her. "You really don't feel anything about this, do you?" said Lucy, glaring at Kara as she worked. "All those smiles and friendships back at Rubicon, that was an act."

"Everything people do is an act," Kara said, distractedly.

"Was it like that when you were with *him*?" Marc threw out the question, deliberately fishing for a response. "The numbers, Kara." He saw the bracelet tattoos in his mind's eye again, and the image of them shifted, became *clear*. "The numbers that are letters . . . Yeah. I think I got it."

She walked back toward him, glancing nervously at Fox, Cat and the other silent soldiers. "I don't know what you're talking about."

"*A* and *W*," he went on. "I just figured it out. *Alexander Wetherby*. Obvious, when you think about it. The ink . . . People don't make that a part of themselves unless there is a deeper meaning behind it. Not unless they—"

"Don't say it." For one brief moment, Kara's expression shifted back to that of the vulnerable, real, human person he thought he knew. "Don't say *love*. You don't get it." He saw pain and regret in her eyes, and then it vanished as a mask of indifference fell back into place.

"The other letters. *W, F* and *S*." He stared at her. "That's you, isn't it? *Song*. The person you used to be."

"Wong Fei Song is the name I was born with. It's who I always was," she corrected. Kara thrust an armor vest into Lucy's arms and tossed her a small radio earpiece. "Put those on. Do what Madrigal tells you." She turned to Marc with the same items for him, but rather than hand them over, she put the vest on his shoulders and fastened it herself. It rested uncomfortably there, pressing into his ribs, as if something wasn't fitting correctly. Before he could stop her, Kara leaned close and looped the radio unit over his earlobe.

Her lips were very close to his face, and when she whispered to him, he could barely hear her. "This is all I could do," she said quietly.

*What hell did that mean?* She pulled away before he could question her.

Marc watched Kara jog back toward the parked Antonov. By now the Halo had been hauled out on to the apron in front of the hangar, and the running lights blinked on as the helicopter started up. The silent black-ops troops began to board via a hatch at the rear.

Fox pointed toward the Halo, and reluctantly Marc started walking. "I guess we don't get helmets," said Lucy, coming up alongside him.

"She wants someone to be seen," he told her. "We're the lucky marks who get to be the faces caught on camera, yeah?"

Lucy filed that thought away without comment. "Any time you want to dazzle me with some clever improvised plan, go right ahead."

"What, you can't come up with an idea on the fly for a change?"

She managed a smirk. "I shoot stuff and I hit people. You're supposed to be the smart one."

There was a click from the comms gear and Madrigal's voice was in their ears. "*Cute. You two should get a room.*"

"Piss off," Marc spat reflexively, his mood darkening.

"*Now, now. Be nice. There's still time for me to make sure a little girl in Ohio becomes an orphan tonight.*"

He felt Lucy tense and saw her hands contract into fists, but the woman said nothing.

Ahead of them, Cat boarded the Halo, her movements still a little stiffer than the other black-clad soldiers. Another of the masked figures stood by the hatch, and the blank face of their helmet tracked Marc and Lucy as they climbed into the helicopter's cargo bay. The Halo's engines were humming now, the big rotor blades chopping sluggishly through the wet air, gaining speed with each turn.

*"This is going to be simple,"* Madrigal went on. *"You'll be taken to a location and given a task to accomplish. Do as you are told and it will be over quickly."*

Fox and another of the soldiers were the last to board the helicopter, and now the rotors were spinning at take-off speed. Fox gave Marc a shove toward a set of folding chairs built into the wall of the cargo bay. He sat and snapped a safety belt into place. Lucy took the spot next to him, doing the same.

*"If you deviate from my directions in any way,"* continued the voice in their ear, *"there will be consequences."*

Fox and Cat bracketed the two of them so they couldn't move freely, and Marc looked back out through the Halo's open rear. The Antonov was visible as a wall of white fuselage through the driving dawn rain. "You're not going to come see us off?"

*"There are live video feeds streaming from a camera in each helmet,"* she replied. *"I've got eyes everywhere. So don't try anything dramatic."*

The Halo's turboshafts growled as the pilot applied power and the big helicopter lurched as it left the ground. The rear hatch stayed open, a sure sign that the soldiers on board were going to make a fast deployment when they reached their destination, and the downdraft blew a swift squall through the cargo bay as they gained height. Marc saw a flash of the Antonov's broad wings and the drab green of the hangar roof before the view swept around as they sped away.

He watched the airport vanish as the Halo left the artificial island where Incheon International was located and turned east toward Seoul. They raced under the low cloud, moving fast along the line of the Ara Canal that led from the Yellow Sea to the heart of the South Korean capital.

Marc looked down into the ribbon of green water and thought briefly about making a break for it, but they were over a hundred meters up, and a fall from this height would be fatal.

Instead, he cast around the interior of the helicopter, watching the troopers prepare. His instinctive tech-head mindset rose to the fore as he clocked their gear, tried to read intentions through the loadouts carried by the masked figures. Marc noted that they had American M4 carbines rather than the Daewoo K2 assault rifles used by soldiers in the South, or the Type 58 Kalashnikov-copies employed by the DPRK army in the North. A deliberate choice, he guessed. Using US-made weapons loaded with NATO-standard ammunition would obscure the origins of any attack.

A cold, creeping realization marched over him. He and Lucy were in the middle of some kind of *false flag* operation, so called because the aggressors would act directly under cover of another actor's identity and seek to fool their targets into thinking they were someone else.

"Right. We're in this up to our necks now." Marc spoke so the radio earpiece would pick up his words. "You going to tell us what the target is? Or do I have to guess?"

*"It's a surprise,"* said Madrigal. *"But go ahead, try to figure it out. It'll keep you occupied."*

There were hundreds of sites in the city where a force of armed killers could wreak havoc, but this wouldn't be as blunt and as violent as the Soldier-Saints' attack on a San Francisco park. Madrigal's plans were too layered, too complex for anything so basic. Taking lives would not be enough for her. Ghost5 were already doing that, sowing confusion with the first stages of their paralyzing hack against Seoul's infrastructure.

The Halo pitched as the pilot brought the nose up in a sharp, climbing turn, and Marc's head thudded against the hull. He twisted in his seat, watching the view to the rear as they skimmed over a railyard. Something pressed into his chest beneath the tac vest, but he ignored it, knowing that the soldiers all around were watching his every movement.

He looked down and saw hundreds of inert commuter trains in their sidings, the network terminus choked by the forced shutdown of the system. Then they were over the water again, the wide expanse of the Han River this time, snaking through the middle of the city. The helicopter flashed over the faded red arches of a highway bridge and it too was a mess of stalled vehicles, a solid traffic jam reaching from one side of the waterway to the other.

Still gaining altitude, the Halo cut through wisps of gray cloud, skimming the bottom of the gloom hanging over a cityscape of residential apartment buildings and smoke-blowing factories. From the air, Seoul resembled a crowded spread of colored building blocks, arranged in patchwork patterns around splashes of dark jade parkland.

The rotors slapped at the air as the aircraft rolled into a hard pivot, perhaps to avoid another helicopter flying nearby, and through the drizzle Marc caught sight of a domed building on the far shore of the river, lit up by spotlights that made it gleam in the dawn light. He recognized it as the National Assembly, a core part of the Republic of Korea's governmental structure. *Was that the target?*

It didn't seem right. This early in the morning, the place would barely be staffed. An assault on it would be symbolic, but it wouldn't draw blood, and having looked Madrigal in the eye he knew that was what she wanted.

"*Not far now*," said the woman, like she had read his mind. "*There's only one more thing that needs to happen.*"

The hairs on the back of Marc's neck stood up, and he felt an irrational dread. It was as if Madrigal were at his shoulder, her icy smile widening as she set the last pieces of her plan into motion.

"*Here we go.*" The Halo dipped again, trading height for speed as it raced past the Assembly building without slowing, leaving it and the river behind to thunder southward. A sprawl of densely packed buildings blurred past below the tail rotor, and Marc distinctly heard the near-sexual anticipation in Madrigal's voice as she spoke again. "*Lights out.*"

From the north of Seoul, receding into the distance, came a wave that advanced over the city in patches of darkness. Irregular, jagged chunks of the landscape dimmed as the power failed in district after district. The buildings became shadows as the grid went down for ten million people. With the rain and the thick cloud smothering the rising dawn, Seoul was caught in a strange half-night.

One of the masked soldiers opened a case at their feet and Marc saw a set of black quadrotor drones in vertical cradles. He watched the soldier pull them out and toss them into the helicopter's wake one at a time. As each drone tumbled away, it righted itself on four buzzing blades and zipped off out of sight.

"What's going on with those?" said Lucy.

"Eyes in the sky," Marc replied. "Good way for them to keep watch on everything."

"Same type we saw at Hite's place?"

Marc nodded.

The Halo continued to power south, as the sprawl thinned into suburbs and then became the rust-hued flanks of a shallow hillside. Marc heard nothing, but he saw the silent soldiers react as one to a new order. They stiffened and readied their weapons as the helicopter pulled into a sharp nose-up attitude, rapidly burning off forward motion.

The aircraft pivoted and dropped like a stone, the ground rising up to meet them. "Where are we?" grated Lucy, straining to see out of a nearby window.

As the Halo rotated to make a combat landing, Marc saw another distinctive building, this one made up of curved sections and low blocks, set in the middle of a great circular space cut out of the hillside. Visible through the sheeting rain, the darkened windows of the place reflected the stony sky overhead.

He spotted an identifying plaque sporting a version of the *taegeuk*, the yin-yang swirl from the South Korean flag, overlaid with a stylized flame and flanked by the forms of a tiger and a dragon. And then he knew exactly where they were.

Madrigal had brought them to the headquarters of Korea's National Intelligence Service, the organization that forty years ago had been the KCIA.

# — SIXTEEN —

The squad of masked soldiers deployed from the back of the Halo in fast, clean order, covering their sectors as they spread out and secured the immediate area surrounding the helicopter. As Lucy followed them down to the tarmac, she tried to take in everything at once, searching for a weak point in their arrangement, for a chink in their armor that could be exploited. There was nothing. These men and women moved with silent purpose and she couldn't help but wonder how long they had been training for this day.

*What the hell are we in the middle of?* She glanced back as Marc emerged from the helicopter into the rain, another of the soldiers following behind him to make sure they didn't hold anyone up.

The Halo had landed on the edge of a wide parking lot sparsely populated with commonplace subcompacts and SUVs. In one direction was a low outbuilding, a four-story office block isolated by lines of discreet concrete crash barriers disguised as ornamental planters. Looking the other way, she saw what had to be the main complex. Much larger than the outbuilding, it had a blank, seamless facia of blue glass reflecting the nearby hillside.

It reminded her of the blandly monolithic architecture she'd seen at places like the NSA's "black box" in Fort Meade or the CIA's Langley headquarters. Characterless but still threatening, the NIS campus looked like what it was; a concrete slab built to house a nation-state's spooks. There was a landing pad on the forecourt, occupied by a spindly silver helicopter a third the size of the hulking Halo, and the uniformed guards milling around it were already starting to break away and move in her direction. Lucy tensed. Any second now, and contact would kick off. She felt exposed and vulnerable without a weapon to hand. The heavy shock bracelet Kara had locked around her wrist weighed her down.

The two soldiers closest to Marc and Lucy shoved them into cover behind a parked car, and she took a closer look at their kit. One of them, the largest of the group by a clear margin, carried extra pouches on his tactical vest, each one filled with demo packs of C4 explosives. A cylindrical, variable-fuse grenade hung off a loop on one of the vest's straps, and Lucy recognized the purple banding around the device immediately, the text INCEN written above it standing out a mile. She glanced at the other soldier, a woman. She too carried a single thermite grenade, a powerful high-temperature incendiary device capable of burning through the engine block of a truck. Why they needed them here wasn't clear, and Lucy was in no hurry to find out. The female soldier cocked her head, then looked down at a display on the smartwatch on her wrist.

Lucy heard a now-familiar high-pitched whining sound, and another pair of black quadrotor drones flashed past overhead. Someone in the Halo or back at the airport was using them to coordinate the attack.

A male voice called out in Korean, and although Lucy couldn't understand the words, the tone was clear. *Confusion and surprise.* With the unexpected power outage, the guards would be scrambling to figure out what was going on.

The masked soldiers did not allow them the chance to learn the answer. Under the thudding of the Halo's idling rotors, the attackers opened up on the guards with short, precise blasts of fire. Three-round bursts laid exactly on target spat from the muzzles of their suppressed M4s, and the NIS men fell sprawling in puffs of red fluid. None of them got off a round in return. One of the soldiers drew a silenced pistol and dashed out of cover, quickly putting a shot into the heads of the fallen men to be sure.

"Fuck . . ." muttered Marc. "These assholes aren't messing around."

"*It's what they are trained for.*" Madrigal's silky tones seemed to pour like poison into Lucy's ear, and she winced at the sound. "*You have to admire their efficiency.*"

"Right . . ." She watched the group hesitate as they listened to an order coming in over their headsets. One of them tapped the same device on their wrist that Lucy had seen on the female soldier. They were clearly working to a precise timeline.

Above, the two little drones settled into a steady hover, watching the approaches while the soldiers moved in their inhuman manner, communicating without appearing to speak. After a moment, the group parted into two units, the first moving off toward the main complex at a run, the rest falling back to form up and deploy toward the nearer outbuilding.

The masked female gestured for Lucy to follow the second group, and to underline the point Madrigal gave the order. *"Go, hurry on now."*

Lucy glared into the camera eye mounted on the soldier's machine-like helmet. "How about we don't?" She searched the mask's dark lenses for some inkling of the person beneath, but could see nothing.

*"Then you'll never know how this ends,"* snapped Madrigal.

The soldier raised her rifle, threatening to strike Lucy with the butt of the weapon.

"Come on," said Marc, pulling Lucy away. "Don't give them an excuse."

"Fuck this puppet-and-mime shit," Lucy retorted, but walked on regardless. She knew he was right—they had to play along with Madrigal's dumb little games until an opening presented itself to turn this around. But the odds on that happening were growing longer with every passing moment.

Up ahead, the first line of the silent soldiers were pushing through the doors to the isolated building and into the atrium within.

"Power cut makes sense now," said Marc, thinking aloud. "Blowing out the candles for the whole city, that's not because they want to cause havoc." He jerked his thumb at the main building behind them. "They couldn't pull the plug on the NIS campus by targeting the local grid, that's too small. It had to be a total shutdown across the whole region."

"I don't follow you . . ." Lucy shot him a questioning look.

"Bigger blackout, different systems protocol," he explained. "When everything goes out, it takes that much longer for the emergency back-ups to cycle, so—"

As they passed by two parked minivans, a black blur exploded out of the gap between the pair of vehicles and gunfire sounded. Lucy reacted, seeing Marc dive away as a man in an NIS guard uniform came out of nowhere with a semi-automatic pistol in his hand.

The guard must have been one of the group that had come out to greet them, smart enough to circle around the back, lucky enough to avoid the hail of bullets that had cut down his colleagues. The soldiers escorting Lucy and Marc were nowhere to be seen. The situation narrowed abruptly to the immediate space around her and the will to survive the next few seconds.

The man snarled as he turned on Lucy as the closest target, bringing the pistol up to aim at her face. He saw no difference between her and the soldiers, helmet or not. She was an intruder like the rest of them.

Lucy didn't wait for the guard to complete the motion and deflected his gun-arm with a forearm block. The pistol discharged harmlessly into the air, and Lucy kept up the momentum, punching the guard in the throat, trying to blunt the energy of his assault. His eyes locked with hers and she saw fury and hate. He'd seen the other men killed, it was right there in his expression, and he believed that Lucy was one of the people responsible.

She bit down on the human response, the impulse to tell him *No, not me, I'm sorry* and reached for a violent reaction instead. Lucy trapped his wrist and twisted it the wrong way, drawing a howl of pain from the guard. She made it so the only way he could move to disengage was to step into her next attack, trapping him. He realized that too late, as she grabbed at his chin and slammed the man's head back, cracking the passenger window of the minivan with the back of his skull. He staggered, dazed and disorientated, and she did it again. The second time his head connected with the glass, the window shattered and the man's eyes rolled back to show the whites. He slumped against the flank of the van, slipped down the wet metal and on to the ground.

Lucy saw where the guard's gun had landed and took a step toward it, but a powerful grip tightened around her arm and yanked her back. The bigger of the two masked soldiers held her firmly, while the other one, the woman, came in and kicked the fallen pistol out of reach beneath the van.

Marc came back into view. "Are you hit?" He looked shaken.

She gave him a worried look. "Are *you*? I thought . . ."

"Close. Parted my hair." He shook his head. "*Shit*. Where'd he come from?"

Lucy's reply was swallowed by a report from the masked woman's gun as she calmly executed the unconscious guard.

"Motherfucker!" She spat the insult at her.

"*Stop stalling*," Madrigal's ghost-voice demanded. "*Unless you want to end up the same way.*"

Madrigal would have them killed no matter what. If there had ever been an iota of doubt in Lucy's mind, it melted away as she looked at the dead guard. Blood streamed down his face from the entry wound in his skull, thinning as the downpour washed it away.

As they entered the isolated building, lights on the ceiling blinked back to life. The NIS campus's independent generators had finally reached the activation point in their cycle and power was returning, but not quickly enough to prevent the North Korean strike team from blowing through the facility's outer defenses.

Marc's heart hammered in his chest from the near-hit of the security guard's bullet. He hadn't been exaggerating when he told Lucy how close it had come; he felt the round cut past his temple, the hum of it making him flinch away. A centimeter or two the other way and the guard's shot would have buried itself in his face. The sense of death passing so close to him made Marc's gut twist and he swallowed a deep breath.

He felt heavy and uncomfortable in the ill-fitting tactical rig Kara had hung on him. Something jabbed him in the ribs. He pulled at the vest, failing to make it sit more easily. Reaching inside, his fingers touched a foreign object there and he hesitated. *What is that?*

Marc heard a strangled moan from close by, and tasted cordite and blood in the air. A handful of NIS staffers—some of them armed guards like the men in the car park, others suited office workers who had made the fatal mistake of coming in early—lay scattered across the reception area. As before, one of the silent soldiers moved among the fallen, administering an extra shot to the head, to leave no chance of any witnesses. The moaning ceased as the soldier's pistol spat out another round.

But what happened here would not go unseen. Marc looked up and saw the black hemispheres of security-camera pods mounted on the ceiling, above the main reception desk, security station and the doors leading deeper into the building. With the power restored, those monitors were working again, and everything the strike team did was being recorded. He looked away. His face was now committed to that same record.

One of the silent soldiers had been cut down in the advance. A body lay slumped over a chair a few meters away from a dead guard, who had taken down his attacker with a burst from a submachine gun. The soldier with the pistol moved to the side of his dead comrade as the rest of the group advanced through the security checkpoint. Marc turned to watch as he was marched with them, under the bleating alarm from an untended metal detector arch.

The soldier behind them took a cylindrical grenade from the vest of the corpse and pulled the pin, dialing down the timer on the fuse before stuffing it back in the dead man's gear and backing swiftly away. A jet of virulent orange fire surged out and wreathed the body in smoke and flames. In seconds, the corpse was burning in the grip of the thermite discharge, and the cloying stink of melting flesh curdled in Marc's mouth. "They torch their dead," he gasped.

"*Leave nothing behind*," Madrigal's voice reminded him.

Ahead, a pair of the soldiers had used their weapons to blow out the locks holding shut the doors to the corridor beyond, and there were more dead NIS guards lying slumped along the walls. Marc looked down at them as he passed, then shot a look at Lucy. She pretended not to notice, but he knew she had seen their guns lying next to them.

If they made a move for the weapons, how long would they have before Madrigal saw it happen and triggered the shock bracelets on their arms? Marc tensed, feeling the bite of the bracelet's contact tines against his arm. Could he risk it?

At the end of the corridor behind another set of sealed doors was an anteroom, visible through a pane of bulletproof glass. These doors were much thicker, heavy-duty panels with their hinges and locking mechanisms mounted on the inside, more suited to a military bunker than an office building. A second set of them were built into the far wall on the other side of the anteroom. It would be possible to blow the doors open with cutting charges, but that would be a lengthy and destructive process.

Inside the anteroom, shielded from the previous exchange of fire by the glass, there were two men, a stern-faced guard with an SMG and a younger guy in a jacket and tie clutching a pistol. Both of them warily watched the approaching intruders.

The body language of the soldiers changed again as they received new orders. The big guy and the woman who had marched Marc and Lucy from the Halo, and two others remained in the corridor as the rest fell back, disappearing toward the reception area and out of the building.

One of the masked figures moved to the bulletproof pane, shouldering their carbine on a sling, and tap-tapped on it like they were looking into a fish tank.

The guard with the SMG snarled and aimed his weapon at the intruder. He didn't see the expression change on the face of the man with the tie, didn't see the flicker of cold intent. The man with the pistol turned his gun on the guard and shot him through the back of the head, spattering blood and brain matter over the inside of the glass. A few moments later, he was working a control panel and the locked doors began to swing open.

"DPRK deep cover agent," said Lucy quietly. "Makes sense they'd have people in the NIS."

"Yeah," agreed Marc. "And if they were willing to burn them for this operation, you have to wonder . . ."

"What's in there that's worth the cost?" Lucy finished the thought.

The second set of doors opened behind the first, and once more Marc got a push in the small of the back to propel him forward. The object pressing into his chest shifted and he tensed. *If it is what I think it is . . .*

The double agent led them inside, beckoning with one hand. The chamber on the far side of the anteroom security doors was a long, rectangular space with gray walls of poured concrete, and the air inside had the dead, flat quality of a rigorously climate-controlled environment. Weak illumination fell from grids of thick square skylights in the ceiling, sluices of rainwater washed across them by gusts of wind.

A line of five large metal cabins were set along the length of the chamber, each the size of a standard cargo container like those found on ships or the flatbeds of trucks. Each of the cabins had a door with a window in the narrow end, and they were mounted on raised jacks at each corner. The lines and ovals of Korean ideograms designated each of the units with an individual code. Some of the cabins were connected to power cables snaking through gutters in the floor, disappearing beneath the support jacks.

Marc's curiosity led him closer to the nearest unit and he craned his neck to look in through the window. Inside, he saw skeletal wire racks stacked with hard-sided containers and what looked like an isolated computer server.

"These . . . these are SCIFs," he said, putting it together.

Like the secure information room he and Lucy had broken into inside the offices of Horizon Integral, the cabins were a series of compartmentalized, armored data stores. Each one held a library of information that South Korea's intelligence agency wanted to keep off the grid. The bounty of secret information they represented was huge.

"This is what this whole deal has been about, right from day one." Marc turned to Lucy. "Every dirty little secret the NIS don't want the world to see. This is where they keep them."

"*I knew you'd get there eventually,*" breathed Madrigal, and he could hear the smile on her face. "*This is the truth behind the lies. And when the world sees what they've been hiding—what the American government and their lackeys in South East Asia have been colluding to cover up—it will start a fire that will topple nations.*"

The masked female soldier abruptly jerked into motion and raised her carbine, finding the camera domes mounted on the ceiling. Taking careful aim, she shot them out one by one until all the monitors in the chamber were destroyed.

"What was the point of that?" sneered Lucy. "All of a sudden you don't want anyone watching?"

"*No*," said the hacker. "*Not for what is going to happen next.*"

One at a time, the silent soldiers reached up and unhooded, removing their helmets and clipping them to magnetic hooks on their belts. The older man and the woman with the scalded face from the attack on Hite's house were there, and the biggest of the masked figures went next, looming over Marc as he twisted off the sealed headgear, presenting another unpleasantly familiar aspect. Null, the thug from the Antonov, the one with the tattoos who had been so generous with the stun baton, leered at him and showed his teeth.

Ice crawled up Marc's spine as the last of the soldiers revealed themselves, and he knew who he would see before it happened. Metallic red hair pulled in a tight cluster spilled out and a pale face smiled wolfishly back at him.

"Surprise," said Madrigal, relishing her unmasking like the performance of a magic trick. "You were right, back at the plane. I couldn't watch from a distance." Her lip pulled into a crooked, victorious sneer. "I couldn't stay away."

"I get it," Marc replied, and jerked his chin at the cabins. "This is your motherlode, yeah? Your pot of bloody gold at the end of the murder rainbow."

"That's funny," she offered. "You're not far off." Madrigal walked toward the cabins, scanning the ideograms on the side until she locked on one unit in particular. "Here we are," she breathed, her face lighting up with anticipation. "Watch them," she ordered Null.

Madrigal produced a plastic injector from a pouch on her belt and jammed it into the lock of the third cabin along. Thick, glutinous liquid spurted through the mechanism, turning acidic as it was exposed to air. Sizzling and bubbling, the lock gave off a chug of white vapor and the metal frame collapsed in on itself.

Lucy called out to her. "What do you think you're gonna find in there?"

"Enough dark data to tear open the NIS and break what little trust the people of South Korea still have in their corrupt government," said the other woman. "For starters. And then there are the lies that track back to Washington DC, the CIA and everyone else who collaborated." Madrigal hesitated, and when she spoke again there was a momentary catch in her voice. "They're going to pay for their sins." She wrenched open the door and became very still as she stared at the contents within.

Marc thought he saw a flash of emotion on Madrigal's face, but then it was gone. "And the North will get their cut of the action, right?" he added, glancing at Fox, who stood nearby with his weapon on the two prisoners. "That's the deal you made."

Madrigal spread her hands and took a deep breath. "Everybody gets what they deserve."

Cat and the double agent were near the doors, the woman covering the man in the suit as he dragged the body of a dead guard into the chamber and dumped it up against a support stanchion. The man went out again and returned with guns looted from the NIS personnel.

Marc traded questioning glances with Lucy and she made a subtle gesture with her hands, as if she were pulling two ends of a string away from one another.

The meaning was clear: *Play for time.*

In turn, she nodded toward the SCIF cabin that was the focus of Madrigal's attention, directing Marc to look. He saw the big guy crouching by the support jacks, wiring up pads of C4 explosive to the feet of the metal frames. After all the effort it had taken to get into this place, the last thing he expected the hacker to do was blow up her long sought-after prize.

"See here," he began. "You have the same problem as someone breaking into a gold vault. There's a metric fuck-ton of materials in each one of those container units and you can't carry it out of here on your back."

The whole reasoning behind the NIS's use of this kind of secure store came down to a single factor—their contents were not linked to any outside database or internet connection. The stand-alone servers some of the cabins contained could only be accessed by physically entering the SCIF and using a terminal inside, and the others with cases full of hard copy contained files that existed nowhere else but here. It was deliberately offline, disconnected, old tech. Impossible to hack, unless someone was capable of crashing an entire city to get to them.

Madrigal turned to study Marc. Her eyes were shining. "You're mistaken," she said. "And anyway . . . I don't want it all."

Gunfire blared and Marc tensed, but the shots were not aimed in his direction. He saw the woman, Cat, empty the clip on her carbine in random bursts into the walls and the ceiling.

When the weapon's magazine ran dry, she pivoted and threw the rifle to Lucy, who caught it awkwardly. "What am I supposed to do with this?" she said.

Cat didn't answer her. She drew a SIG Sauer handgun from her belt and did the same as she had with the M4, firing at nothing until the slide locked back and the ammunition was expended. The woman crossed to Marc and pressed the smoking gun into his hand.

When the other assassin took one of the South Korean weapons from the double agent and loaded a fresh magazine into it, Madrigal's finale for Marc and Lucy became horribly apparent. At once, Marc saw how it would play out: Fox would gun down the two Rubicon operatives and make it look like they had perished in an exchange of fire with one of the NIS guards, leaving their bodies in the SCIF chamber as a false lead for the Koreans to chase while Ghost5 and their allies from the North melted away.

Allowing the cameras to capture their faces in the reception, then shooting out the cameras in here so the deception would remain unseen, Madrigal had designed the scenario to drop the blame squarely at their feet. The NIS would eventually figure out their identities, and then the mother of all shit storms would break loose. South Korea's security services, the Central Intelligence Agency, all of their forces would drop the hammer on the Rubicon Group. Solomon would never see it coming. Even if someone did eventually piece together the truth, by the time that happened Madrigal would be long gone.

"Aw, hell no." Lucy's lip twisted in a sneer as she saw the same thing that Marc did. "We're not gonna be your goddamn patsies, Red."

Madrigal smirked. "It's amusing how you think you have a say in this." Behind her, Null had finished his work on the supports of the number three cabin and scrambled up on to the roof of the unit. He pulled the last of the demolition packs from his webbing vest as Madrigal went on. "I won't lie to you, I'm impressed by what you have done," she said. "The only people who ever get this close to me are the ones I recruit . . . or the ones I have to delete."

"Like Kara?" said Lucy. "Like Lex Wetherby?"

"Now you're getting it." Madrigal paused and pressed her hand to a radio bead in her right ear. Marc heard the faint crackle of an incoming transmission, saw her nod to herself.

"With all due respect, *Marie*," said Marc, using Madrigal's real name to get a rise from her, "you can go fuck yourself. We're not playing your games anymore." He tossed the empty pistol into the shadows with an angry flick of the wrist.

"Weren't you listening, Dane? You never had a choice." She threw a nod at Null, who had finished attaching his last few charges in a ring around the skylights in the roof.

The thug jumped down and backed away, producing a radio detonator. "*Feuer im Loch*," he grunted, and mashed a button on the device.

Marc barely had time to cover his ears before the C4 around the base of the cabin blew in a cracking roll of percussion. The SCIF slumped off its mountings as the second set of explosives on the ceiling went off a heartbeat later. These were shaped charges, their detonation configured to blow up and away, and they took a great circular section out of the roof, blasting reinforced glass and concrete into the rainy air. Dust and fragments billowed back into the chamber, but the debris was almost immediately damped down by the heavy rain that lashed through the ragged hole in the ceiling.

His thoughts caught up with him and Marc started forward, hoping that the wake of the blast would give him vital seconds to get the drop on Madrigal and her team, but from the haze came Null, brandishing that wicked-looking knife of his. He gave Marc a mocking shake of the head, stopping him dead.

Marc heard a low roll of thunder and from the corner of his eye, out through the hole in the roof, he saw a blink of white light. The rainfall abruptly became a torrent as a powerful downdraft of air blasted into the chamber. He realized that the light was a tail indicator on the Halo, and the thunder was the sound of the massive rotors.

The hulking cargo helicopter drifted across to float above the shattered ceiling, and cables dropped down from a hatch on its belly, bouncing off the top of the damaged SCIF.

Null moved away, grabbing the cables and fastening them to thick steel eye-bolts in the metal cabin's frame. Nearby, Madrigal watched him work with a beatific expression on her face, letting the rain wash over her.

The big man quickly finished his work and waved at the helicopter. After a moment, the cables began to slowly draw up as the Halo took the weight of its new cargo.

"Well," Madrigal called out, turning back to Marc and Lucy. "We have to be leaving." The woman slipped a small device into her palm, a remote-control switch similar to the one Null had used to blow the charges. "I'm not without compassion," she went on, pitching up her voice to be heard over the noise. She nodded toward Fox as he raised the stolen rifle. "He'll make this quick. Unless you misbehave."

Lucy held the spent M4 like a cudgel and shook it at the other woman. "You can kiss my ass, you skinny—"

"Never mind," snapped Madrigal, mashing the trigger for the shock bracelets.

Marc braced himself for another onslaught of nerve-shredding agony, the memory of the pain from the stun baton strikes weathered on board the Antonov still fresh in his mind. It didn't come.

The moment of confusion on Madrigal's face was a new expression. She hit the button again, more forcefully this time, and still the bracelets did not trigger.

A crooked grin spread on Marc's face and he slipped his hand behind his tactical rig, grabbing at the object hidden in the lining of the webbing.

"Kara . . . ?" said Lucy, pulling at the inert shock device before giving him a sideways look, her eyes narrowing.

"*Kara*," he repeated, meeting Madrigal's gaze.

The woman's face turned stony and cold, a shadow passing over her features as she ground out the words. "Ungrateful little whore . . ." There was the briefest flash of a deep, wounded sorrow that faded under a murderous scowl. Marc saw the same killer's face from the tape of the Cooper murder, a raw and naked hate exposed to the light. Behind her, the SCIF cabin had pulled free of its moorings and hung suspended in the air. "Erik!" she shouted, tapping the radio bead in her ear. "Erik, anyone on comms, respond!"

"Ah, I reckon she cut you off from the plane, didn't she?" Marc shifted, using the moment to draw away from Lucy, making it hard for Fox to target the two of them together. "Looks like we weren't the only ones she was keeping things from."

Marc's hand dropped into view, and in it he held an EFL, a device that resembled the pistol grip of a large handgun, minus the barrel and receiver assembly. The emergency flare launcher could shoot off a half-dozen 19mm signal cartridges in rapid succession. Kara had slipped it into his gear, back at the airport. Not quite a weapon, but *all she could do*. It had a trigger and a safety, which he flicked off as he brought the EFL up to aim in the direction of Madrigal and the others.

"That's all you've got? A flare gun?" Madrigal shouted back at him, then turned away, ignoring him as she moved to grab on to the cabin before it rose out of reach. "Get rid of them!" Madrigal barked out the order and hauled herself into the SCIF, climbing inside as it rose up through the ragged gap in the ceiling.

Marc saw the split-second decision in Fox's expression as the gunman evaluated and then chose which target he was going to kill first, and, as Marc had gambled, the DPRK assassin swung the gun toward Lucy. She was the trained Special Forces soldier, she was the one Fox would have been briefed on as the greater threat, armed or not.

But Marc Dane was used to being underestimated. Instead of aiming the EFL like a regular pistol, he fired off the first two cartridges in a shallow angle at the concrete floor, and the rounds skipped off where they hit. Bursting into searing bright points of crimson fire, the flares ricocheted away on trails of chemical smoke. Fox could only recoil from the dazzling flames and his shots toward Lucy went wild.

The third cartridge spat from the launcher rocketed across the chamber, fired as Marc burst into motion through the haze, the rain and the Halo's rotor wash. He heard a high-pitched, mewling cry as the flare struck the double agent in the chest, burning through his white shirt. The man had come storming toward Marc, gun raised, and run straight into the shot. Screaming, he clawed wildly at his torso as a thousand-degree fireball burned through flesh and bone into his chest cavity.

Marc caught sight of Lucy diving for cover toward one of the other SCIF cabins as Null and the others opened fire, bullets whistling through the choking, smoke-wreathed air. Marc threw himself in the other direction and out of the line of attack, running, stumbling, determined to survive.

Overhead, the Halo and its cargo slipped away into the gray sky and vanished, the thud of the rotors swallowed by the rainstorm.

# — SEVENTEEN —

The chemical smoke from the flares seared the back of Lucy's throat as she gulped down breaths of air. She fought against the reaction of her body, smothering the urge to cough. Skidding out of the line of fire, she heard the snap of bullets deflect off the corner of the nearest SCIF cabin. Fox had her in his sights, but Marc's diversion gave Lucy vital seconds to break for cover before the North Korean assassin could end her.

The question of where the flare gun Marc used had come from, and of what that meant about Kara Wei's betrayal, did not have time to fully form in Lucy's thoughts. She couldn't waste a moment on worrying about who to trust. Right now, her focus was on the next sixty seconds, then the minute after that and the minute after that. *The other shit I can deal with later.*

She heard shouts and more braying snarls of gunfire. Lucy weighed the empty M4 carbine in her hand. With no rounds in the magazine it was nothing more than an inert lump of metal and plastic, but like her instructors in Basic had drummed into her, in times of crisis anything and everything could be used as a weapon.

Lucy flattened herself against the side of the number four SCIF, hiding in the shadows of the far corner so anyone who thought to drop to their feet and look below it wouldn't see her boots. She twirled the carbine around and gripped it by the handguard and the lower receiver, the muzzle pointed at the floor.

Shouts rebounded off the concrete walls and crimson light from the burning flares danced, casting jumping shadows in all directions. A gun barked again and she wondered about Marc. If either of them tried to make a break for the doors leading out of the SCIF chamber, they would be cut down. Lucy wanted to believe that Dane wouldn't be that reckless, but where the impulsive Brit was concerned all bets were off.

She heard boots thudding as someone came racing up around the side of the cabin. Without hesitating, Lucy rocked off her heels and rushed to intercept them, bringing up the carbine in a motion like swinging an axe.

The punk thug with the metalhead tattoos rounded the corner and Lucy belted him as hard as she could with the M4's buttstock. Plastic splintered as she caught Null across the cheek, hitting the man with enough force to break his nose. Blood smeared his lips and he staggered back, fumbling for his own weapon and missing. She kept up the momentum, giving him no time to recover, hitting Null as hard as she could.

He was ready for her this time, and he brought up his hands to deflect the broken rifle away. Null took blows to the face and neck, and he bellowed angrily, swearing at her in gutter German. Lucy jolted back, wary of overextending, but he was on the move, surging into her. Null smacked the M4 out of her grip and clawed at her chest, gaining purchase on a handful of her webbing vest and the black jumpsuit beneath.

Lucy fired a shotgun double-punch into his broken nose, feeling the bone grind and crunch as she landed the blows. Her knuckles came back bloody as Null kept advancing, raw rage driving him on. His other hand drew across Lucy's neck and she couldn't stop him from twisting her about, drawing her close into a violent embrace.

She felt his chest heaving with effort against her back as his arm tightened around her throat. Lucy's hands became talons and she clawed at the exposed skin of Null's face, tearing his flesh, trying to gouge out his eyes.

Breath stalled in her throat and her lungs turned leaden as she gasped for air. The sensation was horribly familiar. More than once an assailant had tried to take her out this way, and each time it was as terrible as the first.

She saw movement from the other side of the cabin. The female DPRK assassin swept around and caught sight of them locked in their struggle. The woman raised her rifle, unconcerned that Madrigal's thug was in her sight picture as much as Lucy.

Lucy shot back her elbows into Null's gut and he reacted, momentarily easing his grip on her neck. As Cat squeezed the trigger of her weapon, Lucy let her weight shift and deliberately sagged forward, pulling the big man off-balance. Null twisted and Lucy dragged him sideways before he could arrest the motion, turning so he was between her and the muzzle of Cat's rifle.

A burst of fully automatic fire stitched a line up Null's back as he briefly became Lucy's human shield, and he choked out his last breath into her face.



Marc sprinted down the narrow gap between two of the SCIF cabins as shots screamed through the hazy air. Sparks flashed orange-yellow as Fox came after him, bracketing Marc with paced shots from his weapon.

He blind-fired the compact flare gun over his shoulder, aiming to disrupt the assassin's attack and gain the time he desperately needed to escape amid the smoke and the rain streaming in through the ruined roof. Marc wanted to believe there was still a chance he could get out of this in one piece.

The signal flares cracked from the blunt muzzle of the launcher, bouncing off the floor and the flanks of the nearest SCIF. Each one was a tiny, blinding sun of searing crimson, sputtering as it produced streamers of gray-white smoke. Marc felt the last flare leave the device and the hammer fall on the empty magazine. The cartridge struck the ground behind him, close enough for the heat of the discharge to make him flinch as it burst into a fountain of dazzling ruby fire.

Dropping the empty launcher, Marc slipped around the back of the SCIF to his right and grabbed at a handhold welded into the frame. He had only seconds to react, and it took a flood of adrenaline to push him up and on to the top of the metal cabin, sliding low across the corrugated steel surface.

Holding his breath, willing himself to be invisible, Marc flattened his body as much as he could, hoping that the shadows and the smoke would conceal him, if only for a few moments.

From the far side of the SCIF chamber he heard a clatter of metal and plastic and a man shout out in pain. *Lucy did that.* He grinned, in spite of the dire situation. Knowing she was still alive, still fighting, gave him the impetus to do the same. *Not dead yet*, he told himself.

Fox moved past below him, waving a hand in front of his face to waft away the acrid smoke from the hissing, sizzling flares. Marc stole a glance over the lip of the cabin and saw the assassin looking the wrong way, aiming his rifle into the darkness.

He knew he wouldn't get another opportunity. Marc coiled his legs and leaped from the top of the SCIF, diving at the gunman. Fox must have seen the motion of shadows in the red light, because he turned quickly, but not fast enough to avoid Marc slamming into him in a blunt, forceful collision.

The rifle went off with a flat crack, the barrel knocked away and the round pinging harmlessly along the low ceiling. Marc's attack sent Fox into a reeling backward tumble, putting the assassin down on the concrete floor with a crash, the two of them wrestling with one another as they fell. Still, the North Korean was not on the defensive but chose to attack, flicking the skeletal wireframe stock of the weapon up to strike Marc across the chin.

Marc's head snapped back with an eye-watering jolt and before he could recover, Fox punched him hard in the ear. Fresh pain sang through his skull, knocking him off balance and costing him vital split seconds of reaction time. The moment of shock and surprise he had torn from Fox was gone, burned away by the assassin's resilience and grit.

The North Korean agent was fifteen, perhaps even twenty years his senior, and he was every inch the career killer that Marc was not. As their eyes locked for one brief instant, all Marc saw behind them was a cold void, the utter nonexistence of empathy. Fox was the DPRK's ultimate killing tool, a man trained from childhood to serve Party and nation in the business of secret murder. Marc looked into those eyes as the two of them struggled against one another, the rifle trapped between them. It was this man who killed Crowne at the house, who shot Lex Wetherby in Malta and as many others as his masters in Pyongyang commanded.

Then the instant shattered as Fox jerked his arms forward and savagely slammed the rifle frame into Marc's face, knocking him back and away.


Null literally became dead weight as the life faded from his eyes and his body went slack in Lucy's grip. Before the big man's mass could slump forward and knock her down, she braced her feet and shoved him the other way, giving out a cry of exertion.

The bloody, bullet-riddled corpse lurched back toward Cat and caught the other woman off-guard. Null's body slammed into the slight North Korean and she lost her balance, staggering under the unexpected impact.

Lucy saw her opening and flew at her, jack-knifing in a jump kick off the wall of the SCIF to give her height and velocity. She led with her good right cross and punched Cat in the middle of the reddened, swollen patch of her face where she had been scalded. As the dead man crumpled in a heap on the floor, already forgotten by both the combatants, Lucy whipped her other arm around to deflect the assassin's rifle. The strike knocked the weapon from Cat's grip—or perhaps she let it go deliberately, it didn't matter.

Cat brought up her hands and unleashed a wave of sharp, fast hits, each one punctuated by a high-pitched yell. They traded blows, repelling most, some landing with precise impact on soft tissues and other vulnerable spots.

Lucy made a cutting motion, the blade of her hand falling across Cat's forearm, deliberately striking at the point where the assassin's limb had been dislocated in their earlier fight at the house. The strike landed, but Cat seemed to barely react to the hit, fighting on, breath hissing through her gritted teeth.

Lucy saw her eyes were contracted to dark pinpoints, and the assassin's lack of response immediately made sense. Whatever painkillers Cat was dosed up on, they were potent ones. Any punches that Lucy landed had to feel like love taps.

Cat hit her, a lightning-fast blow to the nerve cluster below Lucy's right shoulder. A rolling shock of pain rippled down her arm, a bone-deep sting making her joints twitch and stiffen.

Bright metal glittered in the weak light through the broken ceiling and the combat dagger that Cat had pulled in Hite's house emerged once again. The blade flickered and swam in the wet air, cutting at nothing. The assassin wanted this rematch. She wanted to finish off what had been interrupted back in Sydney. Lucy had no choice but to oblige her, instinctively backing off to open the distance between them.

Cat lunged and slashed at her face. It was a feint, a big and showy move designed to make Lucy react more than to injure her. Before, Lucy had disarmed Cat by letting the assassin's overconfidence get the better of her, making her extend too far into the fighting space. This time, the assassin would not fall for the same trick, and she kept up her speed and motion, shifting from foot to foot, never staying in one place long enough for Lucy to make a grab for her.

Cat dodged away each time Lucy tried to blindside her or step inside her guard and go for the weapon. With every failed attempt, she left Lucy with a shallow cut across her hand or forearm, slicing through the palm of her glove or the sleeve of her over-suit.

Each stinging wound leaked bright blood and sent fresh fire down Lucy's nerves, and part of her screamed at herself to get in there and finish this quickly, before Cat cut across an artery.

She fought down the impulse and weathered the attacks, knowing that there would only be one chance to defeat this woman. Cat had been driven to participate in this mission even though the swollen joint of the arm Lucy had dislocated should have benched her. But fighting an enemy pumped up on sense-deadening drugs was nothing like engaging with a clear-eyed opponent. The predictable, rational patterns of attack and defend, strike and riposte, became irrelevant. If Cat's pain receptors were cloaked in a chemical fog of opiates, then she would not respond as she had before. Lucy could break bone, tear flesh, and the assassin would barely feel it.

That was what Lucy would use to beat her. Despite the drugs in her system, Cat was still a product of her training, a lifetime of techniques drilled into her by whatever teachers the DPRK had employed to make the woman an executioner. The painkillers were making her feel invulnerable, a sensation Lucy had experienced herself in a darker part of her past, but they also affected Cat's judgment. Her mind would move a step behind the old, ingrained reactions of muscle memory. Lucy watched for the fractional delay she knew was going to come, deflecting the blade over and over, taking cut after cut. And when it happened, she moved without hesitating, letting her own deep-rooted experience take control.

Cat saw what her instinct identified as a gap in Lucy's defenses and lunged forward, leading with the arrow-sharp tip of the combat dagger, intent on burying the blade to its hilt in the other woman's breast. The knife would go into Lucy's heart, tear it in two, end her.

Lucy had been waiting for the stab to come, inviting it. Cat's moves from the fight in the house were there in her mind, ruthlessly broken down and countered, each step in the dance ready to be turned back against the assassin.

She caught Cat's wrist as the dagger came in, gripping and twisting, applying pressure to joints and nerves so that her opponent couldn't maintain the impetus. In a flash of reflected light, the blade was torn from the assassin's numbed fingers, spun around, its axis reversed.

Putting all her strength behind it, Lucy stabbed Cat through the eye with her own weapon. She pushed the knife through the socket and into her opponent's skull with a jerk, making the kill with ruthless precision.

Marc scrambled wildly to haul himself up off the damp, rain-slicked floor of the chamber, knocking aside fallen fragments of roof supports and jagged pieces of glass skylight. Fox raised the assault rifle in his hands, drawing out the moment by taking careful aim at his head.

Marc's hands rose up in front of him, as if the gesture could somehow ward off the killing shot. "Wait—!"

Fox glared down the iron sights and his finger tightened on the trigger, but there was no fatal shout of discharge, no final bullet. In the struggle between the two men, part of the rifle's mechanism had become unseated and fouled the shot. Irritably, the assassin pulled hard on the slide to eject the bullet in the breech and rack another.

As the dud round pinged from the ejection port, Marc exploded into motion. He skidded as he fell forward, his rough and clumsy attack fueled by the energy of sheer desperation. For the second time, he body-checked Fox with every effort he could muster and snatched at the rifle, forcing it back so the muzzle aimed toward the SCIFs and away from his face. There was no artistry or elegance to this ugly engagement, and it devolved into a mad flurry of push and pull as the two of them fought over the weapon. Fox slipped against a chunk of broken masonry and Marc shoved him harder, trying to get the upper hand before his fortunes reversed once again.

All the violent experiences Marc had gone through—dust-ups on the streets of a South London council estate as a youth, training to fight with the Navy and later with the Security Services, months of endless sparring with a Krav Maga instructor during his time in Croatia—none could prepare him for combat against someone who would stop at nothing to end his life. Each time it happened, whether there were punches raining down on him or bullets screaming through the air, the raw animal need to *live through this* was the impetus that kept him moving.

Leaning into his opponent, Marc pressed the frame of the assault rifle into Fox's neck, trying to choke him. He had the height advantage but the assassin showed hidden reserves of stamina, gripping the barrel of the gun and fighting back, struggling to push it away.

It seemed like the stalemate between them lasted for an eternity, the muscles in Marc's arms twitching with effort. He knew he would lose this contest if it went on any longer, he could feel the fatigue spreading through his limbs. His bones felt like lead. He had to finish it.

Marc dug deep for a last burst of energy and shoved forward, kicking out at Fox's leg as hard as he could. The assassin twisted, letting the blow slip uselessly off his shin, the effort wasted, but his boot came down on another piece of rubble and it cost him a second of balance, his eyes widening in surprise.

A wordless shout escaping his lips, Marc pushed harder and Fox stumbled. Locked together, the two men fell, and Marc pressed his body weight into the motion, letting gravity give him the extra force he needed.

Fox's head struck the ground with a jolting convulsion, the rifle frame crashing down over his trachea. A sickly crackle of breaking cartilage escaped his lips in a gust of breath, and the light in the assassin's eyes dimmed. Marc kept on pushing down, holding the rifle in place until it was over.

He rolled off the dead man, his gut churning and his hands twitching. Smoke was everywhere, and with the red light of the guttering, fading flares, the chamber had taken on a hellish, infernal cast.

Shadows moved, coming closer. Marc grabbed at the assault rifle, wrenching it from Fox's death-grip, ready to face the next enemy.

The shadow resolved into Lucy Keyes. Her dark features were drawn and wreathed in sweat. "Marc . . . Damn. Did we get them all?"

"I think so . . ." His gaze dropped to her hands and he saw the cuts there, the sheen of blood from the wounds. "Oh shit. You're hurt!"

"I noticed," she said, with a gasp. "Don't worry about me, we have to get out of here. The NIS will be sending reinforcements. And they're not going to wanna hear what we have to say."

"Yeah," he agreed, staggering after her, his heart hammering in his chest. "This isn't done yet. Not by a long chalk."

Lucy found a first-aid kit behind the front desk in the atrium and took the bandages. Discarding the ripped gloves and tearing open the sleeves of her over-suit, her mouth twisted as she looked at the ugly mess of weeping cuts that Cat had left her with. Working on the move, she dressed the wounds as best she could, but crimson fluid had already spotted through the bandages by the time they were back out in the parking lot where the Halo had put down.

She felt the first symptoms of blood loss, her skin clammy, breath coming in gasps. Lucy blinked away a moment of dizziness and pressed on, tilting her head back to let the rain hit her face. The cold droplets gave her something to focus on.

"Here, you take this, you're the better shot." She turned as Marc pressed the assault rifle into her hands. Lucy took it from him and he stooped by the body of a fallen NIS guard, pulling a Daewoo submachine gun from the dead man's two-point harness. He gestured ahead. "You see anything?"

"Fires," she replied. Several of the vehicles in the parking lot had been set aflame, either through random damage or deliberate action, and thick columns of black smoke rose up to meet the low rainclouds. A curtain of haze drifted in front of the main NIS campus building, making it hard to pick out any movement. The damp air was acrid with the smell of burning gasoline and scorched rubber.

Marc shook his head. "No, no. The chopper, I mean. The Halo. You see it?" He looked around, scanning the nearby hillside.

There was no sign of the hulking cargo helicopter, the drones or the other soldiers. Lucy held her breath, and strained to listen. She thought she could hear the faraway thudding of rotors. "Madrigal didn't stick around."

"I'm not letting her go," grated Marc, and he jerked his chin toward the smaller silver chopper on the helipad near the main building. "I can fly that Dauphin."

"That so?" She forced a smirk. "Last time you told me you could fly a thing, we almost ended up as a grease mark across half of Mogadishu."

"I don't tell you how to shoot," he retorted. "Come on!"

They sprinted to the other helicopter, coming across more bodies in NIS uniforms scattered at the edge of the landing pad. Lucy evaluated the kills dispassionately. All of them had been killed by shots from medium range, tight groupings and center-mass. Close by were the remains of two of the masked soldiers, their bodies destroyed by a thermite charge like the dead man back in the outbuilding. The falling rain sizzled off the blackened and twisted corpses as they cooled.

Lucy swallowed her reaction, turning her thoughts to other questions. "Why'd they leave this bird intact?"

"My guess, so the team going after the SCIF had an exit strategy." Marc climbed inside the aircraft and ran his hands over the controls. "Get in, I'll spin her up."

"Do it fast!" Lucy saw men moving out from the main complex, more of the NIS guards coming to back up their dead comrades. The reinforcements had clearly stopped off at the campus armory on the way. They wore body armor and helmets over their uniforms, and all of them carried assault rifles with extended magazines.

Someone saw the Dauphin's rotors moving and called out in alarm, sending a squad of the guards to break off and come running toward the helipad. Lucy swore and snapped the selector on her rifle to burst fire setting. Aiming over the heads of the approaching men, she let off a salvo of shots that sent them diving for cover.

In a few seconds, the ducted blades on the Dauphin's tail filled the air with a high-pitched scream, and Lucy hauled open the sliding door to the helicopter's rear compartment, scrambling inside as the main rotors picked up speed. She fired again, this time aiming at parked vehicles, deliberately blowing out windshields to create sprays of shattered glass and distract the guards.

The rotor howl meant she didn't hear Marc when he shouted to her from the pilot's seat, but she understood the thumbs-up gesture he flashed and quickly grabbed a safety handle as the Dauphin rocked on its undercarriage. The silver helicopter lifted off the ground and pivoted as it climbed straight up. Lucy saw the bright yellow blinks of muzzle flashes as the guards fired after them, and felt more than she heard the metallic thuds of rifle rounds hitting the fuselage.

Marc hauled the control stick hard to port and the Dauphin's blades smacked at the air. He side-slipped the helicopter back over the parking lot and across the top of the outbuilding. Seen from above, the damaged roof was a mess of broken concrete and twisted rebar.

Lucy dragged the side hatch shut as the helicopter shot forward and continued to climb toward the underside of the low cloud base. Every breath she took was labored, but she ignored the sticky blood seeping through her bandaged hands as she checked the assault rifle and reloaded it. The Dauphin tilted as it changed course again, and she shouldered the weapon, glancing over the back of the empty co-pilot's chair and out of the rain-dashed canopy.

They were cresting the hill, heading back toward Seoul. Although dawn had broken, the sunrise made little impression through the thick layer of the slate-colored storm cell smothering the city. The lights of stalled vehicles shimmered below them, marking out the grid of the streets. Save for a few buildings operating on their own generators, the residential blocks, shopping malls and offices remained dark and unlit.

"Power's still out," she called. Marc spared her a questioning look, unable to hear her voice in the helicopter's noisy cabin. She pointed at the city and made a throat-cutting gesture. He nodded in return and quickly made a sign of his own, shading his eyes in a *look-see* motion, then pointing at the horizon.

Lucy returned his nod and scanned the sky by sectors, scanning for the distinctive shape of the Halo. It was hard to pick it out with the increasingly poor visibility, a gray whale of a shape against a gray sky, but the cargo helicopter soon revealed itself as a slow-moving shadow at their eleven o'clock position, slightly below their altitude. Lucy could make out the hijacked SCIF cabin dangling below the Halo's belly, a tan rectangle swaying in the downdraft.

She pointed it out to Marc and he nodded, turning them on to a pursuit path, descending and closing the distance. The Halo was heading west, and for a moment Lucy tried to fathom where the North Koreans intended to take it. Heading back to the Antonov at Incheon seemed like the most likely option, but there were other possibilities. If it came to it, the Halo had the range to carry the SCIF to a ship at anchor out in the Yellow Sea or even chance making a fast run toward the Joint Security Area and the military border that cut the Korean peninsula in two.

*Would they risk that?* Even now, the nearest South Korean air-base would be scrambling its Blackhawks to secure the NIS campus, and their next objective would be to intercept the Halo. *And us along with it*, she thought grimly. Now the wild rush of contact had faded, she could think past the immediate moment and try to figure out what their next move would be.

Out of nowhere, a faint crackling buzz tickled her throat and she instinctively reached for it. The radio earpiece she had been ordered to wear dangled at the end of its cord by her neck, vibrating against her skin. She snatched at it, eyeing the device with distrust. Neither she nor Marc had made use of the comms gear since the firefight in-side the SCIF chamber, both of them knowing that the signals were on a party line that Ghost5 and the North Koreans could also access.

Cautiously, Lucy pressed the blood-smeared radio bead into her ear in time to hear someone saying her name. *"Keyes? Are you there? Dane? Do you hear me?"* It was Kara Wei's voice, hushed and intense.

Marc gave her another searching look, and she responded by tap-ping his discarded earpiece. In turn, he put it on and listened.

*"I hope you are listening,"* said Kara. *"I'm sending this signal directly to the digital receivers in your gear, in the clear. I don't have long."* She paused. *"Can you answer?"* Kara added, almost plaintively.

Lucy and Marc exchanged glances, and she shook her head. For the moment, Madrigal and the rest of the strike team were operating on the assumption that the two of them were dead. If Kara was on Madrigal's side, then the moment either of them uttered a word, that error would be revealed. Lucy and Marc would lose any element of surprise.

Up ahead, the Halo still followed its course, low and fast above roof-top level, showing no sign that the crew had spotted their pursuers.

*"This will sound hollow,"* Kara continued, *"but I want you to know that I regret what I have done."* Lucy's hand tightened on the back of the co-pilot's seat in anger at her words. *"It was the only way that I could do this,"* Kara went on. *"Turning against Rubicon—giving you up—I had to find something that would get me back in deep with Ghost5. Mad-rigal always wanted me to return, but she wouldn't have believed it . . ."* For the first time in a long while, Lucy heard what sounded like real emotion in the other woman's voice. *"So I had to betray you. Sacrifice my friendship, like an offering."*

Marc looked at Lucy, and she glared at him, silently warning him not to speak.

*"I am sorry,"* said Kara. *"I am so bad at this."* She paused again, and then the crackling buzz built, smothering her words. *"I'll make this right."*

The radio channel went dead. Lucy's jaw hardened and she pulled the comms bead from her ear. Marc did the same, his eyes never breaking her gaze.

Lucy leaned in and spoke loudly enough so he could hear her over the droning of the rotors. "Get us nearer. Let's put these assholes down."

Marc nodded, turning back to the controls to apply more power.

The Dauphin's nose dipped and it closed the gap with the other helicopter.

Kara slipped the walkie-talkie radio into the inner pocket of her leather jacket as she pulled it tight over her shoulders. She walked quickly up the Antonov's open cargo ramp and past the masked soldier standing guard inside, observing him without making it obvious. The North Korean black-ops trooper carried an assault rifle in a ready-to-fire stance, and he was constantly scanning the apron in front of the cargo hangar for any signs of approach. On the other side of Incheon's runways, the airport itself was in disarray, a victim of the same massive power outage that had brought the city of Seoul to its knees.

A security car had ventured out to check in on the Antonov after the Halo had departed, doubtless sent by the air-traffic control tower when no response had been given to their increasingly worried radio calls. The airport had switched over to battery power for communications, but it had done next to nothing to alleviate the situation. With the mains cut, they were struggling to stay on top of things. That was likely why no one had questioned why the men in the security car had not returned. Anyone up in the tower looking in the Antonov's direction with powerful binoculars would only see the rear of the car, still parked next to the hangar. They wouldn't see the two figures slumped in the front seats, their faces masks of blood, wouldn't see the bullet holes in the windshield.

In the middle of the big jet's cargo bay, Pyne and the other hackers were agitated, snapping at one another or typing quickly into their laptops. They were trying desperately to figure out why the encrypted communications between the Antonov and Madrigal's strike team on the Halo had been cut off. Some of them were panicking, certain that the operation was falling apart, that the NIS or the local military had reacted faster than anyone expected and were coming to kill them.

They weren't looking for betrayal from the inside. Such misdirection was, Kara reflected, a talent she was showing an aptitude for. There had been ample time on the flight from Sydney for her to find an opportunity to map the temporary network Ghost5 were using. Hacking their covert comms protocols had taken her less than thirty minutes. Kara picked apart the encryption programs that made the group's radio messages into garbled noise and inserted an implant subroutine of her own. She made it so the decoder software that turned the radio signals back into normal speech would stop working after a certain time. Both ends could send and receive, but what they got back was a mess of unintelligible, randomized noise. It was a piece of digital judo, turning the tech's strength against itself. She'd effectively changed the locks on the radio net, cutting off Madrigal's means of contacting Erik or any of the others. For now, Kara owned the airwaves.

But sooner rather than later, somebody on the Halo would figure out that the helicopter's civilian radio could still talk to whoever was in the Antonov's cockpit via regular, unencrypted frequencies. And when that happened, Kara's latest duplicity would be revealed.

She glanced around, looking for Erik, and didn't see him. *Was that a bad sign or a good one?* Her hand went into one of the pockets of the jacket and closed around a thumb-sized USB memory stick she had hidden there. She tried to ignore the tremor. A lifetime of distant emotions were closing in on her, as if they had been held back just to break through in this moment.

Kara walked toward Madrigal's place at the jury-rigged work bench, where one of the woman's computers lay untended. A slim silver laptop without a single hard edge to it, it resembled a piece of extra-terrestrial technology cast against the mechanistic and unlovely hardware of the Russian cargo plane's interior.

Madrigal's machine was a symbolic representation of her presence among the group, like a queen's crown resting atop a vacant throne. No one would touch it. No one would *dare*. The Ghost5 collective had few rules for its members to adhere to, but one of the inviolate ones was *don't hack where you live*. To mess with another person's kit was tantamount to an invasion of the most personal kind, and to put your hands on Madrigal's computer was the equivalent of high treason.

When she had first been drawn into Ghost5's orbit and Lex was still alive, Kara had thought it foolish of Madrigal to leave her machine in plain sight. It invited trouble. But Lex had been the one to explain it. Madrigal left that temptation around because she *wanted* someone to reach for it. To find out who couldn't be trusted to follow the rules she laid down.

Kara knew there was another reason. No one in Ghost5 was good enough to break through Madrigal's firewalls. Anyone who tried would be stymied, taught the lesson of their own fallibility in no uncertain terms.

*Anyone but me*, Kara noted, and sat down before the machine, booting it up and snapping the USB stick into an open port.

Andre was the first one to notice, and from the corner of her eye, Kara saw him hesitate and try to frame his response. He was momentarily shocked silent that she would dare to sully the crown. "What . . . the fuck is going on? Get away from that!"

"Shut up," she snarled, breaking the first layer of encryption with ease. The USB stick enabled itself with a clever bit of trickery, fooling the laptop's disabled auto-play subroutine into reactivating. A weighty shot of intrusion software built to Kara's own designs, some of it borrowed from Rubicon tools developed by Marc Dane and Assim Kader, bored into Madrigal's computer and began hammering down its firewalls.

Pyne's head bobbed on the end of her thin, birdlike neck. "You shouldn't be touching her stuff." At her side, Billy tugged nervously on the back of his trapper hat and mutely shook his head. The others stopped what they were doing.

"I am going to tell you something," Kara spoke with force and conviction, her voice loud enough to carry as her fingers became a blur over the keyboard. "And you won't want to hear it." The next firewall went down, then the next. Madrigal's virtual fortress crumbled beneath Kara's hands. "Ghost5 has changed. Once it was about balancing out the world. Good for bad, bad for good. Not for money but for the fame."

"What the fuck is she going on about?" Andre made a move to grab Kara's arm, but Billy held him back.

"Let her talk!" said the other hacker, and there were a few nods of agreement from the rest of the group.

Kara went on, picking up momentum. "That's not what Madrigal was ever about. It was a means to an end. Ghost5 was always her tool. *We* were her tools." She looked up briefly. "What do you actually think you're all doing here?"

"Getting rich," said Andre, "am I right? Fuck with Seoul, crash the Asia stock market, make bank!"

"No! This is about what she wants. Madrigal sold you out!" Kara shot back.

"*Bullshit!*" Andre shouted. "Where's Erik? Someone get Erik! This is bullshit!"

"We all see those North Korean stormtroopers in here with us," said Pyne, nodding toward the masked men at the front and rear of the plane. "Full on Dark Side. I'm . . ." She hesitated, before finally finding the words to finish her thought. "I'm not okay with that. Fuck it. I don't care who knows it!"

"Pyne is right! These black-ops puke with all their guns, man!" Billy added. His voice rose, the misgivings he had clearly been bottling up until now spilling out. "What are we even doing here? I didn't sign up for this!"

"You don't want to be rich, you fucking prick?" Andre snarled. "I do! Who gives a damn if the Norks are the ones picking up the tab?"

"They murdered Lex." Kara's next words hit like a body blow, and no one had an answer for them. Saying it out loud felt weird. There was a peculiar flutter in Kara's chest, a strange moment of dislocation. On the screen, she was into the root directory of the computer, searching for the handshake protocol that would allow her to talk directly to the Arquebus program. She was very close now. "Madrigal had Lex killed because of this."

And for an instant, she wasn't there anymore, not in front of the keyboard, staring into the cogs and gears of a virtual weapon. She was somewhere years ago, in time past and lost.

*Lex, tentatively reaching a hand out to touch her face, somewhere secret where none of the rest could see them together. He smiled and she caught it too, the emotion pulling her along. It was real, it was true. No one had ever made her feel like he did. She had never wanted to share herself with anyone before him. He made sense to her.*

She blinked, her gaze misting, and angrily pressed the heel of her hand into her eye, killing the tears.

"Lex stole from us and he ran," Andre said doggedly, as if he was reading from somebody else's script. But the fire in his defiance ebbed with each word. "He was going to rat us out to Interpol. The Greek mob got him—"

"That's what Madrigal told us," countered Billy. "I didn't think . . ." He trailed off, unable to finish the thought.

"No. Lex is dead because he was going to blow this whole operation wide open." Kara looked up at them and her gaze turned fierce. "I destroyed everything I had to come back here and finish what he started. I think I loved him. I *know* Lex was right. So I have to make *this* right."

Billy glanced away and she followed his look. The masked soldier standing guard at the cargo ramp had noticed them arguing and was coming their way. "They'll shoot us," he said quietly.

"That was always going to happen," Kara told him, a note of coldness returning to her words. On the screen in front of her, the search protocol had found what she was looking for, and she worked at rewriting the IP address for the attack program's command and control site.

Weaponized virus software like Arquebus and its forebears Stuxnet, Duqu, Shamoon and countless others employed a control hub hidden in the recesses of the internet. Like an assassin contacting a handler for new targets, the programs would "call in" and drop off reports of hacks completed or in progress, and listen for new orders. All Kara needed to do was redirect the program that had crippled Seoul to a new site, this one loaded with an ENDEX protocol—a shut-down command. It took a few seconds to upload the data from the USB drive, and as the progress bar filled, Kara felt the flutter again.

This was Lex's legacy, his final act after abandoning Ghost5. There on the data chip he had hidden inside himself, concealed in phantom code where only she would be able to find it, he had left her the key to killing Madrigal's grand plan. Undoing everything the woman had set in motion seemed like a fitting revenge.

She hit the execute command, and Pyne let out a low whistle. "Oh shit. You did it. It's done." She dashed to the portal window in the Antonov's fuselage and peered out. "I see lights going on. Oh man."

Across the flat expanse of the airport apron, the bright indicators lining the runways began to reappear, and in the distance the dark blocks of the terminal buildings illuminated one by one, floor by floor. The digital switches in the power grid that had been jammed shut, halting the flow of electricity to the city and its surroundings, were reopening.

"Arquebus is dead." Kara's voice caught as she spoke again. She felt horribly drained and she wanted to weep. The storm of powerful, unfamiliar emotions threatened to overwhelm her. "You need to run. Because I'm going to kill the plane." She looked down at the smart-watch on her wrist. "Go. No time now."

The soldier was at her shoulder, and he knew something was wrong. He snatched at Kara, grabbing the sleeve of her jacket to haul her roughly out of the chair.

Billy hit the man across his facemask with a tablet computer, the blow hard enough to smash the screen into splinters and knock the soldier aside, sending him stumbling into the airframe.

There was shouting and a frenzied blur of motion. Andre bolted toward the rear of the jet and the open cargo ramp, and others went after him. Panic shocked through the group and Billy almost knocked Kara to the deck as he fled before the soldier could react to his surprise attack. She staggered into Pyne, and the other hacker's face was paler than it had ever been.

"Stop them!" A shout full of rage washed over her, and Kara turned to find Erik charging down the length of the cargo bay toward them. Two more of the soldiers ran out after the fleeing hackers, and gunfire crackled in the air.

Erik had a heavy pistol in his hand and the anger that constantly fueled him ran high. "You," he spat, sparing Kara a hateful snarl before shoving her into the workbench. "You actually thought you could betray us *again?*" He glared at the display on Madrigal's laptop and his voice rose to a thundering roar. "I should have killed you at the start!"

"But you didn't," Kara said, in an accusing voice. "Because you're Madrigal's dog. And you do what mistress says, animal. Because you love her and you can't have her."

"You've done nothing but get in the way," Erik hissed, showing no reaction to her words. "Wasted your effort. We still win."

"Erik," began Pyne, reaching out a hand to him. "Look, man, this is all wrong! You must know it—"

Without looking at her, Erik aimed his gun at Pyne and pulled the trigger.

## ── EIGHTEEN ──

Marc could feel the layer of sweat on his back as he brought the Dauphin down toward the Halo, tilting the nose of the smaller helicopter until it was at a steep angle of attack. Trading altitude for speed, he was breathing hard as the distance closed between the two aircraft, acutely aware of the pressure of the situation.

But the fear running through him wasn't panic. It gave him focus. Marc felt his senses sharpen as he let his reactions guide him. And in a strange way, it calmed him. Hand-to-hand combat with a lethal opponent, firefights and open battle, these were outside his comfort zone and it was always a struggle to hold on to his edge. Here, the collective and cyclic sticks in his hands, his eyes on the horizon, Marc Dane felt *correct*.

He balanced on that brink between fear and control, letting one fuel the other. There was old anxiety buried deep in him, strong, potent memory that would well up from the past if he let it. Marc knew if he closed his eyes that heart-stopping instant would replay, as real as if it were happening now.

*Before Rubicon, before MI6. The storm over the South China Sea that had brought down the Royal Navy Lynx he crewed. The impact with the waves. The cold ocean filling the cabin. The first time in his life he truly believed he was going to die.*

He forced it to fade, tuning it out like a radio channel that could only be dialed down but never silenced. Marc worked the controls, letting his senses extend out to fly the Dauphin as if it were a part of himself. His gaze fixed through the rain-spattered canopy, he aimed the helicopter at the larger Halo and poured on the power to catch up with it.

The cargo helicopter raced over the course of the Han River, doubling back along the same route it had taken to its target. Its whale-like bulk wallowed in the downpour, the aircraft's center of gravity grossly offset by the weight of the SCIF hanging beneath it. Marc saw the hatch in the side of the metal-walled cabin dangling over the water, wondering if Madrigal was still aboard the container unit. He could picture her in there, oblivious to everything else, poring over decades' worth of unredacted files and covert reports on the worst excesses of the collaboration between the governments of the United States and South Korea. These were toxic secrets that trailed untold numbers of deaths behind them, and Marc briefly wondered if they were better left buried and forgotten.

"Hold us steady!" Lucy shouted over the droning of the rotor blades.

He nodded, levelling out the Dauphin as they pulled alongside the big Russian helicopter. Marc chanced a look over his shoulder as Lucy pulled open the crew bay hatch again and dropped into a kneeling stance. She brought up the assault rifle and squinted down the weapon's tactical scope.

The slower-moving Halo drifted off to port, and Marc saw movement in the cockpit as one of the crew caught sight of the Dauphin's rotors whirling against the rain.

Muzzle flash from the rifle's discharge reflected off the inside of the canopy as Lucy paced pairs of double-tap shots into the side of the Halo, leaving black marks punched through the fuselage where the rounds penetrated. She walked the shots toward the nose and a triangular cockpit window turned white as the glass cracked. The other helicopter abruptly rolled into a side-slip and sank as the pilot reacted in shock.

A square panel ahead of the Halo's forward passenger hatch folded inward and Marc glimpsed a figure in black venture out to aim a rifle back at the Dauphin. More strobing blinks of yellow light flared across the canopy as the gun lit off at full-auto, and reflexively Marc stood on the Dauphin's starboard pedal. The smaller helicopter pivoted hard into a yawing motion that swung the tail away and presented a smaller target. He heard Lucy curse at him as the unexpected motion threw her around in the back.

The Dauphin's curved windscreen grew a trio of bullet holes before the nose lifted up and they passed over the Halo's huge rotor disc.

Wash from the cargo helicopter's massive blades shuddered through the airframe, and Marc rode it out, gaining height, coming around.

"What part of *hold steady* did you not understand?" Lucy yelled.

"Back-seater," he retorted, catching sight of a hollow in the empty co-pilot's seat where a stray round had gone the distance and embedded itself in the cushion.

Off to the side, the Halo hunched forward, the rotors tilting to give it more forward momentum as it passed the riverbank, and rode over the roofs of bland residential blocks and garishly decorated minimalls. Marc completed the pedal turn and then angled them after the bigger aircraft, his eyes narrowing as he saw what the Halo's pilot was doing.

The cargo helicopter sped dangerously low along the lines of the city street, its rotors lashing at the air barely meters above the tops of the six-story buildings that crowded in along the roadway. The SCIF swung like an enormous pendulum, level with the upper floors of offices and apartments.

It was a chancy ploy, risking the aircraft by putting it so close to the ground that any mistake would not only be fatal to the crew but also claim many civilian lives into the bargain. It was also a deliberate one, Marc realized. The Halo's pilot gambled that his pursuers would not take a shot when the possibility of collateral damage was so high.

"Bastard," muttered Marc, easing off the throttle to extend the distance. Every second they wasted tailgating the Halo instead of trying to stop it meant that Madrigal was one step closer to escape.

Rain and cold wind gusted into the Dauphin's interior as Lucy hauled open the other crew hatch to give herself a clear line of fire in all directions. From the corner of his eye, Marc saw her find a tether and snap the D-ring on the end to her tactical vest. "We have to risk it!" she called, and he knew she understood the danger at hand. "Marc, she can't get away!"

"Wilco," he replied, tensing against the straps holding him into the pilot's chair. Twisting the throttle control on the collective stick, Marc put power to the Dauphin's twin Turbomeca engines and started in on another approach.

The Halo's crew were ready for them this time. Marc saw the

bigger aircraft sway as the pilot shifted the controls. The smaller Dauphin dropped to blades-level with the cargo helicopter and Marc kept them in a nose-on position. Lucy went semi-prone, hanging her upper body out of the crew cabin and along the line of the fuselage as she took aim.

Then out of nowhere the Halo killed most of its forward motion with a hard flaring maneuver that kicked the nose up sharply. A less-skilled pilot would have back-slid into a terminal stall, but even with the unpredictable extra mass of the SCIF, the Halo performed a tight pivot that seemed to briefly defy the laws of physics. Marc had once seen a huge twin-bladed Chinook do a similar stunt, the big choppers the Army lads called "wokkas" after the distinctive sound of their rotors moving in ways that seemed impossible. It seemed that the North Koreans had adapted the same dance moves for their bird.

As the Halo settled back, the SCIF cabin swung hard into the frontage of an office block, shattering a line of blue-tinted windows as it glanced off them and away. Marc pulled on the Dauphin's cyclic stick to avoid a collision when Lucy shouted out the acronym that all military helicopter pilots dreaded. *"RPG!"*

He glimpsed the white flash of the launch as he heard the call. Lucy must have seen the soldier who had shot at them moments before, now leaning out of the Halo's gunner hatch with a rocket propelled grenade launcher.

Residential buildings hemmed them in on both sides, and there was nowhere to veer off to that wouldn't put the Dauphin right into someone's living room. Pulling back or climbing would be too slow to save them. Marc rolled the dice on his own skill and accelerated toward the flash instead, hoping that the sturdy Eurocopter's airframe would take the punishment.

He flicked the cyclic in a sharp lateral motion and the Dauphin briefly twisted into a half-roll, leaping aside like its ocean-going namesake in a bow wave. The unguided RPG spiraled under the belly of the silver helicopter and looped away, finally exploding against a billboard atop a nearby multi-story car park.

Marc overcorrected, veering dangerously close to a chain-link fence around an apartment block's rooftop garden, hauling back and away before the tips of the helicopter blades kissed the metal. Wrestling the Dauphin into a hover, he tried to recover, but more gunfire lanced across from the Halo, thudding into the fuselage. Rifle rounds pinged off the cabin interior, and Marc knew that the moment the shooter reloaded the RPG, another deadly rocket would be on its way.

Lucy was a step ahead of him, and the sniper took that option out of play with another double-tap from where she lay sprawled on the floor of the crew bay. Aiming with the assault rifle down the length of her body, she put her shots straight through the Halo's open gunner hatch. Marc saw a figure in black tumble out into the air and fall, the rocket launcher going with him, deflecting off the hanging SCIF and on its way to the street below. With a hurricane roar of downwash, the Halo pulled away, evading.

"We have to force them down!" Lucy shouted.

He didn't answer her. Crimson warning indicators flashed across the control panel in front of him. The shots they'd weathered had hit vital components, and unlike the over-engineered, boiler-plate heavy design of the Russian cargo chopper, the smaller Eurocopter wasn't designed to operate under combat conditions. Marc smelled hot oil as the controls vibrated alarmingly in his hands.

"No problem," he lied, aiming the Dauphin after the fleeing Halo.


The gun bellowed inside the close confines of the Antonov's cargo bay, and Pyne was shocked backward by the force of the shot.

Kara grabbed her before she could collapse to the deck, her hands finding a spreading bloom of dark blood soaking through Pyne's threadbare sweater. Her eyes were wide and streaming with tears of pain, her mouth open in a trembling, endless gasp. She shivered in Kara's arms as she set her on a chair as gently as she could, guiding the stricken hacker's hands to keep pressure on the ugly wound.

Erik raised the smoking muzzle of his revolver and aimed it in Kara's direction. "You are going to be next," he told her, grinding out the words. "It does not matter what you did to the communications. Madrigal will be back soon."

Kara was so close that she could see flecks of dark fluid on Erik's knuckles and the barrel of the pistol, the blowback from where the bullet had entered Pyne's belly. The shot had been a through-and-through, which meant the Polish girl was going to die from blood loss unless she received urgent medical attention.

All these details came to Kara in a stream of analytical thought, in the same dispassionate manner that she would have looked at a piece of computer code. She saw them like the IF and THEN logic statements in a data string. The burly German hacker could not get past the bond between Kara and Madrigal, and he hated it. Coming back to Ghost5 had made that worse, and now Erik was going to run his program to the only end condition that would satisfy him.

"You were never part of this," he went on, barely sparing Pyne a look as she continued to die by inches. "Any of you. *Tools.* Nothing more."

Kara gave him a questioning look, her words oddly calm and level. "Really? Because you are without doubt the biggest fucking tool I've ever met." She peeked at the smartwatch on her wrist, trying to factor time and survivability.

Erik put the bloodstained muzzle of the gun against the center of Kara's forehead and pulled back the hammer. "When Madrigal returns, I am going to kill you in front of her. She will see what you really are."

"Because that will fix everything for you?" She stared blankly at him. "That's what you want. To be the important one in her eyes."

"You keep talking and I won't wait," he warned.

Kara leaned into the gun, pushing back against it. "So do it. If you aren't afraid to be beholden to Madrigal. Do it. Shoot me. You didn't hesitate with her." She waved at Pyne, bent forward in the chair and panting like a wounded animal. "You think you're tough. That you have a strong will and a keen mind. You don't. You're just above average. All you can offer is the willingness to hurt people without hesitation." She glanced back at him, then away again. "There's a transient electromagnetic device built into this plane." Kara pointed at the deck. "It'll put out an electromagnetic pulse that will fry all digital hardware within two hundred meters, give or take. Madrigal's doomsday protocol, in case Interpol or the NSA ever caught up with us."

Erik hesitated. Of course he knew about the pulse device, there was no way Madrigal would have kept that from him. But it was a secret to most of the members of Ghost5, and he hadn't expected Kara to be aware of its existence.

She watched the reaction cross his face. "I was one of them before you came along, remember? Who do you think helped put the thing in there?" She let her hand drop so it floated over Madrigal's laptop.

He glared back at her. "If you try anything with that, I'll end you."

"You think so?"

Erik's reply was a snarl, and he fired a shot into the laptop, blowing a crater in the middle of the keyboard. Hot splinters of plastic stung Kara's hand as she snatched it away. Erik showed his teeth in a feral grin.

"Idiot," she told him, rubbing her wrist, looking at the watch again. "You can't think further than you can see. That's why she doesn't let you hack. I set it up hours ago." Kara tap-tapped the smartwatch's touch-sensitive screen. In a fraction of a second it sent a control signal to a Bluetooth intercept receiver she had secretly spliced into the Antonov's main circuitry bus, when the cargo plane had been somewhere over the Philippine Sea.

The transient electromagnetic device wasn't only designed to render the hard drives and circuits on board the aircraft useless. Kara had not lied when she described it as Madrigal's weapon of last resort. Up in the service crawlspace where the Antonov's wings connected to the fuselage, the drum-shaped TED activated. Powered by a small explosive-shaped charge, in an instant the device super-compressed the magnetic field generated by a high voltage capacitor. The energy of the focused explosion transferred through the field, creating an electromagnetic release ten times the power of a lightning strike. All of this happened in an instant, the TED blowing a hole through the top of the Antonov's airframe, burning into the fuel lines, shocking a wave of crackling electric discharge down through the fuselage and killing every electronic device within the range of the pulse wave.

Fire and sparks flashed inside the cargo bay as all on-board power went out, and the big jet rocked on its undercarriage with the force of the blast. Above their heads, a sheet of orange flame peeled back curls of hull metal as the blaze took hold. Erik was momentarily disoriented by the detonation, and Kara used the distraction to snatch at a portable fire extinguisher fitted to the airframe. It came free in her hands and she swung it around in a hard arc, cracking him across the face with the flat of the cylinder. Erik fell and Kara let the extinguisher go, grabbing Pyne with both hands.

The other woman let out a screech of pain, but she was too weak to resist. Pyne was so slight she barely weighed anything. Kara got her into an ungainly shoulder carry and half-ran, half-stumbled down the Antonov's open cargo ramp. The heat of the burning fuel pushed at her back as the fire spread, eating into the fuselage, gutting the aircraft from the inside out. Thick black smoke stinking of gasoline choked the air around her as Kara kept running, making for the cover of a nearby hangar.

Another explosion sounded as one of the Antonov's wings sagged and collapsed, the fumes and fluid in the near-empty fuel tanks still enough to combust with a dull boom of ignition. Her hands wet with Pyne's blood, Kara shoved at a door in the side of the hangar and disappeared inside.


The Halo crew had decided that a shootout wasn't the way they wanted to handle things, and now the chopper was running with the throttle at full, veering back over the buildings until it went feet-wet over the Han River.

Lucy tried to keep the other helicopter in the middle of the tactical scope atop the rifle, but Marc had difficulty holding them level. Her sight picture bounced around like she was on the Cyclone at Coney Island, and the weapon's laser ranger was next to useless.

The rifle's magazine had only a third of its rounds remaining, so she couldn't afford to waste them. Both aircraft were heading north again, back in the direction of Incheon and the border. Lucy had a brief and nasty vision of a flight of North Korean Hind Attack helicopters crossing the demilitarized zone to meet them. If that happened, the unarmed Dauphin would be scrap metal in seconds.

The Halo fell out of her sight-line once more, and this time it didn't return. She looked away and realized that the Brit was taking them up, trying to gain altitude. Lucy stared down at the blurred disc of the cargo helicopter's main rotors. Could she put a shot into the hub, maybe get a round into the engine intake? Or would it be smarter to go for the tail rotor and try to hobble them that way? If she could blow through the gears and mechanisms back there, it could force the Halo's pilot into an auto-rotate crash landing. "I wish I had a Stinger right now," she said aloud, her voice lost in the coughing and droning of the Dauphin's wounded engine.

She squeezed through the gap between the seats in the cockpit and dropped into the co-pilot's chair, dragging the rifle with her. Finding an intercom headset hanging on a hook, she put it on.

Marc shook his head at her, then looked down at the controls. His knuckles were white where he was holding on tightly: translation— *I can't take my hands off these.* Lucy took the pilot's headset and put it in place for him, flipping the mic down to his lips.

"Shit," he said, his voice sounding in her ears. "Damn it." Every couple of seconds, Marc ground out another swearword as the helicopter fought against him to say airborne.

"That bad?" Lucy replied. Her only flying experience was jumping out of aircraft, not keeping them in the sky, but she understood well enough that the multiple red lights blinking from the control panel were trouble.

"Fuel is gushing out the back from a bust line." Marc's reply was clipped. "Oil pressure is falling. We have maybe ten minutes of flying time at best, and that's if fortune smiles."

"Open to suggestions," she noted.

He spared her a sideways look. "You never like my ideas."

"I'll like anything that takes Madrigal out of play . . ." She trailed off. Out of the side of the cockpit, she could see lights flicking on along the far bank of the river. "Hey, the power's coming back up." Was that part of Ghost5's plan as well, or more evidence of the spanner that had been thrown into the works? She thought briefly of Kara, and then dismissed it.

"I'm going to force them down," said Marc, nodding in their direction of flight. "See the bridge there?"

She leaned forward, looking through the rain. Ahead of the Halo

was a crossing made up of two three-lane highways, with a subway
line sandwiched between them. A long series of curved blue truss
frames extended along over the railroad, and she could see traffic
grouped in clusters of stalled cars, but for the most part the bridge
was empty.

"How are you gonna do that?" she asked, already dreading the answer.

"I set it up," Marc replied, through gritted teeth. "You knock them
down." He reduced the Dauphin's altitude in a swift rush and the
helicopter dropped like a stone, right into the vortex from the Halo's
bigger rotors.

The cargo bird's blades were wider tip-to-tip than the entire footprint of the Dauphin, but still the smaller aircraft's downwash was
enough to disrupt the smooth airflow over the lifting surface. For
one giddy second, Lucy thought the Brit was going to actually crash
them right into the Halo's rotors, but at the last moment the other
pilot reacted and tried to side-slide out from under his descending
pursuer.

Marc cursed loudly as he feathered the controls and mirrored the
Halo pilot's move. The blue truss bridge came up fast and the bigger
helicopter was swiftly running out of room to maneuver.

Lucy saw her opening and rammed open a sliding panel in the
window beside her, poking the assault rifle's barrel out into the air.
Holding the gun across her chest, she steadied it against her bicep
and waited for the moment she knew was going to come, the moment when the Halo pilot would panic and make a hasty choice.
Her sniper self took over, the clinical and predatory spider-mind
that saw the world only through crosshairs. She imagined she was
in some silent hide in the middle of a forest, invisible beneath a suit
of ghillie camo, coldly watching the will of a target break in that
instant before they made a fatal mistake and became exposed. She
put the bright red pinprick of the rifle's laser sight on the target and
took half a breath.

The Halo jerked, the heavy whale-shape veering off, the SCIF
dangling below it drifting dangerously close to the top of the blue
framework of the bridge.

She fired down through the blur of the spinning rotors, through the cockpit windows of the Halo, turning them crazed and fractured. Lucy saw a splash of red against the inside of the broken glass, and the cargo helicopter's engine note became a keening wail.

Marc wrenched the Dauphin away in a juddering turn as the Halo sank too low to clear the top of the bridge trusses. The SCIF slammed into the end of one of the metal arcs and scraped across the steel frame. The side of the reinforced cabin tore open and it tumbled to the road in disarray. The cables trailing up to the Halo snagged in the gap between two of the trusses and snapped tight.

Now fatally anchored, the Halo's own power brought it down over the middle of the bridge to strike the highway on the opposite side at a shallow angle. The cargo helicopter's chin scraped the asphalt in a flash of sparks and fire, tearing off the nose wheel. The fuselage tilted wildly, turning on to its side. The eight massive rotor blades, each nearly fifteen meters long, came down and chopped into the road bed and the bridge frames, one by one splintering and disintegrating into a storm of shrapnel.

The Halo rolled over and sagged under its own weight, bound in a snare of cables. Flames and black smoke bloomed from the engine compartment.

Marc held the Dauphin in a shaky hover over the stretch of the bridge where the SCIF had landed. The downdraft caught papers strewn from the storage racks inside the broken cabin. Materials so secret that they passed beyond conventional classification were whipped up and blown into the river below.

Lucy looked through the assault rifle's scope, scanning the wrecked cabin for movement. She saw nothing.

"We can't leave," said Marc over the intercom, and the Dauphin dropped down toward the road. "Not until we're sure."

They made it to the far side of the hangar's vast open space before Pyne wept that she couldn't go any further and collapsed in a heap.

Kara dragged her into the first place that could generously be called "safe," the open cabin of a twin-engine Beechcraft up on a maintenance stand. She pulled Pyne inside, pausing to survey the trail of red spatter that wound its way across the hangar to this spot.

"I'm going to die," whispered the thin girl. "Oh God, I don't want to go out like this. I don't even know where I am."

Kara wiped her bloody hands clean on the material of one of the passenger seats in the cabin and looked around for a first aid kit. She found a green plastic box in a compartment on the bulkhead and pawed through the contents. Taking bandages and sterile pads, she did her best to dress the ugly wound in Pyne's side, but it was grotesque, sickening work. The other woman faded in and out of awareness.

When she was done, Kara dared to look out through the oval windows in the Beechcraft's fuselage and saw smoke gusting into the hangar from the doors on the far side. Out there, the Antonov was alight and distantly she wondered about Andre and the others. Were they already gone, or had the masked soldiers put them down before they made it to the safety of the terminal buildings? It didn't matter. They couldn't help her.

Kara pulled the walkie-talkie radio from her pocket and weighed it in her hand. It was as good as a brick now, having been caught in the wave of the TED's electromagnetic pulse. She tossed it aside and looked at her smartwatch. It too was inert metal and glass, useless to her.

*Like Pyne?* The question came from nowhere as Kara's gaze settled on the other woman, whose shallow breathing was rasping softly in the silence of the cabin.

The callous impulse behind the thought was crystal clear. Kara really didn't owe Pyne anything. When she had fled Ghost5, she had not dared to share that intention with the girl. She had not trusted her. But did that reluctance say more about Kara Wei—*about Wong Fei Song*—than it did about the other hacker?

Pyne was less than an hour away from death, at the best estimation. But Kara was uninjured and free to escape. If she left the wounded woman now, she could survive, get away, recover.

The thin girl shifted and moaned, gasping in breaths of air. Her eyes fluttered open, briefly seeing Kara before clouding, fading again.

*What were the last words Lex said to me?* The thought rose from darkness, like the one before, and Kara knew it was some fraction of herself speaking back at her, echoing the questions she didn't want to acknowledge.

She couldn't remember what Lex had said. It had been such a swift and brutal decision to break with Ghost5, coming on the heels of an acid, cutting argument with Madrigal about the future of the group. In that conversation, Kara had known that her mentor would take them down a dark path from which they would not return.

*What had Lex said that day, on an overcast Sunday in a squat off the Montmartre? Did he say he loved her as she frantically packed? Did he try to convince her to stay?* Both; neither. The memory wasn't there, only the phantom ache of an emotion Kara couldn't experience.

She had left, though. He hadn't stopped her. Then he was dead, and Kara would never be able to reconstruct that moment. The missing piece had been lost forever.

If she left Pyne, that would be history repeating itself. Another loss. If it wasn't her lover she abandoned, did it matter? But she *had* abandoned him.

Kara crouched next to Pyne and gently laid a finger on her throat, feeling the hacker's weak pulse, then glanced back at the open hatch.

*If I leave again, what does that make me?* A shadow passed over her face as the answer emerged from the same place. *It makes you like Madrigal.*

"Song? Do you smell smoke?" whispered Pyne, slipping out of lucidity. "Not the good kind, like barbecue."

"Yeah," said Kara. "It's okay. Sit tight." She moved down the cabin and opened the door to the grounded Beechcraft's cockpit. She experimented with the switches, hope blooming in her. The edges of the electromagnetic pulse had not reached this far, their force spent on penetrating the metal walls of the hangar. That meant the light plane's circuits and its radio would still be operational. From memory, Kara dialed in the guard frequency the strike team had been using.

It would be in the clear. There was no guarantee anyone would be listening, and it was possible that anything she *did* say would be picked up by the people who wanted her dead.

But she had to reach out. She had to try.

Marc guided the Dauphin into a shaky touchdown on the bridge, easing the helicopter between two streetlamps until the wheels bumped off the roadway. The nearest civilians were a few hundred meters away, staying back by their cars, too afraid to venture any closer. He saw one guy trying to capture the scene on his cell-phone camera, and Marc pulled up his collar in a half-hearted attempt to conceal his identity.

Lucy was out of the cabin before the helicopter had settled, bringing up the rifle as she advanced on the damaged SCIF. Marc scrambled out after her, snatching the submachine gun from its strap and checking the safety.

The wind pushing the dark clouds in from the sea had finally deposited the core of the growing storm cell over the city, and the deluge angled down in hard, hissing curtains. It felt like a dark monsoon, pulse after pulse of rain washing across the bridge from the river, battering at the pair of them, streaming off their faces.

Marc and Lucy shared a look and made their approach to the ruined cabin. Backlit by the flares of orange fire from the stricken Halo on the far side of the bridge, the cables still connected to the SCIF flexed and rattled against the steel arches over the subway line.

Where the SCIF struck the bridge, the force of the collision had ripped it open along a welded seam that ran the length of the rectangular cabin. It resembled a box torn open by a hungry animal desperate to get at whatever was inside.

Marc walked over a swath of soaked briefing documents and military satellite photos scattered across the road, spilled from the inside of the smashed cabin. Hidden secrets, kept locked down across decades of intelligence operations, lay bleeding out of the container.

"Look at this shit," Lucy muttered. "It's a goddamn spy piñata."

He nodded, spotting other objects among the debris. Marc saw portable hard-drive modules, splintered and broken open in the impact, cases of old micro discs and shimmering streamers of magnetic tape.

"Cover me," said Lucy, moving around to the far side, where part of the cabin's facia had been ripped open, hanging twisted and bent.

The SCIF slumped at a shallow angle, and the contents that had broken loose filled the interior with a snowdrift of papers, plastic cases and scattered files. Marc held his weapon at the ready, flicking the fire-select to three-round burst, prepared to shoot at anything that moved.

The wind whipped at the debris, but nothing human stirred inside the shattered SCIF. Lucy shouldered her rifle and climbed into the container. "Proof of death," she said, without looking back at him. "If her body is in here, I'll get it."

"Right," replied Marc, somewhat relieved to be leaving Lucy to the grisly business of digging through the wreckage in search of a corpse. The damaged container unit shifted and groaned under her weight as she disappeared into the dank gloom between the storage racks that were still standing upright.

He clambered up into the cabin after her and found the remains of the workstation bolted to the inside of the nearside wall. The computer console was smashed beyond use, but the server rack above it was still relatively intact. He reached out and ran a hand over the faces of the hard drives still resting in their secured mounts. If he wanted to, it wouldn't take long to remove the locks holding them in place, pull the modules and get them back to the helicopter. Madrigal had spent years of her life preparing to steal this SCIF, and he couldn't help but wonder what kind of deeply buried secrets were swarming inside it. Stored in these media were reports of black operations conducted by the precursors to South Korea's National Intelligence Service, stretching back to the bad old days when they had been the KCIA and their reputation for doing whatever the hell they wanted was notorious.

Behind him, Lucy shouldered a fallen rack aside and it clanged against the hull of the SCIF. "Blood here," she called from the darkness. "Lot of it."

Marc nodded, only half-hearing her, his gaze still locked on the memory modules. He knew some of the tainted history they contained from his service with British Intelligence, mostly relayed in war stories told to him by an older MI6 officer named Leon Taub. The Cold War veteran had been part of Marc's OpTeam, one of the crew killed by a Combine assassin two years ago in France, but in his youth the man had served in the South East Asian sector and seen the KCIA's combative operational style at close hand.

It was an organization born out of a coup d'état. A secret police by any other name that had no qualms about conducting illegal renditions of persons of interest from halfway around the world, interfering in domestic politics, engaging in extortion and bribery, even going as far as implementing the assassination of their own president. Characterized by unchallenged conduct and opportunistic overreach in every incarnation of its existence, first as the KCIA, then the Agency for National Security Planning and finally as the NIS, there was little doubt South Korean Intelligence had a lot of dirt to keep under wraps. By any lights, the contents of the stolen SCIF were politically explosive.

But it wasn't only South Korea's government that stood to suffer from the blowback from any leaks. The anger and the loss that had driven Madrigal to brutally murder an elderly man had grown out of the aftermath of a clandestine mission run by the KCIA and their opposite numbers in the intelligence organs of the United States. She wanted to make that collusion public, in her own twisted search for some kind of justice. Whatever the SCIF contained had to be devastating.

*Evidence of collusion between America and South Korea in unsanctioned attacks on the North? Deniable operations and soldiers killed by their own allies? All that and worse still?* It wouldn't matter that it happened over forty years ago. It would be the pretext Pyongyang would need to go to the next step, to military action. And with a US government engaged in saber-rattling and the fractious political climate in South East Asia, the end result would be open war.

Marc hesitated, hearing the hiss of the rain through the roof of the broken cabin. It was hard to believe that all of that could come from this, that here and now on this windswept bridge in the middle of a thunderstorm, a tipping point turned around him.

There was only one logical course of action. "We've got to destroy this lot," he said to himself, staring at the hard drives. "It's the only way." Madrigal may have been a cold-hearted schemer, but she had been right. And if that corrosive truth was released, it would be like throwing a lit match into a fireworks factory.

He felt a prickling at his throat and he reached up to scratch at it. The radio earpiece hung there, and beneath the ceaseless sound of the rain, he thought he heard a faint sound.

Marc pressed the radio bead into his ear. "Who's out there?"

"*Dane.*" Kara Wei's voice was faint and full of static, but unmistakable. "*I didn't think you'd still be alive.*"

"That makes two of us," he retorted. "Where are you?"

"*Airport,*" she said. "*I need your help.*" Behind him, Marc heard another crash of shifting containers and ignored it, straining to listen. "*Come and get us. Please.*"

"I'm right in the middle of something—" he began.

"You really are," said Madrigal.

He jerked back at the sound of the woman's voice issuing out of the shadows, dragging up the SMG dangling from the sling over his shoulder, aiming as he turned.

"No," she warned, weary and pained and angry all at once.

Lucy came into sight holding her hands down and away from her gun, her dark face like thunder. Gripping Lucy from behind in a smothering embrace, forcing her to shuffle forward, Madrigal glared at Marc with open fury. Her face was smeared with blood and she had snaked her arms under Lucy's in a cross over the other woman's chest. In one hand, gripped tightly, she held a gray metal cylinder stenciled with purple warning text. In the other hand she held an arming pin, and with a flick of her fingers she threw it at Marc.

"We are not finished here," spat Madrigal, pressing the base of the live thermite grenade against Lucy's throat.

## NINETEEN

D ane," Lucy said firmly, "shoot this witch in the face and put her out of my misery, will ya?"

"Be quiet," sneered Madrigal, her knuckles whitening around the grenade's spring-loaded safety lever. The fuse had been dialed down to zero. All she needed to do was release that grip and the "spoon" would flick off, instantly triggering the device.

Bile rose in Marc's throat as he recalled the sickly sweet reek of scorched human flesh, and the blinding flare of the thermite charge that had torched the corpses of the dead North Korean soldiers. That sun-hot fire would be a horrific, agonizing way to perish, but Madrigal seemed ready to accept that if it meant Lucy would burn with her.

"I'm serious," Lucy continued. "I mean, if you gotta, shoot the hostage. Just end her."

"We will both die," said the other woman, baring her bloodstained teeth. "Right here."

Madrigal's arch, cold mask slipped, and once more the furious, murderous reality of her that Marc had glimpsed on the police video was revealed. Her pale face flushed pink with rage, and the blood and soot matting her wine-dark hair gave the hacker the look of some revenant spirit bent on revenge.

Marc aimed the submachine gun, holding his finger off the trigger. The two women were only a few meters away from him, and instinct told him that he could make the shot with the first bullet, even if the others went astray. But the second he started to analyze the angles, his confidence evaporated and doubt crept in. A degree the wrong way and Lucy would be fatally struck. Even if his aim was true, hitting Madrigal would make her drop the grenade and set it off. *Too many variables. Too much risk.*

"C'mon, do it," Lucy implored. "She got the drop on me back there. It's embarrassing. I don't want anyone to know—" Her words were choked off as Madrigal hauled her closer and rammed the cylindrical grenade into her throat.

"You are going to back off," demanded the hacker. "I am going to get what I came here for. No one is going to stop me."

"How's that?" said Marc, willing himself to remain still, to keep on target. "The Halo is wrecked. Your playmates from the North aren't here to back you up anymore."

"Should I give up? Let you turn me over to Interpol?" she snorted.

"You have nowhere left to go." Marc's reply was matter-of-fact.

"You don't choose when this ends!" spat Madrigal, with raw heat. "I choose! I always get what I want!"

"*That's a lie,*" said a static-laced voice in Marc's ear.

"Kara . . . ?" Belatedly, he realized that the radio earpiece was still on, the channel still open. "Madrigal has Lucy," he said quietly.

"Everyone who failed me is dead," Madrigal was saying. "I buried them all."

"*That's a lie, too,*" Kara whispered. "*Tell her.*"

"That's a lie," repeated Marc, trying to buy time. He saw a flicker of dark emotion, a jolt of surprise crossing Madrigal's face. He pushed on. "Kara . . . *Song* . . . she gave you up. Betrayed you."

"No," Madrigal shook her head. "She came back to me. She made a mistake. I'll correct her."

"*You have to break her to end this,*" said Kara. "*She's brittle. She will flinch if you put the pressure in the right place. Do you get it, Dane?*" He didn't respond, his mind racing to grasp what she was telling him. "*You trust me, don't you?*" They were the same words Kara had spoken to him back in Chamonix, the last thing she had said before she sent him to Malta. Before she lied to him.

If Marc uttered the wrong word in the next few moments, this would end in fire and death. There was a hollow in his chest when he imagined Lucy Keyes being torn out of his world. He couldn't grasp the possibility. It seemed impossible, inconceivable. He could not let that happen. *Too many variables. Too much risk.*

The voice in his ear had gone silent, the channel hissing quiet static. He saw Kara Wei in his mind's eye, trying to square his memory of the sparky young hacker he thought he knew with the reality of the distant, damaged woman he had encountered on board the Antonov.

Which of them was the false front? Marc wanted to believe that she had been playing a long game all through this mess. He wanted her to still be one of them. He loathed the idea that Kara had played everyone in Rubicon. He felt that same hollow in his chest at the prospect of her treachery.

*Did he trust her? Did he have a choice?*

"I am going to tell you the truth." Marc let the words come without hesitation. He didn't measure or gauge them, he just spoke, digging deep and turning what he found there on Madrigal. "You think Song is something she's not. I don't know what she meant to you, Marie. Maybe she is the kid sister or the daughter you never had." He leaned in, using the woman's real name to hook her attention and hold it fast. "You have that dead, empty space in you and you want someone to fill it."

He knew that feeling intimately. The reckless, grinning face of someone he had deeply cared for ghosted through Marc's thoughts, the echo of Samantha Green so close that in the moment he thought he could hear her laughing through the rainfall.

"But you chose wrong," he continued. "What you saw was what you projected on to her, not what there is. And when it goes away, it's no one's fault but your own."

"Song returned," growled Madrigal, biting out each insistent word like a bullet. "I knew she would."

"She came back to destroy you," managed Lucy, forcing out the words in a rough gasp. "Yeah, I get it. Not to join you, Red. And damned sure not to forgive you or *become* you."

Marc stared into the pale woman's dark eyes. He saw a flash of the hidden fragility that Kara had warned him about, the smallest fraction of it appearing and disappearing on Madrigal's taut features.

He nodded toward the wreckage around them. "You were so set on this, you didn't see it. You didn't want to."

"Stop talking," said Madrigal.

"You murdered somebody she cared about." Marc saw all the pieces fall into line, all the tragic connections slotting into one another. "Maybe the only person she ever had cared for. And then you were arrogant enough to think she wouldn't know."

"Lex was *weak*!" Madrigal's face twisted. "It had to be done! She understands! She didn't care about him—"

"You're wrong." Marc remembered Kara's face from that day in France. She had known her lover was dead then, and she hadn't said a word to him about it. Instead, she'd buried the raw pain, turned it into fuel for herself in the same way he had when the Combine had killed his team, killed Sam Green and ripped her out of his life. Kara had spun the elaborate lie that had sent Marc after a truth she must have dreaded hearing, the first step on a road that meant destroying the trust she had accrued with everyone at Rubicon. All that to reach a truth that on some level she must have known from the very beginning.

"Kara isn't who you think she is," he said, as much to himself as to Madrigal. "And you're the echo of what you lost forty years ago, clawing for some meaning. Trying to make her fill that void. And failing."

"*You don't fucking know me!*" Madrigal's last fraction of control splintered apart and for a split second she shook with a lifetime of pent-up anger. She broke beneath the pressure of the truth, exactly as Kara said she would.

Lucy saw her moment and shot her elbow into Madrigal's gut. The hacker flinched, jerking back against one of the SCIF's metal racks. Her hand twitched around the thermite grenade as Lucy threw herself forward and away from the other woman.

As Lucy cleared his line of sight, Marc squeezed the SMG's trigger and put three bullets into Madrigal's chest. The hits spun her around and the thermite grenade tumbled from her hand, the safety lever releasing with a loud click.

Lucy slammed into Marc and shoved him back as the device detonated. He couldn't close his eyes or look away from the flare of metallic light, and was briefly dazzled by the searing brightness. The two of them tumbled out of the SCIF and on to the wet asphalt.

Despite the downpour, the piles of papers inside the torn-open cabin were ready kindling for the thermite and in a heartbeat they were a raging bonfire. Madrigal and her spoils alike were consumed in the flames.

Marc scrambled to his feet, still clutching the submachine gun, looking into the crackling, hissing heart of the inferno. Purple retina burns clouded his vision, only the writhing shimmer of the fire moved within the SCIF.

Lucy put a hand on his shoulder and pulled him back a step. "She got what she wanted. What she *deserved*."

"Yeah," he managed, the weight of his actions settling on him. For a moment he was afraid to turn from the flames, convinced that Madrigal was still a threat. Then slowly he walked to the edge of the bridge, the rain hammering down around him. He reached up to the radio bead in his ear and tapped it. "Kara. Are you there? It's . . . done."

The dead air answered him with static.


"I can hear you," called Erik, his deep voice rebounding off the walls of the hangar. "You won't get away. *Nein*." He slipped back into his native language, growling out threats. "*Ich werde dich langsam töten . . .*"

Kara crouched low in the Beechcraft's cramped cockpit until only her eye line was above the control console. Staring out of the sloped windows, she tried to look in every direction at once, but it was impossible to know where Madrigal's thug was. His words echoed back and forth, mingling with the rattle of rain off the roof high above and the sullen rumble of the burning Antonov.

She turned the aircraft radio down even as she thought she heard Marc Dane's voice. She couldn't answer him. Any sound could draw Erik to the plane, and if he found them now, Kara knew he would not hesitate to murder her and finish off Pyne.

Keeping low, moving as quickly as she dared, Kara crawled back down the length of the Beechcraft's cabin to where the girl lay propped up against the back of a passenger chair. Pyne's breaths came in short, panting gulps, and her gaze wavered in and out of focus as she looked up at Kara. "Are they . . . coming to help . . . us?" She labored to get each word out.

Kara's mask-self, the carefully prepared personality she showed the world, told her that now was the time to lie. Give Pyne some predigested falsehood about how *everything would be fine* and *this would be over soon.* Flash a plastic smile. Touch the wounded girl's arm in a gesture of solidarity and support. But those were part of an act, and Kara was sick of being the ghost of something false instead of what she really was.

"I know you are in here!" Outside, Erik bellowed the words and Pyne stirred in fright as she heard him. "I see blood," he shouted, and now they both his heard footsteps coming closer. "I can see you!"

"He's lying," Kara whispered.

"I want to go home," wept Pyne, all the girl's hard edges and strength torn away by her pain. She clutched at the sleeve of Kara's jacket with bloody fingers. "I don't want to die here."

All the trite promises she could give faded before Kara could voice them. She shrugged off Pyne's grip and pulled away. The girl gasped in shock, and tried to call out to her. Kara ignored her and vaulted out through the half-open passenger hatch in the side of the Beechcraft. She landed in a cat-fall on the hangar floor, boots scraping on the ground as she pushed off again into a full-tilt run.

"*Song!*" Erik's furious shout came in her wake. He was close, behind one of the nearby maintenance trucks, catching the motion of her flight from the corner of his vision.

She heard him roaring after her, the heavy thudding steps as the big man broke into a sprint. Gunshots barked at her back and the rounds whistled past her as Erik fired on the move. Kara pivoted around a dismantled engine block and hurdled a low tool chest, scattering spanners and bolts across the floor as she went.

The gloom at the rear of the cavernous hangar promised some kind of cover, and she fled toward it, trying to put as much distance between her and Pyne's hiding place as she could. Another shot cracked at her heels as she ducked out of sight behind a dismantled airframe. Kara's heart hammered at the inside of her ribs and fear swirled around her.

"I never believed you," Erik called, slowing as he stalked her. They both knew she was running out of room, and would soon be cornered. "I knew you were *falsch*. A fake." Kara heard him give a low grunt of callous amusement. "It infuriates me so much. Madrigal is blind to you. Cannot see what I see." He hesitated. "Does she feel sorry for you, is that it?"

Kara held her breath, staring into the shadows, straining to listen. A few meters away, hidden where the hangar's overhead lights didn't reach, there was a fire exit door secured by a push-bar. Between here and the door there was no cover, but if she could reach it, she might be able to draw Erik away. The emergency services from the airport hub had to be on their way by now, coming out to deal with the burning cargo plane. They would discover Pyne, get her to a hospital. But only if Erik did not find her first.

"I saw what you were the moment you showed your face in Teufelsberg," he called, closing in. "I have heard the stories about Wong Fei Song. But I will show Madrigal what you really are."

"She's dead by now." Kara threw out the words before she realized she was saying them. "Broken. Like the plane and everything else. Ruined." She aimed herself at the fire exit and tensed like a runner on the starting blocks. "You followed her, Erik, and she let you down. Like she let me down. Madrigal never cared about anything but herself. She's the one that is empty. And nothing can ever fill the blackness inside her."

"*Ligend hure . . .*" He came marching toward her, sweeping around the flank of the skeletal airframe with the heavy shape of a huge revolver in his hand.

The gun barked as Kara exploded into motion, racing for the exit door. If it was secured, or blocked from the outside, then her escape would end in the next ten seconds. She had no weapon to defend herself with, and no place left to hide.

Kara slammed into the push bar with both hands and for one heart-stopping moment, it resisted her; then the ill-maintained mechanism gave and the door popped open with a grinding clatter. She was almost through the gap when a bullet grazed the top of her right shoulder, tearing open her jacket and pulling a sharp shriek of pain from her lips.

Staggering forward, Kara lurched into a barrage of wind and rain. Hot, searing agony enveloped her shoulder and flames burned along her nerves, down her arm and across her chest in an expanding wave. Her back felt wet and sticky beneath the crimson leather jacket.

*This is new.* The clinical, robotic thought pressed itself to the front of her mind.

Kara had been on the wrong end of violence more than once. Growing up a mixed-race child in the social-care system had made that a certainty, but she had never been shot before. The pain seared her flesh, and every stumbling movement resonated up to the wound and made it worse.

She lurched over a grassy quad behind the hangar and found herself at the edge of a service runway near the airport perimeter. The endless torrent from a sky full of menacing black clouds hissed over the asphalt and into the gale. A hard gust blew her off her pace and she twisted to see Erik striding out after her. Slow and purposeful, he advanced, the gun swinging at the end of his arm as he flicked open the cylinder and shook out the empty brass cartridges. Methodically, he loaded in new rounds with each step he took.

"You may be right," he called, raising his voice to be heard over the storm. "Perhaps she is gone. But Madrigal . . . Marie was . . ." Erik struggled with the words, and Kara wondered what kind of compulsion the other woman had held over him. It was her way. She tied people to her by their own weaknesses. "Ghost5 will not die. I will rebuild it." Erik flicked the cylinder shut and cocked the gun, raising it to aim.

A light came down through the rain, glittering at the edges of Kara's vision. She blinked, trying to focus in it. A crimson thread, appearing and disappearing, wavered over her. The bright dot at the end crossed her face and flickered away.

The wind howled and beat at Kara, a heavy clatter pounding at her ears as the shimmering thread lanced across the runway and rose up Erik's chest. He saw it and flinched, reeling back, bringing up the revolver to aim skyward. The red spark danced over his cheek.

In the next second he was spinning away in a welter of blood and brain matter, crashing back into the muddy grass.

Kara drew in her arms, hugging herself as she turned toward the noise from the clouds. She saw a sleek silver shape dropping out of the storm, a blur of rotor blades whirling in the air.

Sitting with her feet dangling out the side of the helicopter's crew cabin, Lucy Keyes looked down at Kara through the scope on an assault rifle, a targeting laser dancing through the raindrops.

The thread of red briefly connected the two of them once more, and Kara waited, afraid of what would come next.

The storm held the city in its teeth and shook it.

A long rumbling growl rolled from one side of the sky to the other, pads of slate gray cloud briefly illuminating from within as captured lightning flared in the distance. Ingrained reflexes, that battlefield instinct to be watchful for muzzle flashes, drew Lucy's attention to the panoramic windows looking out from the fiftieth floor.

Seoul's skyscrapers captured the dull white blinks of light, reflecting them back at the storm. The city was shrouded in shadows, even with the power now restored to full function. Whole districts were still dark as the authorities combed the streets looking for damage to the infrastructure. Ghost5's silent assault would take weeks to deal with, not only the electrical grid but also the traffic control, the metro and a dozen other systems. And then there was the human fallout, the injuries and the lives that had been lost in the confusion, the panic the hackers had generated to cover their attack.

On the way through the offices on the lower levels of the building, Lucy had seen screens with rolling news coverage from the TV stations first to get back on the air. While she didn't speak or read Korean, she didn't need to in order to understand what they were saying. Footage of people swarming the streets, of police officers barking orders, the burning Antonov cargo plane at the airport, grainy cell-phone video of two helicopters chasing each other over rooftops. It told the tale well enough. The citizens of Seoul lived with an enemy forever breathing down their neck, but on days like this, the danger that was commonplace became real and present among them.

Two fast-moving specks in the distance crossed her sight-line, a pair of F-15 fighter jets from a base outside the attack zone pressed into combat air patrol over Seoul's city limits. They were watching for the North to make a move, to take advantage. Elsewhere, Blackhawk helicopters from the garrison at Seongnam were crisscrossing the Han River, each one carrying squads of rapid-reaction troops, to both calm the populace with a visible military presence and be ready for any follow-up attacks. One such squad had already found the silver Dauphin where Marc had been forced to ditch it in the middle of a vacant construction site.

It had been a close-run thing, but the four of them had made it to the Rubicon offices in a stolen car and not lost anyone along the way. Lucy looked down at the fresh bandages on her hands, flexing them experimentally. She could still smell the stale blood from the wounded hacker's injuries in her nostrils.

*What was her name? Pyne, like the tree, Kara had said. With a "Y."* The girl was so ashen, Lucy thought at first sight she was already dead. But not so. Her gaze drifted away, back across the room to the glass wall and the space beyond it.

Rubicon owned three floors of this downtown office complex. The uppermost was vacant for renovation, so the Special Conditions Division co-opted it as a temporary crisis center. Across the way, a conference space had been repurposed as a field hospital. Pyne was in there, behind sheets of painter's plastic hung over the windows, being ministered to by a team of medical staff who asked no questions and worked with brisk efficiency. The same team had looked over Lucy and Marc, skilfully dressing their wounds and contusions. All the while, Lucy had been unable to stop herself from staring across at Kara, as a medic sewed up the bullet graze on the younger woman's shoulder.

Her hands contracted into fists as she thought about Kara and what she had done, making the bandages tighten and the healing cuts on her hands ache. Lucy pressed down on her churning anger and took a breath.

An encrypted comms rig had been set up on the table in front of her. The gear spread out of an armored case, a flip-up video screen built into the inside of the lid and wires leading from it to a collapsible satellite antenna by the window. After a moment, a cue on the screen announced that a successful scrambled connection had been made and she folded her arms across her chest, straightening. *Back to work,* she told herself.

Henri Delancort's face filled the display, as he leaned close to the camera feeding an image from Ekko Solomon's private A340 jet, currently speeding northward from Australia. He settled back and Lucy saw her employer nearby, watching impassively from a seat in the jet's ops room. *"Secure,"* said Delancort, adjusting his spectacles with one hand. *"Lucy. C'est bon. We thought we had lost you both."*

"It all went to hell," she said flatly. "The lead that pointed us to Hite's house was a set-up. If they hadn't wanted Dane and me for scapegoats, you would have been picking our corpses out of the rubble, the same as those other poor assholes."

*"Quite so."* Solomon gave a grave nod. *"We are in the middle of a very serious matter. I will need a complete debriefing from Mr. Dane and yourself when we arrive . . ."* He glanced at Delancort.

*"Sunset, local time,"* said the other man. *"That is, of course, if we can expedite a landing at Incheon. The airport is still operating under emergency protocols at the moment."*

Lucy had already sent an audio file to the jet via burst encryption, a terse after-action report that covered the high points of the assault on the NIS campus, but there were details she had left out, and they were largely questions over what to do with Kara Wei. She studied Solomon's face. On his order, Lucy had been willing to terminate Kara on sight if the situation had come to that—and the choice had been there, right in front of her as Marc braved the storm front to get them to the airport. She still wasn't sure if she had made the right choice.

*"We are monitoring the situation in Seoul from here,"* Solomon intoned. *"Very serious indeed."*

"Have they given a casualty figure?" Lucy dreaded hearing the reply. "I can't get a straight answer from anyone."

Delancort seemed to intuit this and he deflected. *"Still to be determined. But it could have been far, far worse. You made a difference there today."*

She shook her head. "Kara's the one who shut down the software weapon. Dane flew the chopper and I shot some guys."

*"You need to be made aware of certain facts."* Solomon fixed her with his steady gaze. *"I am presently in contact with members of the South Korean National Assembly, the office of the Prime Minister and senior figures in the National Intelligence Service. We are attempting to find a mutually agreeable resolution to Rubicon's involvement in this crisis."*

"Right." Unsaid under that was the reality that Marc and Lucy were foreign nationals who had been closely embroiled in a terrorist attack on the Republic of South Korea, and right now their legal status in the country was south of "fugitive," veering toward "enemy of the state."

Delancort explained that Rubicon would be offering to trade the intelligence the SCD had on Madrigal, Ghost5 and their collusion with the North in return for immunity from prosecution. A full accounting of everything, from Wetherby's assassination in Malta and the Soldier-Saints' attack on San Francisco, to the train crash in Taipei and all the rest. Lucy was dubious, aware of tensions running high in the South, but Solomon's aide noted that with the deterioration of political ties between the country and their traditional allies in the United States, the ministers of the National Assembly were looking for new friends. The Rubicon Group, as a stateless, transnational entity, especially one with its own military contractors and intelligence gathering capacity, fitted that bill.

Lucy listened and said nothing, wondering how generous the South Koreans would have been if the contents of the stolen SCIF had *not* been destroyed, saving their secrets from global exposure.

*"Martin Wehmeyer is using his local contacts to help us make headway,"* concluded Delancort. *"Horizon Integral have close ties within local political circles that are proving useful."*

She nodded. Wehmeyer would be extremely motivated to do whatever he could to mollify the South Koreans, especially after a weakness in his company's industrial control software had plunged their city into disarray.

Solomon followed the same train of thought. *"Horizon Integral's stock will go into freefall if the truth about the zero-day exploits is made public. I have offered to take them into the Rubicon fold. Their board of directors will be voting later today on the matter."*

Taking advantage of a corporate rival in a moment of weakness was cold, but Lucy couldn't bring herself to voice the notion. Wehmeyer and his people had been complacent in allowing Hite to undermine them, and innocents had paid the price. She wouldn't lose any sleep over their changed fortunes. "I guess Sunny won't be buying any ten-grand dresses for a while," she said, after a moment.

*"We have been informed that the local police have made a few arrests,"* continued Delancort, glancing down at a digital pad in front of him. *"Several cyber-criminals known to be associated with the Ghost5 collective have been caught inside the city limits."* He paused. *"Interpol are aware. A number of extradition orders are already being drawn up. They are wanted by a lot of people."*

*"The Central Intelligence Agency are at the head of that line,"* added Solomon.

He didn't need to remind them that the CIA's relationship with Rubicon in general, and Lucy Keyes and Marc Dane in particular, was not a friendly one. A while back, the Brit had run a spur-of-the-moment prison break from one of their black sites in Poland, freeing a terrorist asset named Jadeed Amarah in return for vital intelligence on a greater threat. Lucy was only too happy to be responsible for Amarah's later termination, but the agency were not so sanguine about it. And before that, when Rubicon had thwarted the bombing of a political rally in Washington DC, the CIA had smarted at being out-maneuvered by Solomon's team. She didn't doubt that they would want her head on a spike and Marc's alongside it, even if the two of them had ultimately protected the CIA's secrets along with those of the South Koreans.

"On that . . ." she began. "We have two members of Ghost5 here with us. We'll have to deal with them."

Solomon's answer didn't come. Lucy heard a rapping sound and looked over her shoulder. Marc stood outside the office with a tablet computer in his hand, and he took her expression as an invitation to enter. The Brit appeared as tired as she felt, strung out, running on caffeine and raw adrenaline.

"Hey," he said, nodding to Lucy and then to the screen. "I thought I should be in on this."

"*Of course,*" Solomon allowed. "*I am glad you are well and whole, Mr. Dane. After the fire in Sydney, we feared the worst.*" He carried on, returning to business. "*Henri was bringing Lucy up to speed on our conversations with the Assembly.*"

"Oh yeah?" Marc threw her a glance. "Well, I talked to the doc here and he says that the girl, Pyne, she's stable. But they need to get her to a proper hospital. There's a trauma center down in Busan, they reckon they can get an air ambulance to take her—"

Solomon gestured to Delancort. "*Authorize it.*"

Delancort made a notation on his pad, then looked out of the screen at Marc. "*And . . . what about Kara Wei's status?*"

"She'll be okay." Lucy watched Marc as he said the words, and the way he very deliberately didn't look back at her. "Most importantly, though. *Arquebus.*" He waved the tablet computer. "I checked the data in the software weapon's command and control page . . . that's the website that the program reports back to for new orders and whatever. The self-destruct order is embedded in there. If there are any other iterations of the modified Arquebus code drifting around out on the internet, they'll read that and erase themselves."

"*You are certain of this?*" Solomon sat back in his chair, considering the ramifications.

Marc gave a quick nod. "And if we give Horizon Integral's programmers everything from Hite's files on the zero days for HIOS Sigma, they can patch it and this hack can never work again. The vulnerabilities will be eradicated." He paused. "Well. At least until someone finds a new one somewhere else."

"So the weapon is useless? Just like that?" Lucy raised an eyebrow. She wasn't convinced.

"It's been fed a digital cyanide pill," Marc replied. "I also have the address protocol of the cloud server Ghost5 used as their central data store. Think of it as having the keys to their virtual armory. I took a fast pass over the directory in there . . . I found intrusion tools, encryption software, activity logs and more besides. We turn this over to Assim and he can send a wiper program in there. Blank every single drive, erase all their assets. Ghost5 will cease to exist."

Delancort made an approving noise. *"So then the question becomes, what would benefit Rubicon best? To allow the South Koreans to take credit for that? Or the Americans? The US Navy already has ships on the way."*

Lucy scowled at the man's mercenary attitude and turned her full attention on Marc, pointing at the table. "That's fast work, Dane. Where did you get the address data?"

She knew his answer before he said it. "Kara."

"And you accepted that?" Lucy's lip curled. "After everything she did. After she lied to all of us. Abandoned us for Madrigal."

"She went back to Ghost5 because of Lex Wetherby's murder," Marc retorted. "She wanted to bring Madrigal down, don't you get it?"

"Evidently not. Kara was willing to use us as meat-shields, Dane. I can't look past that." The anger she had been holding down was pushing back up once more. The pressure of it built, and Lucy knew that if she let it show, she would say something she couldn't take back. "I don't trust her," she said at length, distilling it down into four words.

"Maybe. But we saved her life," Marc countered. "And her friend's, too. That alone means she owes us." He held up the tablet. "I believe in this."

Anger turned to motion, and Lucy could not fight the impulse to leave the room, leave this conversation. "I hope you don't regret it," she said, and marched out of the office.

"Shit." Marc ran a hand over his face, feeling all the fatigue he had been trying to ignore wash over him in a rush. Alone in the room with the video screen, he felt exhausted and strung out.

Solomon cleared his throat from a thousand miles away and cut the tension in the air. *"Is there anything else to add?"*

"Yeah," said Marc, glancing after Lucy and then back to the tablet computer. He tapped out a command string. "I'm going to send you a file packet, some communications that jumped out at me when I scanned the Ghost5 servers." He pressed a tab and dispatched the data. "Have a look. You'll see what I mean."

Marc heard an answering ping from Delancort's tablet, and the other man's expression shifted as he read the file. "*This cipher text. I have seen it before.*" He looked up at Solomon. "*Sir, this is from a communications blind used by the Combine.*"

"*But they were not involved with these attacks,*" said Solomon. "*Did we not confirm that fact?*"

"This has nothing to do with Arquebus or the infrastructure hacks," Marc insisted. "Back on the plane, after those assassins grabbed us, Madrigal said it to my face. She said she knew the Combine." He drew up the memory. "The phrase she used was 'mutually beneficial associations.' I think their interests have aligned in the past. Someone inside the Combine paid them to do a job, and I reckon I know who."

Delancort adjusted his spectacles as he read on. "*I am looking at money transfers. Tens of thousands of dollars, paid through a Swiss bank.*"

"Recognize the routing, do you?" said Marc. "That's a shell account belonging to G-KOR. Pytor Glovkonin's oil company. And we know that slippery bastard is in with the Combine up to his neck." He could picture the Russian as he spoke his name, with that wolflike face, expensive suit and the attitude to walk the earth like he owned it.

Glovkonin and the other members of his cabal were the hand behind the deaths of Marc's team two years earlier, and recalling that horror brought up a whole tide of dark thoughts that swirled around him, mirroring the storm outside the window.

"There's no record in there of the actual material they stole for him," continued Marc, "but the metadata points to what he was after. Glovkonin paid Madrigal to do two jobs for him. The first was to break into a covert database belonging to the Chinese State Security Service."

He saw Solomon stiffen. "*Why?*"

"We can take a guess," said Marc. "The server they hacked is part of a cluster that stores information on secret detainees. It's the prison roster for every black site and deep dark hole in the People's

Republic. Only hackers as good as Madrigal's team would be able to get in there."

Solomon's gaze drifted to the middle distance as he processed this information, and Marc got the sense that he had revealed something that troubled the man.

"*You said two jobs*," prompted Delancort. "*What about the second?*"

"Another server hack," he explained. "And this one I recognized straight away, because *we* tried to get in there ourselves a few weeks ago, and bounced right off the firewalls. Ghost5 were paid to map out the security set-up for a particular luxury villa in Saint-Tropez."

Delancort eyed him. "*Who owns the villa?*"

"Someone we know," said Marc. "Celeste Toussaint."

# — TWENTY —

The slow lap of the water washed over her body as she turned back for the ninth length of the swimming pool. Blood-warm and crystal clear, it flowed across her naked flesh and drew her hair back over her scalp. Each over-arm sweep propelled her forward, her legs kicking gently below the surface. The exercise made her ache, but in a pleasant way.

Celeste relished the simplicity of the activity. The repetition allowed her a moment to relax, and she cherished these all-too-rare opportunities.

Soft lighting cast shimmering forms off the water and on to the walls, the artistically minimal bare concrete and sparse brick patterned with motion. As with the rest of the villa, the design of the sunken room was geometric and full of strong angles. The place had no softness, in echo of the will of the woman who owned it. Once, in an ill-considered moment, one of Celeste's lovers had referred to it as resembling an exhumed nuclear bunker. She dispensed with her the next day.

This place was a citadel, Celeste decided. Armor and shield and holdfast combined. A fitting place for a leader, for one who formed the opinions of millions, to call their home.

The glow of morning grew through the slot-shaped windows at the top of the walls, giving everything a peculiar ghostly resonance that the world only seemed to show in the moments around dawn. She dipped her head under the water and swam the last part of the length without surfacing, indulging the fantasy that it was the strange light she moved through instead of the water.

As she surfaced, Celeste heard the low chime of a tiny bell. She

glowered at the intrusion of it, her elegant and expensively cared-
for face momentarily betraying her age. She was fifty-five, but had
traded away hundreds of thousands of euros to clinics and beauti-
cians in return for an aspect that seemed ten years younger. The bell
sounded again.

By the side of the oval pool, on a low table next to a lounger, a
small drum-shaped object resembling a piece of abstract art emitted
a pulsing emerald light. Celeste suspended herself on the water's edge
and spoke to it in French. "House. What is it?"

"*Good morning, Mme. Toussaint,*" said the device, in a lilting female
voice with a Parisian accent. "*You have an incoming call from Pytor
Glovkonin on your private line. Shall I accept or dismiss?*"

Her frown threatened to become a scowl, but she caught herself
before she reflexively ordered the house's computer to ignore the call.
With a gasp, Celeste pulled herself out of the water and walked to the
table. She disliked ending her exercise early, but the regrettable truth
was, if Glovkonin had called, it was probably important. "Tell Cook I
will be having breakfast now. Transfer the call to my phone."

"*One moment, please . . .*" The voice-recognition device obeyed and
the iPhone lying on the lounger next to Celeste's towel blinked on.

She tapped the smartphone's answer key as she shrugged into a
bathrobe. "Pytor," she began. "Up early, I see."

A gentle, self-amused chuckle issued out of the phone. "*Ah, Celeste.
Nobody sleeps late in Moscow, you know that. Too much to do.*" She pictured the smug cast he would be wearing, his canine smile. "*How is the
weather in Saint-Tropez?*"

She glanced up at the windows, pulling back her wet hair and securing it with a toweling band. "It will be a lovely day." She was already
starting to become irritated by him. "What do you want?"

"*Business,*" he said solemnly. "*Some matters have come to my attention, and I wanted to speak to you about the situation there. The threads of
the web are twitching, yes? I have heard disturbing rumors about the state
of your personal security. Regarding attempts to compromise it.*"

"Someone is always trying to compromise my security," she retorted,
picking up the phone. Celeste walked out of the pool room and down a
connecting corridor, her bare feet slapping on the tiles as she climbed

the wide, shallow stairs to the main floor. "It is the price of success. Someone is always looking for a way to knock me off my plinth." She took a breath, reframing her thoughts, remembering to be cordial. "I appreciate your concern. If you have information my protection detail should see, perhaps you could forward it—"

"*Of course, of course,*" he interrupted. "*Am I presuming? Perhaps I am. But then that is a failing of mine.*"

"Quite." Celeste looked down at the phone, raising an eyebrow. She wasn't sure where this conversation was going, but it made her uncomfortable. The Combine had clear protocols for contact between its members, in order to maintain the isolated cell structure of the organization. No one person knew the identities of more than two other members at the operational level, so that any failure of security or action by the group's enemies would not cripple them. Glovkonin was being overly familiar and borderline reckless by using her private line for a matter that could have been dealt with in a more circumspect fashion.

She entered the lounge, the thick white carpet enveloping her feet as she moved across the wide room. She caught the scent of fresh coffee brewing and wandered toward the window.

"Is there anything else?"

"*Have you seen the news today? I assume your people keep you well informed about global events.*"

Celeste paused in the middle of the lounge and held her hand over the phone's audio pickup. "House," she called. "Television. News."

"*One moment, please . . .*" said the synthetic voice, from another of the little speakers sitting in the middle of a low table. On the far wall, a large flatscreen display blinked on to show a patchwork of smaller video windows, each one tuned to a different global twenty-four-hour news channel. Along with the networks she controlled, France24, CNN, BBC World, NHK and several others were also present. The audio feeds were muted, but she saw the commonality instantly. Footage of police and emergency services on the streets of a Far Eastern city dominated the current news cycle. She read a headline off a ticker scrolling along the bottom of one window. TERRORIST CYBER-ATTACK CRIPPLES SOUTH KOREAN CAPITAL.

"We're not involved in this," she said, more to herself than to the phone in her hand.

"*It would appear not. Naturally, you would know if something on this scale had been facilitated by the other members.*" The Russian's tone was hard to read. Was he accusing her, or trying to intimate that he had inside knowledge of this event when she did not? "*We can't be held responsible for everything, can we?*" Glovkonin chuckled. "*But the Combine can take advantage of it nonetheless. Our kingdom is that perfect edge state between chaos and order, don't you agree?*"

Celeste's tolerance for the man's games wore thin. "The Combine adapts to every outcome, Pytor, that's why it has survived for nearly a century." She eyed the TV screen, then stalked away to the floor-to-ceiling windows of the lounge. "Whatever this is, we will monitor it."

"*Yes,*" he agreed. "*We do not want terrorists controlling their own agendas. Bad for business.*"

Her attention drifted from his voice to the immaculate stretch of lawn on the far side of the glass, and the gray gravel of the driveway leading off through the trees. One of her security staff lay face down on the manicured grass, a dark patch of fluid glistening around his head where it soaked into the earth. His gun was close by, fallen out of reach.

Celeste's breath caught in her throat.

"*Is something wrong?*" said Glovkonin. "*Hello?*"

She ignored him and shrank back from the window, scanning the densely packed trees. The glass was bulletproof, of course, but even that would not be enough to stop an armor-piercing round from a high-powered rifle. A rush of fear shocked through her, a charge of fight-or-flight instinct that made her want to find a weapon, anything she might use to defend herself.

"House!" Celeste barked the command. "Emergency. Emergency. Emergency." Saying the word three times in a row set the voice trigger to activate the villa's silent alarm in the event of a home invasion. The computer system would automatically alert every member of her security detail on site, the staff at her office and the local police station.

"*Understood,*" replied the artificial voice. "*Please proceed immediately to the safe room.*"

She moved quickly across the lounge, eyes darting toward every corner in search of any potential threat. Her fatigue from the morning swim was forgotten, and in its place she was caught by cold terror, and anger that someone had dared to violate her privacy and attack her staff. She put aside questions of how the unseen assailant had broken through the villa's security perimeter and concentrated on self-preservation. There would be time to find someone to blame once the situation had been resolved.

Whoever had done this, she decided, would be made an example of.

As Celeste made for the stairs that would take her up to the second floor, she belatedly remembered that she was still clutching her iPhone. The line was still open. "Pytor? Are you there?"

"*Celeste. Yes. I thought the call had dropped for a moment. What is going on?*"

"Someone is here. An assassin." Saying it out loud made her blood run cold.

"*Oh! I am afraid I was right.*"

Celeste was about to speak again, but a dull buzzing noise caught her attention as she made it to the stairwell at the back of the entrance hall. The sound came from a watch around the wrist of another of her bodyguards, the device's display flashing the word *Alerte* in crimson. The man lay slumped in a corner by a large ornamental vase. He had been shot at close range through the right eye.

The body of a third person, one of the kitchen staff, had been dumped out of sight nearby, behind an ornamental chaise. The woman's white linen jacket was wet with blood from the bullet wound in her throat.

"They are in here with me," Celeste whispered. She ran back to the dead bodyguard and found the man's pistol still in its shoulder holster. The weapon felt huge and unwieldy in her long, thin, fingers, but she knew enough to make sure that there was a round in the chamber and the safety catch was off.

"*Celeste, talk to me!*" Glovkonin said urgently, and she winced, reducing the volume on the phone.

"I have a gun," she whispered. "I don't know where they are . . ."

*"There is a panic room in your home, yes? Go there and stay there. I'm already contacting my people. Help is on the way!"*

"Yes . . ." She took the stairs up to the second floor two at a time, and when she reached the balcony on the upper level, she risked looking back down. From up here she could see into the media room as well, and saw no movement there. Outside, the drive was still and empty. The realization settled on her that she might be the only person left alive in the villa. The men supplied to her by the private military contractor ALEPH were paid too well and they feared her influence too much to have put their lives before hers. If they were not at her side, then they were already dead.

She hesitated at the top of the stairs, briefly considering a different tack. The sporty red Porsche she used as a run-around on those rare days she wanted to drive herself was in the garage, close by. Could she risk making a run for it? But that would involve going outside through the front door, or taking the long way through the service area and kitchens.

She rejected the thought, refusing to give in to raw fear. The safe room was nearer, hidden behind a bookcase in her study. Only ten meters away.

It took monumental effort for Celeste to stop herself sprinting that final distance. Instead, she took careful, quiet steps, leading with the gun grasped in one hand and the smartphone pressed to her ear.

*"Don't worry,"* Glovkonin told her, a silken smile ghosting beneath the words. *"This will be over soon."*

She froze. Pytor Glovkonin was accomplished in many arenas, but Celeste had learned on their first meeting that the man simply could not hold fast over his arrogance. He had a compulsion to show off his superiority, even in the smallest of ways. It was the Russian's greatest tell, and she heard it coming to her across the distance from Moscow. All at once, the horrible reality of the situation caught up with her.

"You have done this." It was not a question. The moment of drawn breath she heard down the line was the confirmation she needed.

It made sense. This abrupt contact out of nowhere, outside their pre-arranged schedules for communication, the stilted pace of their phone conversation. He had called her because in some way, he wanted to be *present* for this moment.

"*I have always admired how perceptive you are, Celeste. A pity that your attention is forever aimed outward. If not, you might have seen this coming.*"

She edged toward the study in silence, her mind racing as she tried to pick apart the Russian's motivation and intent. If her security was breached, then it was likely that the alarm call had been intercepted as well.

A power play, then. How like the man. Anyone else would have had her quietly drowned in the pool, but Glovkonin liked theater. He wanted to be part of the sport of this. And that gave her an opportunity.

Celeste was very close to the study now. The door was ajar, as she had left it. The slice of the room she saw beyond, undisturbed and empty. She could still survive this.

The safe room operated on an independent, self-contained control grid, isolated from the villa and equipped with its own electrical, communications and security systems. Enough food and water supplies for a month. Walls thick enough to weather the impact of a bomb blast. Once Celeste made it inside, Glovkonin's little game would blow up in his face. In this moment, she wanted that more than anything in the world.

"*I need you to understand,*" he began, irritated that she had fallen silent. "*This will serve a greater purpose. The Combine is a great and powerful organization, but it moves too slowly. I am going to help it along.*" She held her breath, waiting silently for him to continue. "*I told you the truth when I said your security has been compromised. I have learned that intelligence about your activities, your dealings with certain people, has been passed to the Police Nationale by those Rubicon fools. That makes you a liability. I could have warned you, given you time to go to ground, but I saw a more useful solution. It is better this way, quicker.*" He paused again, letting that sink in. "*Your place will need to be filled. And I will make certain that the others discover it was the African who sent his people to kill you today.*"

The final piece of the puzzle slotted into place. Glovkonin's hatred of Ekko Solomon and the Rubicon Group had been the Russian's *bête noir,* ever since their involvement in thwarting the Washington attack initiated under his stewardship two years ago. More recently, the situation with Glovkonin's failure to procure an ex-Soviet nuclear weapon had once again been laid at Solomon's feet.

The Combine did intend to deal with Rubicon, but like all of their projects, it proceeded at the correct pace. It seemed the Russian was unwilling to wait. He would make this incident look like Solomon's operatives were behind it, in hopes of stirring the other members of the Combine into quicker action.

"You won't succeed," she told him, tossing the iPhone on her desk as she rushed into the room.

Powerful hands came from out of the gloom and ensnared Celeste before she made it halfway to the bookcase. Lying in wait, concealed in the shadows, Glovkonin's assassin wrestled the bodyguard's gun from her and broke three of her fingers in the process. She cried out as the weapon discharged a round into the ceiling, and then it was gone. The assassin's hands were broad and strong, the acrid tang of spent cordite coating the leather gloves that shrouded them. He grabbed Celeste by the throat and the collar of the bathrobe, lifting her off her bare feet.

She was thrown through the air, crashing against the far wall, tumbling back to the carpet as books and framed pictures clattered down around her.

Celeste tasted blood in her mouth and shakily drew up, pulling the torn robe back over her shoulders to cover herself. She blinked and saw the assassin for the first time. Dark and imposing, perhaps even handsome, he was a hard-eyed Arab with the face of a soldier. He seemed familiar, but she couldn't place him.

A silenced pistol emerged from inside his black jacket and he pointed it at her. "You are making a mistake," she said, in Fush'ha Arabic. "If you are his ally, you will be dragged down with him."

"I am not his ally," replied the man, in flawless French. "And I will not be yours or that of your collaborators."

"A trade, then. I can make you a better offer than he did," she told him, switching back to her native tongue. "Name your price."

"I do not want money." The assassin's face twisted. "There is no way to buy yourself out of this. I loathe your kind, with your lies and pacts and secrets! You are a cancer on the world. I want you destroyed."

It came to her then whom she was talking to. "You're Khadir . . ." Celeste shook her head. The terrorist was a wanted man on every continent, personally responsible for dozens of bombings and assassinations. "But . . . Your organization, Al Sayf, it is gone. Broken apart by the Americans. They said you were killed in an airstrike in Syria."

"Lies," he repeated. "No better than yours."

She held out her hand, grasping at a slim thread of hope. "The Washington attack . . . I know the Combine promised Al Sayf we would make that work, and we fell short. That cannot be denied. But we can still find common ground—"

"I left Al Sayf behind," Khadir told her. "To walk my own path. They were as blinkered as you. I will finish the work I began there on my own. I do not need them or you."

She choked out a breath. "But you're working with Glovkonin? Killing for him?" Celeste let her hand drop and gathered up what defiance still remained in her. "How is he any different from me?"

"He is not," agreed Khadir, taking aim. "And one day, this will also be his fate."


Lighting the cigarette in his mouth with one hand, Glovkonin used the other to press on the Bluetooth earpiece he wore, straining to pick out the sounds coming to him from the other end of the line.

Voices spoke softly in French, a language he had never troubled himself to learn. That irked him. If Toussaint had any final words, he wanted to hear them for himself.

Then, very distinctly, he heard the chug-chug of a silenced weapon. Presently, a solemn lion-growl of a voice addressed him. "*It is done.*"

"What did she say to you?" Glovkonin crossed his hotel suite and made for a half-open window. He wore silk night-clothes, the garments hanging off his tall frame in disarray, the remnants of his brisk and forceful pre-dawn encounter with the young woman still dozing in the bedroom.

"*Nothing of import.*"

"Humor me," he insisted. Leaning on the window ledge, Glovkonin exhaled a puff of blue smoke out into the chilly Moscow morning. He stared toward the domes of the Kremlin without really seeing them. His mind was in Saint-Tropez, imagining Celeste Toussaint as her last breath left her body.

Khadir sighed. "*She bartered for her life.*"

Glovkonin grinned briefly, running a finger over his manicured beard. "The offer was not to your liking?" He didn't need to remind the Egyptian that their agreement was predicated on the assassin's obedience. Khadir would get what he wanted after Glovkonin's ultimate desires were fulfilled.

Predictably, the other man did not rise to the barb. "*I will sanitize the area. There will be no traces.*"

"Well," Glovkonin corrected, "there will be *one.*"

At great expense, his people had procured a copy of a Europol personnel file on Marc Dane, and from that it had been possible to artificially duplicate a partial fingerprint from Dane's right thumb. Khadir carried a plastic pad that could apply the false print to a shell casing, and he would leave the spent brass behind in the villa to be discovered by ALEPH's response team. In the fullness of time, the Englishman would become a person of interest in Toussaint's murder, and that would cast suspicion on his employer, the Rubicon Group. When the moment came, Glovkonin would be there to use the woman's death to further his own agenda.

"Finish up and head for extraction," he ordered. "Return to me."

"*That will take time. I have to travel via indirect means.*"

"Of course." Glovkonin made a dismissive gesture. He wasn't interested in the details. "I must prepare for the next step."

"*Is there another . . . impediment to be removed?*"

"No. Quite the opposite." He ended the call with a tap on the earpiece, removing it and dropping the device on a low, glass-topped coffee table.

Glovkonin sat and poured himself tea from a small samovar, a sense of undeniable anticipation welling up in him. He was in control again, and with the woman out of the picture, he would no longer be subject to her whims in accessing the rest of the Combine hierarchy. It had grated on him to be forced to bend to the needs of others. The displeasure of the experience was so rare that it was a novelty, one that he was glad to be rid of.

He reached for a secure digital tablet resting on a pile of the day's papers. As a sensor in the device registered his fingerprint, he spoke his name aloud and the screen blinked on. Madrigal's data packet lay there, spread out in panel after panel of illicitly captured information. Gathered for him by the elite hackers of Ghost5, the packet contained pages of machine-translated Mandarin and hundreds of digital photos. He flicked through them with swipes of a finger.

The files told the story of a single man, a man who had not taken a breath of free air in decades. This man's existence was a twisting path of random jaunts between nameless prisons, of endless days and nights confined in dark places. It was the story of a single life, one that a great and pitiless agency had decided to punish with indifferent malice. Trapped in the grinding cogs of a monolithic covert power, this man was prisoner, victim and object lesson.

His name was Lau. The men who had taken away Lau's freedom were an agency within an agency, a "star chamber" concealed inside China's Ministry of State Security who were not beholden to the established chain of command in Beijing. The full details were unclear, but the facts were these: he had earned their disapproval and he would spend the rest of his life paying for that error.

Most of the pictures of Lau showed him in grimy prison fatigues, out in work gangs or sitting alone in a tiny cell, but there were others from the time before he had angered his masters. In a few of them, he wore an officer's uniform of the Army of the People's Republic. In others, his garb was business suits of a cut that had been popular during the 1980s. Lau smiled in some, was serious and thoughtful in others. In each of the earlier photos, he had the look of a man of purpose.

Glovkonin found his way to the picture that kept drawing his eye over all the others. The scene was a grassy wilderness, most likely Zambia. Two men stood framed in the shadow of a low miombo tree. Lau, dressed in tropical fatigues, squinted into the sun with a fierce grin on his face. At his side, decades younger and sharing the same expression, stood Ekko Solomon.

The Russian flicked back and forth between this image and the most recent one of Lau, trying to frame the changes the man had been through in the intervening time. What sorrow in that older face, what dejection. But not only those emotions. Glovkonin looked closely and saw an aspect he recognized from himself. A glimmer of *rage*. Contained, guarded and carefully ministered, like a naked flame protected from a windstorm.

After a moment, Glovkonin sat back and drew on his cigarette once more, musing on the future. It would take time and there would be costs, but eventually he would find this prisoner. And when he did, he would be in possession of the perfect weapon with which to destroy the Rubicon Group and the man behind it.


If the world still had any hard edges, whatever drugs they had pumped into Pyne's veins had softened them into a kind of fuzzy dullness.

The brutal, savage agony that had engulfed her back on the Antonov was a blurred memory now. When she looked down at the place in her belly where the point-blank shot had ripped her open, there was a great white wad of bandages that seemed to bloom out of her like fungus on a piece of tree bark.

Her mind took hold of that image and sailed away with it, buoyed on winds of disconnected thought. Pyne had a waking dream full of grass as tall as trees, trees as high as mountains. She saw blue skies and felt a cool breeze on her face.

Eventually the dreamy haze ebbed and she came down to earth. Slow, lumbering icebergs of thought shifted through her mind and came together. After the pain, she remembered jagged fragments of what came next.

Kara dragging her through the hangar, the sound of thunder and rain. Blades spinning over her head. Glass walls and people wearing paper masks. Then the flash of lights and the sense of falling upward. Had that been the drugs?

She turned her head, her body coming into focus, moment by moment realizing that the buzzing in her ears was coming from outside. She lay on a medical gurney on a train. No, *a plane*. A small one. A jet, like the ones rich dicks in rap videos showed off.

Out of the oval windows she saw gray cloud scudding past, and blinks of dream-blue sky. Pyne remembered more. A woman, a doctor with a thick Asian accent, telling her she would be fine. *You will lose some kidney function, but you will heal. The bullet missed everything vital.* Was that true, or did she imagine it? The doctor said they were taking her to a hospital. Somewhere called Busan.

She blinked at the bandages. Hadn't she been in a hospital already? Where did the doctor come from? *Busan?* That sounded like a long way from home.

"Hello, stupid."

Pyne turned her face toward the sound of the voice.

"Kara?" The other hacker sat across from her in a swiveling chair, typing rapidly on a tablet computer resting on her knees. A Wi-Fi sniffer had been haphazardly duct-taped to the side of the tablet. Kara wore the same kind of smock that the doctor with the accent had been wearing. "Why are you . . . dressed like that?" It was an effort for Pyne to make the words join up and leave her mouth. "Are you my doctor now?"

"It's my disguise," said Kara. "Why did you get yourself shot?" Pyne wasn't sure if she was supposed to answer the question, so she didn't. She wasn't completely certain that Kara was really sitting next to her at all. "You shouldn't have stood up to Erik. Look what that got you."

Pyne managed a nod. "Lex would have done it."

Kara's blank expression flickered like a light—sadness there, on and then off again. "People are waiting for you in Busan," she told her. "The CIA. They haven't forgotten what you did."

"Oh." Prior to falling into Ghost5's orbit, Pyne's biggest solo hack had been outing a CIA source, an ISIS turncoat whose bounty of intelligence had come with the price of overlooking his multifarious dealings in sex trafficking. After Pyne leaked his new identity on the dark web, he hadn't lasted long, much to the chagrin of his handlers. "That's bad."

Kara shook her head. "It's not." She looked up as a Korean man in a pilot's shirt entered the cabin from the cockpit and shot her a hard glare. He did not seem happy. "Well?" Kara snapped, brusque and unfriendly.

The man in the shirt glanced at Pyne, then away again. "I did what you asked. But Busan Air Traffic Control are already on the radio, demanding to know what is going on. And once we get close to the Japanese coast, the SDF will send up interceptors to see what the hell we are doing!"

"Leave that to me," Kara said firmly. "By the time we get into their airspace, we'll have an authorized flight plan and everything."

"Nagasaki," said the man. "We barely have enough fuel to reach it."

"Bullshit." Kara held up the tablet and showed the man the screen. Pyne's gaze snapped back and forth between the two of them, as if she were watching a tennis match. "Don't try to play me. I'm tapped into the control systems on this aircraft. If I don't keep entering a code every ten minutes, the ailerons will lock and we will go right into the sea." The man paled as she spoke. "I know exactly how much fuel is in the tanks. And my friend and I, we don't have anything to lose. You get it?"

"I get it," said the man. "Don't do anything stupid, okay?"

"Go fly the plane and let me work." Kara went back to her typing, and after a moment the man sighed and returned to the cockpit.

Pyne tried to sit up, but it was too painful, so she sank back into the gurney's mattress. "You've hijacked us."

"I couldn't stay there." Kara's eyes lost focus as she typed, and she became remote, almost robotic. "I've done a lot of bad things, Pyne." She made a strange noise in her throat, like swallowing a sob before it could fully form. "I don't like what I've turned into. So I should get away. You too."

"Where are we going?"

"A safe place. I'll figure it out."

Pyne blinked. "Those people who came and rescued us . . . your friends. They'll be super-pissed."

"Yes." Kara stopped typing for a moment. "Yes, they will. But it's okay. I left a note."

By sunset the storm had dissipated and the skies over Seoul were clear and cold. A few patches of the city, visible from the windows of the office tower, were still dark. The army had been called in with portable generators and the forecast was good for full restoration of the grid in the next few days.

But a kind of stillness hung over the streets, manifesting itself in the hurried steps of the population as they made their way to their homes and locked themselves in with their loved ones. The attack on Seoul had been a strange kind of almost-war, and the old folks with long memories who recalled blackouts from the battles with the North told their grandchildren to be wary. No one had yet put a name to it, but the engineered collapse of the power grid here and Ghost5's test-run attack in San Francisco were the latest refinements of a new means of battle.

State-sponsored hackers had been attacking infrastructure targets in the Middle East and Eastern Europe for years now, but with major cities in South Korea and the United States becoming targets, the rest of the world could no longer overlook the threat.

Marc reflected on what that would mean for Rubicon, an organization now inextricably linked to these events—and for all its power and money, an organization that existed in the gray shadow margins where the authority of nations thinned to nothing.

"Where do we go from here?" he wondered aloud.

"Damned if I know." Lucy stood in the doorway, arms folded, watching him intently. "You looking for me?"

"I was," he admitted, then nodded at the view outside. "Got distracted for a minute."

"You okay?"

He gave a crooked smile. "About to ask you the same."

"Tried to get some sleep. Didn't take."

"I meant . . ." He held up his hand, trailing off.

Lucy shrugged. "Blood washes off. Scars fade." She looked down at her palms. "I'll manage."

He wanted to question that, but for the moment he held off and gestured with his smartphone. "Delancort pinged me. Solomon's plane touched down at Incheon twenty minutes ago. They should be here in an hour or so, give or take passing through the police checkpoints."

"Where's Kara?"

His smile faded. "Yeah. About that." Marc met her gaze. "She must have slipped away while no one was looking. It looks like she snuck on board the air ambulance taking Pyne south, and diverted—"

"*Fuck!*" Lucy snarled, showing her teeth. "Did you know about it?" She advanced toward him, eyeing him angrily. "You help her?"

"What? *No!*" Marc blew out an exasperated breath. "Shit, if anyone is responsible for making her bolt, it's *you*. And *Solomon*."

"How'd you figure that?" demanded Lucy.

"Despite evidence to the contrary, I'm not an idiot," Marc retorted. "You think I didn't know you were willing to end her if you thought Kara had gone over? You'd already decided when she first cut and ran. You wrote her off."

"Don't tell me what I know," Lucy shot back. "You're a smart guy, Dane, but sometimes you're too trusting. Like it or not, Kara Wei— or whatever the fuck her name is—played us from the start."

"I refuse to believe that."

"That so?" She made a show of looking around. "Then why did she sneak away? *Again?*" Lucy went on, before he could frame a reply. "I trusted Kara. I considered her a friend. And how did that go? She turned rogue. She deceived me, deceived all of us." Some of her anger faded. "Kara . . . did not trust me. She lied. And now, instead of trying to make amends, she does it all over again." Lucy sighed heavily. "Solomon is gonna be pissed as hell when he finds out we lost her twice."

"This time, it's different," he told her, activating an audio player app on his phone. "Listen. She sent me this from a blind server."

Marc held up the phone and increased the volume. A tinny, far-away version of Kara Wei's voice spoke to them.

"*I had to go,*" she began. "*And the reason is because I don't want to look at you every day and know you're wondering when I will lie to you again, run away again. So I'm doing it now. It's the best way.*" There was a long inhale of breath, and Marc sensed she was frustrated at being unable to articulate her feelings. "*I keep saying I am sorry. This is the last time I will do that. If you don't believe me by now, then you never will.*" There was another long pause. "*You're asking yourselves why you didn't see what I was before this. I'm good at masks. You want to know why I didn't neutralize Arquebus before Ghost5 triggered it. I had to wait until it went active before I could kill it. Before Madrigal committed to the hack, I couldn't be sure if the data Lex left behind for me would work. Then I would have been dead and no one could speak for . . . for someone I loved.*" Marc saw Lucy's expression soften. "*I had to play a long game,*" Kara continued. "*I put everyone at risk to do that, but now it is done and I am* not *sorry. If this was looped, I'd do it over again. No changes.*" She fell silent for a moment, and then Kara said one more thing before the recording ended. "*I am not coming back.*"

Lucy's expression hardened once again. "And that's it? What, we grant forgiveness and then we let her go?" She looked away. "I can't do that. There's a long road from where I am right now to any place where I can give Kara Wei a pass for what she did. Whatever the reasons behind that one-woman battle she was fighting, Kara used us. And that don't wash off easy."

Marc slipped the phone back into his pocket. "I know where you're coming from. But I'm holding enough grudges as it is. I don't want to add another one to the pile."

"You want so much for her to be on the side of the angels," Lucy said dismissively. "And you know why?" She prodded him. "It's because you want to be *right*. You were right when you went gunning for a traitor in MI6, and you were right when you found out about the Exile device. And you want to be right about this too, but guess what? You can't make the call every single time, Dane!"

"I understand what Kara did!" He shot back the words, a rush of emotion bringing heat to his reply. "I didn't see it at first, but now I get it. Kara and that guy Lex, they had something precious. And it got torn away from her. That happened to *me*." He tapped his chest. "I lost Sam, and I'm going to carry that around with me forever." Marc turned away, glaring out of the window. "In her place, I would have done the same as Kara. Damn it, I *did* do the same after Nomad were wiped out!" If he closed his eyes, he knew he would see the fire and smoke of that terrible day, as clear now as when it happened.

Reflected on the inside of the glass, he saw Lucy watching him. "You know what your problem is? You're looking for someone to save." The edge and the anger in her words faded. "But Sam Green is gone, Marc, and you can't bring her back. You have to let that go."

A dozen different retorts formed and died in his mind, but he held off, forcing himself to look straight at Lucy's words.

*Is she right?* Ever since the explosion that had wiped out his team two years ago, Marc had been on the run—either away from hunters or doing the hunting himself. Each time he found himself in harm's way, the drive to get through it, to resolve the threat, had been inescapable. *Is she right about my reasons? Is there a void in me that I'm never going to fill?* He had no answer to those questions.

He pushed on, trying to find his way back. "If you were Kara, if it was your brother dead back there instead of Wetherby . . ." Marc began. "You wouldn't have hesitated."

"I would have told *you*." Lucy's reply was soft, almost wounded.

Marc looked back at her. "I still trust Kara. Like I trust you. Because that's all that we have left." He came closer, compelled by an impulse to reach out and touch her hand, to make a human connection in the wake of the turmoil. "That's what this bloody game takes from you, Lucy. The secrets, the legends and the buried lies, it eats away at truth like acid. Corrodes it."

He took a long breath. *Could she see? Did she understand?* Marc pushed on, regardless. The events of the past few days had brought him closer than ever to death, and even if that storm had passed, he couldn't deny what remained in its wake.

"It's not about *trust no one*, Lucy. It's about *trust someone*. We don't have that, then nothing we do matters. If there's no trust, then we're all . . . hollow things going through the motions." He let go of her hand and looked back out at the dark skyline. "We're all *ghosts*."

# ACKNOWLEDGMENTS

I err on the side of drama when I write, but I've tried my best to give everything in this novel as authentic a texture as possible; so my thanks go to Dmitri Alperovitch, Pauline Bock, Andy Greenberg, Ciaran Fahey, Vince Houghton, Ben Makuch, James Plafke, Jeremy Scahill, Craig Smith, Kim Zetter, Abandoned Berlin, Arch Daily, Boeri Studio, DR1 Racing, the Drone Racing League, ExtremeTech, the Intercept, the International Spy Museum, *Vice*, War Is Boring and *Wired* for the articles, blogs, books and other reference materials I made use of during my writing of *Ghost*.

Much appreciation is due to my fellow authors Peter J. Evans, Ben Aaronovitch and my friends Michael Clarke, Peter Clarke and Shaun Kennedy, for offering advice, moral support and invaluable input during my work on this novel.

Once more, thanks to everyone at United Agents—especially Robert Kirby and Kate Walsh—and all at Bonnier Zaffre, most notably my hardworking and enthusiastic editor Sophie Orme.

And as always, much love to my mother and father, and my better half, Mandy.

(No drones were harmed during the making of this book.)